Love, Honour, and O'Brien

Books by Jennifer Rowe

Fiction by Jennifer Rowe
Verity Birdwood series (1987–1995)
Tessa Vance series (1998)
Angela's Mandrake & Other Feisty Fables (2000)
[published in the UK as *Fairy Tales for Grown-Ups* (2002)]
Love, Honour, and O'Brien

Fiction edited by Jennifer Rowe
Love Lies Bleeding
(Allen & Unwin, 1994), anthology of crime short fiction

Non-fiction by Jennifer Rowe
The Commonsense International Cookery Book (1978)
The Best of the Australian Women's Weekly Craft
(Ed. Jennifer Rowe, 1989)

Novels by Emily Rodda
Something Special (1984)
Pigs Might Fly (1986) (also published as The Pigs Are flying)
The Best-kept Secret (1988)
Finders Keepers (1990) and sequel *The Timekeeper* (1992)
Teen Power Inc. series (1994–1999)
(republished as *The Raven Hill Mysteries* 2006)
Fairy Realm series (1994-2006) (also published as *Fairy Charm*)
Rowan of Rin series (1994–2003)
The Julia Tapes (1999)
Deltora Quest series (2000–2005)
Bob the Builder and the Elves (1998)
(republished as *Bob and the House Elves*)
Dog Tales (2001)
Squeak Street series
Rondo series (2007–2009)

Picture Storybooks by Emily Rodda
Power and Glory
Yay!
Game Plan
Where Do You Hide Two Elephants?
The Long Way Home
Green Fingers

Love, Honour, and O'Brien

A Holly Love Mystery

Jennifer Rowe

Poisoned Pen Press

Poisoned
Pen
Press

Page 42 '(There was I) Waiting at the Church'—music: Henry
E. Pether, lyrics: Fred W. Leight. Vesta Victoria, 1906.

Poisoned Pen Press
6962 E. First Ave., Ste. 103
Scottsdale, AZ 85251
www.poisonedpenpress.com
info@poisonedpenpress.com

Printed in the United States of America

Heartfelt thanks to my daughter Kate Rowe for her joyful and useful research on everything from snake keepers to psychic counsellors, to my good friends Ruth and Steve Moline for their generous encouragement, and to my dear, witty husband, Bob Ryan, for laughing as he listened to every chapter as it was written, and for providing the title that began it all.

Chapter One

Holly Love's life fell apart on a Monday. Somehow this made the whole thing seem even more surreal. Being an optimistic sort of person, Holly had always thought of Mondays as new beginnings, days of promise. For the past three months—since she had begun driving to the Blue Mountains most weekends to stay in Andrew McNish's cute little house in Clover Road, Springwood—Mondays had also been characterised by discreet teasing at work and a feeling of enjoyable fatigue that was only partly the result of a long drive back to Sydney in late Sunday traffic.

The three older women who worked with Holly in the small suburban branch of Gorgon Office Supplies, where she answered the phone and shuffled papers all day, said they envied her weekends in the fresh mountain air. Every Monday morning, without fail, Anne, Paola and Justine remarked on Holly's pink cheeks and bright eyes, and exchanged fragmented memories of hot chocolate, the Echo Point view and the lolly shop at Leura, which was supposed to have the largest range of sweets in the southern hemisphere. Since Holly and Andrew rarely left his bedroom from five minutes after she arrived on Saturday morning till thirty minutes before she left again on Sunday afternoon, Holly couldn't contribute much to these discussions.

Maybe Anne, Paola and Justine had noticed. Maybe they had worried among themselves that Andrew was 'taking advantage' of Holly and would drop her when the novelty wore off, because when she came in one particular Monday morning and told them that she and Andrew were getting married, there was a definite undertone of surprised relief in their squeals of congratulation. Holly told herself that their concern was sweet and funny, suppressing the guilty knowledge that she herself had felt a primitive rush of triumph when Andrew had actually suggested marriage, rather than just 'living together.'

'You're gorgeous,' he'd said to her impulsively as they lay in bed among the toast crumbs while Sunday morning slid lazily into Sunday afternoon. 'I adore you. Let's get married.'

And Holly, stunned and laughing, had said, 'Okay,' literally without a moment's thought.

She had always seen herself as a practical sort of person. As a child, she had always been level-headed. She had been famous for it. Among all the children in her extended family, she had been the sensible one—the one among all the cousins who could be relied upon. But now she was thirty-one, and being sensible had lost its charm. Andrew's sublime confidence had swept her off her feet—or would have done if she hadn't already been lying down.

They might have been Cary Grant and Grace Kelly in a forties movie—except for the being in bed part. In those movies men seemed to think nothing of proposing marriage, sometimes within hours of a first meeting, and women thought nothing of accepting. There was none of this timorous 'let's-live-together-for-a-while-and-see-how-we-get-on' business. But then, of course, Holly reflected, in those days the Virgins' Union had a rigid no-wedding-no-penetration policy.

Andrew had no such reason to propose marriage—far from it. Yet he had proposed—impulsively, warmly, delightfully. It was thrilling, and typical of him. His lack of caution, his absolute trust in his instincts, had attracted Holly to him from the start.

Andrew had picked her up (there was no other term for it) in David Jones' men's shirts department, during the post-Christmas sales. They were both waiting to pay for purchases (his, two Italian shirts; hers, a suitably subdued small-checked number for her father's birthday). Stuck halfway down a fidgeting queue, they exchanged rueful smiles as a hefty woman in green argued about her credit card with the patient man at the cash register.

'Bugger this,' Andrew said after five minutes. He stepped out of the queue, slung his shirts onto a nearby stand of men's cologne, caught Holly's eye and grinned.

'Life's too short to stand in line,' he said. 'How about a coffee?'

Two hours later Holly was back at David Jones retrieving the checked shirt, or something very like it, her blood zinging with caffeine overload, her brain zinging with Fascinating Facts about Andrew McNish.

Andrew McNish, thirty-four, financial advisor, coffee connoisseur, buyer of Italian shirts, had dark brown hair that curled crisply into the nape of his neck, roguish brown eyes and a wonderful smile. Andrew McNish loved hang-gliding and surfing and had once participated in a two-day tango marathon for charity. Andrew McNish had been left in the ladies' room at Woy Woy railway station as a newborn baby—

'*You weren't!*'

'*Bizarre, but true. It was in all the papers. My fifteen minutes of fame.*'

— and adopted by Frank and Mavis McNish, who died in a car crash when he was only eighteen. He had worked as a barista, worked in a call centre, worked in a bar, while he put himself through university.

Andrew McNish knew the ingredients for six hundred different cocktails. Andrew McNish had his own business—had never liked working for a boss. He revelled in the cut and thrust of the sharemarket, and knew all the (legal) ways of minimising tax. He had kicked around in Melbourne, Darwin, Montreal, spent a bit of time in New York, now had a little office in the Blue Mountains. Lifestyle choice. He was over big cities.

He was straight. He was single. And he thought Holly had beautiful eyes.

Andrew McNish was so different from anyone Holly had ever known—so different from her kind, careful parents back in Perth, from her nice but faintly boring old friends, and especially from her stolid ex-fiancé Lloyd, about whom the less said the better.

Really, she never stood a chance.

◇◇◇

Holly's Day of Doom dawned bright and clear. Waking for the last time in the boxy little bedroom of her flat, she saw sunbeams filtering through the cream plastic slats of the Venetian blind, and felt it was an omen. Today she was to cast aside her past and embrace her future. And she was ready. She had made a list, and for the past fortnight she had stayed in town and followed it with single-minded determination.

She had cleared out her flat, amazed at how many household objects she had amassed in a mere half-year. She had paid her bills. She had arranged for her mail to be redirected. She had had her legs waxed and her light brown hair freshly cut and streaked.

On Friday she had said goodbye to Anne, Paola and Justine, who had taken her to lunch at a Turkish restaurant near the Gorgon office and presented her with a china biscuit barrel shaped like a goose. Her replacement, a shiny-haired, anaemic-looking girl called Beck, had manned the office in their absence with an air of competence that Holly found very annoying.

On Friday afternoon, abandoning the pretence that she was going to be married in whatever was clean on the day, she had bought a floaty white dress dotted with butter-yellow spots, and some very cute little flat yellow shoes that cost more than the dress. She had also bought some lacy underwear and a bottle of Moët—Andrew's favourite—for a pre-wedding celebration.

She had arrived home on Friday evening laden with carry bags and filled with elation spiced by guilt, the predictable result of having recklessly spent her last cent. It wasn't really her last cent, of course. Just the money she had left in her personal bank account for exactly this sort of purpose when she and Andrew had ceremoniously opened their joint account and bought their wedding rings during her last, luxuriously three-day visit to Springwood.

Still, it had been daunting to see the modest balance in her old, familiar account shrink so quickly, finally reduced to the point of almost complete disappearance. It had made her feel so insecure, in fact, that she had rifled her wallet for the hundred-dollar cheque her parents had sent her for her birthday, and deposited it just before the banks closed, to make herself feel better.

Afterwards, she *had* felt better, in a foolish sort of way. And not just because the account balance looked more respectable, though the funds wouldn't be available till the cheque cleared. She had been carrying that cheque around for a week, continually forgetting to put it into the joint account, knowing all the time that it wasn't really a memory lapse that kept it in her wallet but procrastination brought about by guilt and divided loyalties.

Her parents would never have known where their money ended up, of course, but Holly was all too aware of how they would feel if they *did* know it was in an account with Andrew's name on it, and that was enough. Now it was where they had always intended. There it would remain, no doubt, a sacrifice to her guilt, being slowly eaten up by bank fees.

The weekend had drifted by in a haze of cleaning and final packing, punctuated by hasty, lonely, takeaway meals. Throwing rubber gloves, some limp cleaning rags, an empty Spray and Wipe bottle and the remains of her Thai takeaway dinner into one of her building's communal garbage bins at nine-thirty on Sunday night, Holly knew that she had left nothing undone. She was ready. Now, on Monday morning, with a strange sense of unreality, she stripped the bed, showered, dressed, and toiled up and down the stairs packing her car—a small, ancient and genteel white Mazda which had previously belonged to an equally small, ancient and genteel acquaintance of her grandmother's.

When she had finished it was still early—too early to drop the apartment key in to the real estate agent's office. She told herself to go out and get some breakfast, then felt sick at the thought. She considered ringing Andrew, but told herself he might think it gormless of her to call so early, bothering him like an overexcited child looking forward to a treat.

Andrew was probably already at the office anyway. He was working hard to clear the week to come, which was to be their stay-at-home honeymoon. He had obviously spent Sunday and half of Sunday night in the office, because his phone had still been turned off when Holly went to bed at ten.

Poor Andrew! Part of the problem was that he had been operating without any assistance for almost as long as Holly had known him. His receptionist, Aimee, had let him down and left with practically no notice, he had told Holly ruefully on her second weekend at the Clover Road house. These local girls were bloody unreliable, unfortunately.

Holly had commiserated, but in truth she had not been sorry to hear that Aimee had departed. Andrew had never mentioned what Aimee looked like, but it was hard to imagine his hiring someone who didn't look good.

No suitable replacement for Aimee had presented herself, and of course as things had turned out, this was lucky. Now Holly didn't have to spend time looking for a job in the mountains. Andrew said that her experience at Gorgon's and, before that, at the bank in Perth, had given her just the experience he needed.

Strangely unwilling to leave the small, featureless space that had been her refuge since she had arrived in Sydney, Holly dithered, closing the blinds, checking under the bed and sofa which, with a surly refrigerator, a coffee table, a rickety dining table and two chairs, had qualified the flat to be described as 'furnished.'

When on the last of several nervous visits to the bathroom her mobile phone fell out of her jeans pocket into the toilet and died, she told herself that this wasn't an omen, just carelessness. But afterwards, she saw the drowning of the mobile phone as the beginning of a downward slide.

At five minutes past nine Holly returned the apartment key to the agent, who was snappy. She bought a takeaway coffee from the café next door to the agent's and discovered, when she got back to the car and took her first sip, that the coffee was weak and very sweet, though she had distinctly asked for a double shot and said she didn't want sugar.

She set off through the Monday peak hour. The other drivers on the road were all in ferocious tempers. They glared through their windscreens, a horn-blast away from road rage. There had been a smash on the M4, and traffic was bumper to bumper as far as the eye could see. The news on the radio was a depressing succession of bomb blasts, government denials, share crashes and abused dogs. And after a while, the Mazda started stalling.

Holly called up the spirit of her grandmother and told herself that it was always darkest before the dawn. She wished her phone were still alive so she could ring Andrew and tell him she was on her way. She wished the car had air-conditioning and a CD player. Then, as the stalls became more frequent, she forgot all other wishes and just started praying that the car wouldn't, like the phone, choose this particular day, of all days, to expire.

The Mazda made it up to Springwood, but only just. When it gave its last gasp on the main street, a teenage boy and a gallant old man who Holly thought might have a heart attack at any moment pushed it to the nearest service centre while she steered. The mechanic at the service centre cast his eye over the car, sucked his teeth and said he'd take a proper decko later on but it looked like the distributor. Plus the points were rooted.

'I'm getting married tomorrow,' Holly said, as if this made a difference.

'Good on ya,' said the mechanic sourly. 'First time, is it?'

Holly said it was and he nodded as if this explained her enthusiasm.

'Want a quote?' he asked, jerking his head at the car.

Holly thought quickly. 'Only if it's going to cost more than—um—two hundred dollars, say,' she said. 'Or two-fifty, maybe.'

The mechanic stroked his chin. 'Might be able to lay me hands on a secondhand distributor,' he offered. 'How'd that be?'

'Fine,' Holly assured him. The whole car was so extremely secondhand that she felt a secondhand distributor would be the least of its worries.

They did the paperwork, and after that the mechanic let Holly use his phone. She rang Andrew, quickly rehearsing some witty remarks about her nightmare journey.

Andrew's mobile was turned off, and he didn't pick up the phone in his office. The home phone seemed to be out of order. Only slightly disconcerted, Holly called a taxi, then lugged all her possessions out onto the pavement and sat on the largest of the cases to wait, cradling the china goose and the bottle of Moët, feeling like a refugee.

The taxi driver was a solid, middle-aged blonde woman wearing a Disneyland cap. She eyed Holly, the goose, the champagne and the luggage dubiously. On the plus side, she didn't ask any questions, or try to chat.

In silence they drove the short distance to Clover Road. As they drew up in front of the house, Holly could see that Andrew's dark green Saab was not in the carport. She hadn't really thought it would be, but she felt a pang of disappointment anyway.

She paid the taxi driver, who then seemed to feel it was safe to unlock the boot and help her unload her luggage.

A bitter little wind blew down the street. A few sheets of newspaper tumbled over the nature strip, wrapping themselves around the grey trunks of the almost naked cherry trees.

Holly ferried her things through the front gate and fumbled for her door key. She was aware of the taxi driver watching her with interest as the cab made a lingering turn, and smiled at this evidence of small town curiosity. Feeling cheered, she let herself into the silent house, kicked off her shoes and padded into the kitchen to put the champagne on ice.

The sink was full of unwashed dishes. The benches were sprinkled with toast crumbs. An envelope marked with her name was stuck to the fridge with the tooth-shaped magnet Andrew's dentist gave away with every clean and fluoride treatment. The envelope contained forty dollars and a note.

Dearest Holly,
    I tried to call you, but your phone was off. Sorry for the short notice, but I have to leave. Something has come up.

Don't try to find me. Just forget I ever existed.
Forgive me.
   Andrew

Standing there in the kitchen with her handbag still slung over her shoulder and the champagne bottle in her hand, a few things occurred to Holly.

The first, and most paralysing, was that her mother had been right.

The second was that when she had called Andrew on Saturday, he had seemed slightly distracted, but she hadn't wanted to appear clingy or lacking in confidence, so she hadn't asked him if anything was wrong.

The third was that she wouldn't be surprised if the ex-receptionist, Aimee, had something to do with this.

The fourth was that she wasn't crying, and she should have been.

The fifth was that it was sort of insulting that the note was on the fridge. It was as if Andrew had assumed that this would be the first place she would head for when she arrived. Well, he was right there, she had to admit. But the fridge wasn't a dignified place for a farewell note. A farewell note should be stuck on a pincushion on your dressing table. Or placed on your pillow, under a single red rose. Holly couldn't help but believe that the fact that Andrew, who valued style above everything, had chosen the kitchen as the place to bow out, said a lot about his opinion of her.

Then there was the money. Forty dollars. Did Andrew think she would be too upset to go to the bank for the next day or two? Did he think she would need money for dinner? Or was it—could it possibly be—some symbolic thing?

Facts absorbed in childhood flashed out of the murk of Holly's unconscious. Forty days' rain caused Noah's flood. Jesus wandered in the desert for forty days. Lent was forty days long. (No meat in Lent. Her mother always insisted on that, though she only went to church once in a blue moon. Forty dinners of fish cakes, salmon mornay, macaroni cheese…)

Could Andrew be hinting that his affair with Holly had been some sort of penance? Desperately she tried to think of another explanation. *The Roaring Forties. Life Begins at Forty. Ali Baba and the Forty Thieves…*

She was shocked, of course. She told herself that, later. Concentrating on details instead of focusing on the main issue. The main issue being that Andrew had gone and, presumably, wasn't coming back.

But that was crazy. The kitchen Holly was standing in was *Andrew's* kitchen. The fridge was *his* fridge. The house was *his* house. She had disposed of her own scrappy array of household goods. All she had brought with her were her personal belongings, a bundle of bed linen, a feather and down quilt and the goose-shaped cookie jar.

Andrew might have felt he owed her something for standing her up more or less on the registry office doorstep—ducking, right at the death, out of his promise to make what her grandmother would have called 'an honest woman' of her. But guilt wasn't usually a problem for Andrew. He didn't seem to have what most people thought of as a conscience. He never looked back, or regretted anything. He lived for the present.

Holly had always found that exciting. In fact, she had envied it, since she herself was quite capable of groaning with shame about things that had happened when she was still wearing long white socks with lace around the tops, and going to Sunday school. It had never occurred to her that one day she herself might end up being a casualty of Andrew's ability to move on. But even if, on this occasion, Andrew *had* felt guilty, she reasoned, there was no way he would leave her in possession of everything he owned.

Well, as she was soon to discover, yes, he would. Because it turned out that Andrew had been living for the present in more ways than one.

Holly had several visitors in the next couple of hours. They were all very polite, and they all apologised for not phoning, but it seemed the phone had been disconnected. She tried to make coffee for the first one, but by that time the electricity had gone too.

Anyway, to cut a long story short, Andrew's cute little house in Clover Road, with its fireplace, its broad polished floorboards, its original kookaburra leadlight front door and its elaborate ceiling decorations, was in fact not Andrew's at all, but rented. The furniture was rented, too. And the fittings, glasswear, china, cutlery…even the fridge, which Holly thought was rather an irony. The rents, it seemed, hadn't been paid for quite a while. Just like the lease payments on the Saab, which according to a note she found in the letterbox had been repossessed earlier in the day. Andrew, it seemed, had owned nothing but his clothes, his shaving gear, his laptop computer, his phone and his watch, and they had gone with him.

The real estate agent, and the men from Home Comforts, the furniture and fittings rental place, seemed rather sorry for Holly. The agent, who had bushy black eyebrows and mournful brown eyes and whose name was Len Land—a fact that only added to Holly's sense that all this must be some bizarre joke—even lent her his phone so she could try to ring Andrew. But Andrew's phone was still turned off.

Mr. Land said it had been off, as far as he knew, for days. He said he didn't want to upset Holly, but unless she could come up with the rent owing, plus another month in advance, she was out by the end of the week. Her name wasn't on the lease, he explained carefully, so effectively she was squatting.

And the furniture and fittings rental men were not prepared to wait. As they said, proffering a yellow form covered in indecipherable writing, they had their orders. They just took everything out piece by piece and loaded it into a truck.

Holly stood there watching, clutching her cookie jar and surrounded by her suitcases, her quilt, neatly packed in its original zippered bag, the bottle of champagne, and a slightly damp bundle of sheets, towel and bathmat. She could see the men felt bad about it, but they kept on going until the house was empty. She supposed they saw a lot of desperate people like her in their job.

Chapter Two

By the time the Home Comforts men had gone, it was getting dark and rather cold. Holly wandered around for a while, listening to the echoes and flicking at the light switches just in case one of them worked. Then she cried a bit. Then she put on the jacket she'd prudently packed at the top of one of her cases, wound a woollen scarf around her neck and went into the kitchen.

The things that had been unloaded from the fridge were neatly stacked on a benchtop. Holly ate some yoghurt, some cheese, a gherkin and some leftover asparagus. Then she opened the champagne. The glasses were gone so she had to drink out of the bottle, but that didn't matter. There was no one to share with, and no one to see her.

I have to be calm, she told herself. She found the champagne helped. By the time the bottle was half empty she felt calm enough to wire the foil back around its top and walk with it, her quilt and a small overnight bag, to Andrew's office in the town centre. There would be light and heat in the office. There was a sofa where she could sleep and a TV set, in case she couldn't sleep. There was a bathroom. There were tea and coffee, and a fridge to keep the champagne cool.

And there was a phone. She could ring someone, tell someone what had happened.

But who could she tell? Who could she *bear* to tell?

No one, she realised, feeling heat rise to the roots of her newly streaked hair. Because she had met Andrew so soon after she arrived in Sydney, and had spent every weekend since away, she had never made any friends—except of course her workmates at Gorgon's, and they didn't really count.

She had liked Anne, Paola and Justine, and they had seemed fond of her, but in her clearer moments she had sometimes thought their friendship was a bit like the camaraderie that might develop among strangers trapped in a lift that had stopped between floors. She was fairly sure that Anne's grandchildren, Paola's girl-guide troop and Justine's irritable bowel syndrome would not have the same conversational appeal for her outside the small, coffee-paper-and-plastic scented world of Gorgon Office Supplies. It was also unlikely that her love life would be of much interest to them in less claustrophobic circumstances. Familiarity and routine had bound them. Once Friday's farewell lunch had come to an end, Holly had officially become part of Anne, Paola and Justine's pasts.

And there was no question of calling anyone in Perth. Closing her ears to her parents' warnings of the muggers, druggies and warring gangs that swarmed Sydney's streets, discarding a perfectly good job in a bank with an excellent superannuation plan, Holly had fled the safety of home, leaving dismay and irritation in her wake.

Her old friends had been offended by her defection and shocked by her ruthless dumping of 'poor old Lloyd' after seven years. Holly had swapped emails with them since, of course, using the Gorgon computer in her lunch breaks, and had told them about Andrew McNish. But their replies had been guarded, relaxing with relief in the final paragraphs to give details of lives that now seemed totally alien.

As for her parents...They had actually met Andrew, early on, when their visit to Sydney for an old friend's funeral had coincided with one of Andrew's rare trips to the city. They had disliked him on sight. During a stiff little meeting 'for drinks,' Holly had read all too clearly in their faces their opinion of Andrew McNish, smooth-talking Sydney spiv, who had told them he could halve their tax bill by various 'perfectly kosher' means, who had told them he always went to a restaurant for Christmas dinner, who said 'Skol' instead of 'Cheers' or 'Here's luck!' when he had a beer.

They had made no comment at the time, but afterwards, safely back in Perth, her mother had said quite a lot on the phone about 'taking things slowly,' and about 'people like us' valuing integrity and plain speaking (versus, presumably, people like Andrew who valued neither). She said that she could see Andrew was very good-looking and all that, but Holly should remember that she and Andrew came from very different backgrounds, and not get 'out of her depth.'

Holly had defended Andrew vigorously. She had said she really admired the way he had made his own way in the world. She had said that Andrew was the most interesting, most stimulating man she had ever met, and she trusted him completely. How could she now ring up and admit that Andrew had left her a farewell note and forty dollars the day before their wedding?

She'd rather die.

◇◇◇

Holly trudged up to the main road, and turned left. There was a bank on the corner. On an impulse that had nothing, really, to do with suspicion but was more to do with making herself feel in control of things, she stuck her brand new keycard into the hole in the wall and asked the machine for two hundred dollars.

It said no. 'Insufficient Funds,' it said.

Puzzled, Holly tried for a hundred. Same result. She tried for fifty. No luck.

Holly stared at the machine. It stared back at her smugly.

'Give me my money!' she said to it. A passing woman smiled, her eyes flicking down to the half-empty bottle of champagne at Holly's feet.

Holly couldn't blame her, didn't resent the smile. No doubt it was odd to talk to a machine, but the woman just didn't understand. Holly's severance pay from Gorgon's, and twelve hundred dollars of her savings, were in that bank. In the new joint account. Weren't they?

Her mind quite numb, she walked on to the office and let herself in with the key Andrew had given her. She tried the lights, and as they flickered on, bland and bright, found tears of gratitude sliding down her cheeks.

The curved white reception desk was bare except for the telephone, and filmed with a fine layer of dust. The computer and printer had gone. Andrew's polished wooden desk, behind its half-glass partition, had been similarly stripped. Holly checked the petty cash tin. It was empty. So were all the filing cabinets.

Stiffly, like a hospital patient taking her first steps to the bathroom after an operation, Holly returned to the front of the office. On the wall of the reception area, directly above a tall vase of slowly fossilising banksias, directly opposite the black leather visitors' sofa, the steel and glass coffee table and the television set, Andrew's face smiled at her from the framed local newspaper article cribbed from his own press release and headed 'From Abandoned Baby to Finance Whiz.'

Holly lay down on the sofa, turned on the TV and pulled the wire off the champagne.

◇◇◇

She didn't have a bad night, considering. She woke up in the morning to the sound of someone changing the locks. And before she had even lurched off the sofa, another real estate agent, Oriana Spillnek by name, was explaining to her, not very politely, that, whatever Holly might have thought, the office was not a flophouse.

Ms. Spillnek also said, her pale blue eyes on the empty champagne bottle rolling under the coffee table, that she, Ms. Spillnek, had bent over backwards to be accommodating, but enough was enough. And that she would very much appreciate speaking to Mr. McNish as a matter of urgency, because his cheque for three months' rent—in arrears, mind you—had bounced sky high.

Holly tried to be dignified but she was at an enormous disadvantage, because she had just woken up, and she was wearing only a T-shirt and panties. Furthermore, she had been so calm the night before, after finishing the champagne, that she had gone to sleep without taking her makeup off, so she knew that her mascara had almost certainly smudged under her eyes, making her look like a raccoon. And clearly her breath smelt terrible, because Oriana Spillnek kept turning slightly aside whenever she said anything, and her mouth felt, as her Great Uncle Tom would have said, like the bottom of a baby's pram—all shit and biscuits.

She told Spillnek about twenty times that she had no idea where Andrew was, but it was clear the woman wasn't convinced. So in the end Holly told her about the wedding, and showed her the note. That worked. Spillnek's pale, shallow little eyes, outlined so firmly in black that they looked as if they had been painted onto her face, stopped snapping and took on a superior, pitying look.

Now that Holly was an established victim, she thought she had a chance of being allowed to go to the toilet, and she was right, though Oriana Spillnek asked her not to be too long, because there was a meeting at the agency in fifteen minutes.

Holly found her shoes, her jeans, her jacket and her overnight bag, and scuttled off. When she reached the little bathroom at the back of the office she locked herself in, leant her forehead against the door and stared at the green paint for a while. Then she went to the toilet, washed her face and hands, cleaned her teeth and pulled on her clothes.

As she combed her hair, a pale, haunted raccoon with pink eyes and blond streaks stared back at her from the mirror above the washbasin. She cleaned off the mascara rings and smeared on some face cream and lip-gloss. The raccoon disappeared and a haunted white rabbit took its place.

She wasn't thinking about anything much, but the terror of her position must have begun to penetrate, because on the way back to the reception area she crept into the kitchenette and stuffed a coffee mug, a knife, a teaspoon and half a packet of chocolate chip cookies into her handbag.

Then she left. The locksmith kept his eyes averted as she passed him. It was out of delicacy, Holly thought, rather than embarrassment. He was about her father's age, and probably had daughters of his own.

The streets were bright, and full of Springwood housewives pushing baby-filled strollers. Also old men in track pants and checked flannelette shirts, and men and women in suits, talking on their phones or to each other as they walked along. They were the same people Holly had been seeing at intervals for three months, she supposed. She had never felt exactly one of them, but now they seemed like members of another species. She would have bet half of her forty dollars that all of them had furniture in their houses, for example. And she would have bet the other half that not one of the women had a coffee mug in her handbag.

Thinking of the forty dollars made her remember the bank again. She went back to it. Checked once more, over the counter this time, that the money in the joint account was truly gone.

It was—except for ten dollars, presumably left to keep the account open. The rest of the money had been withdrawn the day before—just after opening time, apparently. About the same time, Holly thought, that she had handed in her apartment key, bought a cup of weak, sugary coffee, and chugged off toward the mountains in a car that was about to self-destruct. Tears stung her eyes—a bitter blend of rage, grief and shame.

The gawky, doe-eyed teller behind the bulletproof plastic shield, her badge declaring that her name was Leonie, was defensive, scenting trouble. She said that the withdrawal had been quite legitimate, because the account was a joint account for which either party could sign. Holly said she knew that, but this didn't stop Leonie from repeating the phrase 'legitimate withdrawal' twice more, as if it were a mantra that would protect her from despair germs.

As Holly left the bank, her head determinedly high, the heat of Leonie's doe eyes burning into the back of her neck, she remembered that the wedding—or, rather, the nonwedding—was scheduled for midday. It was unlikely that Andrew had bothered to cancel the registry office, or the celebration lunch booking at Angelo's. Holly thought it was probably lucky he had bothered to cancel her.

She bought a takeaway coffee and a phone card, then, near the post office, found a public phone cubicle that still had intact directories. She cancelled the registry office and Angelo's. She said it was because of illness, but was sure that the woman at the registry office, at least, didn't believe her.

There was no one else she had to ring. She and Andrew had decided to get married quietly, without telling anyone until afterwards. Or, at least, Andrew had suggested that, and Holly had agreed. Given how her parents felt about him, a big affair was out of the question. Plus, though Holly had been careful to act very cool, so that Andrew would think that a casual, walk-in-walk-out wedding, with witnesses provided by the registry office, was as normal an idea for her as it obviously was for him, the thought of it had actually given her quite a thrill.

It had seemed daring and romantic to just fill in some paper-work, show your birth certificate and do it, without worrying about bridesmaids, and cakes and lists and endless arguments about whether to have the creamed chicken puffs or the Thai fish balls for the entree. No one else in her family had ever done that, except her second cousin Marguerite, and that didn't count because Marguerite was bipolar and hadn't been taking her medication at the time.

With no one else to call, there was no further reason to stay in the phone booth, but Holly found she was strangely unwilling to leave it. It had become, in the space of five minutes, a refuge. Its smell was familiar. Its smeary perspex half-walls shielded her from the curious stares of the stroller-pushing women, the glances of the suits. She wondered if she was having a psychotic episode. Could it happen so quickly?

She finished her coffee and ate a few chocolate chip cookies, leafing sightlessly through the Yellow Pages so that it would look as if she had a right to be where she was. After a while, she called Andrew again. His phone was still turned off.

Then, quite suddenly, all her confusion, all her doubt, all her fears, were washed away by an enormous flood of anger that left her panting, red to the roots of her hair, but clear-headed. So Andrew had dumped her. Well, he had the right, even if his timing was, to put it mildly, unfortunate. But he had lied to her. He had vanished and left her to cope with the mess he'd left behind. *And he'd stolen her money!*

Forgive me, he'd said. The bastard! Did he think he could get away with this? *Don't try to find me*, he'd said. *Forget I ever existed.* Forget you? Sure, Andrew, thought Holly. No problem. But no way am I going to forget my entire severance pay and twelve hundred dollars. I'm going to find you if it kills me. And when I do...

But, as slowly the rage subsided and the red mist that had clouded her vision began to fade, her breathing slowed and she began to face a few facts.

Other people would soon be looking for Andrew, too—debt collectors working for the real estate agents and Home Comforts, and, for all she knew, dozens of other people and companies to whom he owed money. But when they found him, there would be no money for her. She would be last on the list to get paid. If, indeed—the words 'legitimate withdrawal' echoed in her mind—she qualified for the list at all.

So. If she wanted her money, she had to get to Andrew before anyone else did. Make him pay up. Shame him into it—well, maybe not. Shame had never been a big issue with Andrew. Threaten him with exposure, then. But if they made a deal, she wouldn't be able to pass on his whereabouts to the police, and that would mean becoming an accessory after the fact or something. So...threaten him some other way. Set a trap for him. Surprise him, overpower him, tie him up and then...

Holly bared her teeth, savage pleasure rising in her at the thought of Andrew in her power. Andrew was scared of physical pain. He had told her, chuckling, that he had fainted when he'd had his ear pierced. Andrew was proud of his masculinity, often stood in front of the mirror stark naked, admiring himself.

She imagined Andrew tied to a chair, his pants around his ankles, begging while she smiled and sharpened a knife. Yes! But would he know she'd never go through with that? Maybe. Maybe other, less bloodthirsty threats, threats she could actually carry out, would be more effective. Andrew didn't like moths. Or spiders. Or cockroaches. She could take a bagful of crawlies with her, to the final showdown. There were plenty of possibilities.

How to find him, though? He had no family—or so he'd said. She knew none of his friends. Come to think of it, she didn't even know if he *had* any friends. When she and Andrew had been together, they had been alone. He wanted it that way, and she had been only too happy to agree. When they were apart, who knew what he did? Not wanting to appear possessive, as she gathered some of his past girlfriends had been (the receptionist Aimee for one, perhaps?), she had never asked.

For the first time she realised how cocooned had been their existence, how little she knew about this man she had been about to marry.

Mum was right.

Don't think that!

There were business contacts—Andrew always called them 'contacts'—but Holly didn't know who they were, and anyway she suspected that they would know as little as she did. Australia was large. Her resources were pathetically small. How on earth *was* she going to find Andrew McNish? She didn't know where to start.

And at that moment, Holly always believed, fate raised its middle finger to get her attention and guided her gaze down to the Yellow Pages, open in front of her. There, immediately following *Invalid Aids and/or Equipment*, was the heading that was going to change her life.

Investigators.

Chapter Three

Holly was surprised to see just how many private investigators there were in the Blue Mountains directory. If the industry obeyed the usual rules of supply and demand, untold numbers of nasty little problems were wriggling under the mountains' peaceful, nature-loving surface. Problems that police, social workers, priests and marriage guidance counsellors couldn't fix or wouldn't touch. Many more than she had realised.

She found the thought depressing. Misery loves company, they say. But as Holly pored through the entries, taking in the offers to follow and secretly photograph spouses no longer trusted, to locate runaways, absconding business partners and debtors, to spy on employees, detect embezzlement and collect unpaid debts, she felt as if she were slipping through a crack in the world and into a dark, oily subterranean realm where many other, unknown victims also struggled. She tried to shake off the feeling and focus her mind on making a sensible choice.

Some of the 'Investigators' listings were very brief, confined to a name, address and phone number. Others were large display ads for companies based in Penrith, the large township on the plains at the mountains' base. Using reassuringly sober borders and dignified type, these firms claimed long experience and promised expertise, reliability, integrity and discretion.

They were very similar, in fact, to the ads for funeral directors that Holly had once come across in the Sydney directory while looking for *Furniture, Retail,* except for the long lists of services offered (including debugging of premises, corporate investigations and armed VIP escorts), and their frequent references to state-of-the-art surveillance equipment.

Holly didn't feel comfortable with either of these options. To choose one of the very brief listings would have seemed somehow reckless, a leap into the unknown. On the other hand, she couldn't help feeling that the companies represented by the large ads, up to their ears in the excitement of solving corporate crime, stuffed to the gills with arcane expertise and bristling with guns and surveillance equipment, might regard her loss of severance pay plus twelve hundred dollars as rather paltry.

Possibly, even probably, both these feelings were quite irrational. But even while considering this, Holly found herself automatically gravitating to her natural comfort zone: the middle ground, represented in this case by the small display ads. There were quite a few of these, so Holly narrowed her choice down by considering only those that mentioned reasonable rates and contained the phrase 'No job too small.'

The first number she dialled had been disconnected. Her second call was picked up by an answering machine. The recorded voice, which was very husky and of uncertain gender, said it was sorry that the office was unattended at present, but that Holly's call was very important to it and if she would kindly leave her number, it would call her back. As Holly no longer had a phone number to leave, she could do little but hang up.

Disconcerted by these failures, but still hopeful, she moved to her third choice, dialling what in this case was a mobile phone number, then pressing her finger on the ad in question like a talisman as she waited for results.

O'BRIEN INVESTIGATIONS
*Domestic and Personal *Missing Persons Our Speciality
*15 Years Experience *Friendly, Personal Service
*Reasonable Rates *Discretion Assured *No Job Too Small

'O'Brien.' The male voice sounded tired. Traffic roared in the background.

'Oh, hello! O'Brien Investigations?' squeaked Holly, quite shocked to be talking to a real person.

'That's right,' said the man. 'What can I do for you?' His voice was barely audible. It sounded as if he was standing at the edge of a highway—a highway that carried a lot of trucks.

'I'm—I want someone found,' Holly managed to stutter. 'Could you do that?'

'Husband?' asked O'Brien wearily.

'Fiancé,' said Holly.

'What? Sorry, can you speak up?'

'Fiancé!' bawled Holly. 'The wedding was today, but he left. And he took all my money.'

Passing suits glanced at her then looked quickly away.

'Right.' O'Brien sounded depressed, as if he had heard the story a million times. Was that reassuring or not?

Holly realised that he was speaking again.

'I'm in the middle of moving offices,' he said. 'Chaos, you know?'

'Oh, yes,' said Holly, her heart sinking. Was he going to say he couldn't take the case? Should she have left out the bit about not having any money?

'I'll come to you,' said the voice on the other end of the phone. 'What's the address?'

'I haven't got any chairs,' shouted Holly, meeting the eyes of the passing crowd defiantly.

She thought the man sighed, but it was hard to tell because of all the background noise.

'Okay,' he said, after a moment. 'Where are you now?'

'Phone box in Springwood,' yelled Holly. The phone had begun to crackle.

'I'm breaking up,' said O'Brien ominously. 'Springwood. Okay. The pub halfway down the main drag—the Vicky?'

'You mean the Victory?' Holly roared. 'Near the corner of—'

'See you there in an hour. Beer garden. Name?'

'Holly Love!' shrilled Holly. 'I'm—shortish, and blondish. Sort of. And I'm wearing…' She looked down, to check. 'Black jeans and a pink top. Okay?'

'Okay,' said O'Brien. 'Bring a pic of the loser.'

The phone went dead.

The conversation hadn't gone the way Holly had planned it. She hadn't asked O'Brien's rates, for one thing. But at least he was coming. And he did seem experienced. That tired, gravelly voice had sounded like the voice of a man who had seen it all.

Holly backed out of the phone booth. Traffic noise washed over her. The bright light hurt her eyes. She started walking, her overnight bag heavy in her hand, her quilt bag bumping against her leg. She walked quickly. She had a lot to do. If she hurried she could get back to the house, have a shower, pick up a photograph of Andrew, and still be at the Victory at…

She glanced at her watch and was amazed to see that it was still only eleven o'clock. So she was due to meet O'Brien at midday. That was when the wedding was supposed to have been. The coincidence seemed to her extraordinary, and she found herself snorting uncontrollably with humourless, mad-sounding laughter as she turned off the main road and headed for the shell of her home.

◇◇◇

The beer garden of the Victory was almost empty when Holly arrived just after midday. The lunchtime crowd was still to gather. The desperates needing a quick slug or beginning their daily ritual slide into oblivion were inside at the bar, close to the action.

Groups and couples sat at the few tables that were occupied. So O'Brien hadn't arrived yet. Holly threaded her way to a sunny spot that gave her a good view of the door. Foremost in her mind was the annoyed realisation that she had not needed to give O'Brien a description of what she was wearing. Because she'd done that, she had felt compelled to put on the black jeans and pink top again, after her lukewarm shower, even though the very sight of them made her sick, and they smelt damply of foolish optimism, humiliation and sweat.

On the way to the Victory Holly had stopped at the jeweller's where she and Andrew had bought their wedding rings. It wasn't far from the office. That was why they had gone there. She had paid for both rings, she remembered, because Andrew had forgotten his credit cards. Or so he had said. They had joked about it at the time. Now it seemed a joke in bad taste.

The ring she was to have worn had disappeared with Andrew, but she still had the ring they had chosen for him, in its little black velvet case. The old jeweller, who remembered her, took it back and refunded the money without a word. He was so totally unsurprised that she wondered if he had been expecting her. Maybe in his job you developed an instinct for these things.

As she left the shop, hearing the tinkling of the bell over the door, feeling the jeweller's faded eyes on her back, she remembered that he hadn't smiled at the joke over the forgotten credit cards. At the time, she had just thought he didn't have any sense of humour.

Well, at least she had a reassuring amount of money in her wallet again. More than enough, surely, to pay O'Brien a retainer, or advance, if that was the done thing in the private investigation business, and to bail out her car. What was left would have to support her till her parents' birthday cheque cleared. It would be a near thing. She had to find another job, very soon. And another place to live.

She quickly looked away from that thought by glancing at her watch. It was already twelve-ten. She was attacked by the fear that O'Brien had reconsidered. Got a better offer. Was being stood up getting to be a habit with her?

'Holly Love?'

Holly jumped and twisted violently in her chair. A man stood behind her. He was in his fifties, she thought, and had one of those narrow, slightly swarthy faces which, possibly under the pressure of late nights, alcohol, cigarettes, disenchantment and too few fresh vegetables, had somehow fallen forward and concentrated itself into a humped, beaky nose. Dark sunglasses shielded his eyes. His hair was grey-blond, the layered cut growing out, fluffing slightly over his ears and jutting out over his forehead. He was wearing a faded blue shirt with the top button missing, a crumpled, striped tie with a tiny knot and rather tight cream trousers.

This was O'Brien. She would have recognised the voice anywhere, despite the absence of crackling and traffic noise. She realised that he had come into the beer garden by a door that led from the public bar instead of by the more direct route through the lounge. Because he wanted to sum her up from a distance before she saw him? Or just because he hadn't been able to resist picking up a quick drink on the way to the meeting?

Filled with misgivings, Holly murmured her agreement that she was, in fact, Holly Love. O'Brien sat down wearily, pulling out a packet of cigarettes.

'Mick O'Brien,' he said, sticking a cigarette into his mouth and lighting it in what seemed to be a single movement. 'Want a drink?' Gripping the cigarette between his teeth, he began patting his pockets with both hands, as if looking for his wallet.

'Oh—I'll get them,' said Holly, jumping to her feet. She knew she was being outmanoeuvred by an expert, but felt incapable of resisting, and just wanted to get it over with. 'What would you like?'

'Anything—whatever—Scotch,' said O'Brien. 'Double. No ice.'

Holly went to the lounge bar and bought the drinks. By the time she got back, O'Brien had taken off his sunglasses and pulled the knot in his tie down to about necklace length. He had obviously decided that she didn't need impressing. His eyes were small, pale and strangely blank. He seized the drink and swallowed it in a gulp. Holly sipped her mineral water.

'I brought the photo,' she said, after a moment.

O'Brien nursed his glass and looked at her broodingly.

'The photo of Andrew—my fiancé…ex-fiancé,' she urged, pushing the picture toward him. 'You were going to—'

'Oh, sure, sure,' he said. 'Yeah. So.' He slapped his pockets again and pulled out a chewed pen and a small black notebook.

The notebook's vinyl cover was smeared with something yellow. A picture of O'Brien eating a bacon and egg roll in his car flashed into Holly's mind.

O'Brien picked vaguely at the yellow smear, then flicked open the notebook. He prised a business card from beneath the inside cover flap, scribbled on it, then pushed it over to Holly. 'New cards haven't arrived yet,' he said. 'Bloody printers.'

Gorgon Office Supplies offered a twenty-four hour service on business cards. Of course, Holly thought, things were probably different in the mountains.

O'Brien's shaky printing revealed that his new office was in Mealey Marshes. This was a small village in the upper mountains, he told Holly, between Wentworth Falls and Leura, more or less. Off the highway, in a nice little valley. Not on the tourist beat, which suited him.

Holly was reassured. She had never heard of Mealey Marshes, but the other names were very familiar. Anne, Paola and Justine were always talking about the Leura shops, and Justine had a friend whose aunt had once had a holiday house in Wentworth Falls.

O'Brien's top lip quivered as he suppressed a yawn. He flipped to a fresh page in his notebook and wrote 'Holly Love' at the top.

'So, what's the story?' he said. 'Done a runner, has he?'

Holly cleared her throat. 'How much—?'

'Don't worry. You can afford me.' O'Brien grinned wolfishly. It was suddenly possible to see what he had once been. Much better looking, for a start.

Holly told the story, from beginning to end. O'Brien drew spirals and took a few notes. Occasionally he asked a question. Once he said, 'It always comes down to money in the end, love,' and she thought tolerantly how cynical he was, while another part of her mind wondered if he was calling her by a casual endearment or if by some chance he had remembered her second name.

Halfway through the process O'Brien put his sunglasses back on. Holly didn't know if this was a good sign or a bad one, but she was glad. His eyes had been worrying her. They looked exhausted. Haunted. The irises were dim, grey-blue. The whites were yellow-pink. And when he blinked, his lids stayed shut for a fraction too long. Mornings obviously weren't the best times for O'Brien.

When she had finished, he nodded.

'I'll get onto it,' he said. 'No probs.'

'You really think you can find him? How quickly?' Holly's heart fluttered with hope.

'Couple of days,' he said. 'These guys are amateurs. Trust me.' He licked his lips. 'There'll be a few expenses,' he added.

Holly nodded, gripping her handbag.

In the end, he asked for a hundred dollars. Holly smiled feebly, ignoring the warning signal flashing in her mind. Things seemed to have gone too far for her to turn back. It wasn't that she liked O'Brien, but a strange sort of intimacy had grown between them during the past forty minutes. She couldn't imagine starting again with someone else.

And she did trust him, somehow. The depressed way he'd said 'no probs'—it was very convincing. Holly was certain he had hunted down a thousand men like Andrew in his time. Men avoiding child maintenance payments, men who had faked suicide and left their wives with massive debts, men who had robbed helpless widows and gullible spinsters. (Like Holly?)

So O'Brien lived hard, never re-knotted his tie, and had egg on his notebook. So what? Andrew had dressed like an ad man, wore expensive after-shave, and jogged. And look how he'd turned out.

She opened her handbag. O'Brien leant back in his chair, his hands behind his neck, very casual. The warning signal flashed more brightly. Holly's hand slid over her wallet, seized her cheque book.

'It'll have to be a cheque, I'm afraid,' she said brightly.

O'Brien's top lip twitched.

'Michael O'Brien, wasn't it?' she chattered on, pen poised over the cheque.

'Cash'd be more convenient, if you don't mind,' said O'Brien, flashing a smile. 'Bit of a hassle getting to the bank, little cheques…'

'Oh, I *know*,' said Holly. 'I'm really sorry, but Andrew took all the petty cash, and I can't draw on this account with a card.'

Hard times had toughened her, she realised. Suddenly she could lie through her teeth without a qualm. And she told herself there was nothing to be guilty about, anyway. The cheque she was about to give O'Brien would take up to four days to clear. By that time her parents' cheque would have cleared, and there would be money in the account.

O'Brien sighed, shrugged, and gave in.

Feeling efficient and in control, Holly asked for a receipt. Smiling cynically, O'Brien wrote it on a page torn out of his notebook.

As they parted, he said he'd call her. She told him that she didn't have a phone, and said she'd call him. When?

'Couple of days,' he said again, tucking Andrew's photograph into the pocket of his shirt. 'No probs.'

◇◇◇

Holding tightly to the belief that she had achieved something by hiring O'Brien, Holly bought a sausage roll at a takeaway opposite the Victory and wolfed it down so fast that she scorched her tongue. Then she walked down to the service centre.

The Mazda was parked all alone near the yard gate. It had the air of having been finished with, though in what sense Holly didn't know. Crossing her fingers, she went to the little office where she'd used the phone. There was no one there, but a door behind the counter was open, and loud music pounded from the workshop beyond.

Holly walked around the office to the workshop. A pair of blue-clad legs protruded from beneath an immaculate old gold Mercedes.

'Hello?' Holly called. 'Hello!'

The mechanic slid out from under the Mercedes and got up without haste. He looked at Holly as if he had never seen her before.

'The Mazda,' Holly shouted over the music, stabbing her finger toward the yard gate. 'The white Mazda?'

With no change of expression the mechanic jerked his head and slouched toward the office.

They met again with the counter between them. The mechanic stared at Holly, then his eyes flicked away in what she thought was a furtive manner.

'Had a look at her,' he said, rifling through papers with oil-grimed fingers. 'Couldn't do much with her, but.'

Holly felt a clutch around her heart.

'You mean…it still won't go?' she asked childishly.

The mechanic looked up, looked quickly down again.

'Oh, she *goes*,' he said, and went on thumbing through the papers. He finally found the one he was looking for and slapped it down in front of Holly. She stared sightlessly at the indecipherable scrawls, looked down to the total at the bottom.

The man couldn't meet her eyes. He was obviously cheating her. But she had told him to go ahead if…

'We take cards,' the man volunteered, not looking at her. 'Mastercard, Visa…'

'I'll give you a cheque,' Holly said coldly, wondering if he or O'Brien would get to the bank first.

'Nup,' said the mechanic. 'No cheques. Card or cash.'

That seemed to be that. In silence Holly signed the paper and gave up the contents of her wallet. She watched as the small bundle of notes disappeared into the cash register.

'Thought you were getting married today,' said the mechanic, handing her two dollars seventy-five in change and giving her another fleeting, furtive glance.

'I decided not to,' Holly snapped, feeling her neck grow hot.

'Good on ya,' said the mechanic. His hand jerked convulsively to his mouth. He ran a greasy knuckle over his lips and turned away.

'Take her slow, don't thrash her, don't flood her,' he remarked over his shoulder as he slouched through the workshop door.

It took Holly a split second to realise that he was talking about the car.

She called after him, demanding the car key. He told her it was in the Mazda, on the floor on the driver's side, and it instantly occurred to her, with a stab of bitterness, that she could have taken the car without paying, if only she had known. The thought startled her. Only twenty-four hours ago it wouldn't have crossed her mind. It was sobering to experience at first hand how quickly the veneer of civilisation cracked under stress. Still, she thought, leaving the office, it would have served that shifty bastard right to get dudded himself for a change.

Walking across the yard, she looked over her shoulder. The mechanic was standing outside the workshop watching her, wiping his hands on a rag. Suddenly she became convinced that he hadn't fixed the car at all. But the Mazda started on the first try, purring sweetly as if it had been soothed by the touch of the mechanic's oily fingers.

Holly's eyes suddenly welled with tears of gratitude. Her car, her only territory now, was whole again. The mechanic's shiftiness had not been because he had failed to do a good job, then. It must have been because he knew he was overcharging her.

Well, she could almost forgive him that. And she had shown him she was on to him, anyway. That was a comfort.

She adjusted the rear-vision mirror and saw that a large, curling flake of sausage-smeared pastry clung like a scab to the corner of her mouth.

Chapter Four

That evening, Holly opened the door of the Clover Road house to two dark-suited men—a tall thin silent one with a grey ponytail and a shorter, chunkier one who looked as if he spent a lot of time in the gym. The men had an authoritative manner. They didn't smile. The shorter one asked for Andrew, and seemed unable to believe that he wasn't at home. He said they would like to check for themselves, if Holly didn't mind.

Holly did mind, but somehow the men got in anyway. They just eased firmly past her while she stood gaping at them. The search didn't take long, because there were only two built-in cupboards in the place, if you didn't count the kitchen.

Holly assumed her visitors were employed by Len Land, Oriana Spillnek, or perhaps the car lease firm, but they refused to tell her anything. She didn't like the way they looked at her, or at her small encampment on the living room floor, or at the candle stuck into an empty jar that was her only light. They didn't exactly sneer, but she was sure they would have if she hadn't watched them closely.

As they left, the shorter one said they would make it worth her while if she told them where Andrew was.

The hair prickling on the back of her neck, she said she couldn't help him.

◇◇◇

Later, lying wrapped in her quilt in the dark, echoing house, trying to will herself to sleep while her stomach gurgled, rebelling against a dinner of gherkins and dry breakfast cereal, Holly began to review the impulses and actions that, step by step, had brought her to this pass.

It was hard to know where to start. Had saying 'Okay' to Andrew's sudden marriage proposal been the beginning? Or had her fate been sealed before that, when she had agreed to have coffee with an attractive man she had met in a shopping queue? Or had the fateful moment occurred that Saturday night just over six months ago, when she had decided to leave Perth and flee to Sydney?

No. The real beginning had been a few months before that, when she had ended her engagement to Lloyd Price, her steady boyfriend of seven long years. All their friends had been shocked by the breakup. In an unpredictable, ever-changing world, Holly and Lloyd had made everyone feel safe. They had been together forever—quite like an old married couple, except that Holly lived in a flat above a dry-cleaner's shop, and Lloyd still lived with his parents, 'laying solid foundations,' as he put it, in the firm of solicitors he had joined, and prudently investing his savings against the (unspecified) day when he and Holly would marry.

No one understood how Holly could have made such a rash decision. 'After all that *time!*' people said, as if Holly had left a steady job to join the dole queue just before her long-service leave was due. It seemed to them a mad impulse, and in a way it was, though afterwards Holly realised that trouble had been brewing for quite a while.

The boil-over had happened during the inevitable Sunday lunch at Lloyd's parents' place. Holly, who always ate faster than anyone else and always tried to disguise it, was trying to make a few cooling lamb scraps and half a baked potato last the distance. She was listening absently to Lloyd's mother telling her about a new way of using up small pieces of soap when she happened to glance at Lloyd and his father, who were amiably discussing their golf handicaps.

She knew perfectly well that Lloyd and his father both ate their Sunday roast dinner in the same way—meat first, potatoes second, pumpkin third and peas (mashed in a small, carefully reserved pool of gravy) last. She had seen the phenomenon often. There had been a time when she had found it endearing. But that day, as she watched the two men mashing their peas in unison, their pleasant, long-nosed faces intent, their snugly cardiganned forearms moving in exactly the same way, their forks making identical little squishy sounds, something in her seemed to snap. It was an actual, physical sensation, accompanied by a small, pinging sound in Holly's head.

Holly jerked in her chair and for an instant everything swam before her eyes. As her vision cleared, she sat rigidly, fighting the urge to leap to her feet and run. Little chills were streaking up and down her legs, and her knees had started jiggling under the table. She put down her knife and fork and gripped the seat of her chair to hold herself in place.

It was all she could do to wait for the pea ceremony to end, and help serve the apple crumble and low-fat ice cream. She broke out in a sweat as she helped Lloyd's mother pack the dishwasher while Lloyd and his father took their post-lunch naps in matching chairs in the living room, and racing cars buzzed dully round and round on the TV screen like maddened flies.

But when at last she had made her escape—when Lloyd had driven her home, carefully parked his car outside the dry-cleaner's shop, remarked, as he always did, that parking was easier here on Sundays as long as you made it by four, and turned to kiss her before she hopped out and trotted back into her weekday box—she said she had something she had to tell him...

And there it was, Holly thought now, turning over on the hard floor. At a stroke, she had severed the multiple ties that had bound her to her home, and the life she knew. She had cut herself adrift.

She had explained to her best friend, Angie, and her mother and father, about the fateful Sunday lunch—about the meat, potatoes, pumpkin and peas, and about the cardigans. She had added, for good measure, that Lloyd insisted on reusing teabags so a box of fifty would last twice as long.

Angie looked baffled and said, 'Oh, right...' Holly's mother looked worried and said, 'Well, we've all got our little habits, darling.' Her father thoughtfully chewed his moustache.

They didn't get it. Possibly they thought Holly was having some kind of breakdown. Holly, on the other hand, knew she had finally come to her senses, and didn't understand why she hadn't seen the light years ago. It was all so clear to her now. Like a princess in a fairytale, she had spent seven years in a dream. Now the spell had been broken. Not by a handsome prince's kiss, but by the squish of one pea too many.

She was free. Life without Lloyd stretched ahead of her, broad and straight and shimmering with possibilities—notably romance, a tall, dark stranger and lots of hot, safe sex. She felt exhilarated, sad, guilty, excited and frightened by turns.

She told her hairdresser she wanted a whole new look, and emerged from the salon with her mouse-brown hair blonded and cut into a gorgeous, tousled, 'piquant' style. The style lasted till the first wash, then mysteriously transformed itself into a short bob with a side parting and a bit of wispy fringe, but the blonde look, at least, remained to justify the expense.

Next, beginning as she meant to go on, she bought a very short black skirt, a strapless black corset-style top, high-heeled boots and a red G-string. All were great bargains—less than half-price—and all were fiendishly uncomfortable. It only occurred to Holly afterwards that the two phenomena might be linked.

She began going out a lot, and accepted every invitation, but most of her friends were Lloyd's friends as well, so this meant that the invitations were mostly for coffee, lunch or a movie with her oldest girlfriends. She had dropped off the party A list. Party givers couldn't ask both Holly *and* Lloyd, and Lloyd, as the grieving and bewildered dumpee, had the high moral ground. He was the one who needed support. Besides, an extra single man was always welcome in any gathering, whereas an extra single woman, especially one who was possibly mentally unstable, and who had taken to wearing very short skirts, could be seen as a liability.

Things were also bleak on the romance front. After three months, the only tall, dark strangers who had ridden over Holly's expanded horizon had turned out to be married, gay, too old, too young, hopelessly neurotic, or not interested. The fair strangers, both short and tall, fell into the same categories. Holly's only determined approaches came from swarthy men with lecherous eyes and a lot of gold chains, who propositioned her in bars or sidled up to her in the street.

Feeling she might be projecting the wrong image, Holly stopped wearing the short skirt and the corset top. The red G-string was no longer an issue as it had snapped and turned into a sort of lacy sporran on its first chafe-ridden outing. She also let her hair grow out.

Nothing she did made any difference. Suitable handsome strangers continued to be impervious to her charms. Her job at the bank remained as pleasant and uneventful as ever. She took to going to her parents' place for Sunday lunch. Angie and her other friends kept giving her snippets of news about 'poor old Lloyd' over the cheese melts and coffee cups.

And one dreary Saturday night, when at eight-thirty she found herself in dressing gown and slippers, reading the home decorating section of a women's magazine and seriously considering the suggestion that she paint her fridge with 'zany zebra stripes' to brighten up her flat, she realised that dramatic action was required.

So she had sold her laptop computer and bought a plane ticket to Sydney. And met Andrew McNish. And agreed to give up her job and marry him. And ended up here, on the floor of an empty house in Springwood.

Sow the wind and reap the whirlwind, her grandmother sometimes said. Well, so it had proved, Holly thought dismally. Then she remembered that at least she was no longer alone in the storm. She had O'Brien on her side.

One day I'll laugh about all this, she told herself, and almost believed it.

◇◇◇

On Wednesday morning, half crippled from her night on the floor, Holly laboured up to the public phone by the post office and rang O'Brien for a progress report. His phone didn't answer. On Thursday she rang him twice, with no response. By Friday morning, when still she couldn't get through to him, she'd had enough.

She was tired of sleeping on bare boards, showering in cold water and poring over the classified ads in the *Blue Mountains Gazette* by candlelight. *(Barista wanted min. 2 yrs exp…Farrier, 1st yr apprentice reqrd…Maths Tutor…Piano Tuner…Tuba Player…Bantams at point of lay for sale…Boost Your Self-Esteem… Best Quality Mulch…Indulge Your Fantasies! Call Natasha for sexy phone frolics. No Sundays.)*

She was tired of applying for jobs without the benefit of email or private phone. She was tired of living on cheese crackers and breakfast cereal, and she never wanted to see a gherkin again. Her face still burned at the memory of trying to sell the goose-shaped biscuit barrel to the kindly woman at the Springwood secondhand shop who had said she was sorry, dear, but it wasn't their sort of thing, and then asked if she would like to see a social worker. After her last phone call she had exactly thirty-five cents and a New Zealand dollar left in the world, and she was very aware that on Saturday she would no longer have a roof over her head.

Perhaps by now Andrew had spent her money, sold her wedding ring, blown the petty cash. But her determination to find him had not wavered. She had to confront him with what he had done. She wanted to see the expression on his face when he opened his door and found her standing there. If she had to follow him to Darwin, she'd do it.

O'Brien had said he would find him. O'Brien had taken a hundred of her dollars on a promise. Direct action was required.

Holly looked for O'Brien's card in her wallet and was grimly unsurprised when she couldn't find it. Rage had engraved his phone number on her memory, so she hadn't consulted the card since Thursday morning. Either she had lost it since then, or it had disappeared in a puff of smoke. It didn't matter. She hadn't really needed to check the address. She remembered it—remembered that shaky writing perfectly.

Made cautious by adversity, she transferred her suitcases, bedding and china goose to the car, just in case Mr. Land pounced on the house earlier than expected. Then, gritting her teeth, she set off for 16A Stillwaters Road, Mealey Marshes.

◇◇◇

Twenty minutes later, following in the tracks of thousands of ill-fated adventurers before her, Holly was turning off the highway at the small but confident 'To Mealey Marshes' sign. The road off the highway began with a flourish but quickly degenerated into a narrow strip of crumbly bitumen. The 'To Mealey Marshes' signs, thick on the ground at first, dwindled to nothing, but since there were no side streets, Holly moved on determinedly, certain that eventually Mealey Marshes would be revealed.

The bitumen eventually ducked under the railway line by means of a very low, very narrow underpass. A sign tacked to the blackened stone warned 'Oncoming Traffic Has Right of Way,' as if the council believed that at any one time many more cars would be trying to leave Mealey Marshes than wanting to enter it.

Beyond the underpass a deserted, unnamed road straggled away to left and right, roughly following the line of the railway track. On one side of the road was a wire-fenced, weedy railway embankment. On the other side was scrubby bush pocked with occasional timber and fibro houses that bore no numbers and showed no sign of life.

Holly took a punt and turned right. This turned out to be a mistake, but as she discovered ten minutes later, turning left wouldn't have done her much good either. In both directions the road was a snare and a delusion, tempting the driver on by appearing to be going somewhere, then abruptly ending at patches of vine-hung bush and a 'Dumping Prohibited' sign surrounded by rusted supermarket trolleys, bald tires, sodden armchairs and broken slabs of concrete.

Refusing to be defeated, Holly turned the Mazda in to one of the dubious-looking side streets that wandered away from the railway road. The streets all seemed to head downwards, more or less, and she reasoned that as Mealey Marshes was in a valley, it probably didn't matter much which one she took.

It did, in fact, as she was soon to discover. In no time she was hopelessly lost in a maze of featureless dead-end roads, sweating and cursing as she tried to claw back her usually reliable sense of direction. During this ordeal she saw only one street sign. It was at a small intersection, was half veiled by the drooping, speckled leaves of a gum tree, and bore an arrow and the legend 'Baptist Church.'

In desperation Holly followed the arrow. She never found the Baptist Church, but as she and the Mazda idled, bemused, back at the intersection to which, somehow or other, she had returned without realising she was driving in a circle, a white ute with a brown cattle dog in the back rattled past.

Galvanised by the first sign of life she had seen for ten minutes, except for a few parked four-wheel drives (black), two goats (white) and a couple of magpies, Holly wrenched the wheel, put her foot down and set off in reckless pursuit. The ute clattered on for about fifteen seconds, braked noisily, turned abruptly left, then right, and pulled into the kerb just below a war memorial at the top of a broad, gently sloping street lined on both sides by quirky little two-storeyed shops with old-fashioned awnings. A faded sign in the garden surrounding the war memorial read: 'Welcome to Mealey Marshes.'

Holly wiped the sweat from her forehead and blinked. Here, it seemed, was Stillwaters Road, large as life. There was (of course) no street sign, but 'Still Waters Cakes: Tasty Pies Since 1929' was painted on the awning of the cake shop into which the ute driver was already disappearing.

Holly caught a flicker in her rear-vision mirror and became aware that Mealey Marshes' apparent vehicle of choice, a black four-wheel drive, was idling at a polite distance behind her, obviously waiting for her to move on. She flapped her hand in flustered apology, drove shakily past the ute and backed the Mazda into a parking spot halfway down the street. Thrusting thoughts of Brigadoon from her mind, she got out of the car.

The street had a strangely melancholy air, but this might have been due to the greyness of the day and the plaintive accordion music being squeezed out by a pinched-looking busker standing outside the chemist's shop with an upturned top hat at his feet. Ordinary-looking people meandered along the footpaths, strolled across the road and stood chatting at the doors of shops. Dogs tied to awning posts sat dreaming the dreams of dogs, looking animated only when another dog passed by.

There was no bank. There appeared to be no post office. There were no strollers, and no one was wearing a suit.

Holly saw, with a thrill of excitement, that the hair salon beside which she'd parked actually bore a number—5. All right, O'Brien, she thought. Here I come, ready or not. She crossed the road and set off on the track of 16A like a bloodhound who'd been given a scent.

O'Brien's address wasn't what she had expected. It turned out to be a narrow passage between a butcher's shop and a place that sold secondhand books. The passage was painted with grinning white daisies, their fat green leaves spread incontinently against an iridescent mauve background on which pink clouds floated. The sign over the entrance read:

Abigail Honour, Clairvoyant & Psychic

*Tarot Readings, Aromatherapy, Marriage Celebrant,
Justice of the Peace*

Peering into the passage, Holly could just make out a door on the right-hand side. The door, which bore a rainbow with the sun shining over it, clearly marked the entrance to the clairvoyant's rooms. The remainder of the passage was shrouded in darkness.

She hesitated, considering the possibilities. One, despite the sign on the cake shop awning, this wasn't Stillwaters Road at all. Two, she had misread the number on O'Brien's card.

Three, O'Brien had given a false address, and made off with her hundred dollars. Four, O'Brien's office was somewhere further down the passage.

All these theories had their merits, but the fourth appealed to her the most. She moved forward and immediately, it seemed, lost contact with the outside world. The sound of the accordion receded. Mauve engulfed her, and leering daisies closed in. There was a faint smell of fried onions and patchouli.

She reached the rainbow door and paused. Music, heavy on the panpipes, was playing in the room beyond. The door bore a notice that was a miniature duplicate of the one facing the street. Inside, then, the clairvoyant lurked.

Holly bared her teeth at the door, then screamed as it abruptly flew open. A plump woman with dangling earrings and a curly mass of violently red hair stood smiling in the doorway. She seemed to be clothed in an assortment of scarves.

'Welcome, Christobel!' she cooed, and beckoned invitingly.

Her heart pounding with shock, Holly backed away, babbling about looking for O'Brien. She could feel her face burning. The woman must have seen the bared teeth, yet she hadn't seemed surprised. Perhaps people snarled at her all the time. Or perhaps she just assumed Holly had Tourette's Syndrome.

'Oh.' The woman, presumably Abigail Honour herself, went on smiling, but the smile had lost its gloss. 'I felt searching,' she said. 'I thought you were my ten o'clock.'

She pushed back the scarf that hung over her wrist and blinked shortsightedly at an enormous watch. 'Twenty minutes late. Chickened out, I suppose. They're always doing that. I wouldn't mind, if only they'd ring and let me know.'

Holly resisted the ill-natured impulse to ask why that should be necessary. Now that her eyes had adjusted to the dimness, she could see that the corridor ended in a steep, narrow stairway. The stairs were decorated with painted green vines, and seemed to split near the top, leading away to left and right.

'Mr. O'Brien's office is up the stairs, to the right,' said Abigail Honour helpfully. 'I'm sure he's in. I sense his life force. Very powerful. Like the beating of great wings.'

Grinning and nodding idiotically, Holly turned, walked rapidly toward the stairway and began to climb. As she reached the place where the stairs split, she glanced up.

The four left-hand stairs led to a landing featuring a green door screened in white wrought-iron, a letterbox labelled 'E.N. Moss (Mrs),' a flowered doormat that read 'Welcome to My Home' and a large china donkey, its saddlebags sprouting plastic fuchsias in full pink and purple bloom.

The right-hand flight led to a broader landing, the uneven boards of which had been painted grass green dotted with red-and-white-spotted toadstools. Here the mauve of the wall had been relieved by a large red heart, in the centre of which was a door.

The back of Holly's neck was burning. She looked behind her and saw that Abigail Honour was still standing in the corridor, watching her. The woman clasped her hands as if in prayer, and nodded encouragingly.

Holly scurried up the right-hand stairs. A line of yellow circles led through the toadstools to the heart like a row of stepping-stones. A prudent device by the artist, no doubt, to minimise the effects of wear and tear, but following the yellow circles made Holly feel even more like Dorothy in Munchkin Land than she had before.

She raised her hand to knock at the door, then froze as she heard a cracked, crooning voice coming from inside.

There was I, waiting at the church,
Waiting at the church, waiting at the church.
When I found he'd left me in the lurch,
Lor,' how it did upset me.

Holly felt the blood rush to her cheeks. She rapped sharply on the door. The singing stopped abruptly, but no one came.

Holly waited a few moments then knocked again. 'Mr. O'Brien, it's Holly Love!' she called sharply. 'I need to speak to you.'

Still no response.

Holly pressed her ear against the thick red paint, listening intently. And through the feeble fabric of the door, she heard a faint, sly cackle of laughter.

At that moment, something snapped in Holly Love. Perhaps, if she hadn't heard the laughter, if silence had been preserved behind that flaring red door, she would eventually have turned and crept away, down the vine-twined stairs, along the grinning-daisy corridor, out into the melancholy street. Perhaps then, her mind numb, she would have got back into her car and driven away from Mealey Marshes, never to return. But she had heard the laughter. And after that, it was no more Miss Very-Nice-Girl.

'I heard that! I know you're in there, O'Brien!' she screeched, beating at the door with the flat of her hand.

She heard a noise behind her and swung around. The green door on the other side of the stairwell had opened. A small, sweet-faced, white-haired old lady—E.N. Moss (Mrs), no doubt—was peering curiously through the curlicues of her security screen. She was wearing a fluffy pink jumper, a pink skirt and delicate high-heeled shoes. A large ginger cat sat beside her, looking protective and disapproving.

'It's all right,' Holly gabbled. 'I just want to see Mr. O'Brien. He owes me money.'

The old lady's eyes widened. Giving up on her, Holly flung herself back on the door, grabbed the bright red doorknob and twisted it viciously. The door jerked open, revealing a yawning, stuffy darkness beyond. There was an earsplitting shriek, echoed by the old lady on the opposite landing.

Shaking all over, Holly fumbled for the light switch, found it, flicked it on. Light flooded the long, narrow room. Sitting on the back of a tattered office chair drawn up to a red-painted desk was a large white cockatoo, its sulphur-yellow crest spiked as rigidly as the heavily gelled mohawk on an eighties punk, its round eyes wild, its beak wide as it shrieked again and again.

And lying on the threadbare carpet was O'Brien. Dead as mutton.

Chapter Five

Things became confused for a while after that. Mrs. Moss came tottering over, saw how things were and, convinced that O'Brien had been felled by the opening door, tried to give him the kiss of life. The fact that O'Brien bore no visible sign of injury, and in any case was completely stiff, made no difference to her. The parrot went on screeching. Abigail Honour, attracted by the screams, arrived in a flurry of scarves, believing that Holly had attacked O'Brien and floored him, possibly with her handbag. Abigail said she could smell the anger and fear in the room. All Holly could smell was whisky, but as she could feel her own stomach churning with anger and fear in approximately equal measure, she assumed that she was radiating potent vibes.

O'Brien's wallet, sunglasses and car keys lay in a rather pathetic heap on the red desk. A cardboard box sprouting a tangle of computer leads sagged on a garish green tartan visitors' chair. On a table near the back window, beside the slit of a kitchen, stood a large coffee jar half full of bird seed and an empty parrot cage, its door fastened open by a butterfly clip.

Two empty whisky bottles, a crumpled cigarette packet and a plastic carry bag emblazoned with the name Lorenzo's Liquor lay beside O'Brien's body. A greasy paper bag and a white cardboard box that looked as if it had once held fish and chips were crushed under his elbow.

Behind the dead man's head, three garbage bags hunched against the wall beneath a curtained window that presumably looked out onto Stillwaters Road. The bags were dented in the centre and disgorging what seemed to be a mass of clothes and miscellaneous household items. It looked as if O'Brien had been sitting propped up against his worldly goods, and had gradually slipped down till he was lying flat. Not surprising, if he'd drunk all that whisky.

Mrs. Moss was now pounding O'Brien's rigid chest, attempting heart massage. Holly tried to pull her away, but the old woman clung to the corpse like a limpet.

'It's no good, don't you understand?' Holly begged. 'It's too late!'

'While there's life, there's hope,' panted Mrs. Moss.

'There isn't any life!' bawled Holly. 'Can't you see? He's cold! He's stiff!'

The parrot shrieked. Holly scrabbled in her handbag and found half a chocolate chip cookie. She held it out, murmuring.

'Yum, yum, buttered bun,' said the parrot appreciatively. It nodded several times, and Holly had the strangest feeling that she'd met it somewhere before. It took the cookie in its beak, delicately transferred it to one of its claws, and began nibbling.

Abigail had bent and was gingerly poking O'Brien's hand with one finger. After a moment she sighed, carefully wiped the finger on one of her scarves, then tapped the old lady's heaving back.

'I'm afraid we've lost him, Enid,' she said gently.

When Mrs. Moss paid no attention, Abigail sighed again, seized her around the waist with both arms and heaved her up, carefully balancing her on her high heels before releasing her grip.

'He's at peace, Enid,' she said firmly. 'He has gone on to a higher plane.'

Holly doubted that, but thought it unwise to say so.

'We'll have to call the police,' said Abigail. She glanced sideways at Holly. 'Enid and I are going to turn our backs, now,' she muttered out of the side of her mouth. 'We'll count to a hundred.'

'I don't want to run!' said Holly indignantly. 'I didn't—'

'I know, I know,' soothed Abigail. 'You didn't *mean* to kill him. I can feel that. But, let's face it, he *is* dead. You can't deny that.'

'I don't want to deny it!' Holly said.

'That's very brave of you, dear,' said Mrs. Moss. For the first time Holly noticed what a sweet voice she had. Soft, high and very slightly husky, like a flute.

'It's probably just as well, anyway,' said Abigail. 'You're sure to have left fingerprints and fluff and hairs and things everywhere. We'll say he attacked you first.'

'We won't!' Holly found she was gnawing her bottom lip and forced herself to stop. 'He didn't attack me.'

'He didn't, you know, Abigail,' sighed Mrs. Moss. 'He didn't know what hit him, poor fellow. It was the door, you see. I saw the whole thing. It swung very violently, and—'

'It wasn't the door!' shouted Holly. 'And it wasn't me! Don't you see? He's stiff!'

'Now, try to think calmly, dear,' Mrs. Moss said, which Holly thought was a bit rich, coming from her. 'Mr. O'Brien is certainly a stiff, but that's our problem, isn't it, really? That is, Mr. O'Brien has carked it. And you're here, not denying anything, which is very wise and brave of you, but—'

Holly held up her hand. Mrs. Moss paused courteously and waited, her head on one side. Abigail clasped her hands.

'Mr. O'Brien is cold,' Holly said, slowly and carefully. 'His limbs are rigid.'

'He didn't seem to me a very relaxed sort of person,' Abigail agreed. 'Not that I knew him at all well. He only moved in—'

'His limbs are rigid because rigor mortis has set in,' said Holly, gritting her teeth. 'Rigor mortis—have you heard of that?'

The other women glanced at each other.

'Of course,' murmured Mrs. Moss, with dignity. 'We do *read* you know.'

'Okay.' Encouraged, Holly went on. 'Rigor mortis takes hours to set in,' she said. 'Mr. O'Brien is stiff as a plank. Therefore, Mr. O'Brien has been dead for hours. He died sometime last night.'

She looked from one face to the other, willing signs of understanding to appear. 'Long before I got here,' she added, to be sure.

Finally Mrs. Moss nodded again. 'That sounds very reasonable,' she said approvingly. 'We'll stick to that.'

'It's not a matter of sticking to it!' shouted Holly. 'That's what really happened!'

'I think you're right.' Abigail was looking at her finger, gently prodding the air with it as though calling back to mind the sensation of touching O'Brien's only too solid flesh.

Then another thought struck her. 'But he only moved *in* yesterday afternoon. If he died last night, what did he die *of?*'

Holly shrugged. 'Heart attack?' she guessed. 'Stroke? Drug overdose? Who knows? Maybe he had some fatal disease.'

'Disease?' Mrs. Moss' fingers strayed to her lips.

'We'll ring the police from your place, Enid,' said Abigail. 'If you don't mind.'

'Not at all,' said Mrs. Moss. 'I was just thinking of going back. I don't feel terribly well, as a matter of fact.'

She edged out of the room and began hurrying across the landing to the stairs.

'My name's Holly Love, by the way,' said Holly to Abigail. 'Just so you know.'

Abigail nodded absently. She was looking down at the body of O'Brien. 'It seems awful to leave him here alone,' she said.

'It won't be for long,' said Holly. 'And he's got his parrot with him.'

The cockatoo watched them beadily, crooning to itself.

'It's in mourning, poor thing,' sighed Abigail.

But Holly was fairly sure it just wanted another chocolate chip cookie.

◇◇◇

The police came quite quickly. When they arrived, Holly and Abigail were drinking tea in Mrs. Moss' blue and beige sitting room, every horizontal surface of which was crowded with china ornaments. The ginger cat, which Abigail had addressed as 'Rufus,' was on guard by the security screen. Mrs. Moss was still in the bathroom, swilling, hawking and spitting her way through the bottle of mouthwash she was trusting to kill whatever deadly germs she might have picked up during her attempted resuscitation of O'Brien.

The representatives of the law were a square-jawed young woman who bore an uncanny resemblance to Arnold Schwarzenegger and announced her name as Constable Chloe Gruff with the air of daring them to laugh, and a rather weedy-looking young officer whose head seemed too small for his cap, and whose name no one ever caught at all.

'Where's the deceased?' asked Constable Gruff.

Holly and Abigail pointed wordlessly across the stairwell.

'Is the premises locked?'

'Oh, no,' said Abigail, raising her eyebrows as if the constable should have known. 'That flat doesn't *lock*. The lock's been broken for years.'

She, Holly and Rufus watched through the security screen as the two uniformed figures clumped up to the yellow stepping stones and disappeared behind the red heart door.

'Howdy-doody!' cackled a tinny voice from within. There was a sharp exclamation and a dull thud. Holly reflected that she should have mentioned the parrot.

After a while the police emerged once more, closing the red door carefully behind them. The young man looked rather shaken. Constable Gruff's jaw might have been carved in granite. They tramped back to Mrs. Moss' flat and this time came inside, just as Mrs. Moss emerged from her hygienic exertions, flushed and reeking of peppermint.

'There's a bird in the flat,' Constable Gruff said disapprovingly.

'It's not ours!' gasped Mrs. Moss, in a gale of mint. 'It's Mr. O'Brien's. Who had croaked before we got there. Long before. On the square!'

Constable Gruff regarded her impassively.

'Enid watches a lot of late-night TV,' Abigail explained.

The weedy officer took out his notebook.

◇◇◇

The questioning was brief and to the point. Holly gave a confused account of herself and the reasons for her visit, drawing a veil over the full extent of her financial embarrassment. She saw the weedy officer write 'Unemployed' under her name in his notebook, and felt disreputable. To her own ears, her story sounded highly unlikely, but Constable Gruff made no comment on it.

Abigail gave her profession as 'psychic counsellor,' and described greeting Holly on her arrival, then rushing up the stairs on hearing screams. Mrs. Moss gave her profession as 'widow,' admitted to touching O'Brien's body for the purposes of artificial respiration, and defiantly explained that she had done A Course. The weedy officer paused in his note-taking to stare at her.

'You said Deceased only moved in yesterday. Any idea where he was living before?' Constable Gruff asked, with the air of one who had learned to hope for little.

Abigail hesitated, glancing at Mrs. Moss. 'In a brown Torana,' she said finally. 'It's usually parked in the lane beside the butcher's. In a No Standing zone.'

Mrs. Moss murmured agreement and bent to stroke Rufus, a faint blush staining her cheeks, as though O'Brien's fecklessness tainted her by association.

Glazed, Holly watched the weedy policeman write 'brown Torana' in his notebook. She struggled to face the fact that she had hired a private detective who lived in his car in a No Standing zone. A failed detective who had spent all her money on Scotch and fish and chips, then died.

Constable Gruff sighed. 'How long had this been going on?' she asked tiredly.

'Well, we don't know, do we, in *total*?' said Abigail. 'But he was in the lane about two weeks. He managed it quite neatly, really. He slept in the back seat, and shaved and ate in the front. Sometimes he drove away…'

'There's a public convenience in the park near the marshes,' Mrs. Moss added primly. 'I suppose he—'

'Was the parrot in the car too?' the weedy officer broke in, speaking for the first time.

Mrs. Moss shrugged. 'I really couldn't tell you,' she said. 'I tried not to look too closely, when I went past. Not wanting to attract attention. I mean, we didn't know who he was. He could have been *anybody*. Of course, yesterday, when Deirdre and Skye moved out and he moved in, we realised…'

'Looks like he was waiting for the flat to become vacant,' said Constable Gruff. 'Blew all his cash when he signed the lease. Probably had nowhere else to go. Happens all the time.'

Indeed, thought Holly drearily.

There was the sound of voices below, and feet began to climb the stairs.

Constable Gruff looked alert. The weedy officer put away his notebook.

'I'll be back,' said Constable Gruff, and her mouth twitched as though she'd sworn never to use those words again.

Holly, Abigail and Mrs. Moss watched as a sharp-faced woman in a leather jacket and a man wearing a turban and carrying a doctor's bag reached the landing. Constable Gruff and the weedy officer went out to join them, and the whole party moved toward the red-heart door.

'Do you think they believe us?' whispered Mrs. Moss.

'Why shouldn't they?' Holly snapped. She was thinking of her hundred dollars, and Andrew, and the fact that she was homeless. She was very angry with O'Brien for being dead. She found herself wishing that she'd thought to steal what was left of her money out of his wallet before the police arrived. She wondered if she was going mad.

A mobile phone chimed in the kitchen. Mrs. Moss glanced at her watch and clicked her tongue impatiently. 'Of all the times!' she sighed. 'Let's hope it's Winston. He never takes long, poor fellow.' She bustled out of the room, closing the door behind her.

Holly and Abigail sat down again. Holly felt the need to release some of her aggression.

'You said you could feel O'Brien's life force,' she said to Abigail. 'And all the time he was dead.'

'I could feel *a* life force,' said Abigail. 'I didn't know he had a parrot, did I? I didn't see him bring it in.'

'Surely you can tell the difference between a bird's life force and a man's life force?' Holly sneered.

'We're all living creatures, Holly,' said Abigail gently. 'We all have needs, and longings and joys.'

Holly snorted. In her head she heard her Auntie Meg saying, 'Claptrap!' She saw Auntie Meg's little black eyes squinting in the sun as she hung out floppy washing, two blue plastic pegs clamped firmly between her lips.

Abigail jerked slightly in her chair. 'Blue teeth?' she murmured.

Holly jerked in turn. The woman had read her mind!

'It's my aunt, in Perth,' she said.

Abigail looked at her with respect. 'Unusual,' she said politely.

◇◇◇

There was quite a bit of coming and going after that, and hours drifted by. By the time O'Brien was taken away in a body bag, everything had become a bit of a blur to Holly. This could have been the result of exhaustion, hunger and shock, or because Mrs. Moss had early on taken away the tea things and brought out a bottle of brandy.

'Sorry to have kept you so long,' someone said. Holly looked up and saw a very familiar face looming over her. She blinked, struggling to remember whose face it was. There was a strange, whirring sound in the room. For a moment she thought it was a washing machine. Then she realised it was Abigail Honour snoring. Mrs. Moss and Rufus had disappeared, and the kitchen door was closed. Another phone call, thought Holly vaguely.

'We're all finished now,' said the face. A name floated into Holly's mind and she grabbed at it. Constable Gruff. She really did look amazingly like Arnold Schwarzenegger.

'Was it murder?' Holly heard a voice ask. It was a moment before she realised that the voice was her own.

'No suspicious circumstances,' said Constable Gruff. She sounded regretful.

'What killed him then?'

'Doc's seen him before, a few times. Says he had a heart,' said Constable Gruff. 'Could have gone anytime. He had a Liver too, but it was the heart that got him. Stairs, packet of fags, grog, big meal, bingo!' She snapped her fingers. 'Natural causes. Mind you, some people mightn't think drinking two bottles of Scotch at a sitting was natural.' Her eyes slid sideways to the brandy bottle, slid away again. 'But then, some would, I s'pose. It's a funny old world. Anyhow…'

She thrust a card into Holly's hand. 'Tell her to give us a ring if anyone who knows him turns up, will you?' she said, jerking her head at the unconscious Abigail. 'And maybe the old lady could feed the bird for a couple of days? Just till we find the next of kin? We haven't got the facilities.'

Holly gaped and wet her lips. 'It's okay to go in?'

'Sure. There's nothing worth stealing,' said Constable Gruff, innocently offensive.

'No problem,' Holly mumbled. She stared blearily at the card. By the time she noticed that Chloe Gruff spelt her name 'Graff,' the constable had gone.

◇◇◇

Not long afterwards, Mrs. Moss emerged from the kitchen with a platter of corned beef and tomato sandwiches, three flowered plates that matched the teacups, and three flowered paper napkins. The sandwiches, dainty triangles with the crusts cut off, were sprinkled with finely shredded lettuce. Holly hadn't seen sandwiches like that since her grandmother broke her hip and gave up entertaining.

'I thought we could all do with some food,' said Mrs. Moss, 'so I threw these together while I was talking to poor Nigel. Do you have time to stay, Holly?'

Holly nodded, her eyes on the platter. All the time in the world, she thought. No one to see. No place to go.

Mrs. Moss handed her a plate and a napkin and gestured hospitably at the platter. Holly reached for a sandwich, forcing herself not to snatch. She found she was dribbling.

Abigail woke up with a little snort. 'What's happening?' she asked. 'Have they gone?'

She caught Holly's eye. 'Alcohol affects my sensitivity,' she said. 'I shouldn't touch it during the day.'

'You can't give up *all* the worldly pleasures, Abby,' said Mrs. Moss comfortably. 'You don't have to be on the air all the time, do you?'

Holly was already onto her third sandwich.

'You *were* hungry, dear,' said Mrs. Moss.

'Oh, I'm just being greedy! Delicious!' Holly simpered, filled with shame. She jumped up, glancing sightlessly at her watch.

'Thanks so much for everything,' she gushed. 'I'd better be going. They asked if you could feed the cockatoo, Mrs. Moss. Just for a couple of days.'

Mrs. Moss looked doubtful. 'Do you think it bites?' she asked. 'It's not in its cage or anything.'

'It looks pretty tame,' said Holly untruthfully, edging toward the door.

'You know, O'Brien didn't seem the sort of man to keep a parrot,' said Abigail.

She was right, Holly thought resentfully. It would have been easier to imagine O'Brien with a ferret. Or a rat.

'He never even unpacked,' said Mrs. Moss sentimentally. 'Sad, isn't it? He was so keen to move in, too. I mean, Skye and Deirdre had barely walked out the door with the last of their things when he was walking in. He just couldn't wait.'

Couldn't wait to get down to some serious drinking, Holly thought spitefully. With my money.

'You don't like to think about money at a time like this,' said Abigail, shaking her head. 'But what a waste. A month's rent in advance…'

At that moment it was as if something tapped Holly on the shoulder and whispered in her ear. The ghost of O'Brien? That part of herself which had separated from the mainframe when she found O'Brien's body and had been hovering, watching from a distance, ever since? Whichever, what it whispered made sense.

'I'll pop over and fill the parrot's dishes, or whatever, before I go,' she said smoothly. 'That'll fix it for today, anyway. I might even stay a while, keep it company. Even overnight. Poor thing.'

Her heart beat fast as she waited for them to object, but Mrs. Moss simply looked relieved. 'That's very kind of you, dear,' she said warmly. 'Are you sure you won't be nervous?'

Holly shook her head. 'No problem. It's the least I can do,' she said. 'And the body's gone, isn't it?'

It came out more crudely than she'd intended. Mrs. Moss looked rather shocked, and Abigail Honour went instantly into professional mode. 'The physical presence may be gone,' she intoned. 'But the spirit? Who can say?'

'Oh, well,' said Holly inanely. 'We'll see.' She nodded brightly and zipped out the door.

In seconds she was on the other side of the stairwell. Behind the red heart, the parrot was singing dismally.

Oh, dear, what can the matter be?
Seven old ladies locked in the lavatory…

Holly opened the door and peered in. The curtains had been pulled back and sunlight glowed through the dusty windows, front and back. A red-painted door glowed dully behind the desk.

The room looked larger without O'Brien's body on the floor. The empty whisky bottles and the fish and chips wrappings had been removed. So had the wallet, sunglasses and car keys, and the box of computer equipment. The garbage bags still bulged against the front wall. It seemed the police had searched them because they were sagging open. A few crumpled shirts, two belts, a dingy towel and some doubtful-looking underpants had spilled out onto the carpet.

The cockatoo had retired to its cage. It was staring balefully at Holly through the bars.

'You don't have to look at me like that,' said Holly. 'None of this is my fault.'

She slipped into the room, casually closing the door behind her.

Chapter Six

The parrot poked its head forward. 'Give us a biscuit!' it said.

There was something deceitful about its eyes. It definitely reminded Holly of someone, and suddenly she realised who that someone was.

O'Brien.

The physical presence may be gone, Abigail Honour's voice seemed to whisper in her ear. *But the spirit? Who can say?*

Scenes from *The Exorcist,* quickly followed by the memory of a nightmarish colour plate depicting maddened Gadarene swine, which had been featured in *The Young Person's Illustrated Bible,* an icon of her youth, flickered unpleasantly in Holly's mind. Her skin crawled.

She moved a little closer to the big white bird.

'Are you in there, O'Brien?' she asked in a low voice.

The parrot looked at her coldly.

You're losing your mind! a voice snarled in Holly's head. Suddenly seized with terror that Abigail or Mrs. Moss had somehow sneaked into the room behind her and overheard, Holly glanced over her shoulder.

There was no one there. She was alone—alone with the parrot. Which was just a parrot, and should be treated like one. Holly stepped forward and removed the butterfly clip that held the cage door open. The door slid smoothly down. The parrot, secured behind bars, snapped its beak.

Checking that it had enough water and seed, she noticed for the first time that a limp piece of paper was tied to the ring on the top of the cage with a broken shoelace. The paper was headed 'O'Brien Investigations' and appeared to be an invoice. The top half, nearest to the cage, had been severely nibbled, but the words scrawled on the bottom half were still legible.

Sorry but Uncle Bert dropped dead last Saturday. He was never the same after finding out his Russian tart was carrying on with that window cleaning bloke. Don't blame yourself you were only doing your job. He showed us the photos I've never seen anything like it you wouldn't credit what some women will do. About your bill his pension stopped on account of him being dead & there's nothing else cashwise because the funeral took it all even with plastic handles. He'd have wanted you to have something for your trouble & the Parrot is all there is plus I can't take it on account of my asthma.

All the best, N. Curtis

'Silly old bugger,' said the parrot.

Holly turned her back on it. She strode to the overflowing garbage bags and began pushing clothes back inside, holding them by their extreme edges and wishing she had a pair of rubber gloves.

She picked up a blue shirt and felt queasy when she realised that it was the one O'Brien had been wearing when he met her at the Victory. She remembered O'Brien casually tucking Andrew's photograph into the top pocket. 'Couple of days,' O'Brien had said. 'No probs.'

Holly poked at the pocket, felt cardboard inside, and swore. The photograph was still there! She was willing to bet that O'Brien hadn't touched it in the whole time he'd had it—all the time she'd been waiting in that empty house, eating gherkins and dry breakfast cereal, believing like a fool that he was doing something.

Gingerly she slipped her fingers under the flap of the pocket and extracted the photograph. Before it was halfway out of the pocket she realised that it wasn't her photograph at all. It showed a pair of black wrought-iron gates with a huge old vine-clad house—a mansion—rearing in the background. A letterbox fixed to one of the gate supports bore the large number 9.

The focus of the photograph was a man standing just inside the gates. He was turning away from the letterbox, holding some letters in his hand. Holly looked more closely and her stomach turned over. The man was definitely, quite definitely, Andrew!

O'Brien had found Andrew! He'd actually found him! As she looked down at the date printed in white on the bottom of the image, Holly's vision blurred. She blinked rapidly, but the date remained the same. The photograph had been taken on Holly's abortive wedding day, Tuesday.

Slowly Holly made herself accept the fact that O'Brien hadn't been a dud after all. O'Brien had, in fact, been the goods. He'd found Andrew—not just within days, but within hours. Why, then, hadn't he taken Holly's calls on Wednesday and Thursday? If he had news for her...

He was waiting for the cheque to clear. The still, small voice of reason couldn't be doubted. O'Brien trusted no one. He wasn't going to tell Holly anything until he had her money safely in his hand. He'd probably learned that lesson the hard way.

Holly glared at the image of Andrew. He looked relaxed and happy. He was wearing casual clothes—designer jeans, the black knitted silk T-shirt with the V-neck, and his lightweight leather jacket. They were the clothes he'd wear when he wanted to look particularly cool. When he wanted to impress.

His right arm was slightly raised, as if he were gesturing or waving to someone. Holly squinted at the photograph, following the direction of Andrew's eyes. A pale oval glimmered behind the glass of one of the lower windows of the house. A face. It was vague and indistinct, but it was female, Holly was certain.

Something has come up...

Holly realised that she was grinding her teeth, and forced herself to relax. Slowly she turned the photograph over, but the reverse side was blank.

She slid her fingers back into O'Brien's shirt pocket, felt something else, and drew out a business card. 'MID-MOUNTAINS TAXIS' the card declared, '24 HOURS.' Only one line of the receipt form under the phone number had been filled in. Beside 'amount' someone had scrawled $20 and put a ring around it.

Behind her, the parrot chuckled. Holly ignored it. She turned her attention back to the photograph and stared at the house looming behind Andrew. Somewhere that house existed—that big old brooding house with its showy wrought-iron gates. And it couldn't be too far away, not if O'Brien had photographed it within hours of leaving Holly at the Victory Hotel. And not if it had only cost him twenty dollars to get there and back.

It was in the mountains. Andrew wasn't in London, or Darwin, or even in Sydney. He was lurking quite close by. But not too close, Holly thought, examining the photograph so intently that her breath fogged its surface. Andrew looked very relaxed. Wherever the house was, he felt safe—safe enough to saunter out and get the mail, for example. He would have been more wary if he'd thought there was the remotest chance of Holly cruising by and spotting him—not to mention Len Land or Oriana Spillnek.

A wave of heat surged up Holly's neck, burned in her face, exploded into her scalp. She felt as if her hair was likely to burst into flames, and steam gush, hissing, from her ears.

She walked quickly to the back window and after a few moments' struggle managed to push it open. Cool autumn air gusted into the room, bringing with it the faint, mingled smells of eucalyptus leaves, car exhaust fumes and garbage bins.

Breathing in regardless, she looked down at the unlovely back yards of Stillwaters Road. Next door, in the butcher's yard, double gates stood open, revealing the narrow lane that ran behind the sagging paling fences. A refrigerated van stood in the yard. As Holly watched, a very large man emerged from the back of the van, staggering under the dead weight of a huge pig that he was carrying over one shoulder by means of a hook. The pig was wearing a tolerant, humorous expression. The man looked quite jolly, too, considering.

The yard below Holly was a long space filled with a vast array of tall weeds. Little beaten paths, narrow and secret, like animal tracks, threaded through the weeds. One of them led to a lemon tree flourishing against the back fence, which tilted drunkenly under the weight of a rampant vine with yellowing leaves. Another, less clearly marked, trailed to the gate that opened onto the lane.

A head was impaled on one of the gateposts. It was the head of a man, face bright red, mouth gaping. Holly stared at the head, befuddled by shock and brandy, dazzled by the light, too appalled to scream.

Directly below her there was the squeak and rattle of an old screen door. The head on the gatepost disappeared abruptly as a figure emerged from the shadows into the yard. It was Abigail Honour. She had a cane basket over her arm and a floppy straw hat on her head. Her scarves fluttered in the breeze. She began drifting along the winding tracks like a gaudy butterfly, now and then snipping at the tops of the weeds with a tiny pair of scissors.

Holly jerked in shock as the straw hat suddenly tilted and Abigail looked up, straight into her eyes.

'Dead heads,' trilled Abigail. 'They're the bane of my life.'

Holly gaped at her.

'I suppose you think I'm awful,' Abigail continued. 'But life must go on, mustn't it? I'm sure Mr. O'Brien would understand.'

Holly found her voice. 'It's not that,' she called. 'I saw someone looking over the fence just now, that's all, and for a minute I thought…it gave me a fright.'

'Oh, just a tourist, probably,' Abigail said vaguely, snapping her scissors.

Holly waved and backed away from the window.

'Poor me,' a voice croaked dismally behind her.

It was the parrot. It was hunched in its cage, rocking from side to side.

'Shut up,' said Holly. But the interruption had brought her to her senses—or what were passing for her senses that day. There had been no severed head on the gatepost. And if it pleased

Abigail Honour to prune her weeds with a very small pair of scissors, she could get on with it. Holly had other concerns.

The first, and most urgent, she suddenly realised, was to find the bathroom. She strode resolutely to a door behind the red desk and threw it open. The smell of incense gusted from the dim room beyond. She could see the hulking shape of a double bed directly in front of her.

She felt for the switch beside the door, flicked it on and started nervously as the room was flooded with bilious green light.

The walls were painted with luxuriant rainforest scenes. Painted vines snaked across the cracked ceiling, meeting at the central ceiling rose from which the bare green light bulb swung on its cord like a bulbous seed pod, emitting a poisonous glow. Possibly, with Skye and Deirdre in residence, the room had held a bizarre charm. Or perhaps not, thought Holly uneasily. But now that the forest lovers had departed, taking their own moveable possessions and restoring the landlord's fittings to their appointed places, there was no doubt as to the effect. It was grotesque.

The bed was so massive as to carved oak bed-ends, and so meagre as to sagging mattress, that it looked like a giant, misshapen cradle. It was skimpily covered with a chenille bedspread that might once have been pink. The spread was heavily creased in squares, as though it had been folded and packed away for a long time.

Thick mustard yellow curtains, also heavily creased, covered the window that looked out over Stillwaters Road. Rearing in front of them was a huge dressing table with three tall oval mirrors and three grimy lace mats meticulously spaced across its width. To Holly's right, the doors of the bulky oak wardrobe hung incontinently open, revealing a bent brass rail and two wire coathangers.

O'Brien must have been desperate. The thought floated through Holly's mind as her eyes searched the writhing walls for signs of a doorknob.

The bathroom would be next to the kitchen, to save on plumbing costs. On the back wall, then. Holly turned left and finally found what she was looking for. The door was beautifully camouflaged, its shape disguised by tree trunks, its knob protruding from the deep red centre of a fleshy purple flower that looked carnivorous.

Every tap in the bathroom dripped, and the walls and ceiling were painted to create the illusion of being inside a waterfall. Luckily, the room was so tiny that Holly was able to make it to the toilet without actually wetting her pants.

Washing her hands afterwards, she stared into the speckled mirror above the hand basin, wondering how she had come to this. How could she, Holly Love, apple of her parents' eye, competent manipulator of invoices in Gorgon Office Supplies, have ended up alone and starving in a dead man's flat? She leaned closer to the mirror, fascinated by her unnatural pallor, her sharpened cheekbones, her feverish eyes, fantasising about a hot, home-cooked meal.

It occurred to her that the last person to have looked in this mirror was probably O'Brien—O'Brien, who had used her money to eat and drink himself to death. She imagined what her mother would say if she knew, and found herself snorting with laughter.

Then she heard, coming from behind the bathroom door, an orchestra playing the first bars of Beethoven's Fifth Symphony. The shock was terrific. Holly froze. Her heart gave a tremendous thump. Her laughter died in her throat.

Da-da-da-dah! Da-da-da-dah—

The music stopped as abruptly as it had begun. Holly swallowed. Her heart was still beating wildly. She couldn't breathe. Was she going to have a heart attack like O'Brien? Was this her punishment for laughing? Would Constable Chloe Gruff suspect the supernatural when Holly's death was discovered? Or would she put it down simply to bad luck?

It came to Holly that if she were going to die, it would be better not to die in the bathroom. For a start, the door opened inwards and her body would block it. Also, when you heard of someone dying in the bathroom you always thought they had probably died on the toilet, like Elvis. She didn't want her friends back in Perth thinking she'd died on the toilet. And it would make her mother sad.

With a superhuman effort she made herself move. As she pulled open the bathroom door and stumbled into the bedroom, something buzzed sharply three times. It was an inhuman but strangely familiar sound.

Two words floated to the top of the boiling soup that was Holly's mind: *mobile phone.* Her heart slowed. She took a couple of deep breaths. Her brain began to function.

The buzzing sounds had come from the direction of the bed. Slowly Holly walked over to the bed, peering at it through the green gloom. The mighty headboard reared up against the jungle-painted wall, so absurdly out of proportion to the spindly cane bedside tables that flanked it that they looked like furniture filched from a child's playhouse.

There was no sign of a mobile phone anywhere, but Holly knew what she had heard. She pushed the nearer of the cane tables aside and scored first try. There, perfectly camouflaged against the darkness of the skirting board, was a phone charger sucking juice from a single power point. The charger's cord snaked under the bed. Holly pulled the cord gingerly, and a mobile phone slid from beneath the dangling chenille.

Holly picked up the phone and released it gently from the cord. It was a duplicate of her phone—the one that had drowned in what seemed another life. It fitted into her hand like an old friend. But it was O'Brien's phone, she knew. Plugging his phone in to recharge was probably the only piece of housekeeping O'Brien had thought worth doing before plugging himself into his first bottle of whisky.

The phone had probably been on the little cane table originally. It had vibrated itself over the edge and into hiding the first time it had buzzed to signal a message. That's why the police hadn't found it and taken it away.

What a piece of luck, Holly thought, then gave herself a little shake. What was the matter with her? She couldn't keep O'Brien's phone! She had to hand it in to the police. Apart from everything else, there were probably important numbers in its memory—numbers belonging to O'Brien's friends and relations.

Of course, O'Brien might not have *had* any friends and relations, a sly voice whispered in her mind. He didn't *look* like a man with friends and relations. For all she knew, the only numbers in his phone belonged to his dentist, the liquor store, the person who fixed his car...

Holly decided to check the stored numbers. What harm could it do? She carried the phone out of the bedroom, seeking light.

'Give us a biscuit,' the parrot said, the moment she appeared. It sounded like blackmail.

'I haven't got any more biscuits,' Holly snapped. 'Do your worst.' She turned her attention back to the phone.

There was a tap on the door. Holly jumped. The parrot cackled.

'It's only me,' trilled Abigail Honour, poking her head around the door.

'Hi,' Holly said brightly, resisting with all her might the urge to put the phone behind her back.

'Sorry to disturb you,' Abigail said, easing into the room and averting her eyes from the spot where O'Brien had lain. 'I just popped up to say that if you're *really* staying tonight...well, I was just picking the herbs for my casserole and it suddenly came to me that you might like a nice, hot, home-cooked meal, so I thought I'd—you know, ask?'

Holly felt her eyes bulging. 'Oh...that's really nice of you,' she said, little chills running up and down her spine.

'Of course, you might rather get takeaway or something,' Abigail added hastily. 'But Mealey Meals in Minutes closes at five, and it's not the best anyway, quite frankly. Lawrence at the bookshop swears there was half a mouse in a rissole he got there once, but that mightn't be true. Lawrence is very imaginative. Anyway, I just thought—I mean, after the day we've had...'

Da-da-da-dah! Da-da-da-dah!

Holly goggled at the roaring phone in her hand, then looked up at Abigail.

'Go ahead,' said Abigail, flapping her hands. 'I'm fine.' She drifted over to the parrot's cage.

There was no way out. Holly answered the phone. 'Hello?' she said faintly.

'I'm ringing about the advert,' a cracked voice barked in her ear. 'Sulphur-crested cocky? Talks? Fifty bucks? Has it gone yet?'

'Um—no,' muttered Holly. Over Abigail's plump shoulder, the parrot regarded her balefully. She turned slightly away.

'What sort of stuff does it say?' the voice demanded. 'Dirty words?'

'Not so far,' said Holly. 'It just—'

'Aw,' the voice cut in, sounding disappointed. 'Bummer. It's for me old Mum, see. She's in a home, see, and one of her mates there's got a parrot talks filthy! Cracks the old tarts up. I wouldn't want to get Mum one that's not as good.'

'No,' said Holly.

'Better leave it then,' said the voice. 'Sorry about that.'

The phone went dead.

'Bye,' said Holly. She turned back to Abigail, who was cooing to the parrot sympathetically.

'I hate to see a bird in a cage,' Abigail sighed, straightening up.

'Silly old bat!' said the parrot.

Abigail cleared her throat. 'Anyway,' she said to Holly, 'I've got clients till six but if you feel like a little something after that… very simple, you know…About seven, say?'

'That would be great,' said Holly, her stomach growling. 'Thank you so—'

Da-da-da-dah! Da-da-da-dah!

Holly jumped.

'You're in demand,' said Abigail, a little enviously, Holly thought. 'I haven't got a mobile myself. They're so intrusive! Enid has to have one, of course, but she only uses it for work. Well, I'd better get back and compose myself for my three-thirty.'

She bustled to the door, glancing back in surprise as the phone continued to roar.

Holly met her eyes.

'It might be important,' said Abigail.

Holly smiled weakly and answered the phone.

'O'Brien Investigations?' an authoritative female voice demanded.

'Oh...yes,' gasped Holly, instantly cursing herself for not saying no.

'This is Una Maggott,' the woman announced. 'I spoke to Mr. O'Brien yesterday.'

'Oh...yes?' mumbled Holly. Had the woman really said her name was Maggot?

'See you at seven,' Abigail mouthed elaborately. She wiggled her fingers and left.

'Mr. O'Brien said he would ring me back today to make an appointment,' the voice on the phone went on severely. 'It's past three now and I still haven't heard from him.'

'I'm sorry,' Holly said. 'Mr. O'Brien's—um—he was called away.'

'What?' The voice on the phone cracked, suddenly sounding more human. 'But—he can't just leave me hanging like this! He promised he'd see me about Andrew today without—what did you say?'

Holly realised that she must have made a strangled sound. She felt as if she'd been punched in the stomach.

'Andrew...McNish?' she croaked.

'Well, he's been going by that name, yes,' the woman said coldly. 'So you know about this too, do you?'

'I'm—his...partner,' said Holly. She couldn't say 'fiancée.' It was just too pathetic, under the circumstances.

'I see,' said Una Maggott. 'Well, if I'd known Mr. O'Brien had a female partner I'd have insisted on dealing with you in the first place. I prefer conducting business with women. They're more straightforward. Presumably you're authorised to discuss terms? Are you free this afternoon? Hello? Are you there?'

'Ah—yes,' said Holly, the phone pressed to her ear, her mind racing like a mouse on a wheel.

'Your name?'

'Um…Cage,' said Holly wildly, meeting the parrot's mocking eye.

'Cage,' repeated Una Maggott, obviously writing it down. 'Very well, Ms. Cage, let's not fence any longer. I won't stand for any more delays. We're hard to find so I'll send my driver to fetch you. The address I have is…16A Stillwaters Road, Mealey Marshes. Is that correct?'

'Yes,' Holly said. 'But, Ms. Maggott—'

'Eric will be with you in twenty minutes,' the woman snapped. 'That will be…at three-thirty. Be waiting outside. Eric might have trouble parking. He usually does.'

She paused as somewhere in the background a door slammed in an echoing space, and there was the dim sound of voices, one high and one low.

'Three-thirty,' she said rapidly, and hung up.

Chapter Seven

At twenty-eight minutes past three Holly was standing on the kerb outside the door of 16A, waiting for Eric. A brooding still-ness had descended on the street. The footpaths were deserted. The accordion player had abandoned his post by the chemist's shop. The thick grey sky hung low overhead like a sagging ceiling. The only sounds were a monotonous thumping emanating from the two-pump garage across from the war memorial, and a lone dog barking mindlessly somewhere in the distance. The whole place looked like a stage set waiting for the cleaners to move in.

Holly felt lightheaded but strangely calm after twenty minutes of intense activity. She had filled the parrot's water container and topped up its seed, ignoring its demand for biscuits. She had moved her car to a spot outside the bookshop, and carried her quilt and one of her cases up to O'Brien's flat. She had stripped off her jeans, struggled into pantyhose and shoes with heels, and put on the most presentable of the skirt and jacket outfits that had been her standard wear at Gorgon Office Supplies.

In the bathroom, sternly impervious to the maniacal shriek-ing and cage-rattling drifting through the wall, she had done miracles with her hair, and applied mascara and lip-gloss with a steady hand. When she had finished, her reflection in the spotted mirror had been surprisingly satisfactory. The hectic flush on her cheekbones rather suited her, she thought, and if the glitter in her eyes made her appear slightly manic, that was probably all to the good. The parrot had been impressed, anyway. It had stopped screeching and sulkily watched her leave, its spiked crest the only sign of defiance.

The photograph of Andrew behind bars was in Holly's shoulder bag, and so was O'Brien's phone, prudently turned to 'silent.' She had thought of leaving the phone behind—had gone so far, in fact, as to plug it back into its charger, guiltily rub it all over with the edge of the bedspread to remove her fingerprints, and slide it back under the bed. But at the last minute she'd retrieved it. A stolen mobile phone was better than no phone at all. After all, who knew what would happen when Una Maggott realised that her visitor was not O'Brien's partner, but Andrew's?

Holly watched the top of the road, waiting for a gleaming car to nose past the war memorial and cruise down in search of 16A. Una Maggott, with her bossy, English-sounding voice, her air of authority and her crisp 'I'll send my driver to fetch you,' had sounded like someone whose car would gleam. Just as, Holly thought grimly, she had sounded like someone who lived in a great big pretentious house with a black wrought-iron fence.

There was no doubt in Holly's mind that her search for Andrew McNish was about to reach its tacky climax. Making her rapid preparations for the confrontation to come, she had warned herself not to jump to conclusions. Frowning into the bathroom mirror, ruthlessly pulling her lank hair into shape, she had forced herself to consider other possibilities.

None of them was convincing, for two reasons. The first was the way the woman's confident voice had softened when she spoke Andrew's name. The second was the fact that Andrew had never mentioned Una Maggott to Holly, as he certainly would have done if his relationship with the woman had been innocent—if she'd been a client, for example. Andrew thought odd names were hilarious, and wouldn't have been able to resist making a joke of a name like 'Una Maggott.'

So Una was one of Andrew's secrets. And O'Brien had found it out. He had found out about Una Maggott, and a couple of days later he'd made contact with her. In her present mood, Holly could think of only one reason for that: blackmail. O'Brien had tracked Andrew down, seen him at that big house, and sniffed money. He had then done a little more research and found out the extent of Andrew's financial problems which, for all Holly knew, were far greater than a bit of back rent owing. For all Holly knew, Andrew had embezzled money from his clients' accounts as casually as he'd taken her money from the bank.

It was sobering to realise how very likely this seemed to her, and how little it surprised her. In a way, she was more disappointed in O'Brien for deciding to sell out on her by offering to keep Andrew's hideout a secret in return for wads of Maggott cash. For some reason she had believed that O'Brien, sly, tired and egg-stained though he was, had retained a worn core of professional pride. Well, she'd been wrong about that, apparently. But she hadn't been wrong to trust O'Brien's expertise. She'd trusted O'Brien to find Andrew. O'Brien *had* found Andrew. And fate, in the form of O'Brien's phone, had delivered Andrew into her hands.

Holly watched the war memorial, running over her plans for a ruthless pumping of Eric on the drive to the Maggott love nest. Eric, who usually had trouble parking, sounded elderly. He was probably some respectable retiree making a few extra dollars to supplement his pension. It was possible he actually lived on the Maggott property, providing driving and handyman services in return for free accommodation.

Coldly Holly reflected that while her success with men her own age had always been variable, she definitely had a way with old codgers. Being smallish and blondish and depressingly wholesome-looking, she seemed to bring out their protective streak. If all went well, Eric would be putty in her hands and she'd know all there was to know about Andrew's relationship with Una Maggott before arriving at the house. She'd know what approach to take. She'd be more than ready to 'negotiate terms.'

'Welcome, Carmel!' trilled Abigail Honour's voice behind her. Holly jumped and turned just in time to see a stocky, bristle-haired woman in camouflage pants and battle jacket disappear into Abigail's sanctum. She was rather startled to realise that she hadn't heard the woman approaching or entering the doorway of 16A.

Neither had she sensed the presence of the bald man in the bloodstained striped apron who was leaning against the tiled green wall of the butcher's shop behind her, yet he must have been there for quite a while because the cigarette he was smoking had burned down almost to its filter.

'One born every minute,' said the butcher, apparently referring to the woman in camouflage pants. 'Can you believe a *bloke* was in there just before, making an appointment? You wouldn't read about it! A *bloke*! Didn't look like a pansy, either. Still, you can't always tell. Some of them look just like you or me.'

He sucked the last bit of nourishment from his cigarette, dropped the butt on the footpath and ground it out with his heel.

'Filthy habit,' he commented.

He seemed to expect a response, so Holly murmured and smiled.

'Oh, I know all about that,' said the butcher argumentatively. 'But what I say is, everyone's got a right to go to hell their own way, and it's my choice.'

Holly nodded and kept smiling.

'People should keep their beaks out of other people's business, is what I say,' said the butcher, his voice rising. 'Bloody do-gooders are ruining this country. Don't eat this, don't drink that, this'll give you cancer, that'll give you a heart attack—carrying on like two-bob watches, nagging at a bloke every minute of the day. It's what's causing all this depression if you ask me.'

He jerked his thumb at the maw of 16A. 'Bloke topped himself up there this morning,' he said. 'Couldn't take it anymore, I s'pose. Carried out in a plastic bag, poor bastard. Still, it comes to us all in the long run.'

He fell silent. A strange expression crossed his face, which then became quite blank. Holly stared at him. He moved uneasily and nodded at a point over her right shoulder.

Holly spun around.

A huge, gleaming black vehicle was sliding noiselessly to a halt exactly opposite the doorway of 16A. Holly blinked, desperately tried to make herself believe that it was a vintage stretch limousine adapted for the transport of the handicapped, then focused on the silver rails that adorned its roof and forced herself to admit the truth: the vehicle was a hearse.

A man with slicked-back black hair, his eyes shielded by sunglasses, his plump body encased in a white sequinned jump-suit, slid out of the driver's seat, slouched around the enormous bonnet and opened the passenger door.

'Miz Cage?' he drawled.

'Crikey,' said the butcher.

Holly moved between the parked cars and climbed into the hearse. The door shut on her with a quiet, expensive *thunk*, sealing her in with the smells of leather, musky men's cologne, sweat and hair oil.

The driver got back in, checked his reflection in the rear-view mirror and put on his seatbelt, adjusting it carefully to avoid the stand-up collar at the back of his neck and the deep V of chest hair exposed by his jumpsuit's plunging neckline. He waited, staring moodily through the windscreen, while Holly put her seatbelt on too. Then he released the handbrake and the hearse moved on up the street.

Holly glanced back. The butcher was staring after her. She hoped he had taken the hearse's number.

She cleared her throat. 'Are you Eric?' she asked brightly.

The driver nodded slightly, turning left at the war memorial.

Holly wet her lips. 'Ms. Maggott said you might have trouble parking,' she said, trying to sound casually interested. 'I didn't realise why until I saw the hearse. It's very big, isn't it?'

Eric said nothing.

Holly abandoned subtlety. 'Why does Ms. Maggott drive a hearse?'

'*She* don't drive her,' Eric drawled. 'No one drives her but me.' He turned right and picked up speed.

Holly noticed that her knuckles were white, and deliberately released her grip on her shoulder bag. She pressed her lips together to stop herself asking any more questions. Questions weren't working. Maybe silence would.

Her instinct was right.

'Ol' Maggott held on to the hearse when he sold the business,' Eric volunteered after a few minutes. 'Miz M's daddy, you know? He was Aristo-crat Funerals. Family business, but they never used their own name. Thought it might put people off.'

'Oh,' Holly said weakly. 'Right.'

'That was before I knew him, o' course,' said Eric. 'When I knew him he'd been re-tired for years.'

Holly cleared her throat. 'I gather he's...no longer with us.'

'I drove him to the cem-er-tery a year ago on Thursday,' Eric agreed. 'Rest his soul. He left me this old lady in his will. She was a be-quest.'

He glanced in the rear-view mirror and adjusted his sunglasses. The hearse slowed. Holly looked ahead and saw to her astonishment that they had already reached the railway underpass. When the underpass had been negotiated and the hearse was proceeding serenely toward the highway, she played the only card she had.

'You look amazingly like Elvis,' she said.

Eric didn't turn his head, but his full lips twitched with gratification. 'That's what they say.'

'Awfully like,' said Holly earnestly. 'It's quite eerie, really. I've never met an Elvis impersonator before.'

'Tribute artist,' Eric corrected with a slight frown.

'Oh, right. Sorry. Tribute artist.'

'Comes natural to me,' said Eric. 'Always has. I got the spirit.'

'Do you sing?' asked Holly, hating herself.

'Got a little gig once a month at Twitches in Katoomba,' Eric said modestly, his Southern drawl slipping a bit. 'Friday nights. Nothing much. Forty-minute set. Few of the King's hits. Requests. You know. But people seem to like it.'

'I'm sure,' Holly gushed. 'I had no idea. I'm new to the Mountains. I'll have to come and see you one night.'

'Y'all let me know and I'll get you in on the door,' Eric said grandly. 'You got a favourite number?'

'"Love Me Tender,"' said Holly. She hoped that was an acceptable choice. It was the only Elvis song she could think of at short notice.

Eric smiled. 'I get a lot of requests for that one. We always do it with the spot.'

They reached the highway. Eric waited for a break in the traffic, tapping his pudgy, heavily beringed fingers on the wheel. Holly looked at the fingers, and a scrap of TV-gleaned Elvis trivia floated to the top of her mind.

'You've even got the horseshoe ring,' she said.

Eric actually grinned. 'Never take it off.'

A gap appeared in the traffic and the hearse turned majestically right and headed up the highway.

'I do parties too—birthdays, weddings, anniversaries, stuff like that,' said Eric. He seemed very relaxed now. The recognition of the horseshoe ring had done the trick. Holly decided it was safe to try to extract some real information.

'I don't even know where we're going,' she said girlishly. 'I've got the address somewhere.'

'Medlow Bath,' said Eric. 'Next village up from Katoomba.'

'Oh, yes, Medlow Bath, I remember now. Number 9 Something Street, Medlow Bath,' Holly burbled.

'Horsetrough Lane,' said Eric, looking tolerant.

He hadn't corrected the house number. Holly felt a stab of fierce triumph, which was immediately followed by a wave of nausea. She'd been right. They were heading for the house in the photograph. And Andrew.

The hearse swept along doing a steady eighty kilometres an hour. Holly noticed that the other cars on the road were giving them a wide berth.

'It runs very well, doesn't it?' she said, to break the silence.

Eric nodded, glancing in the rear-vision mirror. 'Not bad for an old girl,' he said. 'I been driving her nearly eleven years—ten of them for Ol' Maggott. Started driving for him after they took his licence off him for being a nutter.'

'Really?'

'Don't know how he kept it as long as he did,' said Eric, who was now so relaxed that his drawl had almost completely disappeared. 'From what I hear he'd been a sandwich short of a picnic for years—even before he sold the fu-neral home. There were a few stories about him getting funny with the corpses and all that.'

Holly's stomach churned.

'He had these ob-sessions,' said Eric reminiscently. 'Corpses. Egypt. Snakes. Steam trains. Teeth. Spooked people, you know? But I could manage him all right. You just had to humour him.'

'I can imagine.'

'He spent a fortune on the Egypt thing after he sold the business. Bought a lot of statues and stuff—real anti-quities, some of them. Built little pyramids and temples in the yard, even. But after he hired me he got to be a big Elvis fan. Started collecting the King's LPs. Liked me to wear the gear all the time. That suited me. This—' Eric tapped the wheel '—this is my living. Being a tribute artist is my life.'

Holly found herself warming to him, and fearing for him too. It was extraordinary that snooty Una Maggott had kept him on after her father died. She could just imagine what Andrew thought of him. Yet Eric seemed sublimely unaware of how precarious his sheltered existence was. Maybe he was on some sort of contract, and Maggott was just counting the days until his time ran out.

'He loved "Blue Suede Shoes," Ol' Maggott,' said Eric. 'I must have sung that number to him a thousand times. I'd knock myself out doing it for him and in half an hour he'd have forgotten the first go and be pestering me to sing it again.'

He laughed with real affection. Holly laughed too, and for a moment the hearse was a warm, safe place, spinning along the highway between walls of secret, grey-green bush.

They passed the Katoomba hospital, a cluster of signs on the next corner ominously directing the way to Casualty, the cemetery and the tip. They passed Katoomba's unlovely skyline pierced with occasional, breathtaking views of green-fringed pink cliffs rearing through blue mist. The highway began winding upward to Medlow Bath.

Time to get some hard information, Holly thought. Easy does it. She gave a little stretch and pretended to smother a yawn.

'The old man sounds like a real character,' she said. 'I don't suppose it's as much fun for you, working for his daughter. Especially with Andrew McNish…' She paused invitingly.

Eric glanced into the rear-view mirror and cleared his throat. 'Look,' he said abruptly, 'how about I take you back to Mealey?'

'What?' Astounded, Holly turned to look at him.

'I'll tell Miz M you couldn't make it—had to go out of town,' he said, staring straight ahead. 'You don't want to get mixed up in this thing. It's not worth it to you, believe me.'

A prickling sensation ran down Holly's spine. How much did this man know? Was he threatening her?

'The place is full of bloodsuckers as it is,' Eric said, his lips barely moving. 'How about we just turn around? You could be home in fifteen minutes.'

It was strangely tempting. Half an hour ago Holly would never have believed that the idea of returning to the sordid apartment on the top floor of 16A Stillwaters Road could have so much appeal. But Stillwaters Road wasn't home. Thanks to Andrew McNish, Holly didn't have a home anymore.

'I'd rather go on, please, Eric,' she said stiffly.

Eric's face darkened. Suddenly he looked more like Elvis than ever—Elvis on a bad day.

'It's your funeral,' he said. He hunched his shoulders, tapped his rings on the wheel, and drove on.

Chapter Eight

Eric preserved a forbidding silence for the rest of the journey, and Holly was left to her own thoughts, which were uncomfortable.

Clearly, unlikely as it seemed, Eric was in Una Maggott's confidence. He knew about O'Brien's blackmail attempt—the contemptuous reference to bloodsuckers couldn't mean anything else. He had given Holly the chance to turn from her wicked, bloodsucking ways and she had rejected the offer. Now he thought she was the lowest of the low.

As the hearse oozed off the highway and purred into the leafy depths of Medlow Bath, Holly told herself it didn't matter what Eric thought. As signs of habitation became rarer, then disappeared altogether, she sustained herself with the knowledge that Eric would soon discover that she wasn't in fact O'Brien's partner *or* a blackmailer—just a penniless, homeless victim of Andrew McNish's perfidy. But as Eric swung the hearse into a narrow, bush-lined lane and a big old house surrounded by a very high, very familiar, black railing fence loomed into view, her stomach turned over sickeningly and her palms began to sweat.

Eric slowed the hearse to a crawl, took his phone from the dashboard, punched in numbers one-handed and put the phone to his ear.

'Comin' in,' he drawled.

Before he had clicked the phone off, the black iron gates ahead had begun to swing inward. By the time the hearse reached them they were fully open. Eric's timing had been perfect.

He turned the wheel languidly and gravel crunched as the hearse cruised through the gateway, passing smoothly over the place where Andrew McNish had stood in O'Brien's photograph. Holly surreptitiously blotted her hands on her skirt and stared straight ahead, preparing for action.

A broad apron of pristine white gravel fronted the house, and gravel drives swept gracefully around to the back on both sides, skirting discreet black light poles. Infant lavender hedges flanked the stone front steps, the individual grey bushes still less of a feature than the mulch heaped lavishly at their roots.

Having taken in this scene and registered 'new work' plus 'must have cost a bit,' Holly raised her eyes and was disconcerted. In O'Brien's photograph the Maggott house had been merely the vine-clad backdrop to the image of Andrew McNish, dressed to impress and cosily collecting someone else's mail. The photograph had given the impression that Andrew had fallen very much on his well-shod feet. The backdrop house had reeked of grandeur and money—qualities that were right up his street. Close up, it reeked of other things.

Bulging with streaked green copper domes, writhing with decorative ledges, arches and palisades, it reared dark, vast and feral above its neatly ordered frontage. The creeping fig that smothered its rendered face had overwhelmed window frames, sealed French doors, clogged the rusty wrought-iron wreathing the balconies, and even crept across the dormer windows of the attic. The ridge of the steeply pitched slate roof was spiky with weather vanes and lightning rods. Every visible window was barred, French doors included.

Number 9 Horsetrough Lane was, in fact, exactly the sort of house in which the teenage stars of a slash movie might have spent the night for a dare, despite knowing, surely, from their own movie-going experience, that this could only lead to mass slaughter, with one traumatised soul left alive to tell the tale.

The hearse swept around in a curve and stopped in front of the steps, which led up to a verandah and a massive front door that was an extravagance of carved wood, speckled brass fittings and leadlights featuring lyrebirds, ferns and waratahs. The engine idled almost silently. Eric idled similarly, looking straight ahead. Clearly he didn't intend to move. Bloodsuckers, presumably, didn't deserve to have their doors opened for them.

'Thank you,' Holly said crisply. She removed herself from the hearse, closing the door behind her with thoughtful gentleness. The dignity of her exit was slightly marred when the lock didn't catch. Without changing expression, Eric leaned over and pulled the door properly shut before easing the hearse on around the house.

Holly looked around, getting her bearings. The grounds of the house were level and park-like, an impression reinforced by the black railings and the fact that there was nothing to be seen beyond the gravel apron but grass and a few massive old trees in full autumn colour. The grass was thick and weedless—not a dandelion or patch of moss to be seen. It had obviously been laid recently. Faint lines still showed between the sods. Holly noted with spiteful pleasure that around the trees the turf's hopeful green was already sickening to yellow beneath circular shrouds of fallen leaves.

She turned back to the house and saw a face move behind the lace curtain of the bay window to the left of the front door. Someone had been watching her. Her heart fluttered painfully.

She took a firm grip on her shoulder bag and walked up the steps. In three strides she crossed the patterned tiles of the verandah, the heels of her shoes tapping purposefully. The crazed white button to the right of the door was marked 'Press,' so she pressed it.

The button sank deep into its elaborate wooden surround, taking half her finger with it. There wasn't a sound. No one came. Holly wrenched her finger free. She lifted the heavy brass knocker fixed to the centre of the door and slammed it down. Once, twice, three times. She could hear the crashes echoing on the other side of the door.

She waited tensely, listening for approaching footsteps, making plans. If Andrew were the one to open the door, how would he react? He'd be shocked, of course, but how quickly would he recover? Would he attempt nonchalance? (*Holly! Hi! Tracked me down, did you?*) Or, appalled at the idea of a squalid scene, would he panic and slam the door in her face?

She clutched her bag to her chest and turned slightly sideways, poising herself to shoulder charge her way into the house the moment the door opened.

A shadow loomed behind the lyrebird glass. A key turned in a lock. The door opened a little. An exquisite face appeared in the gap, intricate earrings swinging like miniature chandeliers, huge dark eyes mildly enquiring. Holly's blood boiled, but the shoulder charge no longer seemed an option.

'Ms. Maggott?'

The young woman stepped back, pulling the door wider. She was a head taller than Holly, and ballerina slim. Her perfect skin was the colour of milk coffee. Her glossy black hair was caught back in a craftily negligent knot at the nape of her neck. Her eyelashes were so long and thick that they actually cast shadows when she blinked. She was wearing a calf-length tunic of peacock blue silk over softly pleated scarlet trousers, and soft red shoes with sequinned toes. Reflecting sourly that if she had worn an outfit like that she would have looked as if she were standing in a hole, Holly clumped into the house.

The woman closed the door behind her and turned the key protruding from the lock. Holly suppressed a mild twinge of panic. She was doing nothing wrong. She had nothing to fear. But still, she was relieved when her hostess left the key where it was when she turned away from the door, faintly smiling.

The floor of the vast, dim entrance hall was tiled in chessboard black and white. The walls were cedar panelled to shoulder height and hung with dark, elaborately framed paintings, the largest of which was a portrait of a black-suited middle-aged man with the mad, cunning little eyes of a wild boar. A cluster of brass chains, from which presumably a light fitting had once hung, dangled from the ceiling, swaying and chinking together in the draught as the front door closed. Through a doorway to her right, Holly could see floor-to-ceiling bookshelves and a long table. Directly ahead, a grand staircase rose into dimness.

A shadow stood motionless at the top of the stairs. Holly's skin prickled. She took a step, squinting up. The shadow retreated, melting away into darkness. Holly lunged forward.

'Ms. Cage!'

Holly froze in mid-stride and looked around. A door to her left stood partly open. The voice, unmistakeably that of Una Maggott, had come from the room beyond that door. Holly glanced in confusion at the beauty in peacock blue, who returned her gaze serenely.

'Here!' snapped the voice, as if Holly were a recalcitrant terrier.

Reining in her irritation, reminding herself that this was Maggott's house, and that it would probably be unwise to go rampaging after Andrew without at least explaining what she was doing, Holly walked to the open doorway and looked in.

Directly opposite the door, a gigantic snake raised its head and looked back at her. Vast, scaly coils shifted lazily, black mottled with yellow. A dull roaring began in Holly's ears. Through the roar she heard herself give a little squeak.

'Don't worry about the python,' Una Maggott's voice said impatiently. 'It's perfectly safe.'

Holly tore her eyes from the snake, which she now saw was enclosed in a glass cage with a wire netting lid, and looked to her left.

A woman sat there, behind a large, uncluttered desk that had been set squarely in the centre of the room, at right angles to an elaborately carved marble fireplace. The woman was impeccably groomed, and ferociously plain. Her clothes were exquisitely cut, but classic to the point of looking slightly out of date. Her smooth cap of hair, with its ruler-straight centre parting and uncompromisingly short, straight fringe, was iron grey. Deep furrows scored the space between her eyebrows and dragged down the corners of her mouth. She must have been at least sixty. And she was sitting in a wheelchair.

Holly gaped, all her assumptions flying apart. Struggling to reform them into a pattern that made sense, she looked quickly back over her shoulder, but the young woman in blue had vanished.

'Lily creeps around like a cat,' Una Maggott said, noting her startled expression. 'I dislike it intensely. Fortunately, after Sunday she'll be gone. I've had enough of her. Shut the door, please. I don't want to be overheard.'

Holly did as she was told. She found herself in what had once been a grand double parlour, the sort that could be divided into two rooms by folding cedar doors. In its present incarnation the front room, where Una Maggott sat, was part office, part sitting room, and the back, only partly screened off by the folding doors, was a bedroom disfigured by a partitioned corner that was probably, Holly thought vaguely, an ensuite bathroom.

It was all very practical and understandable, given Una Maggott's wheelchair status. Less easy to accept was the python—and the fact that the front room had been painted to resemble the interior of an ancient Egyptian tomb. Pharaohs, queens, jackals, cats and numerous sinister-looking animal and bird-headed gods marched around the walls in a hail of hieroglyphics, all apparently intent on escaping through the bay window at the front of the house.

'Hideous, aren't they?' Una Maggott remarked, regarding the stalking figures dispassionately. 'My father got some local artist to come in and paint them. He was a great enthusiast, but he had appalling taste.' She gestured imperiously at an armchair that faced the desk.

Holly didn't want to sit down. She felt an instinctive antipathy to Una Maggott. She knew in her bones that the woman was alien to her—one of those cold, dominating people who, like school bullies and saleswomen in certain dress shops, had always seemed to her to be members of an enemy species. But Una was in a wheelchair. It would be churlish to insist on standing, looking down at her. Besides, Holly had no desire to stay where she was, so close to the snake.

It was still watching her intently. The black and yellow coils had become perfectly still, and it had occurred to her that the creature could very well be poised to spring. She didn't know much about the attack methods of pythons, but she had an idea they could strike surprisingly quickly. She wondered how thick the glass of the cage was, how secure the wire netting lid.

The chair Una Maggott had offered was covered in aged red velvet that had split here and there exposing puffy worms of white stuffing. It had short, bowed brown legs and a low, spreading seat that sagged so dramatically as Holly sat on it that her nose ended up about level with the edge of the desk top.

Una opened a folder and picked up a gold fountain pen. 'Now, your terms?' she asked crisply.

But the subsiding chair had been the last straw for Holly. It was time to seize the initiative. She cleared her mind of hearse, python, mural and wheelchair. She sat forward, trying to gain some height by perching on the front rail of the chair's barely concealed wooden frame.

'I'm not here to extort money from you, Ms. Maggott,' she said firmly. 'I'm only interested in finding Andrew McNish.'

'I'm perfectly aware of that, Ms. Cage,' Una snapped. 'Why do you imagine I contacted O'Brien's in the first place?'

Holly felt her jaw drop. She made a huge effort to pull it up again, but it seemed to have frozen. Her thoughts scuttled round in her head like rats in a trap. *Una* had contacted *O'Brien*, not the other way around! Holly made a mental apology to O'Brien, wherever he was. O'Brien hadn't been a blackmailer. He hadn't sold Holly out after all. But what did this mean? Had Andrew somehow found out that Holly had hired O'Brien to track him down? Had Andrew persuaded Una to ring O'Brien and offer to pay him off?

Una slid a mud-smeared business card from the folder in front of her. It was O'Brien's card, with the Mealey Marshes address scrawled on it in blue biro. Holly's lost talisman.

'Eric found this on the front path of Andrew's house in Springwood on Thursday, when he dropped in to clear the letterbox.' Una tapped the card with the end of her pen. 'Rather careless, I must say, for a detective who promises discretion to leave his business cards lying around for all to see.'

She threw down the pen, clasped her hands and regarded Holly severely. Holly stared back at her, stony-faced.

'However,' Una went on, 'in this case the carelessness could work to our mutual advantage. Obviously your company is working for one of the people trying to trace Andrew. It was therefore sensible to make contact. I have a proposition for you.'

Holly waited.

'Presumably you will be receiving your regular fee from your original client, irrespective of results,' said Una Maggott. 'I don't feel, therefore, that my payment needs to be a particularly large one. Shall we say two hundred and fifty dollars? In cash?'

Holly had been expecting something like this, of course. But the offer had been so bald, so businesslike, that it took her breath away. The woman obviously had no doubt that Holly (and O'Brien Investigations!) would be quite prepared to sell out a client for a bit of cash on the side.

Once, at Gorgon Office Supplies, a sales rep for a company that provided spring water dispensers and paper cups to businesses had hinted to Holly that he would 'make it worth her while' if she took one of his water coolers for the Gorgon's display area on a six-month trial.

Holly had told Anne, Paola and Justine about this on their return from lunch, and they had been satisfyingly scandalised. But over the following weeks the attempted bribery, and the suggestion that Holly would have succumbed to temptation if only the rep had offered something worth having, had turned into a running joke that Holly had found rather wearing. She couldn't help feeling that there was an undercurrent to the teasing, and that Anne, Paola and Justine were looking at her with new eyes, now they knew that the rep, with his shiny suit, his dandruff-dusted shoulders and his insinuating voice, had confidently summed her up as being as venal as he was. Now Una Maggott had without hesitation summed her up the same way.

Holly heaved herself from the embrace of the chair and stood up, squaring her shoulders. It was time to throw off her cloak of sleaze and reveal herself as the squeaky clean champion of justice.

'Ms. Maggott, I'm afraid you don't understand—'

'The two hundred and fifty dollars would be merely your retainer, of course. If your search is successful you will walk away with two, three or four times that. I believe in paying for results.'

Search? Thrown off balance yet again, Holly stared at the woman across the desk and suddenly realised that Una Maggott wasn't as calm as she seemed. She was holding herself rigidly under control. The veins were standing out on her tightly clasped hands.

'Let me explain,' Una said, leaning forward a little. 'Hidden somewhere in this house are three items—a black bag of clothes, a flat blue case containing a dozen sterling silver teaspoons, and a red-glazed pottery mug with *Andrew* marked on it in white. You will receive a two hundred and fifty dollar bonus for each of these items you find. Naturally, if you find Andrew himself, I will pay a great deal more, but it's only fair to tell you that possibility is remote. You'll want to check his room, of course, for clues. In fact, you'd better do that first.'

Holly's skin crawled. The woman was mad. She was proposing some sort of game. Hunt-the-Andrew. Holly had read about people like this. She'd seen movies about them. She never thought she'd actually meet one.

'Well?' Una snapped. 'What do you say?' Her small grey eyes were avid. Suddenly her resemblance to the man in the entrance hall portrait was very marked.

Eric tried to warn me. The thought slid into Holly's mind like a sliver of ice. She shook her head slightly, trying to dislodge it. Una Maggott might be unhinged, but it was ridiculous to think she posed any kind of a threat. She was in a wheelchair, for a start. The deadlock key was still in the front door. And there were other people in the house. Eric himself. The silent young woman, Lily. And even if they couldn't or wouldn't interfere with their employer's bizarre games, Andrew was here too.

Andrew. Who took my money.

Holly pulled herself together.

'That's fine, Ms. Maggott,' she said, using the breezy, efficient voice she had found useful when dealing with troublesome or confused customers in her old job at the bank in Perth. 'If you don't mind, I'll make finding Andrew my first priority. I might get lucky. Where should I start looking? Can you give me a tiny hint?'

The furrow between Una Maggott's eyes deepened. Her top lip twitched. 'He must be upstairs somewhere,' she said. 'But—'

'Oh, right!' chirped Holly. 'Well, I'll just pop up and have a little look-see...' She made for the door.

'Stop!' Una called after her, her voice sharp with exasperation. 'Didn't you hear what I said? You have to check Andrew's room for clues, then look for the bag, the spoons and the mug! Forget about Andrew! If the police couldn't find him, how do you think you're going to?'

Holly froze, her hand on the doorknob. She turned slowly. 'You've had the police here?'

'Of course I have!' Una spun her wheelchair away from the desk and zoomed past the stalking gods with astonishing speed. She pulled up a hand's breadth from Holly's knees. She was panting slightly. Dark red patches mottled her face. Out of the corner of her eye, Holly caught a glimmer of black and yellow as the python moved uneasily. She forced herself not to look.

'Two oafs in uniform came,' Una said. 'They poked around a bit but of course they didn't find him. I told them they needed sniffer dogs, but they said it was too expensive. I said I'd pay for them myself but they just left. I couldn't believe it! I don't suppose O'Brien's has access to sniffer dogs?'

'*Bloodhounds?*' Holly murmured, as a vision of Andrew McNish pursued through the house by a baying pack flashed through her mind.

'The ones I saw on television were labradors, but I don't have any objection to bloodhounds, if that's all you can get,' said Una Maggott. 'You can ask Mr. O'Brien when you report to him.

I'm simply saying, Ms. Cage, that there's no point in looking for Andrew without dogs. He'll be under the floorboards, or walled in by now. They're not silly.'

Holly felt weak. 'Who?' she managed to ask.

'Whichever one of them murdered him, of course!' Una snapped. 'It could be anyone. Maybe they're all in it together. How would I know?'

Chapter Nine

Crazy as a loon, Holly thought. Going the same way as her father. Nodding in what she hoped was a thoughtful, reassuring manner, she surreptitiously twisted the doorknob behind her back, planning a quick exit.

Una Maggott was not deceived. The mottles on her face darkened. She slammed her hands onto the arms of her chair in an agony of frustration.

'You don't believe me, do you? Oh, this is a nightmare! Why will no one *believe* me? I'm telling you, my brother never left this house!'

Holly actually felt herself rock back on her heels, as if she had received a physical blow. This was one shock too many.

'Your *brother*?' she asked faintly.

'Brother, half-brother—what does it matter?'

'But I thought—I was told—Andrew McNish didn't have any family,' Holly heard herself saying. 'He was abandoned in the ladies' room at—'

'Yes.' Una bared her teeth. 'Dumped like a sack of garbage by his floosie of a mother—my so-called stepmother! She'd milked my father of everything he had, so she had to find another patsy, didn't she? She wouldn't have wanted to be lumbered with a child. That would have spoiled her chances properly.'

'You're saying...are you saying that Andrew McNish is your father's son? By a—by his second wife?'

'By the bleached blonde nobody my father moved into this house barely a year after my mother died!' snapped Maggott. 'Yes! But whoever his mother was, he was still my brother—the only close family I have left in the world. We found each other three weeks ago. It was a miracle! It meant the world to me—to both of us. And now he's dead!'

'Ms. Maggott—'

'One of the jealous, money-hungry parasites in this house killed him and made it look as if he'd run away.' Una gripped the arms of her chair. 'And the police fell for it, hook, line and sinker! They were only up in his room for two minutes. They couldn't have searched it properly. They said there was no sign that he hadn't left of his own free will. But there must have been. There *must!*'

As Holly gaped at her, she took a shuddering breath and made a massive effort to pull herself together.

'I'm sorry, Ms. Cage,' she said dully, sinking back in her chair. 'I've been under a lot of strain in the past few days. I haven't explained myself very well. I can't really blame you for doubting me—I'd probably do the same, in your place. But, believe me, I'm not mad, I'm not paranoid and I'm not senile, whatever you might think.'

'Oh, I don't think anything like that,' Holly said, lying through her teeth.

Una grimaced. 'Well, the police obviously do. They wouldn't listen to me. They didn't believe me when I said I slept very lightly, and would have heard the stairs creaking if anyone had come downstairs on Tuesday night. When I told them that even if Andrew *had* got outside, he couldn't have got out of the grounds because I had the remote control for the gates, they said he'd probably just climbed over the fence. Well, you've seen that fence! How could Andrew have climbed it?'

'A ladder?' Holly murmured, against her better judgement.

'If he'd used a ladder, it would have still been there, leaning against the fence, on Wednesday morning, wouldn't it? But there was no ladder, or anything like a ladder. I told those idiot police, but they paid no attention to me at all!'

Una was getting worked up again. Little puddles of foam had formed at the corners of her mouth. Holly could well understand why the police had given her short shrift, but somehow she couldn't stop herself from trying to make the woman see reason.

'I suppose they thought that Andrew could easily have taken the ladder away with him and then dumped it, so you wouldn't realise too soon that he'd gone,' she said gently.

Una clenched her fists. 'Stop making excuses for them! They didn't listen because they'd decided I was a crazy, besotted old woman who wouldn't admit the truth! The others had pulled the wool over their eyes properly. It's true that Andrew's clothes are gone and the silver teaspoons are missing. It's true the spoons are worth something—they're antique. But Andrew wouldn't have taken them—the idea's ludicrous!'

Not really, Holly thought ruefully. Andrew knew a bit about antiques—Andrew knew a bit about most things involving money. Very likely the Maggott teaspoons were worth a lot more than Holly's savings, even with a brand new wedding ring thrown in. Andrew McNish, spoon thief. How have the mighty fallen!

She leaned back against the door, facing the fact that she had arrived too late, that Andrew wasn't in this house any longer. Tension drained out of her as the prospect of confronting him vanished. Suddenly she felt exhausted. She had the absurd desire to close her eyes and simply go to sleep where she stood. But Una Maggott, no longer an enemy but a pathetic, even tragic, figure, was glaring up at her, waiting for a response. She managed to rouse herself.

'Andrew had a lot of debts,' she said.

'I know that!' Una snapped. 'I could have settled all that. I told him I would. Settle the debts and start him off in business again. Why not? What else did I have to do with my money? I was alone in the world—we both were. Why would he go away, when by staying he could have made a fresh start?'

'He told you he was alone in the world?' Holly asked slowly. 'He didn't mention any other family or...or a girlfriend, for instance?'

Una shook her head. 'There was no one. I was glad of that, I must admit. Selfish, I suppose, but frankly I didn't want anyone standing in the way of our getting to know one another, catching up on lost time. Oh, there had been various girls in the past, Andrew said. But at the time we met there was no one special.'

Only the one he was planning to marry on Tuesday, Holly reflected grimly. Till a better offer came along—a crazy, rich old snob of a half-sister who was going to solve all his problems, and was likely to resent a little blonde girlfriend plucked warm out of Gorgon Office Supplies.

Something has come up... She could see exactly how it must have been. Andrew had been skating on thin ice. The ice had cracked and he'd found himself in deep water, with killer whales closing in. Then, miraculously, someone had thrown him a lifeline. So he'd grabbed it, shrugging off any baggage that might have weighed him down. As it happened, the baggage was Holly.

He had probably been quite sorry about it. Looking back with a clear-eyed coldness that rather startled her, Holly found herself quite certain that Andrew had genuinely cared about her, as much as he'd been able to care about anyone. He had proposed to her impulsively, in a moment of enthusiasm, but she was sure he'd meant every word he'd said—at the time.

Yet...hadn't she always known, deep down, that his first loyalty would always be to himself? That he wasn't completely to be trusted? Wasn't that why she had always taken such care to maintain the breezy persona he seemed to find attractive, and keep her various insecurities well hidden?

The one thing she couldn't understand was why he had left Una Maggott's protection. Had he received an even better offer? Or...had he seen O'Brien photographing him, and decided he had no choice but to run? That would be an irony.

'You have to find those teaspoons, Ms. Cage,' Una said, leaning forward. 'If you can find them, it will prove Andrew didn't take them. If you can find his bag, it will prove he never left. Then the police will have to come back and locate his body. I can't look myself. I'm helpless, stuck in this wheelchair, and there's no one else I can trust! Please help me!'

Her face was working. Tears were glinting in her hard little eyes. Holly thought uncharitably that they looked more like tears of rage and frustration at being cheated of something she wanted than signs of grief for a man she'd known only a few weeks. But they were very real, for all that. There was no doubt that she was in terrible agony of mind. It would be cruel to refuse her.

But I have to refuse, Holly told herself. I've got to get out of here. Andrew's gone. This poor crazy woman's just another one of his victims. And I can't help her. I'm not really a detective. I'd be taking her money under false pretenses.

This last thought sobered her like a dash of cold water. Of *course* she couldn't start some mad, useless search of the house. How could she have considered it for a moment? She hardened her heart and considered her options. She had to humour Una— find a way of letting her down gently. It wasn't just a matter of humanity. It would be a long walk home to Mealey Marshes if the woman lost her temper and refused to ask Eric to drive her. In fact, Holly wasn't at all sure she could even find her way back to the highway.

And she didn't want to be thrown out of the house before she'd seen Andrew's room. It was just possible that a thorough search might reveal some clue as to where he'd gone. She knew from experience that while Andrew kept his inner life securely locked away, he was untidy in small things, often leaving fading cash register receipts, dog-eared business cards, charity buttons, bottle caps and little piles of loose change lying around. It was as if some part of him yearned for his secret doings to be revealed. Or perhaps he thought that casually emptying his pockets and leaving the resultant debris in plain sight gave the impression he had nothing to hide.

She thought of a ploy, and felt almost ashamed of her own cunning.

'Ms. Maggott, I'll do a quick check of Andrew's room for you—no charge,' she said smoothly. 'But I'm afraid that searching the house would be a waste of my time and your money. Surely the teaspoons and Andrew's bag of clothes would have been hidden with his body, which, as you yourself said, will be impossible to—'

'No!' Una shook her head decisively. 'At least, not the teaspoons. They're far too valuable. They'll have been put somewhere accessible—so the murderer could retrieve them and sneak them out of the house when all the fuss has died down.'

'Then they're probably already gone,' Holly said, seizing the offered lifeline.

But again Una shook her head. 'It's been too risky to move them. The fuss *hasn't* died down, has it? I've seen to that. They're still here—I'm positive. Wait a minute and I'll get you the key to Andrew's door.'

She spun her chair around and zoomed back to the desk.

Well, that had been a washout. Reluctantly Holly accepted the fact that she'd have to be firmer.

'Ms. Maggott, as I said, I'll do the bedroom but I really can't search—'

'Well, not today, not today, I understand that,' the woman said irritably, spinning the chair around again and speeding back to the door like a paralympic hockey champion going for a goal. 'You're not dressed for it. You can do that tomorrow.'

She slapped an old-fashioned, long-shanked key into Holly's hand. 'I had Andrew's door locked and the key brought to me on Wednesday morning, the moment I realised he was missing,' she said. 'No one's been in his room since, except the police. It's at the end of the corridor, next to the bathroom. Look for clues, Ms. Cage! There must be *something*. Then report back to me, and we'll discuss our next move.'

She was bright-eyed now, quivering with manic energy.

'Be as unobtrusive as you can. If you meet anyone, don't say what you're doing. Say you're in real estate—Bowers and Benn, giving a free valuation, trying to persuade me to sell.'

'Who are you talking about, Ms. Maggott?' Holly asked desperately.

'All of them!' The woman flapped her hands impatiently. 'All the parasites in this house!'

Holly gave up. Without further comment, she opened the door and went out into the entrance hall. It was deserted. The portrait of Maggott the undertaker smirked at her mockingly. The hanging chains swayed, jingling softly. The stairs stretched upward into gloom.

There was a loud hiss behind her and she looked sharply around. Una Maggott was peering at her through the crack in the door, looking madder and more paranoid than ever.

'Keep your eye on that key,' Una whispered. 'They'll get it from you if they can. It's the only key left for upstairs—all the others are lost. It's usually in the bathroom door up there, and they're all complaining because I won't put it back. What does it matter if the bathroom doesn't lock, I ask you? Surely people can knock?'

She pulled her head back and the door snapped shut. Holly made for the staircase.

The stairs, covered by a faded runner worn down to paper thinness, creaked, groaned and cracked agonisingly as she climbed them. It was like stepping on an ancient creature in pain. So much for 'unobtrusive.' The sound must have been audible all over the house.

At the top of the stairs a silent corridor stretched left and right, dimmed by murky green embossed wallpaper and lined with gleaming cedar doors. Each door bore a brass number polished to a high shine, and was disfigured by a rubber draught excluder fixed to its base. Cold light streamed from the open bathroom door. The scent of lavender air-freshener hung in the air, masking, but not quite concealing, a faint, unpleasant odour that hinted at blocked drains.

The place must once have been a boarding house or private hotel. It strongly reminded Holly of the inappropriately named Bella Vista, where her great-aunt Stella had taken refuge after

Great-uncle Herb went off the rails and burned down their house after a bad day at bowls. It had the same depressing ambience, the same air of lives compressed by closed doors.

Barely had this thought crossed her mind when the door marked 5, directly opposite the head of the stairs, snapped open. A short, doughy-faced woman with a mobile phone pressed to her ear peered out. She had protuberant blue eyes, a slightly receding chin, and a helmet of shiny brown hair. Her stout body was encased in beige woollen trousers and a hand-knitted beige cardigan heavily ornamented with chocolate brown crocheted edging. She looked so very like a pug dog in a wig that Holly was temporarily at a loss for words.

'Who are you?' the woman yapped aggressively.

'I'm…doing an inspection for Ms. Maggott,' said Holly, finding her voice.

She wondered who the woman was. Another member of Una Maggot's staff? A paying guest? Whatever, she was obviously one of the 'parasites' Una suspected of doing away with Andrew McNish.

'Did you hear that, Cliff? the woman said into the phone. 'An *inspection* for Ms. Maggot!'

Without waiting for an answer she turned her attention back to Holly, compressing her lips and bunching her cheeks so she looked more pug-like than ever.

'It's not convenient at the moment, I'm afraid,' she said in a high, artificial voice. 'I'm taking an important call. And please don't disturb my son in number 7 either. He's not well.'

She jerked back into her room and pulled the door shut.

'Well, heavens, Cliff, *I* don't know,' Holly heard her say on the other side of the polished wood barrier. 'Obviously it's got something to do with…No! I wouldn't lower myself to…Cliff, you'll have to come! I'm at the end of my tether! Drop in after dinner…Yes, just pretend you're…No she won't, it'll be all right. There must be *something* we can do to stop…'

The voice faded. The pug woman had either begun to speak more quietly, or had moved away from the door.

Holly caught a glimpse of movement from the corner of her eye. She looked quickly to her right, and jumped. A figure was dancing backwards out of a doorway near the end of the corridor. As it moved into the puddle of pale light streaming through the open bathroom door, Holly saw that it was a tall and very buxom woman with a shoulder-length mop of frizzy sand-coloured hair. A lime green tracksuit strained over her ample bottom and jiggling bosom. Her joggers were as brightly white as the pile of sheets in her arms.

The woman bounced around, saw Holly and gave a small shriek. Then she laughed and tugged out the earphone wires trailing from beneath the mass of her hair.

'In a world of me own, I was,' she called in a husky voice with a faint Irish lilt. 'Sorry, I'm sure. Can I help you, at all?'

'Oh, no, no I'm fine, thanks,' Holly babbled, hurrying down the corridor toward her. 'I'm just having a look around. For Ms. Maggott. A real estate inspection.'

'Oh, yes?' the woman said, smiling broadly. She was older than she had seemed from a distance—perhaps a nudge over forty. She had a little gap between her front teeth, like Madonna or the Wife of Bath. Her mouth was wide and generous. Her narrow hazel eyes crinkled at the corners, sparkling under sparse, sandy eyebrows, and fringed by eyelashes that were barely visible. Golden brown freckles speckled her blunt, good-natured face and the backs of her strong, capable hands.

'I'm Sheena,' she said, closing the door on a walk-in cupboard lined with shelves of sheets, towels, pillows and blankets. 'I'm the housekeeper, for me sins. Well, chief cook and bottlewasher in the madhouse, more like it. Not for much longer, though, thank the Lord.'

'You're leaving too?' Holly asked. She had instantly warmed to Sheena. It was a great relief to have come across a normal, cheerful person in Maggott manor.

Sheena blinked uncomprehendingly, then her pleasant face contorted into a wry grimace. 'Oh, you mean Lily!' she said dismissively. 'Yes, she's going, finally, I gather, but that's a different kettle of fish. I'm going of my own accord, but Lily—well, she'd stay on if she could. Who wouldn't, I ask you, with free board and bugger-all work to do? But she's been given her marching orders. About time, too. It's beyond me how she lasted as long as she did.'

Clearly it had not been tactful to group Sheena with the decorative Lily. Holly hurried to make amends. 'So, what will you be doing, Sheena?' she asked.

'Oh, I'm going back to nursing.' Apparently mollified, Sheena adjusted the pile of sheets against her bosom, settling in for a chat. 'I start down at the hospital Monday week. Got a room in a share house organised, just to start me off.'

'You sound as if you're looking forward to it.'

'Can't wait. Well, I'll be sorry to leave this place in a way—it's been home to me for going on six years—but it hasn't been the same since me dear old Roly passed over—Roly Maggott, the present owner's da, that is.'

The husky voice flattened slightly at the mention of Una Maggott. No love lost there, Holly thought. Presumably cheery, blowsy, garrulous Sheena was another of Una's murder suspects. She obviously lived in. She had probably been in the house the night Andrew took off.

Sheena would be worth talking to. She might have some idea where Andrew had gone, and why. Those merry hazel eyes were shrewd. Holly was willing to bet that not much went on in this house that Sheena didn't know about.

'You originally came to nurse Mr. Maggott, did you?' she asked casually, to start things off.

Sheena grinned. 'He didn't need nursing so much as company, really,' she said. 'Female company, if you know what I mean.' She winked. 'Nearly ninety he might have been, but some men never lose the urge.'

Holly nodded and smiled. In truth, remembering the man in the portrait, remembering those cunning, teasing eyes, those thick, smirking lips, she felt rather sick.

'Oh, he was an old rascal, no doubt about him,' Sheena said reminiscently. 'I nursed him in hospital—he was in for a gall bladder. We had a lot of laughs. The day he was discharged he gave me his card and said to me, "Sheena, if ever you get sick of carrying bedpans around, give me a call. I've got a job for you." And one fine morning after that, when I'd been blown up by a crabby patient once too often, I got out that card and rang him. I came to see him that night, saw over the house…and that was it. I gave in me notice at the hospital the next day.'

She sighed, clasping the sheets more tightly to her breast.

'I don't regret it. I was fond of him, daft, dirty old bugger that he was. Maybe at the start I thought something else might come of it—a girl has to take care of herself, doesn't she? But that was a pipe dream. Just my luck.'

Her face fell slightly as she looked down the corridor at the shabby strip of carpet, the faded wallpaper, the gleaming doors.

'This place used to be a bed and breakfast, you know. Roly's parents-in-law ran it for years—his first wife's parents. Made quite a good thing of it, too, by all accounts. Could be a nice little business again, with a bit of spit and polish, some ensuite bathrooms…eight bedrooms there are on this floor, plus the maids' rooms in the attic, and there's a lovely view from the back. I'd have done well with it. I'm not frightened of a bit of hard work. Roly and I used to talk about it all the time…making plans…'

She wrinkled her nose humorously and shrugged. 'But he'd been spinning me a line, the crafty old bugger. Or maybe half the time he forgot the real state of things—he only remembered what he wanted to, it always seemed to me. When he popped off it turned out the house wasn't his to leave. It belonged to this daughter I never even knew existed, because she'd been living overseas. It had been in her ma's name, see, and Ma had left it to her. Roly only had it for his lifetime.'

'Oh, what a shame,' Holly murmured. The response seemed woefully inadequate, but she couldn't think of anything else to say.

'Well, I can't say it wasn't a disappointment,' Sheena said dryly. 'Still—' she shrugged her shoulders again '—Roly did what he could for me. The house was Una's but the contents were his—quite right, too, he'd paid for most of the expensive things anyway—so he left them to me. Una had to buy the lot off me first thing, or she'd have been rattling round in this old place like a pea in a bottle, without so much as a knife to butter her bread.'

She laughed uproariously and shrugged again. 'So I've got a little nest egg for me trouble—can't grumble really. Well, I'd better get on. You too, I daresay—that's the bedroom you want, by the way.'

She jerked her head across the corridor, to a door marked '1.'

Chapter Ten

Holly felt her face grow hot. Sheena grinned.

'Don't fret,' she said, as if Holly had apologised for trying to deceive her. 'You've got your job to do. But you'd better think of another cover story. As if Una would let an estate agent in here! She's mad about this house—not that she isn't mad full stop. Anyway, Eric told me he was being sent to get you. He wasn't best pleased, but as I told him, Una's like a dog with a bone about this thing, and if she wants to spend her money on a wild goose chase, that's her business.'

She tilted her head and regarded Holly quizzically.

'You don't look like a detective,' she said. 'Not that I ever met one before. Have you been at it for long?'

'Not really,' Holly said, with perfect truth.

Recovering her poise a little, she decided to make the best of a bad job. At least she could stop attempting to be subtle. She crossed the corridor and tried the door of the room marked '1.' Sure enough, it was locked. Very aware of Sheena's amused gaze, she slid the key from her jacket pocket.

'So I gather you don't think there's anything suspicious about Andrew McNish's disappearance?' she asked in a businesslike manner, as she stuck the key into the keyhole.

Sheena snorted. ''Course not. Done a flit, hasn't he?'

She wandered across the corridor and watched with lively interest as Holly attempted to make the key turn.

'It was only a matter of time,' she said. 'Andrew's a charmer, and I won't say it wasn't fun having him around the place, but he didn't take me in. I knew he was a con artist the minute I laid eyes on him.'

She returned Holly's startled glance complacently. 'Take my word for it. He was no more Una's little brother than I am, and he knew it. But Una had convinced herself, so he played along. Who wouldn't? She's rolling in it. Then things got too hot for him, so he took off. The police could see how the land lay. Everyone could, but Una. Here, let me do that.'

She plumped the vaguely camphor-smelling sheets into Holly's arms and casually elbowed her aside. Then she pulled the key back out of the keyhole, replaced it, and began jiggling it gently.

'This is the bathroom key, really,' she said. 'It does work in this lock, but only just. See if you can get her to give it back, after this, will you? It's a bugger sitting on the jacks waiting for Dulcie's creepy son to walk in on you. I'm as sure as I can be that he does it on purpose.'

Holly laughed.

'No, I'm telling you!' Sheena insisted, scowling at the key. 'He's a real piece of work, Sebastian. Mind you, you're pretty safe till mid-afternoon because he stays up all night with his computer, downloading the Lord knows what off the internet. He couldn't be more than sixteen, either.'

'Is Dulcie the woman in room 5? I saw her earlier—I think she heard me coming up the stairs. Who is she?'

Sheena's expression became disdainful. 'Oh, some relation of Roly's—fourth cousin twice removed, or something. Lives in Queensland. Except for Una, she and Sebastian are the last of the Maggotts, or so she says. So in her opinion that means they're rightfully in for the dosh—and this house, of course— when Una pops off.'

'Really!' breathed Holly, immediately considering the pug woman in a new light.

'She's been here since Tuesday, looking down her nose at me and Eric, smarming up to Una. She's a pain in the whatsit. Roly couldn't stand her, wouldn't have her in the house. And Una only invited her out of spite.'

'Why spite?'

'Well, Andrew had moved in, hadn't he?' said Sheena, manipulating the key with the concentration of a safecracker. 'Una couldn't resist the chance to rub Dulcie's nose in it that a long-lost brother had turned up, and Dulcie could forget about ever getting her claws on the money.'

She chuckled, her natural good humour fully restored. 'The old girl did it in style, too. Threw a dinner here on Tuesday night with caterers and a waiter and all that. Very formal, and in the library, too, with the big long table, instead of the breakfast room where we usually eat. She invited her solicitor, and all the people in the house—Eric and me included, and even Lily, who must have thought it meant she was back in the good books, because she was purring like the cat who'd swallowed the cream.'

Clearly taking malicious pleasure at this memory in particular, Sheena chuckled again before swearing at the key, withdrawing it, and easing it back into the lock for another try.

'So we all chat like ladies and gents through four courses,' she went on. 'Then over the port and cheese Una makes the big announcement that Andrew is changing his name to Maggott, and she's going to make a will leaving him the lot.'

'That must have been a fun evening,' Holly murmured. She smiled inwardly at the thought of Andrew weighing up whether being heir to a fortune was worth being a Maggott, and deciding it was.

'It was a circus—a real circus!' Sheena agreed. 'Dulcie nearly fainted. Then she and Stiff Cliff—that's the lawyer—'

'Cliff? Oh, I think she was talking to him on the phone just now,' Holly broke in.

Sheena nodded. 'The two of them are thick as thieves,' she said. 'Well, they started carrying on like chooks with their heads cut off. Running round, whispering in corners, trying to get Una alone…And Lily, of course, was looking daggers, muttering to herself like…Ah, there we go!'

The key had finally turned and the lock had released its hold with a sulky clunk. Sheena opened the door, pushed it wide and stood back.

'The police opened the curtains,' she said. 'Otherwise nothing's been touched. Help yourself.' With a mocking flourish, she gestured for Holly to enter.

Feeling very self-conscious, Holly handed back the pile of sheets and went into the room. It was very large. She registered barred windows, a stunning view of green hills and grey sky, a double brass bed, neatly made, a worn but beautiful Chinese rug in cream and pale blue, and a massive mahogany wardrobe with matching dressing table, chest of drawers and marble-topped washstand. Dust motes drifted in the stuffy air, which still bore the faint, lingering scent of Andrew's cologne. Holly shivered.

'Best room in the house, this one,' said Sheena from the door. 'Lovely and big, isn't it? It was Una's when she was a kid.'

The room was empty of life, empty of any *signs* of life. All the surfaces were bare, and very lightly filmed with dust. Holly repressed a sigh. For once, Andrew had cleaned up after himself.

'Roly had number 2, across the hall, before his knees went and we had to move him downstairs,' Sheena went on chattily. 'It's not so big, because the linen room takes up part of it, and it hasn't got the view, but Roly liked to keep an eye on the road. He always slept with the remote for the front gates under his pillow. He had a thing about burglars. Una's got it too now. She didn't when she first came, but it's grown on her.'

Holly went to the wardrobe and opened the three doors one by one. There was nothing to see but a brass rail and some wooden coat hangers.

'You won't find anything,' Sheena said. 'He's taken all his things. Plus two hundred dollars out of Dulcie's handbag—she'd been fool enough to leave it downstairs—twelve silver teaspoons, and who knows what else we haven't found out about yet.' She chuckled.

'I've still got to look,' Holly snapped. She was reflecting sourly that Una Maggott hadn't said a word about any stolen money. It looked as if Una, like old Roly, had a selective memory.

'Sure,' Sheena said kindly. 'Well, I'll leave you to it. Do you want this door shut in case Dulcie—?'

'Thanks,' said Holly, turning round and smiling stiffly to make up for snapping. Not that she really wanted to be closed in with the smell of Andrew's after-shave. But she had promised Una Maggott that she'd search the room, so she felt compelled to do it. And if she were going to make a fool of herself she'd rather do it in private.

'If you need anything, give me a hoy,' Sheena said. 'I'll be in me room across the way—number 4, beside the stairs.'

As the door closed behind her, it occurred to Holly that the key was still on the outside. If Dulcie crept out of her room to find out what was happening, she might snaffle it. And if Una Maggott didn't get the key back, there would be a scene.

She hurried to the door, wrenched it open, and jumped as she saw Sheena still standing almost directly outside. Sheena gaped at her, blinked twice, and whipped an aerosol can from the waistband of her tracksuit pants, her finger on the trigger.

Mace! Holly thought wildly, and jumped backwards.

There was a hiss, and the air filled with the smell of synthetic lavender.

'Rats,' Sheena said, spraying vigorously around. 'Una got a fellow in to lay baits a month ago. They're supposed to go outside to die, but that was a joke. The smell's shocking.'

She sniffed, nodded as if satisfied, and took off toward her room, charging the air with puffs of spray as she went.

Heart still pounding uncomfortably, Holly watched as the lime green figure disappeared through the door marked 4 without looking back. How *could* she have thought Sheena was attacking her? She was getting as paranoid as Una Maggott.

It's this house, she told herself. It would make anyone jumpy. Taking herself firmly in hand, she pulled the key from the door and put it back into her jacket pocket, her fingers trembling only slightly. Still, it had been an odd incident. Her thoughts ran on as she shut herself into Andrew's room again. Why had Sheena been hanging around like that? It had nothing to do with air-freshener, for sure. Had she been listening at the door, curious about what Holly was doing? Maybe she'd been planning to steal the bathroom key herself.

Feeling much freer now she had no audience, Holly checked the chest of drawers, the dressing table, and the drawers of the washstand. She conscientiously searched the rug. She peered under the bed, felt under the mattress, and finally, embarrassed by her own zeal, stripped off the cream brocade bedspread, and the pillows, blankets and sheets. As Sheena had predicted, she didn't find so much as a used tissue. And by now she'd started thinking this was odd. Why would someone planning to make off with his hostess' teaspoons bother to leave his bedroom so pristine? It didn't sound like something Andrew would do. He hadn't left the Springwood house pristine—far from it.

Frowning over the problem, she remade the bed. She could have left it, she supposed, but it went against all her instincts not to restore it to its original, impeccable state. As she smoothed the bedspread, something else occurred to her. Surely Andrew would have at least sat on the bed, after he had packed and while he was waiting for the house to settle down. There was nowhere else to sit. Yet the bedspread hadn't been even slightly disarranged.

She sat down on the bed herself, stood up, and noted the definite rumples she'd left behind her. Perplexed, she sat down again and gazed around the room. And it was then that she saw the small, dark object lying against the skirting board to the right of the door. Her stomach turned over.

She got up and walked slowly to the door, telling herself that she was imagining things. It was insane to think that this could happen to her twice in one day. But it had. The object was a sleek little mobile phone—not plugged into its charger this time, but lying all by itself.

It was Andrew's phone, she was positive. She picked it up. It showed no signs of life. Either the battery was flat, or it had been turned off. She stared at it, and then at the place where she'd found it. How on earth had it got into that spot? How had Andrew, whose phone was like part of his body, left the room without it? And why had no one noticed it before?

The answer to the last question was obvious as soon as she thought about it. No one had noticed the phone for the same reason she hadn't noticed it when she first came into the room. Because when the door was open, the phone was concealed behind it. Because Una Maggott had been right—the police had only given the bedroom the briefest of surveys, to humour her. They had seen that the bed hadn't been slept in and that Andrew's belongings were gone, and left it at that. But how had the phone magicked itself out of Andrew's right hip pocket, where he invariably kept it, and hidden itself behind the door in the first place? It must have happened moments before Andrew left the room, otherwise he would have noticed it was missing.

Holly looked at the dark crack under the door. She remembered the rubber flap of the draught excluder grazing the floor as the door opened. If the phone had been lying directly in front of the door, it would have been swept back against the wall as the door opened, and ended up just where she'd found it.

A nasty, creeping feeling squirmed up Holly's spine. A vivid image sprang into her mind: Andrew's limp body being dragged to the door, the phone slipping from his pocket, unnoticed in the dark. The door being stealthily opened, the phone being brushed aside as its dead owner's body was...

No! Holly shook her head violently. She was stressed and overtired—who wouldn't be, after the day she'd had? But that was no reason to let herself get sucked into the twilight zone of Una Maggott's paranoid fantasies. Firmly she considered the situation. Andrew McNish, faithless lover, con-man and spoon thief, had left this room on his own two feet. That was a given. So how had he lost his phone—and lost it right in front of the door?

Holly had known the phone to slip from Andrew's pocket when he was sitting down. It had happened in a taxi once, and a couple of times the phone had made a brief escape into the cushions of the sofa he sat on to watch TV. But she couldn't imagine Andrew sitting on the floor, especially moments before doing a midnight flit.

*It happened somehow. Reconstruct the scene...*It was as if the ghost of O'Brien had whispered in her ear.

Holly went to the windows and closed the curtains. The room dimmed dramatically. At night, it would have been completely dark.

Right, Holly thought. I am Andrew, packed and ready to leave. I've got a dozen stolen antique teaspoons in my bag and two hundred stolen dollars in my wallet. My phone is in my right hip pocket, switched off or at least turned to 'silent.' It's very late. The house is quiet. Okay, time to go...

She pressed the phone to her right hip, picked up an imaginary bag and crept to the door. By the time she got there, she was right in character. The door rose in front of her, dark except for the faint light from the corridor glimmering through the keyhole. She stretched out her hand to the doorknob and found she was holding her breath. If anyone saw her sneaking out of the room with a bag, the jig would be well and truly up. She hesitated, then impulsively crouched, leaned forward, and pressed her eye to the keyhole.

She saw a slab of empty corridor, the door of the linen store and the door of room number 2 beside it. She relaxed her fingers and let the phone drop. It landed on the rug with only the tiniest of sounds, well within the arc of the opening door.

Holly collected it and stood up, marvelling at how perfectly the reconstruction had worked. The horrible mental picture of a limp, dead Andrew being dragged away had vanished as if it had never been. In its place was the tacky but far more believable image of a furtive Andrew with his eye pressed to a keyhole, checking out his escape route. She could almost feel the ghost of O'Brien patting her on the back.

Briskly deciding that enough was enough, she left the room. Her feeling of being in control seemed to communicate itself to the key, which inexplicably turned at the first twist of her wrist.

On impulse she knocked softly on the door of room 3, next door, as she passed it. Receiving no answer, she quietly twisted the doorknob and looked in. The room was empty except for several strategically placed plastic buckets on the dusty floor. The ceiling was sagging and heavily water-stained. So Andrew had had no next-door neighbour on Tuesday night. That would have made him feel safer. Quietly Holly closed the door again.

The sound of rubber soles squeaking on polished boards and an exuberant female voice belting out 'Mamma Mia' were drifting through the half-open door of room 4, but Holly wasn't tempted to pop her head in to say goodbye as she passed. Since the incident of the air-freshener, she'd rather gone off Sheena.

She reached the head of the stairs and hesitated. There was grim silence behind the door marked 5. Room 7, where Dulcie's son apparently lurked, and rooms 6 and 8 on the other side of the corridor—Eric's and Lily's rooms, presumably—were just as quiet. At the very end of the corridor, beside room 7, a narrow staircase led up to the attic.

Holly told herself firmly that there was no need to investigate further. She had done what she had wanted to do, and what she had promised. That was enough. She ran down the stairs, ignoring their wooden shrieks, and was not surprised to see Una Maggott's door snap open as she reached the entrance hall. The woman had obviously been listening out for her return.

'Well?' Una whispered avidly as Holly entered her room, closing the door behind her. 'You found something, didn't you? I can see it in your face. Was it—blood?'

She had the folder from the desk on her lap. She was patting and stroking it unconsciously, as if it were a religious relic.

Holly shook her head, very glad that she had done the search properly and had no need to prevaricate. 'There were no bloodstains, Ms. Maggott. No signs of violence at all.'

The older woman's face convulsed. She spun her chair around and sped away from Holly, stopping a hair's breadth from the python's cage. She sat there panting, her shoulders heaving.

Holly felt a stab of pity. Then the chair spun round again and her heart sank. Una's trembling lips had firmed and the fanatical gleam had returned to her small grey eyes.

'Then they didn't use a knife,' she said. 'Andrew was strangled. Or poisoned. Poisoned, yes! That would fit! Did you find the red mug? The mug with *Andrew* written on it?'

'No,' Holly said. 'There was no mug.'

Una gripped the arms of her chair. 'You mean you found *nothing* in that room?' she asked dangerously. 'No clues at *all?*'

Reluctantly, keeping her eyes fixed on the woman's face so as to screen out the python coiling in the background, Holly held out the mobile phone.

Una's eyes widened. She zoomed forward and snatched the phone. 'It's his!' she hissed. 'Andrew's! That proves it—proves he never left!'

'Well, no, not really,' Holly said. 'It was behind the door. He could have dropped it, you see, when he—'

'And the mug! You saw with your own eyes that it wasn't there! But it should have been, you see? I gave Andrew that mug as a welcome gift, when he first came here. He always used it. He took it upstairs with him on Tuesday night. I saw him do it! But now the mug's gone. It's disappeared!'

'Maybe he took it with him,' Holly said lamely, though she couldn't imagine Andrew McNish wanting a red pottery mug—even one with his name on it.

'His tea was drugged,' Una Maggott announced, her voice ringing with conviction. 'They drugged him and strangled or smothered him. Then they took the mug away—hid it—in case the dregs were analysed—'

'Ms. Maggott, I have to go now,' Holly broke in. Suddenly she couldn't deal with this. She had to get away. The woman was irrational—completely obsessed.

Maggott's tirade stopped abruptly. She wiped her mouth with the back of her hand.

'Oh, of course you do, of course you do,' she mumbled. 'Yes. It's getting late. Eric will be getting edgy. Presumably you'll be able to find your own way here tomorrow?'

Without waiting for an answer, she took the folder from her lap and thrust it into Holly's unwilling hands. 'I wrote a statement for the police,' she said. 'It was wasted on them—they barely looked at it—but everything's in there. What time will I expect you in the morning?'

'Ah, well, I'm not completely sure,' Holly temporised, feeling terrible. She had no idea what she'd be doing tomorrow, but one thing she did know. She was never, ever going to set foot in this house again.

'Be as early as you can,' said Una Maggott. 'I'm depending on you.'

Chapter Eleven

The trip back to Mealey Marshes began tensely. Eric brooded over the wheel in silence, glancing frequently at the rear-vision mirror. The light had faded, but he was still wearing his sunglasses. Holly refused to worry about it. Presumably Eric was used to semi-darkness, and anyway most obstacles would probably just bounce off the hearse. It seemed to be built like a tank. The main thing was, she had got away from the madhouse in Horsetrough Lane. The relief was incredible.

But as the bush-lined kilometres slipped by, she found herself sinking into a more dismal mood. She'd set off for Medlow Bath full of excitement and purpose. Now she had to face the fact that she was back where she started—penniless, jobless, homeless, and with no idea where Andrew was. She had learned nothing from this afternoon's adventure except that he was even more of a skunk than she'd thought.

She was roused from her reverie by the hearse slowing and the sound of the indicator blinking. She realised that they had reached the Mealey Marshes turnoff. And suddenly she decided to have one more try at getting some information. If Eric snubbed her, so be it.

'Eric, I know you didn't like Ms. Maggott calling me in,' she said abruptly. 'But it was her decision, not mine.'

For a long moment she thought Eric wasn't going to answer. Then the sulky lips unsealed themselves.

'I don't like folks ripping the old girl off,' Eric said, staring straight ahead.

'I'm not ripping her off,' Holly snapped. 'I didn't take a cent from her!'

Eric glanced at her. The sunglasses hid his eyes. She couldn't tell if he believed her or not. She felt like showing him her empty wallet to prove her point, but decided that would be undignified.

'The only reason I agreed to go to the house in the first place was because I thought Andrew McNish was still there,' she said. 'It's him I want. We have...some business to settle.'

Eric considered this, then seemed to relax slightly. He breathed out and nodded, tapping the wheel.

Holly pursued her advantage. 'Do you have any idea where he might have gone after he left?' she asked.

'If I did I'd have gone after the smarmy prick and dragged him back by the seat of his pants so she could see he was alive and kicking,' Eric muttered, Elvis drawl totally absent. 'If you think I like being called a murderer you're dead wrong.'

'Sheena says he left because things got too hot for him after that dinner party on Tuesday night,' Holly persisted. 'But he had Ms. Maggott on side. She seems absolutely certain he's her brother—half-brother. So you can't help wondering why...' She trailed off invitingly.

Eric shrugged. 'He was getting a lot of flak. Dulcie and the lawyer were going on about DNA tests and false pretences and that, making out they were going to get the old girl signed off for being senile and they'd see him in court. Lily was spitting chips, saying he was a plague on the house and she was going to put a curse on him...'

'*Curse?*'

'Yeah, well, Lily's into curses. She cuts Miz M's hair, and helps Sheena in the house and all that—or she's supposed to—and she makes jewellery for the markets, but she's a witch in her spare time.'

'A *witch?*'

'She's in this co-vern,' said Eric, sliding smoothly back into Elvis mode. 'Her ma and both her aunties are in it too. They dance round at full moon, and chant and cast spells an' all.' He smiled tolerantly, adjusting his sequinned collar. 'I think they just like dressing up, really,' he added, with no apparent sense of irony. 'But I wouldn't want to get on the wrong side of them. They have these rituals. You never know.'

A coven! Were there many witches in the mountains? Abigail Honour would know. Holly resolved to ask her over dinner.

At the thought of food, her stomach gurgled. She pressed it in with both hands and willed it to be silent.

'Still,' Eric said, 'Allnut hasn't died or come down with leprosy, so there's probably nothing in it.'

'Who's—?'

'Cliff Allnut. Miz M's lawyer. Lily hates his guts. He was the one who told Miz M about the co-vern, see. Lily had kept it quiet—and her weirdo mum and aunties as well—but Stiff Cliff nosed it all out somehow. He's got a lot of contacts up here, and he's a churchy as well. Miz M didn't thank him, but she went right off Lily after that.'

He smirked. He was obviously about as fond of Lily as Sheena was.

'I had a word with McNish myself, as a matter of fact,' he said, returning abruptly to his point. 'I told him my old man was from Sicily and had a few friends in the ce-ment business. He didn't like that much.'

'I can imagine.' Holly regarded her companion's shadowed profile thoughtfully.

'So he took off,' said Eric, as the hearse slid through the Mealey Marshes underpass. 'That proves he was a con artist. But the old girl won't believe it. She just can't face it that he did her down.'

He sighed, and abruptly became confidential. 'When she first came I thought she was normal. A bit bossy and up herself, but you'd expect that. She'd worked in France for thirty years for some hot-shot finance guy before the accident put her in the chair, and you know what the Frogs are like. But after a while I realised she was going the same way as Ol' Maggott.'

'Losing her marbles, you mean?' said Holly. Possibly she could have phrased it more tactfully, but she wasn't in the mood.

'Heading that way. She's about the age the old bloke was when he started to go loopy, by all accounts, and I know the signs.'

He adjusted his sunglasses. 'She gets crazes on things, just like he used to. She gets in a fever, say, about getting the yard back the way it was when she was a kid. Doesn't matter the house needs work and the roof leaks, all she cares about is getting Ol' Maggott's pyramids and o-belisks and stuff pulled down and new grass put in.'

'Well,' Holly began, 'I can understand—'

'But before this grass she's been carrying on about is even laid she's bored with the yard. She's decided half of the stuff in the house is rubbish, and she doesn't want coffins in the place and all that. So then we've got secondhand dealers and moving guys crawling all over the place for weeks.'

'*Coffins?*'

'There were only a few,' Eric said defensively. 'Ol' Maggott held on to them after he sold the business, because he'd made them himself. He was great at woodwork. A real craftsman, you know?'

'I'm sure.' Holly shifted uneasily. Was it a sign of madness to want to get rid of a coffin collection?

'Some nights he'd get me up in the attic to try them out, show me how comfortable they were, and all,' said Eric, his eyes full of memories. 'He was buried in one of them. He'd picked it out before he went.'

'Right.'

'But Miz M got rid of the ones that were left—and a whole lot of other stuff too. The old boy's embalming kit, the spider collection, the train set, the armour, the bear trap, the old dentist's chair…She'd have got rid of Cleopatra as well, but Ol' Maggott had left Cleo to me so she couldn't.'

'Cleopatra?'

'The python.'

'Oh. I didn't realise the snake was—'

'Mine, yeah. That's part of the deal,' Eric said vaguely. '*Then* she gets all het up about the rats. Ol' Maggott used to breed them for Cleo and they were always getting away, so the walls are full of them. Well, Miz M suddenly decides she can't stand it and for a while the rat guy's her best friend.'

'That doesn't really sound unreasonable to me,' Holly said cautiously. On the contrary, she thought, shuddering at the image of teeming rats. White rats, she supposed. White rats with little pink eyes...

Eric shook his head. 'It *sounds* all right, but it's the way she goes on that's screwy. She gets in a fever, you know? Gets obsessed, then loses interest, just like Ol' Maggott. Like, by the time the rat guy's out the door, Lily's been a couple of times to cut her hair, and she's seen these earrings Lily makes out of gumnuts and feathers and stuff, and she's got a bee in her bonnet about being a patron of the arts.'

He snorted. 'Next thing, Lily's moved in to the best room in the house—the one McNish had when he came—and she's swanning around the place thinking she's set for life. And no sooner has Allnut knocked that one on the head than Miz M sees a picture of some loser in the paper, decides he's her long-lost brother, boots Lily into the crummy little room next to mine and puts the loser into the good one. Now she's into murder, and you've seen what *that's* like.'

He glowered, hunching over the wheel. 'It wouldn't matter if she wasn't loaded. If she was like her old man and didn't have a bean Dulcie and co wouldn't give a stuff about what she did. They'd just go away and leave us alone. Then she'd forget about McNish, and go on to something else. But the way things are, nothing's going to settle her down except hard evidence that McNish is still alive.'

'The police might trace the teaspoons,' Holly said, thinking aloud.

Eric shook his head. 'It'd be a miracle. And even if they *did* turn up, Miz M wouldn't believe it was McNish who'd nicked them. She says one of us took them to frame him. Says he was too smart to have left the cupboard door half open so any fool could see they were gone first thing.'

Holly frowned. That made sense, actually. She couldn't imagine Andrew making a mistake like that either.

Eric glanced at her again, hesitated, then seemed to make a decision.

'Look,' he said. 'No one knows this—not even Sheena. But the old girl's rings have gone, too.'

'*What?*'

'They were her mother's. One's an engagement ring—an emerald big enough to choke a horse, with six diamonds round it in a circle. The other one's two emeralds and three diamonds in a line—an e-ternity ring, the old girl called it. They were made to go together. The bands both have "Forever" en-graved on the inside.'

'They sound very valuable,' Holly said faintly.

'Worth a packet,' Eric agreed. 'Ol' Maggott was a great one for jewellery. The wife who bled him dry and then took off—the one who's supposed to have been McNish's mother—they say she used to get around so loaded down with stuff that she jingled like a Christmas tree.'

'But Ms. Maggott's rings…' Holly prompted.

'Yeah, well, the old girl didn't wear them anymore. They'd got too small for her. She kept them in a little bag hanging behind the snake tank, stuck on with masking tape. I saw them there dozens of times, when I went in to clean the tank, and they aren't there now.'

Holly felt sick. It seemed worse, so much worse, for Andrew to have stolen Una Maggott's rings than to have taken the tea-spoons. It was so cruel. Such a *personal* betrayal.

Andrew McNish took all the money I had in the world, and more or less abandoned me at the altar, she reminded herself. *You can't get much more personal than that!* But it wasn't the same. She wasn't a sick old woman, like Una Maggott. Andrew would have known she'd be okay in the end.

And suddenly she knew she *would* be okay. However black things seemed now, in the end she'd put her life back together again. She had youth and energy on her side, plus keyboard skills, common sense, a good head for figures, and a reference from Gorgon Office Supplies. She also had a loving family back in Perth, who would send her the fare home in an instant if she could swallow her pride for long enough to call them reverse charges. Una Maggott, confused, betrayed and helpless, despite all her money, was a very different matter.

Cold anger swept through her, clearing her head. 'Does Una know—about the rings?' she asked.

Eric nodded sombrely. 'I told her, when I noticed they were gone. That was on Thursday—yesterday—in the afternoon. It shook her, I could see that, but she tried to cover it up. She said not to tell anyone. She said she must have just put the rings somewhere else and forgotten where. But she wouldn't have moved them. And no one else could have nicked them. McNish and I were the only ones who ever went into that room. The others won't go past the door. They're all too scared of Cleo.'

Holly noted that it hadn't occurred to Eric that he could be suspected of taking the rings himself. This was a point in his favour, she decided.

The hearse turned a corner, and the Mealey Marshes war memorial loomed ahead.

'I said I'd keep my trap shut about those rings, and I've done it, up till now,' Eric said in a low voice, as they cruised past the war memorial and purred on down Stillwaters Road, which was now as silent as the grave. 'If Dulcie or Stiff Cliff find out they're gone there'll be hell to pay.'

'So why are you telling me?' Holly asked bluntly.

'The thing is,' Eric said, 'the more Miz M carries on with this murder business, the crazier she looks. Next you know, Dulcie and Cliff will finally convince the doc to have her carted off to some home for old loonies. That's what they want.'

He slapped the wheel in frustration. 'The poor old tart's losing it, sure, but why should she end up in a home? Ol' Maggott never did, and he was a lot madder than she is. I can look after her. Sheena's going, and Lily—not that Lily's ever been much help—but we can hire someone else.'

The hearse did a smooth U-turn and came to a halt in front of the daisy-infested passage that was 16A. The bookshop next door had given up for the day. The butcher's shop was in the process of closing. The parsley-decked trays of cutlets, sausages and rump steak had been removed from the window, and plastic ferns had been tastefully arranged in their place.

The bald butcher was standing outside, smoking, in exactly the same position as before. It was as if he hadn't moved since Holly saw him last. He regarded the hearse with interest.

Eric turned to face Holly and, in a supreme gesture of sincerity, whipped off his sunglasses. His eyes were brown, soulful and slightly watery.

'I don't know why you people are after McNish, and I don't want to know,' he said, his lips barely moving. 'It's something heavy, I can see that. Way out of my league. But you're professionals, and you've got the manpower. So I'm giving you the tip. There can't be many fences who'd handle those rings. They're too unusual, and they must be worth a fortune. If you can trace them, they might lead you to McNish. You can do what you like with him. All I want is proof that he was alive when you found him.'

Holly didn't know what to say. She found it endearing that Eric, who had obviously been around, and whose father had a friend in the cement business, could be at the same time so naïve as to be impressed by her work suit and an office above a clairvoyant's premises in Mealey Marshes. She felt strangely unwilling to shatter his illusions. It was balm to her bruised self-esteem to be regarded as a tough professional by someone, even Eric. On the other hand, she knew she was no more capable of tracing Una Maggott's rings than O'Brien's parrot was.

And on the third hand, the last few minutes had made her realise that in fact she no longer had any interest in finding Andrew McNish. All she wanted now was to put the whole sordid business behind her and get on with her life—such as it was.

'I'm not sure—' she began carefully, and broke off as Eric's face froze and he raised his hand warningly. He was looking past her, through the passenger window. She looked around.

The butcher had prised himself from the wall and was approaching the hearse.

'Think about it,' muttered Eric, putting his sunglasses on again. 'I'll be in touch.'

He leaned over Holly and clicked the passenger door open. As she wrestled with her seatbelt, which had caught in the strap of her handbag, the butcher dropped his cigarette butt, ground it out with his heel and pulled the door wide.

'G'day, mate,' he said to Eric, far too heartily. 'Impressive vehicle you've got there. Runs sweet, eh? Must eat up the gas, but.'

Eric nodded broodingly.

His masculine social duties having been discharged, the butcher addressed himself to Holly. 'Glad I caught up with you,' he said. 'Old Mossie upstairs, Enid Moss, was in the shop earlier to get her cat's rabbit, and she gave me the drum that you've moved in upstairs where the bloke topped himself, and you're a private dick! Dickess, I suppose I should say.' He guffawed.

Inwardly cursing Mrs. Moss, Holly simpered, mumbled and tore at the seatbelt. Eric sat like a statue, back in idling mode.

'You could have knocked me over with a feather,' said the butcher, who didn't look as if a charging bull would do more than rock him back on his heels. 'What a bit of luck! Thing is, there's a bloke at the club—nicest bloke you'd ever meet, heart of gold. He's having a bit of trouble with his old lady, but he's not too flush with the readies. Thought you might help him out—mates' rates.'

Freeing herself at last, Holly slithered untidily from the hearse. The butcher caught her as she stumbled and hauled her out of the gutter, slamming the door behind her.

'She's right, mate,' he called to Eric, slapping the roof of the hearse familiarly. Without a flicker of acknowledgement, Eric pulled away from the kerb.

'Funny sort of cove,' the butcher commented, as the hearse purred up the hill. 'Anyhow, about this mate of mine—'

'Actually, I'm—I'm just up here temporarily,' babbled Holly. 'On a job, you know? I'll be going in a day or two.'

'Fair enough,' said the butcher, showing no sign of disappointment. 'Well, I'd better get back and do me bit before Harry comes after me with a cleaver. Hoo roo.'

With a cheery wave he waddled back to the shop, deadheating at the door with a tiny, frantic old woman carrying a string bag.

'Just made it, Mrs. Halliday,' Holly heard him say, as he pulled the door open and waved the little woman through. 'Sleep in, did ya? Hungover again? You want to watch it. Harry nearly sold your kidneys twice this arvo. I had to fight him for them, in the finish.'

Giggling and twittering, the tiny woman preceded him into the shop.

Holly found herself smiling as she walked into the maw of 16A. She had almost reached Abigail's rainbow door when it opened and a large young woman came out. The woman had dull skin and short, lifeless dark hair. Her most outstanding features were her eyebrows, which joined over the bridge of her nose to form a single, thick black bar, giving her heavy face a pugnacious, lowering expression. She had a small brown bottle in her hand.

'Now, don't forget, Dimity,' Abigail's voice cooed from inside the room. 'The burnt offering tonight, under the full moon, and ten drops of the potion in a glass of warm water every morning.'

The young woman nodded, turned to go and saw Holly. She jumped, hid the bottle behind her back and flushed scarlet. Abigail popped out of the door to see what was wrong.

'Oh, never mind about Holly!' she trilled, sizing up the situation instantly. 'My colleague, you know? She's been out… on a house call. Holly, this is Dimity, a new client!' She made anguished faces at Holly behind the blushing woman's back and mouthed incomprehensibly.

'Pleased to meet you,' Holly heard herself saying.

The young woman mumbled a greeting. The painful blush began to subside.

'Give me a ring in a week to tell me how you're going, won't you?' Abigail said brightly.

Dimity mumbled again, flashed an astonishingly sweet smile that transformed her whole face, and hurried past Holly to the street.

Chapter Twelve

'Thank you for that,' whispered Abigail, drawing Holly into the warm, patchouli-scented little room beyond the rainbow door. 'They don't mind Enid Moss, but they get so embarrassed if it's someone their own age.'

'What did she come to see you for?' Holly snapped. The room was claustrophobic. Backing onto the bookshop as it did, it had no windows, and it was very dimly lit. Candles flickered here and there, and crystals gleamed on low shelves crammed with books. In the centre was a small table draped in black velvet, with two chairs facing one another across its midnight surface.

All the trappings, Holly thought, remembering Lily, the soft-footed, hairdressing witch. She felt very sorry for Dimity, and disgusted with Abigail for preying on her, feeding her a lot of hocus-pocus.

'Oh, she wanted a love potion,' sighed Abigail. 'The poor girl's lonely. Extremely romantic, but terribly shy. The grandmother who brought her up is very old-fashioned.'

'So you sold her a love potion, did you?' Holly asked coldly.

'Oh, no,' said Abigail, staring at her. 'There's no such thing, sadly. Most of those old recipes were actually aphrodisiacs, and an aphrodisiac is the *last* thing Dimity needs. No, I made her up a mixture of St John's Wort, to cheer her up, plus some vitamin B for energy and some cleansing herbs for her skin. That should help. It will give her confidence, which is half the battle, really, isn't it?'

Holly readjusted, then flew back into the attack. 'What about the burnt offering under the moon?'

'Oh, that should help, too,' said Abigail serenely. 'Dimity was very keen on the idea of burnt offerings making wishes come true. She'd read about it somewhere. Well, I told her it never hurt to try, but the offering should be something personal. Fingernail clippings, for example. Or hair. So we decided that she'd sacrifice fifty of her eyebrow hairs. I told her to take them from the middle.'

As Holly gaped at her, she winked. 'A bit of hocus-pocus makes the medicine go down,' she said. 'Listen, now you're here, why don't you stay? We could have a drink before dinner. I've put the casserole on to heat. All I have to do is make the salad.'

'That would be…nice,' said Holly faintly. 'But I'll just have water, thanks.' The thought of food made her weak at the knees. The thought of alcohol made her head swim.

Abigail regarded her thoughtfully. 'In fact, would you mind if we ate a bit early?' she asked. 'As soon as the casserole's hot enough? I'm starving.'

Holly shook her head, speechless.

'Wonderful!' said Abigail. 'And while we're waiting, why don't I read the cards for you, Holly? It seems to me you've got a few things on your mind.'

'Oh, it's okay,' Holly mumbled. 'Really, I don't want…I don't need…' But she didn't resist as Abigail led her to the velvet-draped table. Her sudden anger on Dimity's behalf, and the realisation that the anger had been unjustified, seemed to have drained the last drop of adrenalin from her reserves, leaving her feeling listless, and strangely uncaring about what happened to her next. Why not? she found herself thinking, as she sank into the chair Abigail pulled out for her. Let her do her thing if she wants to. At least there'll be food at the end of it.

She watched blearily as Abigail went to a shelf littered with crystals, stood perfectly still with her back turned for a moment, then picked something up and returned to the table.

She was holding a small bundle wrapped in black silk. She put the bundle onto the table and unwrapped it. A pack of cards was revealed. The cards were black with a central gold design, larger than normal playing cards, and a bit furry around the edges.

Abigail folded the silk square carefully and put it to one side. Then she presented the pack to Holly.

'You shuffle,' she said. 'And I'd like you to focus on the key question you want answered, if you can.'

Holly wasn't good at shuffling cards. She'd never picked up the knack, though her mother, her grandmother and most of her aunts played solo and could shuffle like card sharps. She did her awkward best with Abigail Honour's outsize deck, catching glimpses of the pictures on the cards as she manipulated them. From those images, Abigail Honour would presumably tell her future. Or, perhaps, answer the question she was supposed to be thinking about.

She certainly had questions. The main one was: 'How am I going to get out of this mess?' Others were, in order of importance: 'How am I going to get some money?' 'Where is Andrew?' and 'What is Una Maggott going to think when I don't turn up in the morning?'

She put down the cards, feeling they'd been shuffled enough. Badly, but enough.

'Now cut them, with your left hand,' Abigail instructed. Holly did as she was told, wondering vaguely if it mattered that she was left-handed to start with.

'Fine,' said Abigail, drawing the pack toward her across the black velvet, and pushing the cards' flabby edges meticulously into line. 'Now, let's see...'

And, drawing cards from the top of the deck, laying them down one by one, she began to talk. She didn't set out the cards in a pattern, as Holly had expected from various magazine articles she'd read. She merely put them down in front of her in groups of three, as if she were playing some sort of patience.

Holly tried to focus on the cards herself. The images were upside-down for her. She couldn't make much sense of them.

Colours and shapes blurred in the candlelight. She glimpsed a ruined building, what looked like a game wheel, lots of swords, some golden goblets, a dark figure with a scythe over its shoulder…that one didn't augur well.

'Your life changed, quite dramatically, not long ago,' Abigail said slowly. 'You've lost your feeling of security. Death's involved, but it isn't the main issue for you at the moment.' She looked up. 'You've broken up with someone recently.'

Holly nodded, unnerved.

'It's good you got rid of him,' said Abigail, wrinkling her nose. 'He was unreliable—attractive and charming, probably, but not worth having. A Gemini, I think. A great one for the grand gesture, but no good on the long haul.'

Quite, Holly thought, and inconsequentially remembered asking Andrew to sponsor one of her little Perth cousins whose primary school was doing a charity walk. Andrew had insisted on pledging five dollars per kilometre. Holly had been overwhelmed, almost embarrassed. It was five times what anyone else had promised. And of course, that had been the point. She doubted he'd ever actually paid up.

Abigail turned over more cards. 'I can see secrets and lies around you. Shadows. And a snake.'

'That was a real snake,' Holly blurted out, startled into speech. 'A python. I saw it this afternoon.'

Abigail's expression didn't change. She went back to the cards, staring at them intently. 'There's an issue about money. Money lost or stolen. Was it yours?'

'Yes.' Holly felt her face grow hot.

'You should forget about getting it back,' Abigail said, frowning slightly. 'I can see searching, but the searching won't benefit you. A strong-minded older woman—damaged in some way—is going to come into your life. Or perhaps she has already?' Again she glanced up, eyebrows raised.

'Yes,' Holly squeaked. She cleared her throat. 'I met her this afternoon. The snake lives in her house.'

Abigail looked unsurprised. 'This woman will exert a pow-erful influence over you, if you let her,' she said. 'She wants something from you—it's very important to her. She's very determined. You'll have to decide what to do about that.'

'She wants me to help her with something,' Holly said. 'But—but I can't. So I'm not going back.'

Abigail made no comment, but turned over three more cards. One of them, Holly noted queasily, showed a man hanging upside-down.

'You should trust your instincts,' Abigail said. 'Your instincts are good. The path ahead of you is difficult—even dangerous—but your instincts will guide you safely, if you listen to them. You'll be receiving some small sums of money from unexpected sources very soon. And…there's a handsome stranger waiting in the wings. You might have met him already. An attractive, fair-headed man with a practical streak.'

She glanced up at Holly again. Holly shook her head. The only men she'd met lately were Eric and the butcher, and neither of them was fair-haired—or remotely attractive.

'Then you'll meet him soon,' said Abigail, unperturbed. 'And he's not the only man interested in you. There seem to be several of them circling around, waiting for you to notice them. It looks to me as if you're not going to be alone for long.'

She gathered up the cards, returned them to the pack and folded her hands. The consultation, it seemed, was over.

Holly had been far more impressed than she'd expected. The bits about Una Maggott and the snake had been extraordinary. So had the stuff about stolen money. But she had found the summing up disappointing. Trust yourself? Money coming? A handsome stranger? Apparently the union of tarot-card readers adhered to the old Hollywood 'Send them home happy' rule.

'Thank you, Abigail,' she murmured, hoping this was the appropriate response. 'That was really—interesting.'

Abigail nodded casually, wrapped the deck of cards in the black silk again and took the little bundle back to the shelf. As Holly stood up too, she saw that instead of putting the bundle back in the box, Abigail was arranging crystals on top of it. Disinfecting the cards of me, I suppose, thought Holly, and felt oddly insulted.

She watched Abigail's profile, wild-haired and witchy in the candlelight.

...secrets and lies around you. Shadows. And a snake.

Not anymore, Holly promised herself. Her stomach gurgled.

'Well, the casserole should be hot enough by now,' Abigail said cheerfully, turning away from the shelf. 'Come through and we'll eat.'

She led the way through a door at the back of the consulting room. Holly followed, and to her surprise and relief found herself in a large, welcoming, brightly lit space that was part kitchen and part living room, and had a broad view of the dark back garden. A sturdy wooden table stood in the centre of the room. It had been covered in a blue gingham cloth and set with two places. The air was filled with a savoury smell. Holly's heart sang.

◇◇◇

Abigail's vegetable casserole was a dark brown mush that tasted of fennel and not much else. It was impossible to tell what was in it, though Holly was fairly sure the orange lumps were sweet potato, and the black bits were mushrooms. Not that she cared. The food was hot and filling, and that was all that counted as far as she was concerned. She had eaten a third of what was on her plate without drawing breath.

'I don't know where the cauliflower went,' said Abigail, trawling through the sludge on her plate with her fork. 'And I can't taste the garlic at all. Maybe I should have left out the juniper berries. What do you think?'

'It's great,' said Holly sincerely. She was feeling better. Much, much better. She had feared that Abigail might want to talk about the consultation—ask her questions, maybe, or give her advice. But to her relief, Abigail hadn't referred to her predictions, or the tarot cards, at all. She had just busied herself getting the meal on the table with all possible speed.

'My first husband, Fergus, said I had no feeling for food,' said Abigail. 'He insisted on doing all the cooking. He only used fresh ingredients—no processed food at all. That's how he died, really.'

'Oh, I'm sorry,' said Holly, swallowing hastily.

'Yes, it was very sad,' sighed Abigail. 'Fergus had aichmophobia, you see. That's a morbid fear of knives. He'd had it for as long as he could remember—only ever ate with a fork and spoon. Or chopsticks. He wouldn't have a knife in the house. So if a recipe called for ingredients to be sliced or diced, it was tricky.' She helped herself to salad.

'I suppose he could have used a food processor,' Holly suggested tentatively, wondering how this story was going to end.

Abigail shook her head. 'Fergus started hyperventilating if he even saw a *picture* of a food processor. All those blades, you see. Scissors were out for the same reason. It made things a bit awkward.'

'It must have.'

'He managed quite well, really, just tearing things apart,' said Abigail, her eyes growing a little misty. 'He had his mortar and pestle. And very hard things he broke up with a little hammer. He was very stubborn—wouldn't let anything beat him. He was a Taurus, of course.'

She paused. 'I did wonder about that—the Taurus thing—before I married him. But I thought it would be good for me to have a steady, reliable partner, and I convinced myself that the brick walls I kept seeing in front of me when I was with him meant security. Ah, well. More casserole, Holly? Salad? Bread?'

'Thanks,' said Holly, gratefully accepting all three. 'What happened? I mean, how did Fergus…?'

'It was a pumpkin,' said Abigail. 'A Queensland Blue. A man was selling them out of the boot of his car near the station—practically giving them away. Well, Fergus loved a bargain, so he bought one. He must have chosen the biggest one the man had. It was enormous! It's a wonder he didn't give himself a hernia carrying it home. He'd been planning to bake it whole, but it wouldn't fit into the oven. So he tried to break it up with his hammer, but he didn't have a chance. That pumpkin was hard as a rock.'

She took a celery stick from her plate, propped her chin on her hand and chewed thoughtfully.

'I begged him to give up on it. I told him I had a really bad feeling about it. But he wouldn't listen. He worked on that pumpkin for hours. He must have thrown it down the front steps a dozen times. They were stone, but they didn't make a dent in it. He tried to run the car over it, but it just kept rolling away. It was getting dark by the time he hauled it up to the roof.'

'And—he fell?' Holly prompted, unable to bear the suspense.

'Yes,' Abigail agreed. 'Two floors, into the vegetable garden. I saw him come past the kitchen window. It was amazing. He wasn't hurt at all. Sat up, good as gold, spitting out lucerne mulch. Then the pumpkin came rolling down after him and landed on his head. Killed him instantly. And do you know, it didn't break even then?' She took another celery stick.

'That's...awful,' Holly said.

'Oh well, it was a long time ago,' Abigail sighed. 'I got over it in the end. Mind you, I swore I'd never eat pumpkin again. Or marry a Taurus, for that matter. And I never have. Carl, my second husband, was a Scorpio. He was a salesman. Very magnetic. He swept me off my feet, and we married a month to the day after we met. I didn't have a moment's doubt, because the first time I saw him I heard wedding bells as clearly as I can hear you now.'

She sighed. 'Of course, it turned out that I'd misinterpreted that. What it really meant was that he was married already. Very married, in fact. He had five wives, including me. All in different states.'

She registered Holly's appalled reaction, and shrugged. 'You're probably thinking I can't be much of a psychic if I made such hopeless marriages,' she commented, with devastating accuracy. 'But I seem to be able to help other people quite well. It's just that when I'm emotionally involved, my gift can lead me astray. My third husband—'

'You married *again*?' Holly gasped, then bit her tongue.

But Abigail just laughed. 'Oh yes. I was a sucker for punishment in those days. I know better now. Anyway, my third
husband, Prosper—who strictly speaking was only my second
husband, really, since Carl was a quintigamist—was an older
chap, and an Aquarius. I honestly thought I was safe with him.
I met him at ballroom dancing class. He wasn't very passionate,
but he was very gentle and sweet, and he loved dancing. I could
sense a redheaded female in his life, and I was going to ask him
about that, but then I went to his house and met his red setter,
Lucinda, so I thought, well, *that's* all right.'

'But it wasn't?' Holly asked, absent-mindedly taking the last
piece of bread.

Abigail shook her head.

'It turned out there was more to his relationship with Lucinda
than met the eye,' she said primly. 'In fact, if only he could have
danced with her, he wouldn't have needed to marry me at all, if
you know what I mean. Coffee?'

Holly gulped, and nodded. As Abigail pushed back her chair
and went to fill the kettle, she stood up herself and mechanically
began to clear the table.

'Just leave that,' Abigail called over the sound of the running
water. 'I'll do it in the morning. I haven't got a client till ten. It's
a man, for a change—I hope he turns up. I found him hovering
around in the corridor this afternoon, too nervous to knock, I
suppose, and more or less *forced* him to make an appointment.
You've never been married, have you, Holly?'

'No,' said Holly, carrying the plates to the sink and glancing
out the window into the darkness that had fallen outside. 'I've
been engaged twice but…it didn't work out. Well, you know that.'

And suddenly, with no warning, hot tears welled up in her
eyes. She struggled to hold them back, but it was no use. Her
throat was burning and aching. There was a terrible, bursting
pain in her chest.

She heard a sound behind her and felt an arm around her
shoulders.

'Oh, I'm sorry,' she heard Abigail say. 'Oh, poor Holly!'

And the next minute she was sobbing on Abigail's shoulder, and Abigail was patting her back murmuring, 'Never mind, Holly. Never mind…'

Holly just wept. She wept because Andrew McNish had deceived her and left her. She wept because Andrew was a conman and a thief. She wept because Una Maggott had lost something money couldn't buy. She wept for the old, safe times in Perth, and her friends, and Lloyd, who had never done anything to deserve her betrayal, except to be boring.

And then, at last, the terrible ache in her chest and throat eased. The storm of tears subsided into snuffles and shuddering breaths. She drew away from Abigail, accepted a tissue, and blew her nose.

'Sorry,' she said. 'I'm—I've been a bit stressed out lately.'

That was the understatement of the year, she thought, and almost smiled. She blew her nose again, avoiding the other woman's eye.

'Do you really want a coffee?' said Abigail. 'Or will I open a bottle of wine?'

So Abigail opened a bottle of wine. Then she remembered a box of orange peel dipped in chocolate that one of her grateful clients had given her. Carrying this booty between them, she and Holly moved to the enormous, old-fashioned three-piece lounge suite that almost filled the far end of the room. And there, sitting in an armchair so comfortable that you could have slept in it, at a pinch, Holly told her story, from beginning to end. The only thing she instinctively kept to herself was her total lack of funds. She shrank from the thought that Abigail might think she was asking for a loan.

'Well!' said Abigail, when she'd finished. 'You *have* had some fun, haven't you?'

And Holly laughed. It was the first time she had laughed since finding Andrew's note on the fridge. Actually, she realised, it was the first time she had laughed properly for months. It had been a strain, preserving the casual, cool, confident persona she'd invented to please Andrew McNish. It had been very stressful, preparing to run away and marry a man she hardly knew. This discovery amazed her.

'I don't think I've been in my right mind for ages,' she said aloud.

'Probably not,' said Abigail, draining her glass. 'We're all a bit unhinged when we're first in love. And obviously this Andrew was offering something you wanted. Obviously you weren't happy with the way things were in your life, and were looking for a way out. Otherwise you wouldn't have suspended your judgement like that.'

She was right, of course. Holly leaned back in her chair. Suddenly she was having trouble keeping her eyes open.

'Would you like to sleep here, on the couch, tonight, Holly?' Abigail's voice sounded as if it were coming from a long way off. 'You're very welcome, and I'm sure the parrot will be okay on its own.'

'Oh, no, thanks very much, but I'll be fine. Truly.' Holly struggled out of the warm embrace of the chair. The idea of the empty flat upstairs wasn't appealing, but she knew she couldn't impose on Abigail any longer. She had to gather the shreds of her independence together and act like a grown-up. She had a bed, at least for tonight, and she should sleep in it.

'Well, if you're sure,' Abigail said doubtfully.

She took Holly back through the front room and opened the door into the passageway. The door to the street had been closed. A single light hanging from the ceiling at the foot of the stairs did little to relieve the prevailing dimness. The passage with its grinning daisy faces reminded Holly of the interior of a ghost train.

'I can't thank you enough for dinner and—everything,' Holly said, and had never meant anything more sincerely in her life.

'Oh, it was nothing,' said Abigail. 'But, Holly, I've been thinking. There's nothing to stop you staying here, you know, while you decide what you want to do. Enid and I would be pleased to have you.'

Holly blinked. 'What about the landlord?'

'Oh, what old Droopy Drawers doesn't know won't hurt him. He won't be here till the rent's due again. Never comes near the place between times. He kept the whole of Skye and Deirdre's bond, you know, because of those gorgeous murals, even though they paid for all the paint themselves.'

'I'll think about it,' Holly temporised. The offer was strangely tempting, but she knew she couldn't accept it. Abigail's revelations over the tarot cards had made one thing very clear to her, at least. She had to get away from poor, mad Una Maggott, and while she stayed here Una could always find her.

'Sleep well, then,' said Abigail. 'See you in the morning.'

As the rainbow door closed, Holly felt a pang of regret. She trudged along the corridor, reached the stairs and wearily began to climb. There was a line of light showing under Mrs. Moss' door, through which TV screams and gunshots drifted. She found this oddly comforting.

Her own landing was dark, and the only sound was a soft, repetitive buzzing. The cockatoo snored, apparently. Smiling wryly, Holly moved forward, and ran straight into a dark figure sitting slumped at the top of the stairs.

Chapter Thirteen

With a strangled scream, Holly staggered back, grabbing the flimsy banister for support. The dark figure snorted, shook itself and lurched up, revealing itself to be a small, weedy, balding man with a prim, stubborn little mouth and very large ears.

'Oh, my arm's gone to sleep!' the man said, making an anguished face. He cradled his left arm with his right and eyed Holly resentfully. 'I must have dropped off I've been waiting a *very long time.*'

'What do you want?' Holly demanded, taking a cautious step down. The man looked harmless, but she'd seen enough movies to know that looking harmless was the serial killer's secret weapon.

'Purse,' the man said incomprehensibly.

Holly gaped at him.

'Trevor Purse.' Wincing, the man felt in the inside pocket of his anorak, pulled out a black vinyl wallet and extracted a card. He held the card out to Holly. She took it and strained to read it in the gloom.

TREVOR PURSE. PEST EXTERMINATOR.
BEDBUG SPECIALIST.

Holly's skin crawled. 'I don't need a pest exterminator,' she said, hoping very much that this was true.

Trevor Purse clicked his tongue impatiently. He leaned toward Holly. 'Keith Bone sent me,' he muttered out of the side of his mouth.

'Keith Bone?' The name meant nothing to Holly. She wondered if she'd been having blackouts.

'Keith said I should come straight away or else I'd miss you,' the man mumbled. 'So I did. I haven't even been home. I've missed the news.' He lowered his voice even further. 'Keith said you could help me with…ah…with a small personal problem.'

And suddenly Holly saw the light.

'You're the butcher's friend!' she blurted out. 'His friend from the club, with wife problems.'

She felt graceless as the man shrank back into his anorak like a tortoise retreating into its shell.

'I'm sorry, Mr. Purse,' she said, making an effort to sound friendly, despite her instinctive dislike of the man. 'But I'm afraid—'

'We'll talk about this behind closed doors, if you don't mind,' Purse mumbled, snatching up a bag that strongly resembled a doctor's medical case. 'I do understand that you modern, professional women have been forced to develop a hard carapace in order to survive, but it's beyond me to be so cavalier about discussing deep personal feelings in public, I'm afraid.'

Oh really, thought Holly, very irritated. She folded her arms, remembered this was a classic defensive gesture, and unfolded them again.

'It's after business hours, Mr. Purse,' she said. 'And I've had a very long day…'

Long day? It seemed like a week since she'd set out for Mealey Marshes.

'I could inspect your rooms for bedbug infestation while we talk,' Trevor Purse suggested cunningly. 'I gather you're only visiting, and you can't be too careful about strange beds, believe me. Bedbugs are multiplying to plague proportions internationally, and it's not a matter of simple hygiene. There have been cases of bedbugs in four-star hotels, you know.'

Holly thought of the sagging bed in O'Brien's flat. Her skin crawled again. She made a lightning decision.

'It's a deal,' she said, sounding hard, brittle and modern even to herself.

Trevor Purse drew back, clutching his bag to his chest, as she moved up to the landing and strode past him to the door with the red heart.

'I couldn't help noticing you'd left the radio on in there,' he said, following her. 'You think it will discourage burglars, I suppose, but I really should warn you that there is always the danger of an electrical fault. I insist on my wife unplugging every power point when she has to leave our home unattended.'

'Really,' said Holly, through gritted teeth. She pushed the door open and switched on the light.

'Howdy!' screeched the parrot. 'Give us a biscuit!'

Holly scowled at it. It raised its crest and regarded her roguishly. 'And the hairs on her dicky-di-do hung down to her knees,' it crooned.

'Oh, dear, dear, dear!' exclaimed Trevor Purse. 'A bird! I would never have a bird in my home. The seed attracts vermin.'

He placed his bag on the red desk and looked around, narrowing his eyes at the sight of the bulging garbage bags propped against the wall.

'That's not garbage, just clothes and things,' Holly said instinctively, then gave herself a mental slap on the wrist.

Purse made no comment. He glanced through the open bedroom door and a fanatical gleam appeared in his eyes. He snapped his bag open and withdrew a pair of polythene gloves.

'The light's not very good in there, I'm afraid,' said Holly.

Purse shook his head. 'I can't tell you how many times I've heard that,' he said, pulling on the gloves. 'People *will* insist on subdued lighting in the bedroom. They've got no idea! Darkness conceals, light reveals, that's what I always tell them. It's not just bedbugs, you know. I've seen it all—clothes moths, fleas, cockroaches, silverfish, crickets, carpet beetles, mice, rats, white-tailed spiders…'

He dipped into his bag again and pulled out an enormous torch cloaked in black rubber. It could have passed for part of a submarine.

Striding to the bedroom doorway, he felt inside for the light switch. The green bulb came to life, its sulky glow barely illuminating the jungle foliage writhing on the walls. Purse clicked his tongue. He flicked on his torch and trained a beam like a searchlight onto the bed.

'Follow me,' he said. 'Stay back.'

Slightly crouched, holding the torch in front of him with both gloved hands and swinging the beam from side to side like an FBI agent entering an unsecured crime scene, he stole toward the bed.

Keeping a safe distance behind him, Holly watched as he bent, pinched the trailing hem of the chenille bedspread between gloved fingers and fastidiously folded the spread back, exposing part of the dingy mattress beneath to the merciless glare of the torch.

'My wife Leanne and I have been married for eight years, Miss Love,' he said, without turning around. 'She was twenty-nine when we met and I was...a little older. Waiting for the right woman to come along, you see.'

Sighing, he straightened, felt in his shirt pocket and drew out a pair of glasses, which he settled on his beaky little nose before bending again to the bed.

'For eight years we've lived happily together, never a cross word. We're not rich, by any means, but we own our own home, and my wife has never had to go out to work. She has been free to pursue her various little hobbies and keep our home as we both like to see it. I've always prided myself on that.'

'Children?' Holly hazarded, feeling as if this was the sort of question that O'Brien would have asked.

'Not at present,' Purse said, wincing as if she had said something indelicate. 'We both feel we need to secure our position thoroughly before bringing a child into the world. Education expenses alone...' He clicked his tongue.

He had begun edging round the bed, peering intently at the raised side seam of the mattress, pressing the seam out with his gloved fingers.

'They also hide in the cavities of the frame, of course,' he said. 'But if the bed is infested, they can usually be found in the cleft of the mattress seam. They keep hidden, you see, until someone goes to bed, and to sleep. Then, attracted by exhaled carbon dioxide, they crawl out to feed.'

Holly shuddered. She realised she must have made a sound, too, because Trevor Purse looked over his shoulder at her. His face was so thin and his eyes were so hugely magnified by the thick glasses that for a moment he looked like an insect himself. A giant cricket, perhaps. Holly twitched, beating away the illusion.

'Have you found anything?' she asked.

'Not so far,' Purse told her. 'But it's early days yet. Early days.'

He turned back to his examination of the mattress seam. 'My problems all started a month ago, when my wife began going out on Saturdays. She *said* she was going to her friend Petula's place, to babysit while Petula went to work. Petula is one of those single mothers and—'

He froze like a pointer, glaring down at the mattress. Holly held her breath, but after a moment he shook his head and moved on.

'—and I can't say I've ever been too keen on her,' he went on, as if there had been no interruption. 'But though I've always been the head of our home, I wouldn't interfere with my wife's choice of friends.'

Big of you, Holly thought sourly.

'And as for Saturdays—well, my model train club meets every Saturday, regular as clockwork, and it seemed quite reasonable to me that while I was away my wife should go out and enjoy herself,' Purse continued. 'But then, last Tuesday, I had to take the day off work. I suffer dreadfully from haemorrhoids.'

Holly wasn't surprised.

Purse had reached the end of the bed. He skirted the corner carefully, folded the bedspread back, and continued searching the mattress seam.

'By lunchtime I was feeling a little better, and my wife took the opportunity to pop out to the shops,' he went on. 'While she was out the post came, so I hobbled out to get it. I never like mail being left in the box for any length of time. Any passer-by could break the lock and take the letters, getting access to all your personal details. And as I'm sure you know, identity theft is a growing problem.'

Holly was starting to feel very uncomfortable. Purse's thin, precise voice had slowed. Obviously he was reaching the climax of his story, and was unconsciously delaying getting to the point. But he'd get there sooner or later, and Holly found she didn't want him to.

'Mr. Purse, I don't think—'

'There was a postcard,' Purse said, in a rush. 'From New Zealand. For my wife.'

He straightened abruptly and turned to look at Holly, his thick glasses flashing, his face nightmarish in the glaring white light of the torch he was clutching to his chest. 'Normally I would never dream of reading my wife's mail,' he said, in a pathetic echo of his former pompous manner. 'But this was a postcard, you see. I couldn't help noticing the signature. It was—*Petula*!'

He waited, searching Holly's face for a reaction.

'The friend whose child your wife has been minding on Saturdays,' Holly said, feeling as if the words were being dragged out of her one by one with hot tongs.

'Yes, yes!' said Trevor Purse impatiently. 'But don't you see? My wife *can't* have been babysitting for Petula! Petula and her child have been in *New Zealand* for *six weeks*! Petula said so herself— well, I can't be blamed for reading the message, it was there in the open for anyone to see. *We're so settled I can't believe we've only been here six weeks,* she said. Well, you can imagine how I felt!'

Distractedly he started checking the far side of the bed. In the other room the cockatoo chuckled like a deranged cartoon villain bent on world domination.

'What did your wife say when you asked her about the postcard?' Holly was sure she already knew the answer to that question. Her heart felt as if it had sunk to the soles of her shoes.

Purse looked up again and she saw with horrified pity that tears were leaking from beneath his glasses. 'I didn't ask her,' he whispered, as she'd known he would. 'I put the mail back in the box and let her collect it herself, when she came home. She brought in the other letters and put them on the kitchen table as usual, but the postcard wasn't there. She must have hidden it in her handbag. I couldn't tell her I'd seen it. I couldn't ask her why she'd lied to me. I—I was scared of what she might say.'

This was awful. Holly stood tongue-tied, feeling totally irresponsible, filled with shame, bitterly regretting she'd ever let things get this far.

'She's seeing someone else.' Purse pulled a perfectly ironed handkerchief from his anorak pocket, shook out the folds and blew his nose noisily. 'When I thought about it, I realised I should have recognised the signs. Over the past few weeks she's seemed—happier. Her eyes are brighter. Her hair is shinier. She…she *sings* while she's vacuuming!'

He buried his face in his hands. 'I keep imagining—terrible things. I can't sleep. My work is suffering. I have to know! That's why I've come to you. Tomorrow is Saturday. I want you to follow her…find out…'

Oh no!

'Mr. Purse, please, I'm sorry, but you'll have to find someone else,' Holly gabbled, panic-stricken. 'I don't have time…and anyway I—we—don't handle divorce cases.'

Purse's head jerked up. He looked horrified. '*Divorce?*' he gasped. 'There's no question of *divorce*! My wife and I have been happily married for *eight years*! I won't say a word to her about anything you tell me. I'll try to win her back—I'm sure I can win her back! But I have to know what I'm dealing with, you see. I have to *know!*'

'You could follow her yourself,' Holly suggested desperately. 'You could—'

Purse shook his head violently, wringing his gloved hands. 'She'd recognise my van. It's green. It's got my *name* on it! Please! All you have to do is follow her, then ring me. I'm not asking for a written report. I've got everything ready—here, I'll show you!'

He rushed from the bedroom, the torch beam flashing wildly over jungle-infested walls and ceiling. Holly followed, wondering how she could have been so insensitive, so stupid, as to encourage this poor, sad man, wondering if there were bedbugs in the mattress, wondering if this day would ever end.

'Here!' gasped Purse, pulling an envelope from his exterminator's bag and thrusting it into Holly's hands. 'Here's our address, and everything else you'll need. I leave the house at ten-forty-five. My wife leaves very soon afterwards, or so she says.'

He shoved the torch into his bag, snapped the bag shut, put his head down, and made for the door.

'What about the bedbugs?' Holly bleated, as he pulled the door open.

'This house is clean,' Purse said, and bolted.

'Ah-maze-i-i-ing grace,' the parrot crooned mournfully, 'how sweet the sound, tha-a-at saved a-a-ah wretch lie-ick meee!'

Holly felt drained. Obeying some impulse she preferred not to analyse, she went behind O'Brien's desk and sat down in the squeaky office chair. She tore open the envelope. Inside there were four items. The first was another of Trevor Purse's business cards, the mobile phone number circled in red biro. The second was a photograph of a pretty blonde woman wearing a bright sundress and smiling self-consciously in front of a burgeoning bougainvillea—a holiday snap, perhaps. The third was a piece of notepaper on which a precise map had been drawn. Below the map was written, in tiny, constipated script: *Mrs. Leanne Purse, 15 Wattle Crescent, Bullaburra. Saturday, 10:45 am (approx).*

The fourth was a fifty-dollar note. Trevor Purse's idea of 'mates' rates,' presumably. Holly's heart leapt. She eased the fifty from the envelope, feeling its smooth, reassuring texture beneath her fingertips, pressing one of its sharp corners into the pad of her thumb. She remembered Abigail telling her that money was coming, and a pleasurable shiver ran down her spine.

In that instant, a plan unfolded, ready-made, in her mind. Bullaburra, she knew, wasn't far away. It was the next village down from Wentworth Falls. She had passed through it on her way to Mealey Marshes—or at least seen a sign announcing its presence near a lone little shop that stood beside the crossing to the railway station.

In the morning she would pack the car and fill it with petrol. She would say goodbye to Abigail and Mrs. Moss. Then she would drive down to Bullaburra and follow the pest exterminator's wife. She wasn't a detective, but how hard could it be to follow someone? She'd find a public phone, make her report, and drive on down to the city. What was left of the fifty dollars would feed her for the weekend if she was very careful and resisted buying takeaway coffee. She would have nowhere to stay, but if O'Brien could sleep in his car, she could sleep in hers.

The important thing was, by tomorrow night she would be far away from memories of Andrew McNish, and out of Una Maggott's reach. Safe in Sydney, she would cut her losses and start again. She'd had enough of being Alice in Wonderland.

Feeling incredibly stable and efficient, Holly put the fifty dollars into her wallet, filled the parrot's seed and water containers, made the bed, cleaned her teeth, and had a shower standing on a plastic bag in case Skye or Deirdre had been afflicted with plantar warts.

Back in the bedroom, pulling on the cosy old spotted flannelette pyjamas she had nearly discarded in Sydney but had fortunately been unable to part with at the last minute, she heard the parrot singing lustily in the other room. It had moved from hymns to sea shanties.

'Sixteen men on a dead man's chest,' it sang. 'Yo ho ho and a bottle of rum.'

Warm, clean, the possessor of fifty dollars, and her stomach full for the first time in days, Holly smiled tolerantly. After a minute or two, however, it occurred to her that the parrot sounded closer than it should have. And at almost the same moment she found she couldn't remember replacing the butterfly clip that secured the cage door. Holding tightly to her newfound feeling of wellbeing, she went to investigate.

The parrot had freed itself. It was perched where Holly had first seen it, on the back of the office chair. As she emerged from the bedroom it raised its yellow crest defiantly.

'You can't sleep there,' Holly told it. 'Go back to your cage.' She took a threatening step forward. The parrot spread its wings and launched itself onto the red desk, skidding into Holly's shoulder bag, which tipped over the edge of the desktop and fell to the floor, voiding its contents on the way down.

Highly stimulated, the parrot waddled to the desk edge and peered down at the jumbled objects on the floor. Swearing, Holly went to clean up.

O'Brien's phone, jolted out of silence and buzzing distress calls, was lost in a sea of crumpled tissues, the incomprehensible paperwork from the Springwood service centre, forlorn lists of job possibilities and chocolate chip cookie crumbs. The photograph of Andrew McNish protruded impertinently from a clutter of keys, hairbrush, pen, nail file, lip-gloss, emergency tampons, coffee mug, wallet and diary. Trevor Purse's envelope, bent double, embraced a grimy teaspoon. Directly below the lip of the desktop, Una Maggott's yellow folder sprawled open, face down on the threadbare carpet, flattened beneath the shoulder bag itself.

Taken as a whole, it was a collage rich with symbolism— almost like an installation in an art gallery, Holly thought, staring down at it. It was as if it had been constructed for a purpose, to illustrate the helpless confusion of the past few days, to signal to her that from this moment, if she willed it, those days had ended.

'Thank you, O'Brien,' she said. The parrot bobbed jauntily, its eyes alert.

Holly bent and retrieved the shoulder bag. Then, choosing carefully, she picked through the mess on the floor, extracting only those items she needed for her flight to freedom, brushing them free of crumbs and packing them away. Wallet. Car key. Sunglasses. Hairbrush. Lip-gloss. Pen. Tampons. Nail file. After a moment's thought, she salvaged the diary and three of the freshest tissues. Then, reluctantly, she added Trevor Purse's envelope.

She put the bag aside and picked up O'Brien's phone. It flashed at her importunately, declaring itself to be bursting with voicemail. Not my problem, Holly told herself firmly. Then she felt a little tremor. What if one of the messages was from Una Maggott? Telling Holly that Eric would be coming to pick her up in the morning after all, for example? That would put a spanner in the works.

She listened to the messages. The first two were from people wanting to buy the parrot. Guiltily Holly deleted them. The third was from a woman called Dolly Bliss. She was ringing to tell O'Brien that she didn't want to proceed with the investigation they had discussed the previous week.

'Turns out there's no other woman,' Dolly said brightly. 'Turns out Ian actually bought that negligee for himself! I caught him wearing it this afternoon. So that's all right. Well, thanks very much.'

Holly deleted that one as well.

'Message four,' the phone announced. 'Received…today at… eight-fourteen pm.'

'Ms. Cage!' Una Maggott's voice hissed over the sound of banging and muffled shouts in the background. 'You have to come first thing tomorrow. As early as you can, do you understand me? I need you. There have been…developments—' The message cut off abruptly.

Holly stared at the phone. She realised she was gnawing her bottom lip, and made herself stop. Una Maggott's hysterics aren't your problem anymore, she reminded herself. You are taking back control of your own life. You are leaving here tomorrow, as planned.

Ruthlessly she deleted Una's message. She took the phone into the bedroom, wiped it, and plugged it into its charger. Then she fetched the plastic bag from the shower.

When she returned to the office, the parrot was on the floor prospecting for cookie crumbs, clucking and crooning like the chooks that had been the companions, and occasionally the Sunday dinners, of her youth. Holly knelt companionably beside it and began collecting all the inedible things remaining on the carpet, the things that had now officially become rubbish. Andrew's photograph, torn into four, went into the plastic bag first. The key to his house went next, and then the coffee mug and the teaspoon of despair. The used tissues, the lists and the paperwork from the service centre followed.

Soon the collage had been reduced to the sad, splayed sheet of yellow cardboard that was Una Maggott's folder. Holly picked it up and hesitated, her conscience pricking her at the thought of putting it into the garbage instead of the recycling bin. Then she decided that ritual demanded sacrifices, ripped the folder in half and ruthlessly stuffed it, too, into the plastic bag.

Two neatly printed-out sheets remained on the carpet. They were stapled together. Unable to resist the temptation, Holly glanced at the top sheet.

Statement by Una Maggott, 9 Horsetrough Lane, Medlow Bath.

On Tuesday 23rd March, I held a dinner party to celebrate my reunion with my half-brother, Andrew McNish/Maggott, and to announce that I intended to make a will naming him my sole heir.

Present were a distant cousin, Dulcie Maggott, her son, Sebastian Maggott (16), my housekeeper, Sheena Molloy, my chauffeur, Eric Maglioco, my hairdresser and household help, Lily Hoban, and my solicitor, Clifford Allnut.

My announcement was not well received. My guests apparently resented my half-brother, and were jealous of my natural affection for him. Clifford Allnut and Dulcie Maggott were particularly offensive, accusing me of premature senility and speaking to my brother in an abusive and threatening manner. Lily Hoban, who is a member of a so-called witch's coven based in Katoomba, also uttered threats against him.

At the end of this acrimonious discussion it became clear that Clifford Allnut had overindulged in alcohol to the extent that he could hardly stand. I was forced to offer him a bed for the night. Sheena Molloy and Lily Hoban made up the bed in my late father's room for him. This room, which is usually unoccupied, is directly opposite my brother's room, and is separated only by a linen cupboard from Ms. Molloy's own bedroom. Dulcie Maggott, Sebastian Maggott, Lily Hoban and Eric Maglioco all occupy rooms on the other side of the staircase.

Holly frowned. So the solicitor, Allnut, had stayed on Tuesday night—and had slept in the room opposite Andrew's, and next to Sheena's. No one had mentioned that before.

It doesn't make any difference, she told herself. None of this makes any difference, and none of it has anything to do with you anymore. Stop reading!

But she didn't.

At about 11 pm, Ms. Molloy, with the assistance of Lily Hoban, made tea and brought a tray of filled mugs into the casual sitting room at the back of the house. My brother's tea was in the personalised red pottery mug that I had bought him as a gift, and from which he had drunk since his arrival in the house on Sunday afternoon.

The tray was left on a side table for people to help themselves. I took little notice of it. I do not drink tea at night.

Everyone else took their tea and went up to bed. My brother stayed to say goodnight to me, then followed the others upstairs, taking the remainder of his tea with him. He was yawning, and seemed very tired. By 11:30 I was the only person remaining downstairs. I personally locked the front and back doors and took the remote control for the gates into my room as usual.

> *I can testify that no one came down the stairs into the entrance hall after that. The stairs squeak badly, and I would have heard. I was wakeful in the night. I often am, being troubled by pain, and that night I was excited by events. If I dozed at all, it would have been only lightly. There is no fire escape, and all the windows in the house are barred.*
>
> *My brother did not appear for breakfast the following morning. At 9:30, at my request, Eric Maglioco knocked at his door and, receiving no reply, looked in. The room was empty, and…*

Holly snatched up the papers, folding them quickly to stop herself inadvertently reading another word. Then she saw the five fifty-dollar notes that had been lying underneath them.

'Pieces of eight!' the parrot squawked, waddling over to look more closely.

Holly stared at the notes as if by concentrating on them she could will them away. Abigail's prediction that she was about to receive money from unexpected sources floated again into her reeling mind. It was quickly followed by the memory of her stiffly telling Eric she hadn't taken a cent from Una Maggott, and an image of herself explaining to a clone of Constable Chloe Graff why she had given a false name, pretended to be a detective, and run away to Sydney with an old woman's money. Her head began to throb.

'Don't panic!' she said aloud.

'Don't panic! Don't panic!' the parrot screeched excitedly. It was clearly familiar with the phrase.

Holly collected the notes and stood up. She took a deep breath. Then another.

This is not a disaster, she told herself. It doesn't mean you can't leave here tomorrow. It doesn't mean you have to see Una Maggott again. All it means is that there will have to be a slight change of plan. You put the money into an envelope, addressed to Una, with a note saying that unfortunately you've been called away and can't take her case. In the morning, very early, as soon as you have the petrol—the sign on that little place near the war memorial says it opens at six—you drive to Medlow Bath and put the letter in Una's letterbox. At that hour no one will be awake to see you. You then come back here and proceed with the plan as before. Simple.

'Simple,' she said aloud. 'Cowardly, but simple.'

'Don't panic!' croaked the parrot.

It sounded as if it was no longer behind her. She looked around and saw that while she had been thinking it had quietly retired to its cage. Presumably it had decided the fun was over for the night.

Before it could change its mind, Holly hurried to the cage and fastened the door with the butterfly clip. The parrot blinked at her through the bars and fluffed its feathers sleepily. On impulse Holly turned and went to the garbage bags. She returned with O'Brien's blue shirt and draped it over the cage.

'Goodnight,' she said softly.

'Don't let the bedbugs bite,' the parrot responded, and was silent.

Chapter Fourteen

At nine the next morning, Holly swung her car onto the highway and headed for Medlow Bath.

She was on the road three hours later than she had planned. Against all expectations, she had slept long and soundly in O'Brien's sagging bed. Dreams of black iron bars and faceless men, of pumpkins, witches and hieroglyphics, had crowded her sleep but had not roused her. She probably wouldn't have woken when she had if it hadn't been for the parrot rattling its cage and screeching for a seed refill.

At first she had been appalled that she had overslept. Then, as she began frantically pulling on jeans, shirt and jacket, she had told herself to slow down and take it easy.

In the bright light of day, with a good night's sleep behind her, her resolve to reach Medlow Bath at the crack of dawn seemed melodramatic and unnecessary. After all, it was Saturday, and in her experience, Saturdays began slowly in the Blue Mountains. Mrs. Moss' apartment, and Abigail Honour's, had been utterly silent as she stole down the stairs and let herself out into Still-waters Road. She took this as a promising sign.

Now, as the highway traffic thickened and the nine o'clock news bulletin gave way to music on the car radio, her spirits were high. Trevor Purse's envelope, now addressed to Una Maggott and containing Una's money, the folded statement, and a short, hypocritically regretful note, was in Holly's shoulder bag. The car was filled with petrol. She herself was filled with surprisingly good coffee and an unbelievably delicious egg and bacon pie from the Mealey Marshes cake shop.

The garage at the top of Stillwaters Road, with its two petrol pumps, its battered freezer marked 'ICE,' its stacked plastic sacks of firewood and its bundles of Saturday morning newspapers, had been attended by a shrivelled, toothless old man in finger-less mittens who looked as if he had slept in his clothes, and not for the first time. He had taken Holly's money with an air of deep suspicion, as if serving blow-ins was not part of his job description.

The woman in the cake shop, however, had been brisk and cheery, her glossy black ponytail swinging as she darted around her warm, fragrant domain, seeing to everything single-handed. The cake shop, in fact, had been like an oasis in the chill Saturday morning silence of Stillwaters Road, a fact clearly appreciated by the locals. The comfortingly urban sound of the coffee machine was frequently punctuated by the squeaks, rattles and bangs of the old screen door as men in overalls and paint-spattered jeans strolled in for meat pies with sauce, leaving the engines of their white utes running outside.

The men who waited for coffee, lounging against the back wall of the shop to leave the counter free, all knew one another. They exchanged casual remarks, joked with the ponytailed woman, whose name was Dee, and glanced at Holly in a friendly, mildly interested way. One in particular—tall and rangy, with an untidy shock of fair hair and bright blue eyes—had even nodded to her with a tweak of the lips, as if they were acquainted. Holly felt a spark of interest, which she instantly suppressed. She smiled faintly back at the man, then looked away. Despite Abigail's predictions, men had no part in her immediate future plans. And men from Mealey Marshes, however brightly blue their eyes, were definitely out of the question.

Still, it had been nice to be noticed. And it had been good to feel like an independent woman again, a woman with a purpose, picking up a bite of breakfast before tackling the business of the day, instead of like a piece of flotsam washed helplessly around by the tide of circumstance.

Holly reached Medlow Bath more quickly than she had expected, and in her uplifted mood turned off the highway without qualm, trusting in instinct to guide her.

As it happened, instinct served her well, and she found the way to Horsetrough Lane with only a couple of wrong turns. This was lucky, since she saw no one she could have asked for directions. There was the occasional parked car, but otherwise the area seemed as deserted as it had been the day before. Either the houses behind their screens of trees were holiday homes, untenanted this weekend, or everyone was still in bed. She hoped the members of Una Maggott's strange household also slept in on Saturday mornings.

She eased her little car along the bush-lined lane. Just past a bend, the roof of the Maggott house reared through the trees. A moment later the railings of the fence became visible. Then Holly saw a large, black vehicle hulking in a rough lay-by just ahead.

Her stomach had turned over sickeningly by the time she realised that the vehicle wasn't the hearse, but only the inevitable four-wheel drive, no doubt belonging to some early bushwalkers. The fright, however, had been enough to persuade her that it would be a bad idea to drive boldly up to the Maggott gate. Better to go the rest of the way on foot. She pulled the Mazda off the road and squeezed into the lay-by behind the four-wheel drive.

It wasn't until she had got out of her car that she realised she had been wrong about the four-wheel drive's being the property of enthusiastic bushwalkers. The vehicle's bonnet was spattered with sap and bird droppings, its windows were steamed up, and groaning sounds were coming from inside. Holly quickly averted her gaze and hurried on.

She was within metres of the Maggott letterbox, and was actually reaching into her shoulder bag for the envelope, when she heard a car coming up behind her. She ducked her head and shrank against the fence railings, trying to make herself incon- spicuous. The next moment a gleaming grey BMW had swept past her and parked half on and half off the road just beyond the black iron gates.

As Holly hesitated, torn between the desire to beat a hasty retreat and the urge to make a lunge for the letterbox, a man got out of the BMW and walked briskly back toward her. He was probably in his mid-forties and was vaguely pleasant-looking, like a mild-mannered sheep. He had a ruddy complexion, and his carefully combed, light brown hair was thinning slightly on top. He was wearing a tweed sports jacket, a striped tie and a checked shirt, all in muted autumn tones. Holly stood rooted to the spot, waiting for him to challenge her, but he merely nodded and smiled.

'Lovely morning for a walk,' he said heartily.

As Holly agreed that it was, he strode past her to the gatepost and pressed the button on the intercom panel.

The intercom spluttered with static. 'Yes?' a tinny voice demanded.

'It's Cliff Allnut, Una,' the man said, still in that same hearty, confident tone. 'Sorry to come so early, but I need to talk to you. Could you open the gates, please?'

The intercom spluttered again. 'No!' the tinny voice said. 'Go away!'

The man's cheeks darkened to a dull red. He shrugged at Holly, forcing a smile. 'Difficult client,' he mumbled. 'All in a day's work.' He laughed uncomfortably.

Holly stretched her own mouth into what she hoped was a sympathetic grin and began to edge away. She had remembered that Cliff Allnut was the name of Una Maggott's solicitor. She was painfully aware of the envelope in her shoulder bag—the envelope stuffed with ill-gotten Maggott money.

Before she had taken two steps, the intercom burst into life again. 'Who's that with you, Allnut?' the tinny voice demanded.

With horror, Holly looked through the bars of the gate and saw that the lace curtain masking the bay window had been pulled aside. A pale disc was pressed against the glass. Una Maggott was looking out. Una Maggott had seen her!

'Ms. Cage, is that you?' the intercom yapped. 'Good! Come in! Come in!'

There was a click and the gates began to swing open. Allnut stared at Holly, his mouth slightly open.

A dozen phrases hovered on Holly's lips: *I don't really need to go in...I was just dropping off...I'm afraid there's been a bit of a misunderstanding...Look, please tell Ms. Maggott that I can't...* But none of them were uttered, for at that moment the front door of the house opened and a stocky figure bundled to the knees in an elaborately crocheted maroon poncho hurtled out. It was Dulcie Maggot.

'Cliff!' she cried, hurrying down the steps. She rushed for Allnut, her arms outstretched, the poncho flapping around her like bat's wings.

'Dulcie,' Allnut murmured, standing his ground manfully as she bore down on him.

'I saw your car from upstairs,' the woman gasped, clawing at his tweedy sleeve. 'Thank heavens you've come! Oh, I've had the most terrible night! I can't *tell* you! I didn't sleep a wink! Cliff, we should have called the ambulance last night, whatever Una said. She should be in hospital!'

Ambulance? Hospital? Remembering Una Maggott's urgent, hissing voicemail from the night before, Holly felt a prickle of apprehension. What had been going on here?

'She's refusing to open the door to any of us, even Eric,' the woman babbled on. 'She's still locked in, with that snake. I'm *sick* with worry. She hasn't had a thing to eat—'

She broke off as she registered belatedly that Allnut was not alone. 'Not today, thank you,' she said, flashing a hideously artificial smile in Holly's general direction. Clearly she failed to associate Holly with the formally dressed intruder of the day before.

'Dulcie—' Allnut began.

'I rang that doctor Nguyen this morning, to tell him what was happening, and he was quite brusque,' the woman went on. '"Just leave her alone," he said. "She'll eat when she's ready." Almost rude, really, and *criminally* irresponsible, in my opinion.

Then he had the hide to say that he thought having the house full of people was making Una overtired, and perhaps Bastian and I should go home. As if I'd leave her the way she is! I couldn't *live* with myself.'

Allnut wisely kept silent.

'At least she opened the gates for you,' Dulcie went on. 'For a moment I thought—'

'She didn't open them for me,' said Allnut. He nodded in Holly's direction.

Dulcie's pencil thin eyebrows shot up. She turned to peer at Holly, and the eyebrows drew together as recognition dawned. 'Miss Maggott can't see anyone this morning,' she snapped, her pale blue eyes as hard as river stones. 'She's not well.'

Holly returned the gaze blandly. By now she had accepted that a quick escape was no longer an option. It wasn't just because Cliff Allnut, solicitor, had seen her, and an envelope containing two hundred and fifty ill-gotten dollars was still weighing down her shoulder bag like a burning brick, or just because she enjoyed the idea of defying Dulcie, who she liked even less this morning than she had yesterday afternoon. It was mainly because she knew that she couldn't run out on Una now, without explanation, and without finding out what had happened last night.

Recognising dumb insolence when she saw it, Dulcie pursed her lips, tensed her shoulders like the pug she so much resembled, and made an absurd little spring to the right so that she was standing in Holly's way. Holly was wondering if she'd actually have to wrestle with the woman to get through the gateway when they were both distracted by the sound of a car engine. A dusty white ute with a brown dog in the back was rattling up the lane.

Dulcie clicked her tongue. 'It's that landscaper again!' she exclaimed. 'What's *he* doing here?'

'Una must have rung him,' Allnut said glumly.

The ute braked and turned into the drive. Finding his progress blocked by three people, the driver leaned casually on the wheel and nudged his vehicle's blunt nose forward fractionally, as if to hint that when Allnut, Dulcie and Holly were ready, he'd appreciate it if they'd move out of the way. With a little shock, quickly followed by the lowering sense that she had once again become the hostage of fate, Holly recognised the fair-haired man who had half smiled at her in the Mealey Marshes cake shop.

Tamely she trotted through the gateway with Allnut and Dulcie. The ute followed, rumbling at their heels, herding them as if they were a small mob of sheep. The moment its path was clear, it sped up, rattled across the gravel apron, skirted the right-hand light pole, and disappeared around the side of the house. Slowly the gates began to swing closed again.

'Heaven knows what she's told him to do this time,' fretted Dulcie. 'String barbed wire along the top of the fence, nail up the doors…Cliff, we've got to put a stop to this! You've got to speak to that doctor again, *make* him—'

'Ms. Cage!'

The shriek from the front door made them all jump. Una Maggott, sitting well forward in her wheelchair, was framed in the open doorway. Her left wrist appeared to be bandaged.

'She's come out,' said Allnut, who seemed to be one of those people who relieve their feelings by stating the obvious.

'Ms. Cage!' Una shouted. 'Don't take any notice of them. Come on!'

Holly walked to the house and up the steps, ignoring the sound of two pairs of feet hurrying after her.

Una Maggott's face was grey. There was a small gauze dressing on her forehead, only partly concealed by her fringe, and the circles under her eyes looked as if they had been drawn on with charcoal, but she was as impeccably groomed as ever, and energy radiated from her like heat. Without a word she spun the wheelchair around and sped back toward the snake room, with Holly trotting in her wake.

'Una, wait!' squealed Dulcie from the front door. 'Cliff is here to see you!'

'Leave this to me, Dulcie,' Cliff Allnut muttered, and Holly heard their feet clattering on the entrance hall tiles as they ran forward.

At the same time, obviously attracted by the noise, Sheena, Eric and Lily appeared from the back part of the house. Sheena, looking highly amused, was wearing the same lime-green tracksuit she had worn the day before. Eric was sultry in glittering pale blue, hung with silver chains and holding a piece of toast and Vegemite. Lily was draped in witchy black from neck to toe, so that her exquisite, inscrutable face seemed to be floating in mid-air.

As the two groups closed in on her from opposite directions, Una reached the door of her haven and swung around, at bay. She clutched Holly's wrist with her good hand and drew her closer, as if for protection.

'Una, what are you up to now?' Cliff Allnut asked mildly. 'Who is this woman?'

Una tightened her grip on Holly's wrist. 'For your information, Ms. Cage is a private detective,' she announced. 'She is going to prove that Andrew was murdered.'

'*What?*' shrieked Dulcie, and Lily actually hissed like a cat.

That's torn it, Holly thought. She couldn't believe this was happening. She concentrated on not looking at Eric.

'Una—' Allnut began.

'And what's more,' Una went on, raising her voice, 'until we have the proof we need to call the police back, Ms. Cage will be staying here in this house to ensure that there won't be any repeat of last night's attempt on my life.'

Holly's head was swimming. 'Ms. Maggott—'

'No one tried to kill you, Una,' Sheena said, her Irish accent very much in evidence. 'It was a pure accident. You forgot to put the brake on your wheelchair, that's all. Or maybe the brake is worn. If you'll just let Eric take a look at it…'

Una jerked her chair back into the doorway, shaking her head.

'It was one of you!' she said. 'You all knew I was sitting on the front verandah after dinner. One of you crept up behind me, snapped off the brake, and pushed me down those steps. I heard it. I felt it!'

She brandished her bandaged arm at them. 'If I'd fallen any way other than I did, I'd have more than a sore arm and a cut on my forehead. I'd have broken my neck! At the very least, I'd be flat on my back in hospital right now, with a lot of fusspots checking my bone density, and pneumonia around the corner. Don't tell me that's not what you wanted! I know!'

Holly looked around the semicircle of faces. Sheena, frowning. Eric, worried. Lily, sullen. Dulcie, flushed and outraged. Cliff Allnut, his lips pursed. Was one of them acting? *Had* one of them pushed the wheelchair down the front steps last night? Surely not. Surely it was just another one of Una's paranoid fantasies. Why would any of these people want to kill her?

Because she won't stop saying Andrew was murdered?

The last thought drifted into Holly's mind and clung there. She shook her head, but the thought refused to be dislodged. Remember the rings, she told herself. No one but Andrew and Eric could have stolen them, and you decided it wasn't Eric...

'Una, if you really think there was an attempt on your life, you should speak to the police, not a private detective,' Allnut said evenly.

Una narrowed her eyes. 'Oh, yes, you'd like that, wouldn't you? The police already think I'm irrational, thanks to you people. If I complained to them, I'd have social workers crawling all over me in two minutes, making reports that I'm senile and need to go into sheltered accommodation for my own safety. With you or Dulcie getting my power of attorney, most likely.'

She paused, scowling malevolently as Dulcie spluttered and Allnut shook his head and sighed.

'But it turns out I'm not as helpless as you all think, doesn't it? The police might let themselves be fobbed off with a pack of lies about Andrew, and my sanity, but Ms. Cage is a different story.'

'Clearly,' said Allnut, looking at Holly with distaste. 'But before you invest any more money in Ms. Cage, Una, you may be interested to know—'

'I'll be calling the police again when I've got some hard proof that Andrew never left here,' said Una. 'And Ms. Cage is going to supply that proof. She's going to search this house from top to bottom till she finds his things, those spoons he's supposed to have stolen, and the mug he drank from on Tuesday night. And if any of you object, or try to stop her, we'll know why.'

In the paralysed silence that followed this announcement, there was a knock from the direction of the open front door. The ute driver was leaning against the doorjamb. His vehicle idled on the gravel behind him, the brown dog panting in the back. His face was quite without expression. It was impossible to tell how much he had overheard.

'Sorry to interrupt,' he said lazily. 'I just need a word with Una before I push off.'

'Martin!' Galvanised, Una sent her wheelchair zooming forward, dragging Holly with her and forcing Dulcie and Allnut to jump aside.

The man's blue gaze flicked in Holly's direction, then flicked away again.

'Won't come in, Una. Boots,' he said economically. 'I took a quick look around the boundary, like you said, but I couldn't see anything.'

'Aha!' Una Maggott sat up straighter in her chair. 'You'd swear to it?'

'Turf's still pretty spongy,' said Martin. 'A ladder would have dented it well and truly, especially after the wet. But it's as smooth as when I set it.'

'What about in front of the gates? On the gravel?'

Martin shrugged again. 'It doesn't look like it to me. Unless someone's done a pretty good filling and raking job since.'

Una glanced triumphantly at Holly.

'Thank you very much, Martin,' she said. 'And thank you for coming at such short notice.'

'No worries.' Martin unhitched himself from the doorjamb, nodded casually at the company in general, and strolled toward his vehicle.

'I wonder how much he'll charge you for that?' Dulcie asked spitefully as the ute door slammed and the dog barked.

'I doubt he'll charge me at all,' Una said, pressing the remote control to open the gates and turning her wheelchair around.

'And if he does that's *my* problem, isn't it, Dulcie? Not yours. The main thing is, he's confirmed that Andrew did *not* use a ladder, or anything else, to climb over the fence on Tuesday night.'

'McNish didn't need a ladder,' Cliff Allnut said loudly. 'He had an accomplice who helped him from the outside—threw a rope ladder or somesuch over the fence, probably. A *female* accomplice.'

Holly tensed.

'Rubbish!' Una Maggott snapped.

Ponderously, Allnut drew a minute, leather-covered notebook from his breast pocket.

'Last night was the final straw for me, Una,' he said, in a serious, more-in-sorrow-than-in-anger tone. 'After years of service to your family, like my father before me, to be accused of... well, I decided I had to do something about it. So first thing this morning, I went down to Springwood. I was planning to stay longer, even give up golf if necessary, but as it turned out there was no need.'

He opened the little notebook. 'That's why I'm here. It seems that, whatever he told *you*, Una, Andrew McNish had a girlfriend.'

Chapter Fifteen

'Rubbish!' Una Maggott repeated, after the briefest possible pause.

Allnut consulted his notebook. 'A short, plumpish girl with mouse brown hair, possibly in her mid-twenties, but could be much younger,' he said. 'Wearing a pink and white striped jumper, pink trousers and a pink knitted cap. First sighted with Andrew McNish three weeks ago, cuddling and kissing outside the Commonwealth Bank in Springwood.'

Holly wondered if the age thing made up for the short, plumpish thing. She was glad she'd had her hair streaked. She was glad that after a week of near starvation her cheekbones were showing. She resolved to get rid of the pink and white sweater with the horizontal stripes.

'Who was your informant?' she found herself asking crisply, and marvelled at the way terror could bring out unsuspected inner reserves.

'Mrs. Felicity Wigg, one of the Springwood taxi drivers,' Allnut said, with an air of triumph. 'The real estate agents I wanted to see were still closed when I arrived, so I decided that while I was waiting I'd speak to the taxi drivers parked at the rank beside the railway station. Local taxi drivers, I've found, always know a lot about what goes on in a place.'

Again he consulted his notes. 'Mrs. Wigg knows Andrew McNish by sight. She read that old article about him in the *Gazette*, and now and again after that she noticed him around

Springwood, buying coffee and so on. For a while he was often with a glamorous redhead—she thinks they worked together. Then the redhead dropped out of the picture. And about three weeks ago—she's not sure of the exact day, but she thinks it might have been a Monday—she saw him with this other girl outside the bank.'

Una was looking thunderous. Allnut eyed her reproachfully and flipped over a page of his notebook.

'But that's just the beginning. Mrs. Wigg was in fact the taxi driver who brought McNish here last Sunday—picked him up from his place in Clover Road. She remembers it well because the next day—the *very* next day, mind you, Monday—she had to go to the Clover Road house again, to drop off the *same* girl she'd seen with McNish outside the bank. The girl had tried to disguise herself by bleaching some of her hair, but she was still quite recognisable. She had luggage with her, and seemed in a highly excited state—possibly on drugs. She let herself into McNish's house *with a key*.'

'So!' hissed Dulcie. Lily gave a harsh little laugh.

Una was gripping the arms of her wheelchair, breathing hard, her face a mask of fury. Holly was paralysed. Her inner reserves seemed to have evaporated.

'There's an interesting side-note,' Allnut went on, turning over yet another page. 'The *next* day, Tuesday, Mrs. Wigg was having lunch in her cab when a man she describes as—' he consulted his notes '—"medium height, mid-fifties, looked like a heavy drinker," showed her a photograph of McNish and asked if she'd driven him anywhere lately. She wouldn't admit she'd told him this address, but in my opinion she was lying.'

O'Brien, Holly thought glumly, remembering the taxi receipt she'd found in the dead man's shirt. Twenty dollars.

Una seemed to have recovered some of her poise. *Her* inner reserves were apparently inexhaustible. 'How much did you give this Wigg woman to tell you all this, Allnut?' she growled.

'Twenty dollars,' Allnut said with dignity. 'It's what she asked for, and it seemed only right to pay her for her time.'

'Pay her for telling a pack of lies, you mean,' Una spat. 'I might have been able to believe that Andrew was involved with some glamourpuss redhead, but a fat little teenager on drugs is another matter. When you lie, you shouldn't over-elaborate, Allnut. It's always a mistake.'

Allnut went brick red and literally bared his teeth. For an instant his mild, slightly sheep-like face looked quite savage.

'If I were you, Miss Cage, I would think very carefully before continuing to take instructions from Miss Maggott,' he said to Holly. 'There is such a thing as a professional code of conduct, you know, even for private investigators. Good morning.'

He turned and walked rapidly out the front door, slamming it behind him.

'Great exit, but it won't do him much good,' Sheena murmured to Eric. 'The gates are shut. How's he going to get out?'

'Climb the fence, I guess,' drawled Eric. They both sniggered. Lily confined herself to looking disdainful.

'Una, how *could* you!' Dulcie stormed predictably. 'I've never been so embarrassed in all my—'

'You'd better get that boy of yours out of bed and bring him down here, Dulcie,' said Una. 'Do him good to see what daylight looks like—and Ms. Cage will be up to search his room in a minute.'

Dulcie bridled, then scurried for the stairs.

'Ms. Maggott, I can't—' Holly began in a low voice.

But Una had turned her attention to Lily. 'Why are you still in the house?' she demanded. 'Didn't I tell you to leave?'

'You said I could stay till the weekend,' Lily muttered.

'Yes, well, it's the weekend now, isn't it?' snapped Una.

Lily pressed her lips together, raised her chin and swept to the stairs. When she reached them, she grasped the newel post and turned gracefully, the perfect, tragic picture of a blameless heroine accused.

'Andrew McNish was taking advantage of you, Una,' she said in a trembling voice. 'It's not fair to turn me out, with less than a week's notice, just because I said so on Tuesday night! I only did it because—'

'Because you lost your temper and showed your true colours when I said I was going to leave him all my money,' Una broke in contemptuously. 'I know. I saw your face.'

'I didn't—'

'Don't lie! I know what a sneaking cat you are. I know you'd been trying to pump Andrew for information ever since he'd arrived on Sunday, cosying up to him, batting your eyelashes, inviting him to your room. I know how spiteful you got when he told you he wasn't interested. He told me. We laughed about it.'

Lily's face sharpened with anger. Her top lip curled, revealing small, even teeth. Suddenly there was a squirrelly, feral look about her.

'And if you killed him you did it for nothing!' Una spat. 'I was finished with you a month ago, the moment I found out what a liar you were. Whatever you did, whatever you said, you were never going to get your hands on my money. Never in a million years!'

'You're mad!' hissed Lily, and bolted up the shrieking stairs. Eric gave a low whistle.

'Get about your business, Eric!' Una barked at him. 'You too, Sheena! I don't know what you think you're doing, standing gawping there like a couple of tourists.'

'You're a one, Una, you really are,' said Sheena, shaking her head. 'Why are you going on with this? You can't fool me. You know perfectly well that Stiff Cliff was telling the truth. Andrew had a girl. That's why you're so angry. Your tame detective knows it too. It's written all over her face. If she's got any decency at all she'll leave you to it.'

She gave Holly a hard stare then turned and stomped back toward the kitchen, with Eric slouching after her.

Una Maggott looked up at Holly. Her shoulders slumped. Suddenly she looked almost defeated.

'He swore there was no one,' she muttered, almost to herself. 'He lied to me.'

Holly's heart was wrung with a mixture of guilt and pity. 'Yes,' she murmured.

Now was the time to admit why she was so sure. *I was the girl in the pink striped jumper, Ms. Maggott. I was the girl with the key to Andrew's house. He lied to me, too. He dumped me, and stole my money...* But the words were still framing themselves in her mind when the woman in the wheelchair shook her head and straightened her shoulders.

'I should have known,' she said softly. 'Oh, Andrew was a twister. A user and a twister. A chip off the old block.' She raised her eyes to the portrait of the smirking, black-suited old man on the wall and, bizarrely, she smiled.

Holly stared at her. What was she saying?

'I'll tell you a story, Ms. Cage,' Una went on, almost conversationally. 'I left Australia six months after my father sold his business and installed Lois, Andrew's mother, in this house. My employer, Alexis Delafont, had decided to return to France, and had asked me to go with him. His offer was good, and there was nothing to keep me here. In fact, I had every reason to leave.'

She looked around the entrance hall, her eyes dwelling on the grand staircase, the cedar panelling, the stained glass of the front door.

'Come in here,' she said suddenly. 'I want to show you something.'

She turned the chair around and wheeled herself into her room. Holly hesitated, then followed, hovering cautiously just inside the doorway. The gods and pharaohs, bright in the morning sunlight, stalked relentlessly toward the bay window. She was relieved to see that the snake seemed to be asleep. It wasn't moving, anyway.

Una was fossicking in her desk. She slammed a drawer and rolled swiftly back to Holly's side holding out a large photograph.

The photograph, which looked like a recent enlargement of something much older and smaller, showed a man, a woman and a stocky, dark-haired girl of nine or ten, squinting into the sun on the front steps of 9 Horsetrough Lane. The photograph had been taken from a distance, but was clearly a family group. The mother had her arm around the girl's shoulders. The girl was looking up at her father, who was staring straight ahead at the photographer with that teasing smirk Holly recognised from the portrait in the hall. In front of the three lay a flat apron of white gravel, and stretching away to their left and right was a park-like vista of lawn and trees. The house behind them looked elegant. There were no bars on the windows, and tendrils of creeping fig were just beginning to soften the walls.

'That was how this house looked when my mother, father and I first came here,' Una said. 'It was absurdly large for a family of three, but my mother's parents had left it to her, and my father liked the idea of living in something so grand.'

Her lips twitched, whether in amusement or resignation it was impossible to say.

'I already loved the house when we moved in. I'd often stayed here overnight when my parents went out. I'd help serve the guests' breakfasts, and do the beds with my grandmother and the maids. I thought it was all very glamorous. I grew to love the place even more over the years we lived here, and when I got older, even after I started work and got a flat in town, I always thought of it as home.'

Holly glanced from the photograph to Una's face. The grey eyes had warmed. The harsh lines beside the mouth had softened. Then the face changed again. It was like watching wax harden and crack in cold water.

'Then my mother died, and less than a year afterwards, Lois moved in,' said Una Maggott in a flat voice. 'After that, I couldn't bear to come here. Lois was quite impossible—featherbrained, greedy and common as muck, but my father was besotted with her. She played up to him appallingly, trailing round all day in transparent negligees and high-heeled slippers with swan's-down on the toes. The perfect old man's darling.'

An expression of fastidious disgust flickered across her frozen face.

'The few times I came here after she moved in they went on as if they were alone. Champagne at all hours. Screeching and giggling. Playing infantile games. Chasing each other from room to room. My father had actually bought black satin sheets for the bed. The bed he'd shared with my mother for over thirty years.'

Holly found herself nodding in understanding. Una was a snob, certainly, but she had a point. Live and let live was all very well in principle, but Holly knew how she would feel if her mother died and twelve months later her father was playing slap and tickle with someone less than half his age, who wore slippers with swan's-down on the toes.

'My father was spending money like water,' Una Maggott went on. 'He'd been doing it even before he met Lois, but now he'd become the joke of the district. Everyone knew him, everyone knew that Lois was just a gold-digger, and of course the cleaners and delivery people talked about the goings-on in the house. I was embarrassed, and very, very angry—on my mother's account, and my own.'

She sighed. 'So I accepted Alexis' offer and washed my hands of the whole affair. I didn't even say goodbye to my father. I just left contact details with his solicitor, who was then Cliff Allnut's father, Thomas. I'd been in France for about a year when Lois walked out. My father was devastated. He rang me and begged me to come home, but as far as I was concerned, he'd got what he deserved.'

'Yes,' said Holly. She knew she would have felt the same. But…could she have refused the old man if he'd begged? Maybe not. Probably not.

'I should have come, at least for a week or two, but I didn't,' Una said harshly. 'Not then, and not later. I bitterly regret that now, but what's done is done.'

She was staring past Holly to the portrait on the entrance hall wall. Her mouth dragged down at the corners and her eyes were bleak. She looked a hundred years old.

'I didn't see my father again for thirty-five years. Paris became my base, and my job was my life. There was never anything—like that—between Alexis and me. He had a wife and children. But in every other sense we were partners. We travelled all over Europe, doing deals. I had shares in the business. We made decisions together, took risks that paid off. Money poured in. Alexis listened to me. I was indispensable to him. I protected him from people he didn't want to talk to. People called me "La Dragonne" behind my back. It didn't worry me.'

On the contrary, Holly thought, watching the closed face. You liked it, because it meant you had power. She was repulsed. She remembered why she had instinctively disliked Una Maggott on their first meeting. Then she remembered the empathy she had felt when Una was talking about her lost home, and struggled to reconcile the two opposing feelings.

'But—it ended,' said Una. 'There was a car accident, in Germany. Alexis was killed. I was left—like this.' She patted the arms of her chair. 'I could—can—walk a little, with two sticks, though it's tedious and painful. Eventually I learned to dress myself, shower and so on. But that was all they could do for me.'

There was not a trace of self-pity in her voice. Holly's emotions see-sawed again. The other side of this woman's ruthlessness was her determination. It was impossible not to admire it.

'Everyone was kind, but I hadn't made any friends in Europe,' Una went on. 'Alexis' family and I had never been close. My acquaintances were his friends, and our business associates, and during the long months of my rehabilitation they gradually dropped away. I realised I had no one, and for the first time in many years I thought of home. Then—just over twelve months ago it would be now—I had a phone call from Cliff Allnut. My father had had a catastrophic heart attack and was not expected to live.'

She glanced at Holly's stricken face and shrugged. 'I flew home the next day. Eric met me at the airport. He was in full Elvis regalia. Glittering white. He and the hearse caused quite a stir between them.' Her mouth tweaked into a grim smile.

'We went straight to the hospital. A strange woman was sitting by my father's bed, holding his hand. Sheena. My father had been unconscious since the heart attack, but just after I arrived, he stirred and started trying to talk. I've heard that happens, sometimes, just before the end. Or maybe the nurses were right, and he'd been waiting for me. I don't know. Anyway, they left me alone with him. We had half an hour—that's all. It wasn't a good thirty minutes for either of us.'

Again she looked at the portrait and the smile faded, leaving her face bitter. And when she drew breath to go on, Holly knew that at last she had come to the climax of her story, and her reason for telling it.

'Maybe if he'd said a single word about my mother it would have been different. But he seemed to have forgotten her. He just rambled on about his other women—about Sheena, first, and then about Lois. He went on and on about how beautiful Lois was, how he'd loved her, how losing her was the worst thing that had ever happened to him…on, and on, and on till I thought I'd go mad…the sentimental old fool!'

Her face convulsed. She pressed her lips together, breathing heavily, fighting for calm. When she spoke again, her voice was harsh but steady.

'Finally he got to the point. He told me the secret he'd been keeping for years. Lois had rung him a couple of months after she left. She said she was pregnant—swore the child was his—asked for money. He said she'd had as much as she was going to get out of him and hung up on her. He never heard from her again. And now, thirty-five years later, when he was literally on his deathbed, the thought that he had another child somewhere was preying on his mind.'

She shook her head. 'He tried to make me promise to find Lois and the child, make sure they were all right for money. I refused. Among other things, I said that Lois had only ever loved his money and if she really had been pregnant it was ludicrous to think the child was his. He got…frantic. He begged me, but I was too angry even to humour him. Then he suddenly went quiet. He never regained consciousness. An hour later, he was dead.'

Tears were burning behind Holly's eyes. 'I'm so sorry,' she said.

'Yes, well, it's not the best of memories.' Una's own eyes were tearless. She seemed quite calm now, as if getting the story off her chest had helped.

'Afterwards, I came straight back to this house. Everything looked smaller than I remembered, and much shabbier, and of course my father had done his outlandish best to ruin it. I resolved to restore it to what it had been, and tried to put everything else out of my mind.'

She paused and seemed to suppress a sigh. 'Then, about a month ago, I saw a photograph of Andrew in an old copy of the local newspaper. Eric had brought some old papers in to line the bottom of the python's cage after he'd cleaned it—he kept a stockpile out the back. I happened to glance at the page on the top of the pile. And there, smiling up at me, was a man who was the spitting image of my father. The resemblance was extraordinary.'

Involuntarily, Holly turned to look at the portrait. She couldn't see much resemblance. Except maybe for the reckless twist to the mouth, and the gleam in the small, cunning brown eyes.

'My father when he was younger, of course,' Una Maggott said. 'When I was a child. When we were...close. The article—it was about Andrew setting up business in Springwood—said that he was thirty-four, so the age was right. It also said he had been abandoned as a baby and had no idea who his natural parents were.'

A little shiver ran up Holly's spine. She turned back to Una, who nodded, apparently satisfied with her reaction.

'I contacted Andrew—asked him to come here, pretending to want financial advice. The moment he walked in I knew I was right. He was a Maggott.'

Holly imagined Andrew McNish, elegant in suit and tie, knocking at the door of the grand, decaying, eerie old house, eventually finding himself locked in with the snake, the mural, the avid woman in the wheelchair. Thinking he was onto something. Wondering how much he could get out of it. Doing what came naturally. With no idea...

'I didn't say anything at first,' said Una. 'I let him go through his paces. He was charming, of course, but I saw straight away that he was a twister. I didn't work with Alexis Delafont for nearly forty years without learning to read the signs. But that made me even more convinced. My father was a twister too. Lying was second nature to him, when he wanted something. Andrew had a smooth surface, but underneath he was just like Dad. As I said, a chip off the old block.'

A scale off the old python, thought Holly. She had started to feel sick. For lots of reasons.

'I'm a private woman, Ms. Cage,' Maggott said. 'I haven't told anyone else all this. My motivation isn't their business, and I don't care what they think of me. But I've been frank with you because I have no choice. I have to convince you that I'm quite sane, and deadly serious, because I want you to go on helping me. It's beyond me to start all over again with someone else. I don't want you walking out on me because you think Allnut and Sheena are right, and you'll be taking advantage of a delusional old woman if you stay. Do you understand me?'

Holly nodded. She was finding it hard to breathe. She could almost feel scaly coils tightening around her, crushing her chest, binding her hand and foot.

'All right,' Maggott said. 'Now. It seems Andrew had some girl in tow when he met me. But that doesn't mean he was still in touch with her when he disappeared, does it? It *doesn't* mean she helped him get over the fence.'

'Not really,' Holly managed to say.

It wasn't me anyway, Ms. Maggott. I didn't help Andrew climb the fence. I can't speak for the glamorous redhead, though—Andrew's ex-receptionist, who was probably up to her neck in his funny business. Who maybe decided she didn't want to be ex anymore, when she found out that Andrew was taking off, and in the money.

A reflexive wave of jealousy rose in her but almost instantly subsided, leaving behind only a feeling of cold distaste. She noted this and was grimly glad.

'The fence is a complete red herring anyway,' Maggott went on. 'I only got Martin to come and check it because I could see you were letting it worry you. The stairs didn't creak—that's the important thing. Andrew never came downstairs—he never left this house. Did you manage to contact Mr. O'Brien last night?'

Holly shook her head.

Da-da-da-dah! Da-da-da-dah!

Holly jumped violently and gaped at her bellowing shoulder bag. Surely she'd turned O'Brien's phone to silent! Was she being haunted?

'Get that!' urged Una Maggott. 'It might be O'Brien! Tell him about the attack on me. Ask him about the sniffer dogs.'

Holly found the phone and answered it.

'Cage speaking.'

'Who are you?' a female voice snapped. 'Put me onto O'Brien.'

'I'm sorry, he's not available at the moment,' said Holly, her eyes on Una Maggott, who scowled and sped past her into the bedroom part of the double room.

'Oh really?' jeered the voice on the phone. 'Well, you can tell him that I put his precious bomber jacket in the Vinnie's bin. If he wants it so badly, he can buy it back. Tell him not to call me again. And you can tell him from me to drop dead.'

'No problem,' said Holly.

The caller snorted and hung up.

Una Maggott reappeared from the bedroom. Balanced on her knees was a huge black torch. It was a dead ringer for the one employed by Trevor Purse in his pursuit of bedbugs.

Trevor Purse! Trevor Purse's fifty bucks! Trevor Purse's straying wife! Ten-forty-five!

Holly looked wildly at her watch and was amazed to see that it was still only ten-fifteen.

'Here,' Una said, pushing the torch at her. 'You'd better get started on the search. Don't worry about me. I'll lock myself in again. No one will be able to get at me.'

'Ms. Maggott—'

'Don't bother about the bedrooms at this stage. I just said that to stir them up. It's highly unlikely they've stowed the things in their own rooms—too risky. The attic is a possibility, but—'

'Ms. Maggott, I can't stay,' Holly blurted out, fending off the torch and backing out into the entrance hall. 'I'm sorry, but I've got other commitments today. I tried to tell you before, but...'

Her stomach churned as the haggard face staring up at her went slack with dismay.

'But I'll be back,' she charged on recklessly. 'Don't worry. I'll come back—later.'

'When?' The question was tremulous. Again Holly felt an overwhelming surge of pity.

'Late afternoon...early evening—I'm not quite sure. But as soon as I can. Okay?' She took another step back.

Una rolled her chair partway through the door, then seemed to realise pursuit was pointless and stopped. She nodded in dull acceptance.

'Just try to get some rest,' Holly urged. 'And please let Sheena bring you something to eat, too, Ms. Maggott. You need—'

'I'm not touching anything that comes out of that kitchen,' snapped Una, with some return of her old spirit. 'I've got fruit and biscuits in my room, and they'll do me till you get back. At least I know that nothing in my room's been tampered with.'

She nodded darkly toward the back of the house. 'They won't get me today at any rate,' she added, raising her voice as if to be sure that anyone lurking in the shadows, or listening from the top of the stairs, wouldn't miss a single word. 'I'm locking myself in till you come back. And you'll be here to guard me tonight, won't you, Ms. Cage? That's agreed?'

Holly hesitated. She knew this was crazy. She knew she could search the house till kingdom come and she wouldn't find any trace of Andrew's bag, Andrew's coffee mug, or the silver tea-spoons. She knew Una Maggott wasn't really in danger—couldn't be. All the people in the house were...just normal people. Even Eric. Even Lily. Even the loathsome Dulcie. Underneath all the trappings, all the eccentricity, they were completely ordinary.

But ordinary people did murder. You read about it all the time.

'Please, Ms. Cage,' Una muttered. Suddenly there was fear in her eyes.

'Yes, I'll be here, Ms. Maggott,' said Holly. 'That's a promise.' And she made sure to speak loudly. Just in case.

Chapter Sixteen

Thanks to Trevor Purse's little map, Holly found Wattle Crescent, Bullaburra, with no trouble at all. It was a determinedly suburban street of modest project homes. The only reminders of the bush from which it had been carved just a generation or two ago were the crabbed banksias making aggressive statements on a few front lawns. The houses faced each other across the firmly kerbed and guttered bitumen as if trying to pretend that the dangerous blue-grey wilderness that stretched for kilometres around them didn't exist.

As she drove slowly by Number 15, Holly thought she could have picked it as Trevor Purse's house even without the white numbers on the letterbox. In a street of well-kept houses, it was the neatest. A prim little construction of light-coloured brick with a modestly low-pitched green-tiled roof, its most prominent feature was the fawn aluminium roller shutter that closed off the garage built in to one side. Its frontage featured a low brick fence, a weeping standard cherry tree in brilliant autumn colour and a row of rigidly controlled roses. Not a single fallen leaf marred the perfection of its impeccably trimmed square of grass, its ruler-straight driveway, or the paved area in front of the house.

The driveway gates were standing open, but Holly had no fears that her quarry had already left. A white Mazda, the twin of her own vehicle except that it was very clean, stood in the shelter of a carport that snuggled beside the garage like a poor relation.

A few doors down, Holly did a sedate U-turn and parked on the other side of the street where she had a clear view of Number 15. It was only ten-thirty-five, but having successfully found the house she felt it would be tempting fate to leave it, even in the interests of discretion.

After a couple of minutes, however, she began to feel conspicuous. No one appeared to be watching her, but there was something about Wattle Crescent that gave the impression of eyes peering from behind curtains and between the slats of Venetian blinds. When a black four-wheel drive cruised past, she felt certain that the driver had glanced at her with more than casual interest. Hastily she took out O'Brien's mobile phone and held it to her ear, nodding and moving her mouth occasionally to reinforce the charade.

As time crawled by, Holly's eyes remained fixed on the front door of Number 15 Wattle Crescent while her mind wandered back to the mansion in Medlow Bath.

Cliff Allnut's BMW had still been parked outside when she had hurried through the opening gates, but of Allnut himself there had been no sign. Presumably he had gone around to the back of the house. Maybe, Holly thought uncomfortably, he was pumping Eric and Sheena about her. By now Eric had probably given him the Mealey Marshes address. Eric obviously didn't like Allnut, but at the moment he wasn't keen on Holly, the promise-breaker, either.

Maybe Allnut was even now making calls, trying to get information on a private investigator called Cage who was based in Mealey Marshes. Or maybe he had finally made contact with the real estate agents who had handled the rentals of Andrew's house and office. Holly wondered what Len Land and Oriana Spillnek would tell him. Everything, probably. Neither of them had any reason to prevaricate. She wondered if their descriptions of Holly Love, Andrew's abandoned fiancée, would finally lead Allnut to suspect who Una's protector, Cage PI, really was. What if he asked Land, Spillnek or even Mrs. Wigg the taxi driver to come to Horsetrough Lane, to lie in wait for Holly's return and unmask her? What if he called the police?

The envelope containing Una Maggott's money was still in Holly's shoulder bag. Certainly, the resignation letter was folded with it—which was why Holly had balked at giving the envelope to Una before she left—but that proved nothing, really. Holly could be carrying it merely as a safety measure, with no intention of handing it over unless she was challenged.

She caught a flicker of movement out of the corner of her eye and her stomach lurched as she saw the fawn roller shutter of Number 15 rising like a curtain opening at the beginning of a play. No one had come out the front door. Apparently the garage could be accessed from the house.

Holly threw the mobile aside, started her car and glanced at the clock. It was exactly ten-forty-five.

A small green van emblazoned in bright yellow with Trevor Purse's name, profession and phone number, and decorated with pictures of rats, mice and assorted magnified creepy-crawlies, backed cautiously from the garage. Purse was at the wheel. He got out to close the garage door, then returned to the van and reversed through the gateway. He saw Holly, showed the whites of his eyes, and sped off.

Less than a minute later, the front door opened and Leanne Purse peered out. She seemed to be checking that the coast was clear. Holly grabbed O'Brien's phone and pretended to be listening again, but obviously Leanne was only interested in making sure her husband had gone, because her gaze swept without interest over the white car parked across the road. Apparently reassured, she left the house, a trifle chubby but neat and pretty in a blue floral skirt, lemon-coloured blouse, pale blue cardigan and dainty sling-back shoes. Her fair hair, bouncing in shining waves on her shoulders, looked freshly washed. She was carrying a small overnight bag.

There was definitely something furtive about the way she scuttled to the carport and slung the bag into the boot of the Mazda, shutting it in quickly as if it were something disgraceful she didn't want the neighbours to see. It looked as if poor Trevor Purse was right. His wife was up to no good. His ordered little world was falling apart. Holly felt depressed. She thought of O'Brien, remembered his world-weary eyes, and felt she understood why he had taken to drink.

Leanne got into her car and backed rapidly up the drive. Just beyond the fenceline she halted with a little screech of tires and jumped out to close the gates. Cheating on her husband, but still dutifully following his security rules, thought Holly. Feeling cynical and hard-bitten she clutched the wheel, her hands sweating.

Back in the driver's seat, Leanne put on her seatbelt and reversed into the street. Barely glancing at Holly, she took off at a brisk pace toward the highway. Holly eased her car away from the kerb and followed.

It wasn't difficult to keep Leanne in sight while she stayed on the back roads, but things became more complicated once she reached the highway and turned west. Traffic was heavy. Escapees from the city had now joined the throng of locals heading for the shops or driving their children to Saturday morning sport. Every second car seemed to be a white Mazda.

Holly soon found that keeping a discreet distance behind her quarry was dangerous. Leanne Purse was clearly impatient to reach her destination. She drove as fast as she legally could, changing lanes frequently, and in minutes was much too far ahead for comfort. Holly decided that discretion would have to be abandoned.

She gritted her teeth and began to weave through the traffic, intent on her goal. At last she caught up with the Mazda on which her eyes had been trained for five minutes, only to find that it had a 'Baby on Board' sticker on its back window and was being driven by a large man with dreadlocks.

Holly felt a sort of sickening lurch, exactly as if she was in a lift that had dropped too fast. She goggled, appalled, at the impostor in front of her. She saw him glance at her curiously in his rear-vision mirror, quickly looked away, and by pure chance caught sight of Leanne's car just ahead, turning left at a sign reading 'Misty Views International Motel.'

Holly slammed on her indicator and recklessly forced her way into the left lane. She managed it just in time to swing into the motel entrance herself, to a chorus of angry horn blasts that brought the blood rushing into her face.

She pulled up on the concrete apron, her hands slippery on the wheel, her cheeks on fire. Belatedly she realised that her life-threatening exit from the highway had been totally unnecessary. She could just as easily have driven past the motel and circled back at her own convenience. It might have taken a while, but Leanne Purse obviously wouldn't be leaving anytime soon.

Sending a silent word of thanks to whichever saint it was who protected feckless motorists, Holly peered around, getting her bearings.

The Misty Views International Motel was not the sort of place she would have chosen for a romantic rendezvous. It was a no-frills establishment. A narrow, flat-faced rectangle two storeys high, with a pale blue aluminium awning jutting over the central entrance door, it looked more like a barracks than a lovers' hideaway. A row of dusty succulents and a single, depressed-looking cypress did little to screen it from the highway traffic speeding past toward more desirable locations. The best that could be said for the place was that it was tidy and functional, and looked cheap. Leanne's car was nowhere to be seen, but an arrow directing visitors down a steep driveway to the parking area at the back of the motel told Holly where to go.

She eased her car down the driveway and found herself in a wasteland of bumpy asphalt newly marked with glaring yellow lines. There were only a few cars dotted about. Leanne Purse's Mazda was one of them, nestled inconspicuously in a corner not far from a steep flight of concrete steps that provided a shortcut back up to the motel for those guests able-bodied enough to negotiate it.

There was no sign of Leanne herself. She had obviously wasted no time in hurrying up the steps. By now she had probably slipped through a side door—a fire door, perhaps, opened by her lover. She wouldn't risk walking boldly through the main door and braving the receptionist, Holly thought. Not carrying that overnight bag.

For the first time, Holly let herself wonder what that neat little bag contained. A black silk nightie, perhaps? Red lace lingerie? Fishnet stockings and spiked heels? Smoked salmon sandwiches and a bottle of champagne? Whips and chains? She made herself stop thinking and moved her car into a space that gave her a good view of the back of the motel, the steps, and Leanne's Mazda.

The back of the motel was marginally less brutal-looking than the front because of the railed walkways (no doubt described as 'balconies' on the motel's website) that stretched across the building on both ground and first floors, providing access to the rooms. There were twelve pale blue doors on the top floor, and twelve on the bottom. Having counted them, as if somehow the number mattered, Holly waited in suspense for Leanne, alone or with a companion, to appear on one of the walkways.

Nothing happened, and after five minutes she began to wonder just how long she had dithered at the front of the motel, recovering from her brush with death on the highway. After another five minutes she faced the fact that Leanne, with the speed and efficiency made possible by long practice, must have disappeared behind one of the twenty-four plain blue doors before Holly even reached the parking area.

Holly sighed. All she could do now was watch until Leanne emerged from one or other of the doors. No doubt it would be a long wait.

Feeling at one with the spirit of O'Brien, she sipped from the plastic bottle she had filled in the Mealey Marshes flat, and took perverse pleasure in the tepid water's slightly rusty, slightly chemical taste. This was what being a detective was all about. It wasn't about thrills and dark alleys and guns and fights and being hit on the head. It was about sitting in the parking area of a second-rate motel, putting up with discomfort. *It's a dirty job*, she could almost hear O'Brien saying. *But someone has to do it.*

Another ten minutes passed before Holly, hot, cramped, uncomfortable and bored out of her mind, asked herself *why* someone had to do it, and more specifically, why *she* did. Why couldn't Trevor Purse simply *ask* his wife what she was doing on Saturdays? They had been married for eight years, for heaven's sake! If he'd forgive Leanne anything, why didn't he just tell her so and get the whole thing out in the open?

Holly instructed herself to settle down. She tried playing word and memory games, but found she couldn't concentrate. She didn't dare listen to the radio, in case she ran down the Mazda's battery. Her mind, like nature abhorring a vacuum, had begun buzzing with unwelcome thoughts.

Thoughts of Una Maggottt, alone and afraid, waiting for her return. Thoughts of Solicitor Allnut, insulted and vengeful, pursuing his enquiries about Andrew's accomplice. Thoughts of Eric, disappointed in her. Thoughts of Una's missing rings. Thoughts of Andrew sunning himself by the pool of a tropical hotel while the languorous, long-limbed redhead beside him ordered another round of margaritas. Thoughts of the forty dollars in the envelope on the fridge, the stripped house, the empty bank account, the pitying eyes of Oriana Spillnek. Thoughts of her mother and father, and how appalled they would be if they knew what she was doing at this moment. Thoughts of Abigail Honour reading the cards, telling her that she should trust her instincts.

And what were Holly's instincts telling her now? They were telling her to flee—to shake the dust of this sordid carpark from her wheels, regain the highway and drive down to Sydney with all possible speed. They were telling her to forget Trevor Purse, forget Una Maggott, forget Andrew McNish, forget Abigail…

But she had promised Una that she'd return, and she still had Una's money. Trevor Purse believed that she was going to report back to him on his wife, and she had already *spent* most of his money. Her clothes and other belongings were still in the flat at Mealey Marshes…And by late this afternoon, O'Brien's parrot would have run out of seed and water, and if she left without a word, no one would know she had gone. Trapped in its cage, the parrot might call vainly for hours till at last, parched, its beak gaping, it toppled from its perch…

Holly threw open the car door and jumped out, shaking her head violently to rid herself of the nightmarish dead-parrot images that had taken possession of her mind. The moment her feet hit the asphalt she understood that images of drought-stricken parrots were the least of her worries. She had drunk three-quarters of her water just to break the monotony. This, combined with the large latte of the early morning, meant that her bladder was at bursting point.

She had read that detectives on a stakeout sometimes used bottles to pee in. Well, that wasn't an option for her. She had her talents, but peeing into a bottle wasn't one of them.

It appeared that her next move had been decided for her. She hobbled to the steps and, slightly crouched, began climbing painfully toward the motel.

Chapter Seventeen

The reception area of the Misty Views International Motel featured royal blue carpet decorated with frantic yellow squiggles, two blue vinyl armchairs, a humming drink machine and a long desk that faced the door. Behind the desk, which was equipped with computer, phone and a selection of brochures displaying Blue Mountains tourist attractions, sat a woman with glossy, perfectly straight, copper-coloured hair that just brushed her shoulders, and a face so like a beautifully painted mask that Holly couldn't even guess at her age. She could have been a mature eighteen or a well-preserved forty. She could have been a vampire who had manned the Misty Views reception desk for a hundred years.

The woman smiled professionally as Holly entered, her eyes automatically flicking up and down, sizing Holly up as feminine competition and quickly dismissing her as a serious threat.

Holly smiled brightly back, her own eyes darting around in search of a sign pointing to a toilet. Finally she saw one, directing her into the narrow opening between the reception desk and the stairs leading up to the next floor. She moved forward confidently.

'Can I help you?' the receptionist asked in a breathy, little-girl voice that contrasted weirdly with her glamorous appearance.

'Oh, I'm fine, thanks,' said Holly. 'I'm visiting a friend who's staying here, but I'll just pop into the ladies' room first.'

The receptionist blinked at her. 'All our suites have ensuites, madam,' she said. 'What is your guest's name? Who shall I say?' Her hand moved to the telephone and hovered suggestively.

'Yes, but I'm in a bit of a hurry,' babbled Holly. 'Long drive, you know, heh, heh, heh.'

Without waiting for a reply she bolted past the desk. Just beyond the staircase she found a door marked *Ladies*. She shot through it, locking herself into one of the two meagre cubicles she found inside with a sense of defiant elation.

When she returned to the reception area, much relieved and with a new plan, the receptionist was gazing with absorbed interest at her own fingernails, which were so long and perfect as to be clearly ceramic, and were painted the colour of dried blood to match her lipstick. So great was her concentration that it would probably have been possible for Holly to make a discreet exit. But while Holly had been in the ladies' room it had occurred to her that now she was actually *in* the motel, she might take the opportunity to nose around a bit.

Sure, she could justify her fifty-dollar fee by simply watching and waiting outside, but as her father so often said, if a thing's worth doing, it's worth doing well. In childhood this maxim had irritated Holly no end, applied as it had usually been to jobs like tidying her room, which in her opinion deserved the bare minimum of time and effort, but it suited her to quote it to herself on this occasion. Doing some subtle investigating would be a lot more interesting than sitting in a carpark for hours.

And besides, she told herself righteously, what if Leanne's visit to the motel was perfectly innocent? What if, for example, the motel's breakfast room was the venue for meetings of the local dramatic society? Or a first aid course? Or macramé classes? What if Holly told Trevor Purse that his wife went to the Misty Views International Motel every Saturday, leaving him to draw the obvious conclusion and suffer agonies, when all the time Leanne was only working on a knotted string plant hanger as a surprise for his birthday?

Mix-ups like that were standard fare in the TV sitcoms to which Holly's first fiancé, Lloyd, had been addicted. Holly had seen the same scenario in various guises hundreds of times, watching with glazed eyes as the story creaked to its predictable close, and Lloyd chortled along with the canned laughter. Still, the way life had been going for her lately, the clichés of situation comedy were surely relevant, and she felt it would be wise to take their lessons into account.

She sidled to the desk and stood waiting. The receptionist looked up and blinked at her vacantly. It was almost as if she had forgotten that Holly existed.

'Is there a place here where my friend and I could have a coffee?' Holly asked craftily. 'A café, or breakfast room, or something? Or is it occupied at this time of day?'

The receptionist blinked again. She seemed to blink before every thought. Maybe, Holly thought charitably, it wasn't stupidity. Maybe it was just that all the mascara made her eyelids heavy.

'We don't have a café or breakfast room, madam,' the receptionist said. 'Every suite has complimentary tea and coffee making facilities.' She blinked. 'We don't do breakfasts,' she added, to make sure Holly understood. 'We just do suites.'

'I see. Right.' So much for the macramé classes.

The receptionist was looking slightly uneasy. Her hand strayed to the telephone again. 'If you'll just tell me the name of your guest, madam…'

Holly decided to bring out the big guns. She leaned impulsively over the desk. The receptionist drew back a little and blinked twice.

'Look, I'm going to be frank with you,' Holly said in a low voice. 'I'm not really here to visit a guest. I just want to have a look around the motel. It's very confidential, but actually, I'm a researcher.'

The receptionist looked alarmed. 'For the health and safety people?' she squeaked. 'But the manager isn't here on—'

'No, no, it's nothing like that.' Holly took a deep breath and resisted crossing her fingers. 'Between you and me, I'm a researcher for a film producer.'

The receptionist's mouth fell open.

'We need a motel setting for a movie, you see,' Holly went on, 'and this place could be just what we're—'

'A *movie?*' the receptionist breathed. Little stars sparkled in her eyes. A faint stain of natural colour had appeared beneath the blusher that defined her perfect cheekbones.

And after that, it was easy. Within five minutes, Holly had established (and noted in her diary) that the motel's only rooms were the twenty-four 'suites' accessed from the walkways ('shared balconies') at the back, and that all the downstairs rooms had been booked in a block by a tour party, due to check in at any moment.

She had also learned a great deal about her new best friend, Aimee Rice, twenty-four, motel receptionist and would-be movie star. She had learned more than she'd bargained for, in fact, so that as she climbed the stairs to examine the upper floor of the motel, with Aimee's wholehearted blessing, she was feeling shaken rather than smug.

Aimee Rice, who was proficient at tap dancing, clog dancing, ballet and modern dance, who had seen *Chorus Line* nine times and who was working as a receptionist only while waiting to be 'discovered,' had been with Misty Views International for only a few months. Before that she had been working 'in finance,' in Springwood. She had further to travel to get to this job, but she enjoyed it because she liked meeting people. Also, here she was paid on time. Her previous boss was always behind with her pay.

At first she'd put up with his excuses, because he said he had contacts in the film industry, but after six months she'd started to think that maybe he was spinning her a line, so when she'd seen the Misty Views job advertised in the *Blue Mountains Gazette*, she had applied.

Aimee's old boss *still* owed her a fortnight's pay, in fact, and it looked as if she'd never get it now, because her mum, who had her toes done once a month at the podiatrist's across the road from the office, said the place was closed, with a 'To Let' sign on the door, and according to the podiatrist, Andrew had done a runner owing money all over town.

The coincidence had taken Holly's breath away. Staring with something like superstitious dread at Aimee, the redheaded rival of her jealous imaginings, shockingly sitting before her in the vulnerable, if thickly painted, flesh, she could barely croak the appropriate words of commiseration. It had probably been lucky for her that, at that moment, a half-empty tourist bus had pulled up outside the motel with a squeaky puff of brakes and begun discharging eager white-haired men and women from both front and middle doors.

Bracing herself to face the onslaught, Aimee had merely waved distractedly as Holly made for the stairs. Now, reaching the upper walkway, gazing blankly at the twelve pale blue doors set at regular intervals along its length, each door flanked by a small, high, frosted window below which stood a sand-filled flowerpot for the convenience of smokers, Holly tried to calm herself. So what if Aimee Rice had once been Andrew's receptionist? That wasn't so strange. The Blue Mountains had a relatively small population, after all, and there were only so many jobs, and so many people to fill them.

But it was still a weird coincidence. And—Holly realised that this was her real problem—Aimee Rice had been so very different from the elegant hard case she'd imagined keeping office house for Andrew. More to the point, Aimee Rice wasn't now lying on a sunbed by a pool in Queensland, drinking margaritas bought on the proceeds of Una Maggott's rings and silver teaspoons. Aimee Rice was here, on the desk of the Misty Views Motel, still waiting for her ship to come in.

Holly leaned over the rail of the walkway, noted that Leanne's car was still in its place, then rocked with vertigo as she saw a bulky black bonnet nose into the carpark. But again, it wasn't the hearse. It was only another of the black four-wheel drives that seemed to infest the mountain roads, along with battered white utes and identical Mazdas. Holly could almost hear the parrot cackling.

Pull yourself together, she told herself harshly, turning away from the railing. Do what you came here to do.

She dug in her shoulder bag for her diary and pen so she would look as if she were taking notes if Aimee finished with the tour party quickly and came up to see how she was getting on.

Slowly, diary open in her hand, she paced along the line of doors. Signs reading *Please Make Up My Room* hung on the knobs of the first four, so they were out. The cartoon sounds of Saturday morning TV drifted from behind the fifth door, so that was probably out too. People had strange tastes, Holly knew, but she had never heard of a cartoon fetish.

A *Do Not Disturb* sign hung from the knob of the sixth door. That looked promising. But as Holly lingered beside the flowerpot, the sand of which was liberally scattered with the skimpy butts of roll-your-own cigarettes, she could hear someone snoring thunderously inside the room. Surely it was a bit too soon for that, unless Leanne's lover had narcolepsy.

The seventh door opened just as she came to it, and a middle-aged woman in a bright pink trouser suit bustled out carrying a box wrapped in silver paper and crowned with a white bow. The woman smiled brightly at Holly, showing teeth lavishly smeared with cerise lipstick.

'Lovely day,' the woman said.

Without waiting for a reply she hurried to the eighth door and knocked. 'Francine!' she bawled. 'Are you ready?'

There was a muffled call and a thump from the other side of the door. The woman clicked her tongue, bolted on, and knocked at the next two rooms too. 'Janet?' she called. 'Sue? Come on, we'll be late.'

Holly went to the railing and pretended to be gazing at the view. Once you looked beyond the parking area, it was very pleasant—a storybook vista of little houses tucked amid trees, leading on to the darker outlines of Katoomba, the Edwardian magnificence of the Carrington Hotel. And it did have a faint tinge of misty blue.

She didn't move as for the next few minutes doors opened and closed, high female voices rose, and doors opened again for the recovery of forgotten items amid laughter and expostulation.

She watched out of the corner of her eye as the four women finally departed, chattering like excited birds, their high heels click-clacking on the concrete of the walkway.

Ten rooms had now been accounted for. Feeling that she had done O'Brien proud, imbued with the guilty satisfaction of the successful stalker, Holly turned to examine the remaining two doors and jumped as she saw that the one second from the end was now wide open.

A thick-set, hairy-chested man wearing only a pair of trousers with the belt dangling sauntered through the open door, shaking a cigarette out of a packet. 'Back in five minutes, love,' he called over his shoulder. 'Okay?'

A female voice trilled something indistinguishable over the sound of running water. And suddenly, looking past the man's shoulder into the mean little room with its tumbled double bed, Holly wished she had never set foot in the Misty Views Motel.

The man caught sight of Holly and winked in greeting, his eyes flicking up and down her body exactly as Aimee's had done, though for a different reason.

'Smoke?' he suggested, offering Holly his packet.

Holly shook her head and forced a smile.

'You used to be able to smoke inside in this place,' the man said, lighting up. 'Now it's just like everywhere else—you've got to stand outside like a leper. It's bloody cold up here in the winter, too.' He leered at Holly, squinting through a drifting white haze. 'You here for the whole weekend?'

'I'm not staying here,' Holly said quickly, then realised, as the man looked quizzical, that she had better give some sort of excuse for skulking on the walkway. She proffered her diary and pen. 'I'm just visiting. Working. I'm doing research. For a documentary. About motels, and their customers—and so on.'

'Is that so?' The man looked interested. 'Well, I might be able to help you there. I've stayed in more motels than you could shake a stick at.'

'Really?' Holly asked, trying to sound enthusiastic.

'Sure,' said the man, expanding. 'I'm a rep—well, area manager, really—for Gorgon Office Supplies. Heard of them?'

'I think so.'

Holly wondered if this whole thing could be a bizarre dream. Maybe she'd fallen asleep in the parking area. Or maybe there had actually been a collision on the highway and she was lying in a coma in Katoomba Hospital. Wake up, she told herself. But nothing changed.

'Feldman's my name,' the man said, transferring his cigarette to his left hand and sticking out his right hand. 'Frank Feldman.'

'Cage,' said Holly, taking the hand and shaking it for the least possible time. 'Um…Polly Cage.' The moment the words were out of her mouth she cursed herself.

'Polly want a cracker?' Frank Feldman sniggered. 'Sorry, you must get that all the time.'

'Not really.' Holly glanced at her watch. 'Well, I'd better be—'

'Don't go yet,' Feldman exclaimed, grabbing her arm and pulling her toward his room. 'It'd do me a lot of good if I could get Gorgon's into a documentary. Come and have a look at my sample case. The viewers would be really interested. I designed it myself. It opens out flat, fifteen separate compartments—takes our whole range plus a laptop.'

'No!' Holly tried to shake herself free. 'No, really, I have to—'

'Won't take a minute,' said Feldman, practically wrestling her through the doorway. 'Come on, Pol, be a sport. Don't worry, you're safe with me. And anyhow, we've got a chaperone.' He gestured off-handedly at the bathroom.

The bathroom door was wide open. Holly didn't want to look, but she couldn't help herself. And there was Leanne Purse, in pink rubber gloves, a blue cotton overall and sensible shoes, cleaning the toilet.

Chapter Eighteen

By calling on the spirit of O'Brien, Holly managed to act like a professional. That is, she didn't gape at Leanne for too long, she didn't burst into hysterical laughter, she didn't start babbling about situation comedies, and she didn't stumble blindly into the trolley of motel room supplies and cleaning equipment parked against the wall, though that was a near thing.

But as Frank Feldman heaved a flat black vinyl case onto the bed and started manipulating its many zippers and velcro strips, she couldn't tear her eyes away from the bathroom. She could hear Leanne Purse humming as she worked.

The toilet flushed.

'She must have been cleaning the end room, before,' Holly said aloud.

'What?'

Holly looked around quickly. Feldman was staring at her.

'I didn't see the cleaner come in here,' Holly explained, in some confusion. 'She must have moved into this room when those other women were leaving. While I was looking at the view.'

For a moment Feldman looked blank. Then his face cleared. 'Oh, the cleaning routine, is it?' he said, going back to tearing velcro. 'Yeah, well, they're all different, aren't they? Don't worry, we'll be right in here. She's only doing the bathroom. I told her to leave the rest. The match starts in ten minutes.'

Holly managed to make the appropriate noises while he displayed the intricacies of his one-of-a-kind sample case and its disturbingly familiar contents. Then, politely declining his invitation to stay, have a few beers and watch the footy, she stuffed the many brochures he had forced on her into her shoulder bag, and made her escape. As she left, she saw Leanne Purse finishing off the bathroom by folding the end of the toilet paper into a little point.

Holly almost ran along the walkway and down the stairs. Most of the people from the bus tour were still milling around in the reception area, talking at the tops of their voices, lining up for the drink machine, or trying to locate their luggage in the pile that had been dumped just inside the door. Behind the reception desk, Aimee was blinking steadily, explaining that all the suites were identical, that all the beds faced south-north, that unfortunately the motel did not provide soy milk, and that she was sorry, but she couldn't give change for the drink machine.

Snorting with laughter, Holly made for the ladies' room. Both cubicles were occupied, and there were several white-haired women waiting. Holly splashed her face with water and dried it with a paper towel, trying in vain to suppress the giggles that kept bubbling up from her chest and bursting out of her mouth of their own accord. She knew that the helpless laughter was the after-effect of shock and relief. She was giggling because her suspicions, and Trevor Purse's suspicions, had turned out to be absurd.

Pretty, plump Leanne Purse hadn't been cheating on her husband—quite the contrary. She had been secretly using her Saturdays to earn a bit of money—cash in hand, probably—to buy herself some new clothes, perhaps, or simply to support the monthly maintenance of her crowning glory. It was possible that careful Trevor was a bit mean with the housekeeping money. And it was possible—probable, Holly thought—that he had no idea his wife was not a natural blonde.

Holly would have liked to stay in the ladies' room for a bit longer, to recover her equilibrium, but she was receiving dubious looks from her elderly companions, so after only a few minutes she left, still wracked with occasional bouts of painful, silent laughter. She fought her way through the thronged reception area and out into the open air. The walk down to the parking area, with the sun on her face and a light breeze tossing her hair, calmed her down enough to punch Trevor Purse's number into O'Brien's phone without fear of laughing in his ear.

Purse answered on the first ring, his voice tight with tension. Holly told him the good news. There was a strangled squawk, then silence. Holly wondered if they'd been cut off.

'Are you there, Mr. Purse?'

'A *cleaning* job? *My wife?*'

'That's right. At the Misty Views Motel. On the highway at—'

'I know where it is.'

Purse's voice was shaking. Holly could hear little puffs of air, as if he was breathing hard through his nose.

'Thank you,' he squeaked, and the phone went dead.

Well, so much for that, Holly thought, forcing her phone back into her bulging shoulder bag. She felt rather deflated. Purse hadn't sounded at all amazed that she had found out so much. He hadn't seemed to appreciate how much trouble she had taken on his behalf. A perfunctory 'thank you' and that was it. *Punters! They're all the same.* She could hear O'Brien saying it. She could almost see his world-weary smile.

Holly straightened her shoulders. *She* knew she'd done well. That was what counted.

She reached her car and stood for a moment looking up at the motel. Frank Feldman's door was shut now, and the one next to it—Sue's room—was open. Holly imagined Feldman reassembling his exploded sample case while the TV blared. She imagined Leanne Purse in her pink rubber gloves, humming as she disinfected her third toilet of the day. She felt a sudden rush of warmth for them both. They were triers, like herself. She sincerely wished them well. She wished Aimee Rice well, too. And Francine, Janet, Sue, and the woman with lipstick on her teeth. And the bus tour party, far from home.

She drove from the parking area feeling efficient and in control. By deciding to investigate inside the motel she had gained not only valuable information, but time as well. Now, instead of staring at twenty-four doors for hours, she could go home to Mealey Marshes, get something to eat and pack a bag for her stay with Una Maggott. She could shower and change her clothes. She could check the parrot's seed and water. She could recharge her—or rather, O'Brien's—phone. She could thank Abigail for dinner the night before, and tell her about being away overnight.

The highway traffic had thinned dramatically, as if most people had reached their destinations and settled down to lunch. Between the Misty Views International Motel and the turnoff to Mealey Marshes, Holly saw only one white ute, and two other white Mazdas. There were no black four-wheel drives at all. It was very pleasant not to be following anyone. In no time, it seemed, she was negotiating the underpass. Singing along with the radio, she flew to Mealey Marshes like a homing pigeon.

Stillwaters Road was mellow in the afternoon light. The busker was back outside the chemist's shop, playing an Irish jig. The screen door of the cake shop rattled and banged as pie-seeking customers moved in and out. A whiteboard was propped against the window of Mealey Meals in Minutes, advertising a Saturday special on Singapore noodles with chips.

A station wagon moved out of a parking spot directly out-side 16A just as Holly reached it. It seemed meant. She slid the Mazda into the space with a feeling of entitlement. She glanced at the butcher's shop as she got out and was relieved to see that it was shut. There was no danger that her bald-headed friend of the day before would bound out to interrogate her about Trevor Purse's affairs. One, Holly didn't want to waste her precious time, and two, she might be annoyed with Purse, but O'Brien's did promise discretion.

Abigail, resplendent in an ankle-length green crushed velvet dress and a filmy purple scarf that clashed wildly with her hair, was standing outside the secondhand bookshop. She was talking in an agitated way to a man who was straightening the battered paperbacks in a wire basket hopefully marked *SPECIAL!! $1!!* As the car door slammed, they both looked up, and Abigail's face broke into a relieved smile.

'Holly, you're back!' she cried. 'What luck! Could you possibly drive me somewhere? Right now? I was hoping that Lawrence could do it but Oliver's taken the van to pick up some books. And it's an emergency!'

Holly felt a pang, hoped she hadn't shown it, and hastened to say that of course she could. No problem. As soon as she'd topped up O'Brien's—that is, the parrot's—seed and water.

'Already done!' said Abigail, hurrying to the Mazda. 'I didn't mean to interfere, but I got this awful image of him dying of thirst a while ago, so I popped up to check you were both all right. You were out, and I didn't know when you'd be back, so I filled both containers to the brim, just in case.'

The bookshop man smiled at Holly. He had a very nice smile. His light brown hair was streaked with grey at the temples. Abigail's prediction sprang unbidden into Holly's mind and she found herself wondering if light brown hair counted as fair before sternly reminding herself that she was finished with men. For the time being, anyway.

'So you're the detective from upstairs,' the man called. 'Welcome to the madhouse.'

Holly smiled back. She didn't feel like complicating things by correcting him about her profession. Besides, she was feeling like a detective at the moment.

Abigail was standing with her hand on the Mazda door handle, jiggling on the spot with impatience. Holly opened up for her and got back behind the wheel.

'Straight ahead,' Abigail said. 'Down the hill to the marshes, then left into the dead end. Oh, thanks so much for this!' She leaned back with a gusty sigh as Holly manoeuvred the car away from the kerb, narrowly missing the front headlight of the sports car waiting like a vulture for her parking spot.

'What's the emergency?' Holly asked.

'Oh, it's Reenie, an old client of mine,' said Abigail. 'Her cat's gone missing and she's just about distracted.'

'Cats do wander,' said Holly.

'Not Lancelot. He's ancient, and fat as a football.' Abigail sighed again. 'To tell you the truth, I'm afraid he might have passed over. While Reenie was on the phone I kept seeing him all flattened out, like a tabby fur rug. And I've had the most terrible sense of foreboding ever since I woke up.'

Holly glanced at her. She had closed her eyes and was frowning slightly. Her face looked drawn and tense and somehow duller, as if she really was under some sort of shadow. Or maybe it was just that purple wasn't her colour.

'I was sure it had something to do with that nervous man who made the appointment yesterday, but he didn't turn up so it can't be that,' said Abigail. She opened her eyes. 'Of course, it *might* be to do with this other client I saw this morning. She's got *such* a problem. I can't see it having a good outcome.'

'What is it?' Holly asked curiously. 'Oh—sorry, I suppose you can't talk about it.'

'Oh, April wouldn't mind. She tells everybody. She believes in openness, and sharing. She and her partner, Saul, are old hippies—peace, love, living off the land, scorn for material possessions, and all that. They're quite well off, actually—made a lot of money on shares, April tells me, buying and selling at the right time. But she still has her spinning wheel and so on. And she still wears rope sandals and doesn't shave her legs.'

Holly slowed the car to a crawl as Stillwaters Road showed signs of petering out and the edge of a vine-hung swamp that looked like the habitat of the Creature of the Black Lagoon loomed ahead.

'A bit further,' said Abigail. 'Past the *No Through Road* sign, then left. Well, about six months ago Saul moved another woman into the house—practically a girl, really, compared to April. He told April that men were naturally polygamous, and that free spirits in tune with the infinite were beyond bourgeois conventions.'

'The bastard!' Holly muttered, gripping the wheel.

'Bastard,' Abigail agreed.

They exchanged a look of perfect understanding.

'April claims not to mind,' said Abigail. 'She says it's just a matter of working toward adjustment and acceptance. Calls this other woman her sister in love. Smiles all the time. But of course she's a nervous wreck. She's lost all this weight, and her hair's falling out. I've begged her to see a marriage guidance counsellor or a therapist, but she won't. She won't even talk to her GP.'

'She should talk to her bank manager,' said Holly, from the depths of bitter experience.

'Actually, remembering what you told me last night, Holly, I did just mention that,' Abigail said. 'April seemed to think it was very cynical of me. But there *were* a lot of Pentacles in the cards, so I felt justified. Right—here we are.'

Holly stopped in front of what looked like a giant's abandoned doll's house. Clematis, honeysuckle and Virginia creeper had almost overwhelmed the little cottage. Trees and shrubs grew thickly on both sides of the path that stretched between the rickety picket fence and a flight of steps leading up to the miniature verandah and leadlight front door. Cat's paradise, Holly thought.

The door of the house opened and a tiny old woman tottered out. She stood at the top of the steps and peered down at the car, clasping her hands anxiously. With only the mildest surprise, Holly recognised Mrs. Halliday, the old lady who yesterday had nearly missed the butcher's.

'Well, here we go,' said Abigail. She paused, her brow wrinkled. 'Holly, would you come in with me?'

'Sure,' said Holly, thinking longingly of lunch and mentally crossing the shower and change of clothes off her 'things to do' list.

Abigail smiled and touched her shoulder. 'Thanks,' she said. 'I've just got a feeling it might help. We'll get some lunch when we get back. And this won't take long. Either I'll get a flash, or I won't.'

So they went together to the gate in the rickety fence, and together they walked up the path toward the house.

'He's not outside, anyway,' said Abigail, looking vaguely from side to side. 'That will make things quicker.'

Disloyally, Holly wondered if that was a flash or just wishful thinking. Uneasily, she wondered how much Abigail charged for a home visit. She scanned the bushes, looking for a tabby-coloured shape, but could see only shadows and skinks.

Reenie Halliday greeted them with twitters of distress and gratitude, bobbing and murmuring as Holly was introduced. Trembling with anxiety, she pressed a brown hairbrush into Abigail's hands.

'It's the best I can do,' she whispered. 'I can't find his mouse on wheels. But he does love his brush, and we use it every day.'

'That's fine, Reenie.' Pressing the brush between her palms, Abigail stepped through the front door of the house with Mrs. Halliday hard on her heels and Holly trailing behind, feeling like a fifth wheel.

Two paces down the short central hallway, Abigail stopped dead.

'He's here,' she said.

Mrs. Halliday gave a little scream and looked around wildly, as if expecting her cat to appear out of thin air.

Holly reminded herself that Abigail definitely had some psychic ability, and tried to make herself believe that she was not being party to a rip-off that might end up on *A Current Affair*.

Abigail hesitated then moved slowly on, peering in turn through the doorways of the two small bedrooms on either side of the hall, then moving at last into the over-furnished but exquisitely neat sitting room. She paused, shook her head decisively and turned to go back the way she'd come.

Seeing her standing with Mrs. Halliday in the middle of the hallway, turning from side to side like a wavering compass needle, Holly decided that it was up to her to take more practical measures. She wandered around the sitting room, checking every possible place where a cat could hide, even looking under the sofa cushions, and making sure there were no gaps above or beside the gas heater that had been fitted into the old fireplace. Then she went on into the old-fashioned kitchen at the back of the house. Methodically she opened every cupboard door, checked under the old-fashioned dresser, and peered, ridiculously, into the plastic flip-top kitchen tidy.

No cat. Not a whisker.

As she left the kitchen she could hear drawers being pulled open, and Reenie Halliday calling Lancelot in a pathetic, quavering voice.

It's unfair to put her through this, Holly thought, biting her lip. Abigail's wrong. The cat must be outside somewhere. For sure he's been hit by a car, or bitten by a snake, and he's crawled away into the swamp to die. This dismal thought brought tears to her eyes, so she quickly changed her theory, persuading herself that in fact Lancelot was curled up in a favourite corner of the overgrown garden, having peacefully died of old age.

She found Abigail and Mrs. Halliday standing motionless in the smaller of the two bedrooms.

'He's in here, Holly,' Abigail said in a low voice. 'I can feel him. Definitely.'

'But where?' moaned Mrs. Halliday.

Holly looked around. The bedroom was sparsely furnished with a built-in corner cupboard, its door wide open, a divan bed that stood barely a hand's breadth off the floor, and an old oak dressing table, its empty drawers pulled out. The floor was covered wall to wall with faded linoleum. There was a dusty Venetian blind at the window. A piece of white-painted fibro had been nailed over the fireplace, sealing it off completely.

'Try again, Reenie,' urged Abigail.

'Lancelot!' quavered Mrs. Halliday. 'Where are you, darling boy? Lancelot…fishies!'

And as her voice died away they all heard a faint, piping cry.

'It's him!' shrieked Mrs. Halliday.

Every hair on Holly's body stood on end. The sound had been so thin, so tiny, that there was no way of telling where it had come from. Had Lancelot been sucked into the very fabric of the house? Had he been abducted by ghosts, like the child in *Poltergeist?*

She looked frantically around the drab little room. She looked up at the ceiling, down at the floor. Her eyes fell on the one thing that had not been moved. The divan bed.

When you have eliminated the impossible, whatever remains, however improbable, must be the truth... Sherlock Holmes, the greatest detective of all, had said that. O'Brien had probably said it too, or something very like it.

Holly went to the bed. It was pushed hard against the wall—no joy there—and was skimpily covered by a tie-dyed cotton spread. There were no cat-sized bulges, but she stripped off the spread anyway to expose a thin, buttoned, black-striped mattress.

That left the space beneath the bed. It was very shallow—surely much too shallow for a big cat to squeeze into in any kind of comfort. He'd literally have to crawl on his belly....

I keep seeing him all flattened out, like a tabby fur rug.

Holly's skin prickled.

'Abigail!' she hissed, seizing one end of the bed. 'Help me! We'll have to tilt it back, not pull, or we'll hurt him.'

'He can't be under there!' Mrs. Halliday wailed, as Abigail hurried to grab the other end of the bed. 'Lancelot wouldn't go under there—he'd never fit!'

'He might if he wanted to enough,' Holly said. 'If his mouse on wheels ran under there, for example. And once he was in, not able to move or turn...Okay, Abigail, one, two, *three!*'

The front of the divan bed jerked up from the floor. There was another faint cry. Mrs. Halliday, by now lying flat on the lino, screamed with joy.

'Higher!' she yelled. 'That's it! Now, hold on! *Hold on!*'

And, sweating and straining, Holly and Abigail managed to hold on just long enough to let a very fat, very dusty, very disgruntled tabby cat come crawling stiffly out into the light.

Chapter Nineteen

Reenie Halliday was so overcome by the recovery of Lancelot, and so exhausted by the effort of writhing around on the floor in the spare room, that Holly and Abigail were able to leave quite quickly, without having to stay for tea and a thorough discussion of events.

Once Lancelot was safe, they had dropped the fiendishly heavy divan bed which Reenie said had a cast iron base. After that, Holly had used a broom handle to sweep the mouse on wheels from under the bed, and put it out in the hall. Then Abigail had advised Reenie to keep the spare room door shut from now on, and she and Holly had departed, their ears filled with Reenie's tearful thanks.

Reenie had also thrust a twenty dollar note into Abigail's hand.

'Half of this is yours,' Abigail told Holly, showing her the note as they drove back up the hill to the Mealey Marshes shops. 'If it hadn't been for you, we'd never have found him. I'm sorry it's so little, but Reenie's only on the pension, and she can't afford any more.'

'That's all right,' Holly said absently.

A week ago she would have said that she didn't want the money—that Abigail should keep it, or donate Holly's half to charity. Not anymore. These days, ten dollars was ten dollars, and well worth having. And she knew she had earned the money.

She, student of Sherlock Holmes, apprentice to Mick O'Brien, had thought of lifting the divan bed. But Abigail…

'Abigail, I've been thinking—'

'Enid's got chips!' cried Abigail, pointing ahead to the footpath outside 16A, where Mrs. Moss and Lawrence the bookseller stood chatting. 'Quick, Holly, before Lawrence eats them all!'

Holly picked up speed and zipped into a parking spot just past the one she had occupied before. It was only one of many parking spots. She glanced at the car clock and was surprised to see that it was only two o'clock. She and Abigail had been gone for less than an hour. Yet suddenly all was quiet. The busker had left his post outside the chemist's shop. Mealey Meals in Minutes had taken in its whiteboard. Except for a few customers still wandering in and out of the cake shop, the shopping centre was deserted.

'Just about everything closes at two on Saturdays,' Abigail said, noticing Holly's bemused expression. 'Once the lunch rush is over, there's no point staying open. We're not exactly on the tourist circuit here.'

They both got out of the car and sauntered self-consciously toward Mrs. Moss and Lawrence.

'Well?' Lawrence called.

'Did you find him?' Mrs. Moss asked anxiously. 'Is he all right?'

They both beamed as Holly and Abigail nodded.

'Holly was amazing,' said Abigail. 'He was trapped under a bed and she—'

'Abigail was amazing,' said Holly at the same moment. 'She just stood in this room and said, "He's in here." And he was!'

Neither Mrs. Moss nor Lawrence looked even slightly surprised. They were obviously used to Abigail.

'Have some chips,' said Mrs. Moss, holding out a bulging white paper bag blotched with patches of grease. 'I got to Mealey Meals just before it closed, and they gave me all they had left.'

'Yum,' said Abigail, taking two chips at once.

'That place peddles poison,' said Lawrence, taking three. 'We shouldn't go there. My cholesterol count shoots up just looking in the front window.'

Holly ate a chip. Hot, salty, delicious! She took another.

'Have you heard the big excitement?' Mrs. Moss said to Abigail. 'I was just telling Lawrence. There's been a heist at the Misty Views Motel! You know, the one on the highway just past—'

Holly choked.

'*No!*' exclaimed Abigail, helpfully banging Holly on the back with one hand and helping herself to more chips with the other.

'*Yes!*' said Mrs. Moss. 'Neddy at Meals got the gen just now, from his auntie, who heard it from—Holly are you all right, dear?'

'Fine,' Holly managed to croak. She swallowed and wiped her streaming eyes.

'I knew something terrible was going to happen today,' said Abigail. 'The moment I woke up this morning—'

'There were three of them, apparently,' Lawrence cut in.

'Yes, it was a gang,' said Mrs. Moss, wresting back the role of chief storyteller. 'Two goons and a frail. The frail went in first, to suss the place out. Talked her way in saying she was a film producer, or something.'

'Pretty weak story,' said Lawrence critically.

'Well, it worked, didn't it?' said Mrs. Moss. 'Of course, the new receptionist up there…well, she's a very nice girl, they say, a Warimoo girl, and beautifully groomed, but not too bright. And the poor mug who was robbed obviously isn't the sharpest pencil in the box, either. I mean, imagine inviting a strange woman into your motel room like that! What was he thinking?'

Abigail snorted. 'What do you *think* he was thinking, Enid?'

Lawrence laughed. Holly stood paralysed, her mind a frozen blank.

Mrs. Moss sighed. 'She was quite a young woman too, by all accounts. The mug is in shock—can't remember much, poor chap—but he thinks she said her name was Polly Parrot. Well, obviously that's false. Isn't it dreadful? They think she must have been a hop-head. Some women from a bus tour that had just arrived saw her in the ladies' room, behaving oddly. Making faces and laughing for no reason and so on.'

'A bus tour,' Lawrence said, taking more chips. 'That means a lot of people in reception. Luggage. Confusion. So the woman could get out easily, and the two guys could get in, without anyone noticing. Clever planning.'

'How would they know a tour would be arriving?' Abigail objected.

'It was an inside job,' Mrs. Moss breathed, her eyes wide. 'The perps had a mole in the motel!'

'The receptionist, probably. She sounds a bit too good to be true.' Lawrence picked up the basket of paperbacks. 'Well, I'd better get on. Oliver will be back soon, wanting help unloading. Glad poor old Lancelot lives to sleep another day. See you all later.'

He heaved the basket into the bookshop, pushed the door shut with his shoulder, and flipped the *Open* sign to *Closed. Please Call Again.*

'Not the receptionist,' said Mrs. Moss thoughtfully. 'A cleaner. They say a cleaner who was doing the upstairs rooms took a powder just after the alarm was raised.'

'What?' Holly mumbled.

'She means the cleaner ran away,' said Abigail, shaking her head at Mrs. Moss. 'It's all those old movies she watches in the middle of the night. Enid, the cleaner probably only left because she didn't want to get involved with the police. Maybe her visa has expired.'

'Holly, have another chip, dear,' said Mrs. Moss. 'You're looking a bit peaky.'

Abigail turned quickly to look at Holly. Her brow wrinkled in concern.

'Yes, Holly, you're awfully pale,' she said. 'You must have over-done it, going out so early, and then lifting that heavy bed on top of it. Come in and I'll make you some chamomile tea. I could do with some myself. I just can't get rid of this awful feeling....'

At that moment there was a squeal of tires at the top of the street. Holly, Abigail and Mrs. Moss looked around. A white Mazda swung past the war memorial and hurtled toward them, pursued by a black four-wheel drive and, a few moments later, a small green van covered in bright yellow writing. Holly's stomach turned over.

'Drag racing,' Mrs. Moss said with intense disapproval.

The Mazda skidded to a halt directly in front of them. A man leapt from the passenger seat, leaving the door wide open. He was big, with a shaved head, and wearing sunglasses and a creased black suit.

'The butcher's closed!' Mrs. Moss called to him, making shooing gestures with her chip bag.

'Oh, no!' sighed Abigail. 'It's my ten o'clock appointment! Only *four hours* late! Really, some people—'

And that was Holly's last coherent memory of what Mrs. Moss later insisted on calling 'the snatch.'

The rest was recorded in her mind only as a series of flashes and sensations.

The four-wheel drive braking sharply behind the Mazda. The green van skidding into it with a crunch and a tinkle of glass, then slewing sideways. The big man in his crumpled black suit, his heavy, stubbled jaw set, jumping over the kerb and rushing for her. Her glimpse of a terrified pink face pressed to the back passenger window of the revving Mazda, and her astounded realisation that it was the face of Leanne Purse. The shock and disbelief as the man grabbed her and swung her off her feet. His iron strength, and the synthetic smell of his black sleeve pressed to her mouth and nose. Piercing screams—her own, she presumed, as well as Abigail's and Mrs. Moss'—as she was dragged off her feet.

A moment later she was in the back seat of the Mazda, Leanne Purse's Mazda, with Leanne shrieking and struggling beneath her. Then she was scrambling into a sitting position, gasping for breath and thinking in bewilderment: 'I've been kidnapped!' And the Mazda was racing back up Stillwaters Road, narrowly missing a white ute doing a U-turn outside the cake shop.

The man who had grabbed her was in the front passenger seat. He was rummaging through her shoulder bag, pulling out stationery samples and brochures by the handful.

'Nothing,' he growled, hurling the bag onto the floor in disgust. 'Just more of that Gorgon shit, and two-fifty in an envelope.'

'Shit!' said the driver.

The next thing Holly remembered clearly was the Mazda swinging out onto the highway, heading west. She remembered thinking the car was going too fast for her to try to jump out. She remembered the roll of fat on the neck of the man in the passenger seat, and the scaly, scrawny, bristly neck of the driver. She remembered feeling lumps beneath her and realising that she was sitting on Leanne Purse's sling-back shoes, floral skirt, pin-tucked blouse and pale blue cardigan, and that Leanne's overnight bag, gaping and empty, was under her feet. She remembered Leanne herself, lumpy in her cleaner's uniform, shrinking into the opposite corner of the back seat, whimpering, 'I know you! You're the woman in the motel!'

Holly screwed herself around and looked through the back window. The black four-wheel drive was close behind them—so close that she could see the sap marks and bird droppings on its bonnet, and the gum leaves caught in the windscreen wipers. It was the four-wheel drive that had been parked in the Horsetrough Lane lay-by!

Its driver was wearing sunglasses, but his face was vaguely familiar. Holly knew she had seen him before, and suddenly she remembered where. He was one of the two men who had forced their way into Andrew's emptied house while she was staying there. It came to her that the muscular man who had grabbed her was the other.

Then something else struck her. It was the muscle man who had been looking over the back fence of 16A yesterday! And a little later Abigail had sprung him inside the building. She had thought he was a hesitating client, but he'd probably just been on his way out after searching O'Brien's flat.

While I was in the bathroom, doing my hair and makeup, Holly realised, remembering the parrot's piercing shrieks coming through the wall. The parrot had been warning her there was an intruder! And she had just ignored it.

'Is this about Andrew McNish?' she shouted. 'If it is, you might as well let us out right now. We don't know where he is. We don't know anything!'

'Who's Andrew McMish?' sobbed Leanne Purse from her corner. 'Who are you? What do you want with me?'

'Shut up!' growled the man in the passenger seat. He punched a number into his mobile phone. 'I'll let Moonie know we're on our way,' he said to the driver. 'He worries, and he's got that ulcer.'

'We shouldn't have left him there on his own when we went after her this morning,' fretted the driver. 'You and Bernie could have got her easy, but I thought…Christ, Fen, if this was all a con and McNish has got away while we were farting around—'

'Moonie? It's me,' the man called Fen said into the phone. 'Anything up?' He listened. 'Okay, now, Moonie, don't stress,' he said after a while. 'Take one of your pills….Shit, I'm not calling you anything, Moonie, I'm just saying…Listen, calm down, we're on our way. Five minutes…No, no luck. But we've got his girl… Yeah, she'd gone back to Mealey, like we thought. We picked her up just standing…Yeah, we're watching her, don't worry. She wasn't carrying. Didn't even have a knife, cocky bitch. Plus we got another one….No, another girl. And we got her car as well. We're in it now, Skinner and me. White Mazda….No, another white Mazda. Bernie's in the four-wheel drive…No, don't worry, he's right behind us. Well, Moonie, it's a long story…yeah, well… Five minutes. Ten minutes tops, okay?'

He clicked the phone off.

'Moonie's not happy,' he said to the driver.

'Shit! Has McNish—?'

'Nah. McNish is still in the house with the old woman. The Elvis freak took the hearse out, and the lawyer was following him in the BMW, but the branches we left on the road stopped them all right, so—'

'Are you taking us to Medlow Bath?' Holly broke in furiously. 'To the house on Horsetrough Lane? Did you leave this Moonie person keeping watch in the lay-by in case Andrew tried to escape? While you followed me in the four-wheel drive to Leanne's place, and then to the motel? If so, you've all been wasting your time! Andrew's gone!'

The men ignored her completely.

'So while they were clearing the track,' Fen went on, 'Moonie snuck round and got a good look inside both vehicles. Nothing.'

'The BMW boot?' the driver asked sharply.

'Just a bag of golf clubs. Clean.'

'Andrew McNish isn't in that house!' said Holly, loudly and clearly. 'He *was* there, but he left on Tuesday night. He's probably not even in this *state* anymore. He could even have left the country!'

Probably has, she thought. If he managed to sell those rings....

'Oh, yeah,' the driver jeered, without bothering to look around. 'That's why you keep going back to the Maggott house, is it? And got a heavy to check the boundary? And had a smart-arse lawyer hanging round? Because McNish *isn't* there?'

'Who's McMish?' Leanne Purse shrieked. 'What do you want with me? Why is this *happening*?'

'Shut up!' roared Fen. 'Jeezus H *Christ*!'

'Listen to me!' Holly exploded. 'Obviously you've been following me ever since I left Andrew's house in Springwood, but you've got it all wrong! I'm not his henchwoman, or messenger or enforcer, or whatever you think I am. I'm just his girlfriend—his *ex*-girlfriend!'

Fen laughed. 'So you're going to tell me it's just a coincidence that you visit a private dick who's poking his nose into McNish's business, and the dick conveniently drops dead, are you?'

Leanne gave a little scream.

'Yes,' said Holly with dignity. 'O'Brien died of natural causes.'

This time both men laughed.

'She's good,' said Fen appreciatively. 'You've got to admit it, Skinner. First she nearly loses us on the highway so we have to drive to buggery around in a circle to get back to the motel, and only see her going into that bloke's room by a miracle. Then she gets out and away right under our noses while we're going in to get her. Smooth.'

'It was all those granny and grandpa tourists,' Skinner grunted. 'She'd never have given us the slip otherwise. So, what's up with Moonie, Fen?'

Fen shrugged. 'He just wants backup. Plus he's run out of cigarettes. Plus he doesn't get why we picked up two women instead of one.'

'Yeah. Why did you have to grab the wrong car, you stupid prick?' Skinner muttered.

'It *looked* like the same car,' grumbled Fen. 'I didn't know McNish's bint had already gone, did I? Plus the other bitch came tearing out of the motel like a bat out of hell. Plus she had a bag with her. A blonde bitch with a bag, see? How did I know she was the wrong one?'

'She's a fatso, for a start, dickhead! Her hair's longer. She's wearing different clothes!'

'I don't notice that shit. A blonde with a bag, that's all I saw. Well, I saw the dress but I thought she'd put cleaner's shit on as a blind.'

'Moron!'

'Don't call me a moron. *You're* the moron, Skinner. You're the moron who said we should turn over that guy's room because she'd probably passed him the loot. *You're* the one who ripped off a bag that turned out to be full of paperclips and pictures of office shit! You should've seen your face when Bernie opened it.'

'Shut up!' Skinner glanced in the rear-vision mirror. 'Shit, that dickhead in the van's caught up. Thought we'd shaken him off in Mealey. He was losing oil after the smash.'

'What's his problem?' Fen shook his head. 'Why did he chase us out of the motel anyway? He didn't see anything. He was just coming in as we were leaving.'

'Saw you throw your fag out the window, maybe. Thinks he'll make a citizen's arrest,' said Skinner, and sniggered.

Holly twisted around to look through the back window again. The four-wheel drive was still tailgating them. And right behind the four-wheel drive was Trevor Purse's little green van. As the road curved, she could see Purse crouched low over the wheel, his face grimly intent. Two people were crammed together beside him. Holly's breath caught in her throat. Abigail and Mrs. Moss! Had they flagged Purse down on Stillwaters Road? Had they just forced their way into the van while Purse was still groggy after bashing into the four-wheel drive? However it had happened, they were there. They had come after her! Hot tears of fear and gratitude welled up in her eyes.

'It's this woman's husband!' she shouted. 'Pull over and let us out! He won't give up till you do. He'll never give up. And by now he'll have rung the police!'

'Trevor!' screamed Leanne Purse, kneeling up on the seat and beating at the window with her fists.

'Shit!' said Skinner, and put his foot down.

The little white Mazda responded, surging strongly forward. Glumly Holly reflected that her Mazda wouldn't have done that. No doubt Leanne's had been regularly serviced.

The four-wheel drive kept an even distance behind them. The van quickly fell back. Then a white ute overtook the van, and it was hidden from view.

'That's got him,' said Skinner.

'The Medlow Bath turnoff's coming up,' Fen said nervously. 'Plus it's an 80k limit here, Skinner. If a cop car sees us—'

'Shut the fuck *up!*' snarled Skinner, who seemed to react badly to stress. He gunned the Mazda past the Medlow Bath sign and swung recklessly left at the turnoff that led to Horsetrough Lane. The four-wheel drive followed as if it were attached by a short string to the Mazda's tail. Looking back, Holly could see no sign of the little green van.

'He'll miss the turnoff,' wailed Leanne. 'He won't know where…Oh, Trevor! Trevor!'

'Call Moonie again, Fen,' Skinner said. 'Tell him we'll be with him any minute now. And tell him to get his shit together. We're going in.'

Chapter Twenty

Five minutes later, the Mazda was parked beside the Horsetrough Lane lay-by. Holly was sitting in the driver's seat. Fen was in the back, close behind her, pressing the muzzle of a gun against the nape of her neck, so she was being very careful not to move. As a result, one of her ears had become fiendishly itchy, her nose was running and she had developed an overwhelming urge to cough. The gun could have been a replica, or even a toy, but it had looked real when Fen showed it to her. And it felt real—hard, cold and very bad against the skin of her neck.

The black four-wheel drive was idling close beside the Mazda. The ponytailed driver sat silently in the front seat. Leanne Purse was huddled in the back, having been bundled out of the Mazda as soon as it stopped at the lay-by, where the man called Moonie had been waiting impatiently.

Moonie, who looked like a rugby player run to seed and had a few dozen long, glistening black hairs combed over his balding scalp, was standing on the road with Skinner, squeezed between the two vehicles.

Immediately ahead, the Maggott mansion rose silent behind its railings. Deep shadows lay on the flat green lawn.

'Creepy old dump, isn't it?' said Moonie. 'Who'd want to live way out here?'

'The old woman's a nutter,' said Skinner. 'Her dad was the same. He messed around with Bernie's grandma before he buried her, right, Bernie?'

The thin man behind the wheel of the four-wheel drive nodded shortly. His long grey face was expressionless. So far he hadn't said a word. Holly found him more frightening than any of the others, though it was Fen who was holding the gun.

'I still reckon the rest of us should go in on foot,' said Moonie. 'Then we'd have more chance of taking him by surprise.'

'We've been through that!' snapped Skinner.

'See, once we're in, we don't need surprise, Moonie,' Fen said soothingly from the Mazda's back seat. 'All we have to do is move fast. We'll get McNish easy. He's a cream puff. And we've got the girlfriend, that's the point.'

'Right,' said Skinner. 'Let's do it.'

Dimly Holly wondered if he had watched too many action movies, or if the dialogue in action movies actually reflected the way people like him really talked, which was something she'd never previously considered.

Clutching the wheel of the Mazda, she waited as Skinner climbed into the passenger seat of the four-wheel drive and Moonie got into the back to sit beside the whimpering Leanne. Behind her, she heard Fen breathing heavily through his nose as he punched Una Maggott's number into O'Brien's phone. She heard the tinny sound of Una's voice answering. She felt the gun muzzle shift slightly as Fen reached over the seat and pressed the phone to her ear.

'Hello?' Una was saying. 'Hello? Who is it?'

'It's Holly Cage, Ms. Maggott,' Holly said. 'Could you open the gates, please?'

When Skinner had told her what she had to do, her first thought was that she could give Una Maggott some coded warning, some hidden instruction to call the police, if she chose her words carefully. But then Fen had pulled out the gun, and its pressure on the back of her neck seemed to have emptied her mind.

The phone went dead. Ahead, the gates began to open.

Fen gave a grunt of satisfaction and took the phone back. The gun slid from Holly's neck as he lay down on the back seat to keep out of sight.

'Go,' he said. 'And remember, I've still got you covered. I'm aiming right at your spine. You try anything and you get it. Get it?'

He obviously watched a lot of movies too, but his dialogue needed work.

Holly drove the Mazda forward, leaving the four-wheel drive in hiding. By the time she reached the gates they were almost fully open. She heard the sound of the four-wheel drive revving up, and glanced in the rear-view mirror. The black monster was edging forward, waiting its moment.

'Go!' Fen muttered behind her. 'As close to the steps as you can get, then cut the engine and stay put. Don't move an eyelash.'

Holly turned the Mazda through the gateway and eased it on, the gravel crunching softly beneath the tires. As she pulled up, the front door of the house began slowly to swing open. She stared at it with a sort of horrible fascination.

Una Maggott, bolt upright in her wheelchair, emerged from the dimness and moved out onto the verandah. She looked excited. The remote control for the gates was in her hand. She saw Holly still sitting in the car and beckoned to her irritably.

There was a roaring sound from the road. Una's eyes widened. In the rear-view mirror Holly saw the four-wheel drive thunder through the open gateway, gravel spraying up on either side of it as if it were a speedboat. The next moment it was skidding to a stop beside the Mazda. Skinner and Bernie leapt out, both wearing expressions of intense disgust. Moonie crawled more awkwardly from the back seat, dragging Leanne Purse, who was pale green and seemed to have been sick in his lap.

'What do you people think you're doing?' shrieked Una. 'This is private property!'

'Shut the fuck up!' Skinner bellowed, pulling a gun from his pocket and pointing it at her. She shut her mouth with a snap.

'The woman spewed in the vehicle,' said Bernie. 'She *spewed in the vehicle*!' He seemed unable to take it in.

'Don't worry about it, Bernie,' gabbled Skinner. 'We'll get it detailed—soon as we're out of this. You go round the back, right? Secure the exits.'

As if the final words acted as some sort of trigger, Bernie went at a run, quickly disappearing around the side of the house.

Swearing, Fen heaved himself out of the Mazda, threw Holly's shoulder bag into the lavender bushes and wrenched her door open.

'Out!' he ordered, gesturing with his gun.

He looked very twitchy. Holly slid cautiously from the car, hoping his trigger finger wouldn't convulse and shoot her by accident. He grabbed her and pulled her hard against him, sticking the gun in her ribs.

'Leave the doors open,' Skinner was telling Moonie. 'Let the stink out.'

'It's all over my pants!' babbled Moonie, whose face was fish-belly pale and shiny with sweat. 'It's on my shirt. Aargh! Shit, I hate sick! I've always hated sick. Ever since I was a kid and my little brother—'

Bernie jogged back into view beside the light pole on the other side of the house.

'Done already?' Skinner called.

Bernie held up a key. Presumably this meant that he'd found the key in the back door and deadlocked it from the outside.

All the windows are barred, Holly thought. With the back door deadlocked and the front door guarded, the house is a prison. And Sheena, Lily and Dulcie were in there. Dulcie's son, too, Holly reminded herself. She kept forgetting about him. The thugs didn't seem to know they existed, but they had to be in the house if Eric and Allnut had been the only ones to leave. Why hadn't any of them appeared to find out what was going on? Was it possible that they hadn't heard the noise?

It was, in fact, especially if they were upstairs. Holly remembered only too well how very silent the house had seemed when she was inside it—how its thick walls and sealed, barred windows seemed to muffle sound, shut the world out. If only one of them would look down, see what was happening, realise what it meant, and ring the police. Sheena, at least, had the brains for that. She could be doing it right now! Holly felt a wild flutter of hope, crossed her fingers and concentrated on holding still.

Bernie had almost reached the Mazda. She watched him under her eyelashes, repelled yet fascinated by his weirdly immobile features, the smooth, even greyness of his skin. Then she saw him stiffen, as if he'd heard something. Her heart leapt as he turned his head to stare out at the road.

'*Shit!*' Fen muttered. He was goggling at the road too. Forgetting that she wasn't supposed to make any sudden moves, Holly looked eagerly around.

A small green van covered in bright yellow writing was labouring toward the house.

'How…?' Skinner was staring at the van as if it were an apparition.

'He'll have called the cops!' Fen gabbled in panic. 'Skinner, we got to—'

'Shut the fuck up!' Skinner had returned to high stress mode, but the expression of almost superstitious awe that had crossed his face when he first saw the van had gone. He lowered his voice to a mutter.

'Don't you get it, Fen? The little prick knew where to come! That means he's mixed up in this. McNish must have used his pest extermination setup to wash the money. Offered him a cut. He won't have called anyone.'

'Yes, he will!' Holly burst out in frustration. 'You've got it all wrong! I don't know how he found us, but he's got absolutely nothing to do with—'

'*Shut up!*' Skinner and Fen yelled together.

'Trevor!' screamed Leanne, sighting the van and suddenly coming to life. She twisted and struggled violently, punching and clawing at Moonie with vomit-smeared hands.

'Get off!' yelled Moonie. 'Stay still! You're getting it all over me! Aargh!' He started to retch, but gamely held on to the back of the blue overall as Leanne plunged and strained like a dog on a short leash.

'Shut the gates!' Skinner shouted at Una.

Una folded her hands around the remote control and stuck out her bottom lip, her small eyes glittering. At that moment, Holly thought, she looked exactly like the portrait of her father.

'Bernie, get the remote!' roared Skinner.

Bernie lunged for the steps.

Instantly, Una Maggott dropped the remote control in front of her right wheel and ran over it. There was a sickening crack.

Bernie and Skinner gaped at her. She bared her teeth at them, reversed, and ran over the shattered plastic again.

Two batteries, the only survivors of the ruin, rolled slowly to the edge of the verandah and started bouncing down the steps. Bernie regarded them silently as they passed him. Then he looked back at Una, and suddenly a knife was in his hand. He took a step up.

'No!' Holly screamed. 'Don't hurt her! She doesn't know what she's doing!'

'Shut up!' hissed Fen, but she could tell that his heart wasn't in it.

'Let it go, Bernie!' said Skinner in a level voice.

The tall man looked back over his shoulder, his face as expressionless as ever.

'Let it go,' Skinner repeated. 'We might need her later. You go on in and get McNish. We'll handle the cretins in the van.'

The knife disappeared. One minute it was in Bernie's hand, the next minute it wasn't. Holly shivered—shivered all over. Bernie stalked past Una, ignoring her completely, and disappeared into the gloom of the house. A few moments later the stairs began to squeak.

Holly shut her eyes and concentrated with all her might on Sheena, on sending a message to Sheena. *Hide! Hide and ring for help! Ring for help!* By the time she opened her eyes, the green van had almost reached the gateway.

'It's that rat man again,' said Una Maggott, scowling. 'What's he doing back here?'

'Fen! Get up there and keep the old loony under control. Moonie—' Skinner glanced around, obviously made a snap decision that the gagging Moonie had his hands full wrestling Leanne Purse, and turned to face the gates alone.

'Ms. Cage, who *are* these men?' Una demanded as Fen dragged Holly up the steps. 'What do they want?'

'Andrew,' said Holly dully. 'And the money he owes them. They've been using him to launder cash for them, apparently. Drug money. Or the haul from a robbery. Whatever.'

Una hissed something in French. It sounded like a curse, and probably was. Her face was suddenly mottled with red, ugly with rage.

'He didn't tell me he was involved with *criminals*,' she hissed. 'If I'd known that I would never have…' She clenched her fists.

If you'd known that you'd never have taken him into your house, Holly thought. You'd probably have gone right off him, like you went off Lily when you found out she was a member of a coven. Which is exactly why he didn't tell you, Una. Just like he didn't tell you about me.

She found that she was furiously angry too. Angry with Andrew for being such a shallow, selfish, dishonest slimeball. Angry with Una for being taken in. Angry with herself for being taken in. And, most of all, angry because she had been so stupidly blind to the fact that her movements were being tracked, so that everyone she came in contact with, from Abigail to Leanne Purse, had been smeared with the mess Andrew McNish had left behind him.

'Bastard!' she said aloud.

'Shut *up*!' Fen ordered, digging the barrel of the gun harder into her ribs. 'And you!' He glared at Una. 'Fold your arms! Fold them and keep them folded!'

Scowling, Una obeyed.

The green van swung off the road and, like an exhausted horse making some final, gallant effort, puttered through the gateway. It came to a shuddering halt behind the Mazda. Both doors burst open and Trevor Purse, Abigail and Mrs. Moss spilled out.

The sight of her husband was too much for Leanne. Screaming his name, she made a frantic lunge toward him. The buttons of her blue overall popped and flew through the air like bullets. Wild-eyed, Leanne wriggled out of the overall sleeves and took off. Moonie toppled backwards, clutching a vomit-covered blue rag to his chest as she flew into her husband's arms, her plump breasts and little round belly bouncing under the shiny pink fabric of her camisole and half-slip.

'Leanne!' moaned Trevor Purse, staggering slightly under her weight. 'Oh, Leanne!'

'Holly!' cried Abigail, starting forward. 'Are you all—?'

'*Freeze!*'

It was Skinner. He was talking like a movie character again, and looking like one too, with his gun held in both hands, at arm's length, aimed at the group by the van. His Adam's apple was wobbling up and down. His hair was standing up in a ridiculous little quiff. He looked like a skinny turkey pretending to be tough. It should have been funny, but it wasn't.

Abigail stopped dead. Mrs. Moss gave a little scream. Trevor and Leanne stiffened, locked in a spellbound embrace.

'Check them out,' Skinner snarled at Moonie, who had crawled to his feet and was fruitlessly trying to devomit his pants and shirt with Leanne's unsavoury overall. 'For fuck's sake, Moonie, get your act together, will you?'

'I hate sick,' Moonie said sullenly. He dropped the overall and walked unsteadily to the group by the van. Mrs. Moss wrinkled her nose fastidiously as he patted her over, but Abigail merely stared sightlessly over his shoulder, her face dull with fear.

Moonie moved to Trevor and Leanne. After a moment he held up Trevor Purse's wallet, a key case, a roll of breath mints and a clean white handkerchief.

'Now the van!' snapped Skinner.

The van yielded Mrs. Moss' wallet, the empty chip bag, the van keys, and Purse's mobile phone, which appeared to be very much the worse for wear.

'It was on the floor,' said Moonie, showing Skinner the phone. 'Display's all smashed in. Looks like one of them trod on it.'

Trevor Purse shot Mrs. Moss a reproachful look. Mrs. Moss tossed her head and shifted uneasily in her high heels.

Skinner's lip curled. 'Moonie, truss them up to something. Those light poles at the sides of the house'll do—we only need half an hour.' His eyes slewed to Trevor Purse. 'You first! You and the old girl. Don't try anything or your wife gets it.'

Leanne gave a sort of howl as Moonie prised her husband away from her. Mrs. Moss showed signs of defiance but as Abigail nudged her, murmuring urgently, she seemed to think better of it and allowed herself to be hustled with Trevor to the light pole on the right side of the house.

'Better not do their mouths,' Fen called from the verandah, as Moonie sat his prisoners back to back against the pole and set about securing them with lavish amounts of duct tape. 'They might chuck up and choke on the vomit.'

'Shut up, you moron!' Skinner snarled. He flapped his hand in front of his nose as Moonie, retching helplessly, shuffled past him to repeat the duct-tape performance with Leanne and Abigail on the other light pole.

Inside the house, the stairs shrieked. A moment later, Bernie appeared in the doorway and stood watching the activity below with no appearance of interest. Holly tried not to look at him, but couldn't resist sneaking the occasional glance. Bernie was so still, so self-contained, that he could have been a statue. It was impossible to tell what he might have been thinking, or indeed if anything was going on in his mind at all. Fen must have known he was there but made no sign of it except for a slight tensing of his muscles. He preferred to leave the management of Bernie to Skinner, it seemed.

Skinner at last looked around and noticed the man standing there.

'Got him, Bernie?' he asked eagerly.

Bernie gave the slightest possible jerk of his head and went back into the house. It was an obvious summons, and an imperious one at that.

Skinner checked to see if Moonie and Fen had noticed, and seeing that they had, forced a tolerant grin.

'Old Bern's feeling lonely in there,' he said, and sauntered to the steps, ostentatiously taking his time.

'The one with the knife's a psychopath,' Una Maggott said to Holly in a piercing whisper. 'You can tell by his eyes. He probably murdered Sheena and Lily when he found them. Dulcie and the boy too, very likely.' She didn't sound very sorry about it.

'Shut up,' said Fen, who by now must have been feeling like a broken record. He waited till Skinner had gone past them into the house and Moonie was on the steps behind him, then slowly moved the muzzle of the gun from Holly's ribs to her back.

'You push the chair,' he said. 'Take it slow. Do anything stupid and one bullet will do for the two of you.'

Oh, very dramatic, Holly thought, but she knew she was whistling in the dark. Her knees felt like marshmallow as she turned the wheelchair and pushed it into the house. *How has this happened?* a voice blared in her head. *As if things weren't bad enough! Now you're in danger of getting shot, and all these innocent people are too, and it's all your fault!*

Andrew McNish's fault, in fact, her common sense told her, but she found it difficult to take much comfort in the thought.

The entrance hall seemed very dim after the brightness outside. The chains dangling from the ceiling jingled softly together as Moonie shut the door and turned the key in the deadlock to seal the house completely.

'I'll take that key, Moonie,' said Skinner's voice. 'Give it here.'

He and Bernie were standing together at the bottom of the stairs. They were looking down at a row of people sitting with their backs to the wall under the portrait of Rollo Maggott: Lily. Sheena. Dulcie. And a plump teenage boy with a sulky mouth.

At Bernie's feet, like the spoils of war, lay four mobile phones, a crochet hook and a tangle of bright pink wool, a tube of craft glue, and a can of lavender air-freshener. Holly's last hope gave a final quiver and died.

'Jeezus H Christ!' gasped Fen, surveying the prisoners in amazement. 'Where did they all come from?'

'You tell us,' Skinner said, deftly shifting the blame for faulty surveillance onto the last person to reach the scene.

Bernie, who seemed to be literal-minded, cast his eyes to the ceiling.

'They were all upstairs,' Skinner translated. 'Bernie got the kid first, so the rest of them came down like lambs. No problem.' He paused. 'No problem for Bernie, that is,' he added, and laughed sycophantically.

No one else joined in. Holly had a vision of Bernie's knife at the boy's soft throat, and felt sick.

'The kid was the only one who'd heard us,' Skinner went on, still trying to lighten things up. 'He was in the linen cupboard, trying to hide his stash. Thought we were the cops!' Again he laughed. This time Fen gave a token chuckle in response, and even Moonie brightened.

The boy on the floor glowered.

'*Drugs!*' Dulcie breathed. 'Oh, *Bastian!*'

'It's only weed, Mum,' Sebastian muttered. 'It's nothing.'

'*Marijuana?*' Dulcie pronounced it as it was spelled. Her tear-stained face was bright red.

'So where is it?' Moonie asked Skinner eagerly as he handed over the front door key.

'What?'

'The stash! Where is it?'

'Bernie's got it.'

Moonie's face fell. He glanced at Bernie, who returned his gaze stonily.

'Forget about the stash!' Fen broke in. 'What about *McNish?*'

Again Bernie's eyes flicked to the ceiling.

'One of the bedrooms is locked,' said Skinner. 'McNish'll be holed up in there, with the cash. Has to be. Bernie reckons the other rooms are clean and there's nothing in the attic except a few dead rats.'

Moonie gave a low moan and looked even sicker than he had before.

'Andrew's not in that room!' Sheena said sullenly. 'He's *nowhere*! He left on Tuesday night, and he took all his things with him! How many times do we have to tell you?'

'Shut up,' Fen said automatically. Holly felt him flex the muscles of his powerful shoulders. 'So we break the door down,' he said, sounding as if he relished the idea no end.

'Right,' said Skinner. 'Your department, Fen.'

'No!' Una Maggott snapped.

Bernie's dead eyes swivelled in her direction.

'Those are good cedar doors up there,' Una said, shrugging off Holly's warning hand impatiently. 'I don't want one of them smashed in for nothing.'

Holly waited for her to say Andrew McNish was dead, and to start raving about sniffer dogs, but, as usual, Una surprised her.

'The key's in my desk,' Una said. 'You can have it.'

Skinner's eyes narrowed.

'Over there,' said Una, jerking her head at the door across the hall. 'Top left-hand drawer. Help yourself.'

'Moonie, go and have a look!' Skinner ordered. 'But watch yourself. It might be a trap.'

'A *trap*!' jeered Una. 'Funnel-webs in the drawer? A needle tipped in cyanide? You booby!'

'Shut up!' Fen growled. 'If you know what's good for you,' he added, as a variation.

Moonie showed the whites of his eyes and moved out of Holly's line of sight. She heard him trudging across the entrance hall, the rubber soles of his shoes squeaking on the marble tiles. There was a creak as the door was pushed open, and a sudden yelp of shock.

The gun pressed to Holly's back jerked slightly. She winced.

'Shit!' muttered Skinner, staring through the open door.

'There's a bloody snake in here!' Moonie yelled. 'A bloody huge—'

'It's in a cage, you moron,' snapped Skinner, recovering. 'Don't worry about it. Get the key.'

In a few moments Moonie was back. He handed the key to Skinner, his hand shaking. 'I hate snakes,' he said, with a sidelong glance at Bernie, who remained expressionless.

Skinner looked at the key with satisfaction. 'Right,' he said. 'We're in business.'

'Bit too easy, isn't it?' Fen said, clearly disappointed to have lost his chance to star. 'The locked room might be a blind. McNish might be hiding down here somewhere, waiting his chance—'

'His chance to what?' barked Skinner. 'He can't get out of the house.'

Fen stuck out his bottom lip. 'I still say we should look down here before we go up.'

Bernie made a slight growling sound. It could have indicated agreement, or he could have just been clearing his throat.

Skinner wet his lips. 'Right,' he said. 'We'll look down here first. Now, here's the plan…'

Chapter Twenty-one

After some discussion, which included angry recriminations against Moonie, who had used up all the duct tape on the Purses, Abigail and Mrs. Moss, it was decided to put the unexpectedly large group of hostages in the library for safekeeping. Una's room, with its lockable door, would have been a more obviously secure holding cell, but the pale and reeking Moonie, who had been appointed the captives' guard on the grounds that at present he was incapable of anything else, had refused absolutely to enter what he called 'the snake room' again.

The captives sat around the long table, eyeing one another grimly, sullenly or hopelessly according to temperament, like the ill-assorted board members of a company that was not doing well.

Holly and Sheena were on the far side of the table, facing the bulbous sideboard that stood beside the door to the entrance hall and supported a statue of a naked woman with a stopped clock in her stomach and a glass case of stuffed birds. Lily, Dulcie and Sebastian, on the other side, had a view of the floor-to-ceiling bookshelves. Una sat in her wheelchair at the head of the table, with her back to the barred windows, scowling like an ill-tempered chairman.

Moonie had been given Fen's gun and now leaned against the door, covering his prisoners shakily enough to ensure that none of them felt like making any sudden moves. He looked irritable and extremely unwell. Every now and again there were dim sounds from the other side of the door—the sounds of Skinner, Bernie and Fen searching the ground floor.

Predictably it was Dulcie who finally broke the tense silence, her feverish need to tackle her son over the confiscated stash overwhelming her fear of the gun.

'Where did you get it, Bastian?' she hissed. 'Who gave it to you? Tell me! It was Eric, wasn't it? I always knew he was a—'

'No one *gave* it to me,' muttered the boy. 'I wish.'

'Quite!' said Una. 'I daresay whoever sold it to you got a very good price.' She glanced coldly at Lily, who widened her eyes, the image of outraged innocence.

Una snorted and turned back to Sebastian. 'And what I'd like to know is, where did you get the money from, boy? Out of your mother's purse, was it? Two hundred dollars must have bought you enough to go on with.'

Holly's heart gave a great thump as she saw Sebastian's heavy eyelids flicker.

'*Bastian!*' wailed Dulcie.

Sheena laughed. 'And here we were blaming poor old Andrew,' she said. 'Well, well.'

Moonie stirred. 'What's this about McNish?' he asked thickly.

'Mind your own business!' Una snapped.

Moonie blinked, then seemed to remember who was holding the gun.

'McNish *is* my business,' he growled. '*Our* business.'

Una sneered. 'I gather he was laundering money for you. It's hard to believe you buffoons would have enough cash to make it worth his while.'

'A lot you know!' Moonie retorted hotly, rising to the bait. 'There was plenty.'

'And you gave it to Andrew McNish?' Sheena jeered. 'Lord, you need your heads read!'

Bastian sniggered.

Moonie's waxen face darkened unattractively. 'It was Skinner. Skinner got the word McNish was okay. He made the contact. McNish said he'd do it for a cut, no problem—'

'There you are, Una, what did I tell you?' shrieked Dulcie.
'What did Cliff and I both tell you? The man's a *criminal!* A
criminal, pure and simple!'

'Yeah,' Moonie agreed, glowering. 'Couple of weeks after he
got his hands on the dough he stopped returning Skinner's calls.
Then he went into smoke. He ripped us off.'

Sheena laughed humourlessly. 'Join the club,' she said. 'Well,
he didn't get any money out of me, thank the Lord. Not that
he didn't try. Said he could double me little nest egg in a few
months if I gave him the handling of it, but I said no thanks,
I'd rather leave it in the bank.'

'Very wise,' Dulcie said in a high voice. 'Well, I wish you
joy of your *little nest egg*, Sheena. Personally, *I* wouldn't be able
to sleep at night if I'd persuaded a helpless old man to leave his
property away from his family, and then had the hide to *sell* it
back to his rightful heir!'

Sheena's neck and face flushed bright red. Her eyes snapped.
'What, did you expect me to *give* it away, Dulcie?' she spat. 'It
was all I had to show for *five years* with Roly!'

'Yes, well, and you did very nicely for yourself, too, didn't
you?' Dulcie said nastily. 'Cliff Allnut drew up the sale agreement, and he told me—'

'Allnut had no business telling you anything!' barked Una.
'How I choose to spend my money is *my* affair, Dulcie! It has
nothing to do with you, and never will have, whatever nasty
little plots you and that golf-mad shyster have been cooking up
between you!'

Dulcie boggled, then took refuge in tears.

'You should have auctioned the best of the stuff on eBay,'
Sebastian said to Sheena, coming surprisingly to life. 'You'd have
got a lot more that way. I could have done it for you. I'd have
done it for…20 percent of the sale price.'

'*Twenty percent?*' Sheena's face broke suddenly into a broad
grin. 'Lord, boyo, you're a Maggott, all right.'

'You'd still have done better than you did from Auntie Una,'
said Sebastian, unperturbed. 'People'll buy anything on eBay.'

Holly saw Una give him a sharp glance. Moonie also looked interested. He turned to stare at the case of stuffed birds and the clock. This brought his eyes in contact with Lily's. She batted her amazing eyelashes and wriggled around to face him, bending slightly to reveal a little of her cleavage.

'These people aren't my friends, Moonie,' she murmured. 'I don't belong with them. And I'm so tired. Perhaps...if you could just let me go to my room to lie down? I'd be so grateful. And after all this is over...'

'I hate women,' said Moonie. 'Especially the ones who try to make me do things by flashing their tits at me.'

Lily shot him a look of pure hatred, flounced around in her chair and began muttering soundlessly to herself.

'She's a witch, you know,' Una said to Moonie. 'You want to be careful how you talk to her.'

'Shut up!' said Moonie. But he looked rattled. Keeping the prisoners covered, and eyeing the back of Lily's bent head uneasily, he moved to the sideboard and pulled one of the doors open to reveal a cluster of bottles. He seized a quarter-full bottle of sherry, screwed off the lid one-handed, took a swig, and shuddered all over, looking sicker than ever.

'You're probably poisoned, now,' Una told him calmly. 'I like a glass of sherry myself, and someone's been trying to kill me lately.'

And it was then, when she was turning away from the sight of the gun wavering in Moonie's shaking hand, that Holly saw a face at the library window. She froze. The face behind the yellowed lace curtains and dusty glass was so grotesque that her first thought was that the watcher was someone wearing a horror mask.

She had told herself that Bernie the psychopath was the obvious candidate, and her teeth had begun to chatter, by the time she realised that the misshapen disc she was seeing was a human face distorted by being pressed hard against the security bars. A second later she understood that what she had taken to be bat-like ears were actually hands cupped on either side of the watcher's head like blinkers, to exclude the afternoon sun. Then she saw the dark cockscomb of hair, and slowly recognised the face at the window as Eric's.

Her heart bounded. Eric had come home! Eric had seen the captives tied to the light poles! By now he must have called the police. Relief was at hand!

Terrified that she had given the game away by staring, she looked quickly away from the window and glanced around. To her relief, no one else seemed to have noticed her distraction. Sheena and Una were both looking without sympathy at Dulcie, whose weeping had quickly subsided into a series of exaggeratedly shuddering sobs. Sebastian was staring vacantly at the bookshelves, no doubt calculating how much Rollo Maggott's tomes on embalming, reptiles, steam trains, Elvis and dentistry might fetch on eBay. Lily was gazing down at her hands, mumbling incantations, whether calming or vengeful it was impossible to guess.

Moonie was still investigating the sideboard, pushing aside bottles in search of something he liked better than sherry. As Holly's eyes fell on him he straightened up, holding a bulky padded envelope.

'*Holly Cage,*' he read slowly, squinting at the bold printing on the front of the envelope. '*Per-sonal.*'

Everyone looked at Holly. She stared, confounded, at the envelope.

'What's that, Ms. Cage?' Una demanded, leaning forward.

'Your name's not Cage,' Moonie said to Holly. 'Your name's Love. Holly Love—that's what Fen said.'

Holly shrugged, feeling her face grow hot.

'Well, well,' Sheena said softly.

Moonie put his find to his ear and shook it. Outside the room they heard the stairs shrieking beneath three pairs of feet.

'They're going up to get your boyfriend,' said Moonie. 'Won't be long now.' He grinned sadistically at Holly, showing stained, uneven teeth. Holly, who up till now had thought he was the best of a bad bunch, revised her opinion.

'Boyfriend?' Una Maggott burst out. '*Love?* What's he *talking* about?' Her voice sounded hoarse. Holly couldn't look at her.

'So what's in this?' Moonie asked, holding up the envelope.

'I've got no idea,' Holly said feebly. 'I've never seen it before.'

'Oh, is that right?' Moonie jeered. 'So if it's a shitload of cash, it'll be a big surprise to you, will it? Well, let's have a look.'

He lumbered over to the dining table, ripped the envelope open, and upended it with a flourish.

A very dead white rat, seething with maggots, fell onto the tabletop.

'Ugh!' said Moonie. The blood drained from his face. His eyes rolled back. Slowly he toppled sideways, and crashed to the floor.

Then Holly was on her feet. She couldn't quite remember how she got there. Presumably she had reacted instinctively to the sight of the dead rat. Everyone else had abandoned the table too—everyone except Una, who was still sitting at its head, scowling down at the unconscious Moonie. Sheena was swearing under her breath. Dulcie was babbling hysterically, clutching at her son, who was struggling to get away from her. Lily was gaping, apparently mesmerised, at the maggots wriggling on the tabletop.

'Get the gun! Get the gun!' Holly heard herself gabbling, then seeing that no one was listening to her, ran around the table to get it herself.

She found it pinned under the unconscious Moonie's knee. Gingerly she tugged it free and stood up, feeling its weight in her hands.

'I'll take that,' said Una.

Holly glanced at her uncertainly.

'Give it to me!' Una ordered. 'I can handle a gun, which is obviously a lot more than you can do, Ms. Cage, or Love, or whoever you are.'

'No! Don't let her have it!' squealed Dulcie.

Holly passed Una the gun. Dulcie squealed again.

'Keep quiet!' hissed Sheena. 'The others will hear you!'

Moonie mumbled. He smacked his lips and his eyelids fluttered.

'Keep him covered, Auntie Una,' Sebastian advised.

'I think I'll do better than that.' Una leaned over the side of the wheelchair and hit Moonie smartly on the head with the gun butt. The murmuring and eye-fluttering stopped. Una straightened and tossed the gun onto the tabletop.

Squealing for the third time, Dulcie ducked for cover, pulling Sebastian down with her.

'It isn't real, you fool,' Una said. 'It's just a dummy. No striking mechanism. No bullets. Useless.'

Everyone groaned. Dulcie, Sebastian and Lily stared reproachfully at Holly as if she should have known.

'It looked real,' Holly said, impelled against all reason to defend herself. 'I wasn't going to take any chances.'

'Quite right,' said Una surprisingly. 'So. What'll we do now? The other three will be down any minute.'

She was looking at Holly for instructions. They were all looking at Holly, expectation in every line of their faces. After all, Holly was the professional. Professional detective, or professional con artist, either way she was an aficionado of the mean streets, and therefore the only one of them fitted to lead a battle on the dark side.

It's a dirty job but someone has to...

Holly glanced at the window, but Eric had gone. Her mind raced. No way out of the house. No lock strong enough to keep Fen out. Unless...

She stepped over Moonie's body and darted to the end of the sideboard. 'Help me push this thing across the door,' she heard herself saying crisply. 'We don't have to hold out for long. I saw Eric outside. The police must be on their way by now.'

She put her shoulder to the sideboard. Sheena hurried to join her. Sebastian and Dulcie gripped the end nearest the door as best they could. Lily stood ineffectually in the middle, holding on to one of the drawer handles.

'One, two, three!' said Holly. Grunting with the effort, she and Sheena pushed, Sebastian and Dulcie pulled, and Lily did a bit of both. The sideboard shifted a little, its base grating on the floorboards, the bottles inside it chinking together. Then it ground to a halt.

'Put your backs into it!' Una Maggott hissed, zooming dangerously past Moonie's head to get closer to the action. 'What's wrong with you all?'

'Can't—get—a—grip,' Sebastian panted. He pushed past his mother and hauled recklessly at the drawer nearest to him, jumping back as it slid out abruptly and fell to the floor, just missing his foot.

The drawer's contents spilled onto the boards: chess pieces, poker chips, decks of cards, some bridge score pads, several small, blunt pencils, a few dice, two champagne corks…and a flat, faded blue box with a gold clasp that sprang open to reveal a row of silver teaspoons.

'Ha!' crowed Una Maggott.

Holly's breath caught in her throat, but before she could say anything, Sebastian had kicked the clutter away and taken hold of the edge of the drawer cavity. He gritted his teeth. The unaccustomed physical effort had turned his usually vampire-pale face scarlet.

'Go!' he ordered. Again they strained, and this time the sideboard moved, sliding across the boards with a dull, rasping sound, to within a chair's width of the door.

'Again!' gasped Holly. 'One, two—'

The final word stuck in her throat as the library door swung open.

Martin the landscaper slipped noiselessly into the room, a spanner hanging loosely in his hand. He nodded to the gaping prisoners, as laconic as if he'd come to give a quote on building a retaining wall. Behind him crowded Eric, glittering and manic as Elvis on speed, brandishing a piece of pipe, and Trevor Purse, tousled and intent, gripping his massive black torch.

'Are the police here?' Una demanded, finding her voice.

Martin shook his head slightly and put his finger to his lips. He looked quickly around the room, taking in the rat and the gun on the table. His gaze swept over Holly as if she wasn't there. He didn't seem surprised that Moonie was unconscious, and Holly realised that Eric must have seen the man fall.

'Where are the other three?' Martin asked softly.

'Upstairs,' said Sheena. 'Looking for Andrew.'

He nodded. 'Still clear, Trevor?' he whispered.

Trevor Purse peered around the doorjamb and beckoned elaborately like an elf in a pantomime.

'Go!' said Martin to the room in general. 'Follow Trevor. Out the kitchen window, then up the front. Hide in the bush across the road. Trevor's wife and the other women are there. He'll show you. Quick and quiet as you can.'

Still beckoning over his shoulder, Trevor ran from the room on tiptoe, looking more like an elf than ever. Lily bolted after him, beating Dulcie to the door by half a head only because Dulcie paused to seize her son's arm on the way.

Holly grabbed Una's wheelchair and tried to turn it. It wouldn't budge. She tugged at it, but it was wedged between Moonie's body and the leg of the table.

'Sheena!' she hissed desperately.

Sheena glanced over her shoulder, hesitated, then ran back to help.

'Hurry up, will you?' Una complained as the two women heaved at the chair, trying in vain to free it. 'We haven't got all day!'

Holly could have hit her.

Eric came running. He elbowed Sheena and Holly aside, dragged the table a little to the left and jerked the chair free, lifting the wheels from the ground in the process.

'Be careful, you fool!' growled Una, clinging to the chair arms. 'You'll have me over! Trying to finish what you started last night, are you?'

'You lousy, ungrateful old besom!' spat Sheena. 'It'd serve you right if we left you to rot!'

But Eric didn't miss a beat. Swivelling the wheelchair around he reached for the gun on the table.

'Don't worry about it,' Holly told him. 'It's a fake.'

Eric ignored her. He picked up the gun, shook a couple of maggots from the barrel and began wheeling Una rapidly toward the door, with Sheena striding behind him.

Holly shrugged and trotted after them. Maybe Eric thought the gun might be real after all. It was possible that it was, but Holly didn't think so. Una had seemed to know what she was talking about. In fact, eccentric and obsessive as Una was, she hadn't been wrong about very much so far. She'd been right about the sterling silver teaspoons, for example—the teaspoons that had been hidden at the back of the sideboard drawer, and lay right now under the library table. She'd been right about Dulcie's money, too. Maybe she'd been right about everything.

Holly's skin prickled. The room seemed to darken. Fighting off the unreal feeling that had become very familiar over the last few days—the feeling that she wasn't actually awake, but was in the grip of some long and complicated nightmare—she hurried to catch up with Sheena.

Trevor Purse had reappeared in the doorway. Presumably he'd come back to see what was keeping them. Hopping nervously on the spot, brandishing his giant torch, he now looked less like an elf and more like a feverish cricket.

'What's with the dead rat?' Holly heard Eric murmur.

'Someone's gift for Ms. Cage,' Una said grimly. 'Of course, it turns out her name isn't Cage at all.'

Eric nodded as if he'd suspected that all along.

'If the police aren't here, how did you get in?' Sheena asked him.

'Kitchen window,' said Eric. 'Martin took out the bolts and the bars all lifted off in one piece, easy as pie. Old Maggott got done. He must be spinning in his grave.'

Una gave a harsh bark of laughter. Sheena chuckled.

Martin grinned at them both. 'Let's get out of here,' he said.

And at that exact moment, the staircase outside began to squeak and there was the echoing sound of voices.

Holly's stomach turned over.

'They're coming down!' croaked Trevor, springing back from the doorway and dropping into a half-crouch.

Martin swore under his breath and pushed the door shut.

'Sheena, take Una down the other end. Down to the windows. Get behind the couch if you can move it.' He glanced coldly at Holly. 'You, too!'

'Thanks for the permission,' Holly snapped, very irritated.

Martin and Eric flattened themselves against the wall on either side of the door. Trevor Purse crouched by the sideboard, killer torch at the ready.

'Don't listen to him!' hissed Una, as Sheena spun the wheelchair around and began hurrying past the table. 'He needs to take those lowlifes by surprise. We have to be sitting where we were or they'll know there's trouble the second they open the door.'

Right again, Una, thought Holly. She caught Sheena's eye, darted back to her chair, and sat down. Sheena ran with Una to the head of the table, then ran back to take her own place. They all folded their hands on the tabletop and waited for Martin to notice them and protest.

Martin, however, was busy examining the gun that Eric had passed him.

'Replica,' he said at last, putting it down on the floor.

'We told you that,' Una said impatiently, not troubling to keep her voice down.

Martin looked up. When he saw the three women sitting at the table he raised his eyebrows, but didn't comment.

Mr. Cool, Holly thought sourly. She wondered what it would take to ruffle this man. If she knew, she would take pleasure in doing it.

'I can't speak for the other one, though,' Una went on blithely. 'And the tall fellow, the one with the ponytail, has a knife. He's a psychopath. You can tell by his eyes.'

'Nice mates you've got,' Martin said to Holly. She blinked. Was he joking? He didn't look as if he was. His mouth was hard.

'They're not my mates,' she said. 'They're nothing to do with me.'

'Tell us another one,' muttered Eric. 'I've got eyes.'

Whatever that meant. Holly stared at him, but he turned his head away.

The stair squeaks stopped. The voices were louder. There seemed to be only two of them, but then, Holly reflected with a shiver, Bernie was the silent type.

She noted that a few maggots had squirmed almost to the table edge. She hoped they wouldn't fall into her lap. Then she wondered what a few maggots on her lap mattered when she was probably about to get shot.

The door swung open. Fen lumbered in.

'Get up,' he said, staring straight at Holly. 'You're coming with—'

His voice broke off in a little squeak as Eric's pipe landed squarely on his head. His knees buckled. Martin caught him neatly and lowered him to the ground.

There was a moment's silence, broken by the sound of the front door being unlocked and creaking open. Eric, Martin and Trevor leaned slightly forward. Holly, Sheena and Una sat rigidly still, their eyes on the open doorway.

'Fen!' Skinner called, his voice echoing in the hallway. 'Moonie! Stop farting around! Just bring her out, will you?'

Receiving no answer he swore comprehensively and they heard him hurrying back toward the library. 'Come *on*, you bloody morons! I want her in the car before Bernie comes down. He's not happy, and you know how he gets when—'

He scurried through the door, his head poking forward tortoise-like on his scrawny neck. Martin brought the spanner down efficiently and, without a sound, Skinner sagged into Eric's waiting arms.

'Hope I haven't killed him,' said Martin. 'I didn't realise he was a shrimp.'

Eric shrugged.

'He's the one with the gun,' Holly told them. Her voice sounded strange and breathy.

Martin unearthed the gun from one of Skinner's jacket pockets.

'Another fake,' he said, as he took it out and checked it.

'Are you sure?' Una snapped.

Martin looked at her. 'Pretty sure. The badge on the butt says *Super Spy Junior.*'

Una snorted. Sheena sighed. Eric sniggered. Holly clenched her fists, seething with rage and self-loathing.

'The front door's open,' whispered Trevor, who had crawled to the doorway to look out. 'Do we wait for the other one, or—'

He froze like a hunting dog on point.

'Leanne!' he squeaked. 'Leanne, I told you to stay... *Get back!*'

The stairs shrieked. Heavy footsteps pounded downward, very fast. Trevor sprang to his feet.

'Leanne!' he bellowed, bolting out into the entrance hall. *'Run!'*

As the door swung gently closed behind him there was a thump, followed by silence—a terrible, blank silence. Then slow, squeaky footsteps sounded on the marble floor. The library door swung open again. And there, framed in the gap, was the tall, lanky figure of Bernie the psychopath. He was clasping Leanne Purse close to his chest. The point of his knife was pressed to Leanne's soft white throat.

Eric and Martin stood immobile on either side of the door, their weapons raised. Both of them were sweating. Martin looked at Holly, a question in his eyes. She shook her head slightly. One sudden move and Leanne would be dead. She had no doubt of that.

Bernie pushed the door open and took a step forward, carrying Leanne with him like a life-sized doll. His eyes slid from one side to the other, registering Martin and Eric's presence without surprise.

'Drop them,' he said softly.

As the two men hesitated, he moved his hand very slightly. A bright drop of blood welled up beneath the point of the knife and trickled down Leanne's neck. Her eyes widened, and her mouth opened, but she didn't make a sound.

Martin and Eric looked at one another, and lowered their arms. The spanner and the piece of pipe clattered to the ground.

'Back,' Bernie ordered.

The men shuffled back.

'Further,' said Bernie.

As they obeyed, he took another step forward, hauling Leanne with him. He looked swiftly around, noting Holly, Sheena and Una, the rat on the tabletop, Fen and Moonie sitting up groggily, holding their heads, and Skinner still lying huddled on the floor. He gave Skinner a negligent kick. Skinner groaned, and Bernie kicked him again.

'The police are coming, you know,' Una Maggott said loudly. 'They'll be here any minute.'

Bernie ignored her completely. His eyes were on Holly. 'You!' he said. 'Here!'

Holly stood up. She heard Una order her to stop, but she paid no attention. She skirted the end of the table and moved forward, past the rigid figures of Eric and Martin, past the groaning Fen and Skinner. What else could she do, with the knife point hovering a millimetre above the little cut on Leanne Purse's neck, from which blood still flowed, a scarlet line that ended in a spreading stain on the lacy edge of the pink camisole?

She reached Bernie and in a single, fluid movement he thrust Leanne aside and grabbed her.

Chapter Twenty-two

Holly felt herself pressed hard against Bernie's body. She registered automatically that he used Blue Stratos after-shave, and no deodorant. She felt the knife blade at her neck. She felt a sensation behind her feet, heard a sobbing sound, and knew that it was Trevor Purse, crawling through the doorway and finding Leanne safe.

That's good, she thought hazily. That's very good. Not that she wanted to die, but if it was inevitable, it was nice to know it had been in a good cause.

She realised her eyes were shut, and opened them. The first thing she saw was Martin's face. He was looking straight at her, and his eyes weren't as hard as blue ice anymore. They were agonised, in fact. That was strange. He hadn't seemed to like her much.

'Where's McNish?' Bernie muttered in her ear.

'I don't know,' Holly said.

She felt a stinging pain as the knife pierced the skin of her neck. It wasn't so bad, actually. It was like when old doctor McGrath back in Perth had said, 'Now, you'll just feel a little prick…'—a phrase that had always made her smile.

'Where's the money?' asked Bernie, still in that same low mutter.

'I don't think there *is* any money,' Holly said. 'I think Andrew spent it. Or lost it. Or paid other debts with it. He was skint, at the end. I think he'd been close to the edge for a long time.'

She knew it was true. It was as if, in this moment of crisis, her mind had suddenly cleared on one matter at least. Andrew McNish, thief and swindler, had been fond of her, in his way. If he'd had a fortune stashed away, he wouldn't have taken her money.

She waited for another sting, but it didn't come. Bernie had become very still. He seemed to be thinking. To take her mind off what the final results of his cogitations might be, she focused on her surroundings.

Fen had staggered to his feet and was hauling Skinner up. Trevor and Leanne Purse were sitting on the floor not far away. They had their arms around one another, and both of them were crying. There was an angry red swelling just under Trevor's right eye. Leanne's neck had almost stopped bleeding, but her pink camisole would never be the same, in Holly's opinion, even if she knew the trick about soaking bloodstains in cold water.

Eric was standing with Martin by the bookshelves. Sweat beaded his forehead and his mouth was hanging open. Maybe he had finally realised that he'd been wrong about Holly's motives and allegiances. Maybe they both had. She took grim satisfaction in that, then wondered if she was losing it. If it came to a choice between someone thinking badly of her and having a knife stuck in her throat, which would she choose?

Sheena and Una were still sitting at the table. Sheena's face looked frozen. There was no way of telling what she was feeling. Una was scowling and her nostrils were pinched together, possibly because beside her the odoriferous Moonie had crawled to his knees.

Bernie made a low growling sound and turned very slightly toward the door. The muscles of his knife hand tensed. Holly felt a wave of dizziness. Here it comes, she thought. She shut her eyes again, and braced herself.

But after a while she realised that she was still alive. The knife hadn't touched her again. Or if it had, she hadn't felt it. All she could feel was the iron band of Bernie's arm, and the tickling of the blood running slowly down her neck and on into her cleavage.

She found herself wishing that she wasn't wearing her favourite bra—the white lace one with the embroidered pink rosebuds. She told herself that someone on the point of death should be thinking of more spiritual things than bras, but nothing spiritual occurred to her. It was hard to think when her mind was filled with the pounding of her own heartbeat, vague, echoing whispers, and a clicking sound that reminded her of high heels tapping on a marble floor.

The whispers suddenly became intelligible.

Death! one of the whisperers said. *I feel it! Oh, my God!*

Wait! said another. *Take it steady, dear! We don't know what...*

The tapping sped up, grew louder. Then abruptly it stopped and there was a low, gasping cry.

That's not in my head, Holly thought slowly. That was real.

She opened her eyes.

Abigail and Mrs. Moss were gaping at her through the open door. *'Holly!'* Abigail breathed. She looked haunted and dishevelled. Leaves and little sticks clung to her long green dress, her purple scarf and her tangled hair. Mrs. Moss looked more normal, but her lipstick was smeared and her eyes were round with fear.

'In,' Bernie ordered. Holly felt the knife point just graze the wound in her neck. She winced. It hurt a lot more this time.

Mrs. Moss squeaked and seized Abigail's arm. Together they stumbled past Bernie and Holly, into the room.

'Sit,' Bernie told them, jerking his head at the table. And when he swung Holly around she saw that they had done it, taking the chairs abandoned by Dulcie and Sebastian.

'They've been *torturing* you, Holly!' cried Mrs. Moss, staring in horror at the maggoty rat. 'Oh, the *smell* in here!'

'Some of it's him,' said Una, nodding at Moonie. 'He's covered in vomit.'

'Shut up!' shouted Moonie. A maggot dropped over the edge of the table onto the back of his hand. He yelled and scrambled up, shaking the hand violently and rubbing it on his trousers.

'There, Abby,' Mrs. Moss whispered, patting Abigail's hand. 'A dead rat, that's all you felt. Just a dead rat.'

Abigail looked unconvinced.

'Where did it come from?' Fen asked stupidly.

Shuddering, Moonie nodded at the padded envelope still lying on the table. Fen lumbered over and picked it up.

'*Holly Cage,*' he read aloud. '*Per-son-al.*' His brow puckered.

'That's her,' said Moonie, jerking his head at Holly. 'She gave them a phony name.' He expanded slightly, as if being privy to fresh information would improve his damaged status.

As Fen turned the envelope over, a sheet of paper slid out and flapped onto the tabletop along with several stained rat hairs and a few more maggots. Everyone looked. The message on the paper, made up of words cut out of a newspaper, looked like a poison pen letter in an old-fashioned mystery novel: GIVE UP AND GET OUT OR ELSE.

Holly stared blankly at the message. Her stomach was churning.

'Someone trying to scare her off,' said Moonie, and gave a weird, high giggle.

'McNish?' Fen asked slowly, his forehead puckering. 'What for? She's working for him, isn't she? She's his tart. She was in his house. She knocked off that dick O'Brien who was after him.'

'Shit eh!' Holly heard Eric exclaim with what sounded like respect.

'Holly did *not* knock off Mr. O'Brien,' Mrs. Moss cried indignantly. 'Mr. O'Brien croaked before we got there. Long before.'

Bernie turned his head to look at her. Holly felt his knife hand relax slightly.

'McNish wouldn't touch a dead rat,' said Moonie. 'It's not his style.'

Skinner gnawed at his bottom lip. 'You're right,' he said slowly. 'Plus, whoever addressed that envelope thought her name was Holly Cage.'

Yes, Holly thought. And who is Holly Cage? The private investigator Una hired to convince the police that Andrew McNish hadn't stolen and run, but had been murdered. Persuasion hadn't stopped her. Claims that Una was senile hadn't stopped her. So threats were the next logical step. Death threats, in fact, if that maggot-ridden rat enclosed with the note had any meaning at all. Someone had prepared that nasty little package and left it in the sideboard for her to find. Someone who hoped—who believed—that she was gutless enough to take the warning and go. Cold anger swept through her. Who did they think she was?

'For the last time, I'm *not* working for Andrew McNish,' she spat at Skinner. 'I've been trying to find him, that's all. He ripped me off just like he ripped you off, and I wanted my money back.'

'Bullshit,' said Skinner, but for the first time he sounded uncertain. He was eyeing Holly rather nervously—a bit like Lloyd used to do when, very occasionally, she became what he called 'overexcited.' Possibly she was looking a little wild-eyed. Well, too bad, she told herself. Knife at her throat or no knife at her throat, if anyone had a right to a temper tantrum at this moment, she did.

'Didn't your goons here tell you I was sleeping on the floor in an empty house with nothing but gherkins and dry cereal to eat?' she raged at Skinner. 'Why do you think I was doing that? Because Andrew McNish had cleaned out our bank account and left me flat, that's why! Because I had nowhere else to go!'

Skinner glanced sharply at Fen.

'She didn't tell Bernie and me any of that stuff,' Fen said defensively. 'She just said McNish weren't there.'

He looked at Bernie for confirmation, but Bernie didn't say a word.

'Well, what was I supposed to say?' Holly shouted. 'I wasn't going to tell two complete strangers my private business!'

'You might have told me, however,' said Una.

The rasping voice penetrated the roar that was filling Holly's ears. She forced herself to meet Una's furious eyes and her own rage abruptly died.

'I'm sorry, Una,' she said. 'I meant to, but…things got out of hand.'

The feebleness of the excuse brought the blood rushing to her cheeks. She knew that she had more important things to worry about than being exposed as a lying schemer, but even her awareness of Bernie's knife didn't dull her feeling of burning shame. She was acutely aware of Mrs. Moss, Eric, Martin…She could imagine what they were thinking of her.

'You mean you're not a detective at all?' Trevor Purse burst out. 'But I hired you to follow *my wife!*'

'I trusted you!' Una had begun to tremble. Her face was a mask of baffled fury. 'You lied to me! You took my money! You promised you'd search the house. Get sniffer dogs to find the body.'

'Oh, Lord,' Sheena muttered.

'What body?' Skinner was blinking rapidly. He seemed to be having trouble taking all this in.

'Andrew's body!' Una shouted, her voice cracking into a screech. 'He's been murdered, I tell you! The teaspoons prove it!'

Her cheeks were mottled red. Her tearless eyes were burning.

'Who *are* you people?' wailed Moonie. Holding his stomach, he edged away from Una and made for the door, looking distinctly queasy again.

'Mad as a meat-axe,' Holly heard him mutter to Skinner as he passed him. 'They're all mad as meat-axes. No wonder McNish pissed off.'

'Where do you think you're going?' Skinner demanded feebly, recoiling as the stench rising from Moonie's clothes reached his nostrils at full strength.

Moonie kept moving. 'This has been a balls-up to end all balls-ups,' he called back over his shoulder. 'I've had it with this place.' He disappeared through the door and they heard his shoes squeaking on the tiles of the entrance hall as he made a rapid departure.

Fen stared at Skinner in bovine enquiry, his eyebrows raised, his mouth hanging slightly open.

Skinner bared his teeth, then bowed to the inevitable. 'Okay,' he said. 'So it's a washout.'

'What about that bag Bernie found upstairs?' asked Fen.

Holly's heart gave a sickening thud. Una hissed.

'What about it?' Skinner snapped.

'It was his—McNish's.'

'So what? There was nothing in it—just clothes and shit.'

'But it was stuffed in behind the hot water tank,' Fen persisted. 'Why was it hid? Maybe the old tart's right. Maybe McNish never left. Maybe someone did cool him off.'

Someone in the room moaned softly. Holly thought it was Abigail.

'And maybe he just wanted to travel light,' Skinner snarled. 'Who cares?' He turned to Bernie. 'Let the stupid bitch go. She doesn't know anything. We're out of here.'

But Bernie didn't move and his grip on Holly didn't relax.

'You said McNish was here,' he said to Skinner. 'McNish and the money.'

Fear sparked in Skinner's eyes, and was instantly suppressed. Trial expressions of apology, irritation and superiority flickered across his face in quick succession before he finally plumped for bravado.

'We all make mistakes, right?' he said carelessly. 'I thought the little shit was here, but he's not. So sue me.'

Bernie made a low growling sound and the next moment, miraculously, the pressure on Holly's throat had vanished, and Skinner's eyes were popping like a startled rabbit's as he backed hurriedly toward the door with Bernie prowling after him.

'Now, Bernie,' Skinner chattered. 'Don't take it like that. You're upset, I can understand you're upset, but—' Abruptly he whirled around and bolted. Bernie went after him, taking his time.

Left alone, Fen looked helplessly around the room, opening and closing his fists. Holly felt almost sorry for him.

'You'd better keep your traps shut about this,' he said, with a feeble attempt at a bullying tone. 'You set the cops on us and we'll tell them you snuffed McNish.'

There was a roar outside as the four-wheel drive started up. Fen's lip twitched. He turned and ran.

Chapter Twenty-three

Holly stared at the empty doorway, listening to the sound of the four-wheel drive bellowing and spraying gravel as it reversed through the gates. People were chattering around her and saying her name, but she didn't seem to be able to respond. Her mind was curiously blank.

Slowly she turned away from the door. The room seemed to have begun moving around her. It was as if she were standing in the centre of some weird homemade merry-go-round that featured furniture instead of swans and white horses. Interesting, she thought dreamily, watching the table with Una at its head sail by, closely followed by Mrs. Moss and the sideboard.

She heard an exclamation, and felt movement beside her. An arm was wrapped around her shoulders. The arm was strong and reassuring, so Holly leaned into it and closed her eyes. The next moment she was sitting in a chair. The room was buzzing with voices, but a man was talking quietly to her, close to her ear, telling her to put her head down. Holly thought she might as well do it. She felt very tired.

'That's it,' the man said. 'You'll be right.'

Martin, Holly thought. Martin the ute driver. Martin of the bright blue eyes, who talked easily to Sheena and joked with the woman in the cake shop, but didn't care for Holly Love.

'Poor little thing! What a terrible ordeal!' That was Mrs. Moss.

'Terrible ordeal indeed! What about *my wife*?' That thin, chirping voice was familiar too. Holly couldn't put a name to

it, just at the moment, but it made her think of crickets and…
bedbugs. She shivered.

'Relax,' Martin murmured, squeezing her shoulder. 'It's all over.'

'It certainly is *not* over!' the chirping voice objected. 'Not as far as I'm concerned. This woman led those criminals to that bug-ridden motel and put *my wife* in danger of her life!'

'Now, Trevor, that's *very* unfair!' Mrs. Moss exclaimed.

Trevor Purse, Holly thought, memory clicking back into place. He and Mrs. Moss must have got onto first name terms while duct-taped to the light post.

She was feeling more herself now, but she didn't want to raise her head. The tabletop was cool and smooth on her forehead. Martin's hand on her shoulder was comforting. And she wasn't ready to face anyone yet—especially Una Maggott.

'Holly had no idea those crims were shadowing her, did she?' Mrs. Moss argued. 'As the smelly one said, it was all a balls-up. It could happen to anyone!'

I doubt that, Holly thought glumly, and slowly she made herself sit up straight. She couldn't leave her defence to Mrs. Moss. This was her mess and she had to deal with it. As she had feared, the moment she moved Martin's hand slipped from her shoulder. She felt sad about that, but it couldn't be helped.

She had braced herself to face Una, but Una was no longer sitting at the head of the table. No one was sitting at the table except Holly. More time had passed than she had realised, it seemed. Eric, wearing bright pink polythene gloves that contrasted oddly with his shimmering jumpsuit, was sweeping up the maggots on the tabletop with a dustpan and brush and tipping them into a bulging supermarket bag that presumably already contained the rat. The padded envelope and the absurd threatening letter had gone.

A glass of water appeared in front of Holly, held firmly in a capable freckled hand. She turned a little, saw Sheena bending toward her, and recoiled, pressing her lips together and shaking her head.

'Let me,' she heard Abigail say.

Expressionless, Sheena withdrew. Then it was Abigail offering the glass, and this time Holly drank.

'Thanks,' she said. She looked up into Abigail's shadowed eyes and her scalp prickled.

'It isn't the rat,' Abigail murmured, her lips barely moving. 'The feeling's too strong. Much too strong. It's human. Secret. Hidden. In this house.'

A memory flowed into Holly's mind—the memory of Abigail standing in Reenie Halliday's hallway, clutching a cat's brush and saying: 'He's here.' She remembered how disbelieving she had felt then—and how wrong she'd been. She remembered the question she had almost blurted out afterwards as she and Abigail drove up Stillwaters Road, just before they saw Mrs. Moss and Lawrence gobbling hot chips outside the bookshop. It wasn't quite so easy to ask the question now. Now she was more fearful about what the result might be. But she asked it anyway. How could she not?

'Could you find it, Abigail? Would you try?'

Abigail took a quick breath, nodded, and turned away.

'And don't forget, Trevor,' Mrs. Moss was saying. 'Mrs. Purse put *herself* in danger the second time. The goon with the knife would never have got her if she'd stayed in the bush with us, instead of bolting into the house to find you as soon as she saw that the door was open. And Holly let herself be taken as a hostage in place of her. That was *very* brave!'

'Be that as it may, I would never have hired the woman if I'd known she wasn't a professional!' said Trevor Purse hotly. 'I'll be reporting her to the police the moment they get here. She took my money under false pretences.'

'Don't know where the false pretences come in,' drawled Eric, straightening up with the rat bag dangling from one pink finger. 'Miz Cage did what you paid her for, didn't she? Followed your lady to the mo-tel? Reported back? That's what you said when Martin flagged you down on the highway and told you where to turn off.'

'That's right!' cried Mrs. Moss.

'Well—yes, yes, I suppose so,' Purse spluttered. 'But the point is, the first thing I saw when I got to that motel was Leanne being driven away by two—'

'And whose fault was *that*?' cried a high, trembling voice that Holly didn't recognise.

She turned to look. Just in front of the doorway, Leanne Purse, chubby and bloodstained, was facing her husband, spitting like an angry kitten. Trevor himself was looking astounded. His curved arm was hanging foolishly in the air, as if Leanne had just torn herself away from his embrace.

'It was *your* fault!' Leanne almost screamed. '*Your* fault, Trevor Purse!'

'*My* fault!' her husband gasped.

'Yes!' Leanne stamped her foot. 'None of this would have happened if I hadn't run out of the motel like a madwoman the second that man who was robbed gave the alarm! And I only did that because of you! I was terrified of getting mixed up with the police, so you'd find out I'd taken on one of Petula's shifts.'

Trevor recovered himself enough to manage a fussy little frown. 'Yes, well, Leanne, you know how I feel about my wife working, let alone working as a *cleaner* at a—'

'And what's more,' Leanne raged on, 'those criminals wouldn't have even *been* at the motel if *you* hadn't hired a detective to spy on me—*me*, your own *wife!*'

Trevor went red to the roots of his scanty hair. 'I—I was worried,' he stammered. 'I was out of my mind with worry, Leanne!'

Leanne tossed her head, burst into tears, and stormed past him, out of the room. Trevor spun round to go after her, his face crumpled in dismay.

'If I were you, I'd get her home, Trevor,' Mrs. Moss advised. 'I really don't think it would be wise for either of you to speak to the police. The story would be bound to get into the *Gazette* and it doesn't reflect very well on you, really.'

Trevor stopped in mid-stride and turned around, his eyes bulging.

'We won't say anything,' Mrs. Moss said reassuringly. 'Your secret is safe with us. Isn't it, Holly?'

Holly swallowed, and nodded.

'They took the Mazda keys,' croaked Purse. 'And the van will have to be towed. It's—'

'Oh, I'm sure our friend here can hot-wire the Mazda for you, Trevor,' Mrs. Moss said, smiling at Eric with little-old-lady confidence. 'He knows all about cars. He was Mr. Maggott's chauffeur, you know.'

'Eric's got his hands full. I'll do it.'

Holly turned and saw Martin easing himself away from the bookshelf. She hadn't realised he was still in the room. She'd assumed he'd left with Sheena. She was absurdly glad that he hadn't.

'You *are* kind,' said Mrs. Moss, beaming.

With a little wail of thanks, Trevor Purse departed in pursuit of his wife.

'That was neat,' Martin commented, as he went by Holly's chair. 'But Purse was the least of your worries. Una's gone to ring Allnut. Feel like a bit of fresh air?'

Holly shook her head. 'I'm okay.'

He looked at her quizzically. 'If you change your mind, the ute's parked in the lay-by,' he remarked, and followed Trevor.

Holly stared after him.

'I think he's suggesting that we should split, dear,' whispered Mrs. Moss. 'He's offering to help us make our getaway. It will be a squeeze in that truck, but it might be best.'

'No.' Holly shook her head again. 'I've got to talk to Una.' She stood up and took Abigail's arm. It was quivering as if something were buzzing inside it.

'But the fuzz will be here any minute,' said Mrs. Moss. 'In fact, I can't understand why they aren't here already. It's disgraceful, really. For all they know we're lying here wallowing in our own blood!'

'Oh, Enid, *don't*!' Abigail shuddered.

'Oh, sorry, dear.' Mrs. Moss tapped her lips as if to reprove herself and noticed Eric was staring. 'Abby saw blood when we came into the house, you see,' she told him brightly. 'Blood and death. She thought it was Holly's.'

'I was *sure* it was Holly's!' said Abigail.

'Well, it wasn't, was it?' Mrs. Moss soothed. 'Holly's here, alive and well. I was just saying that it's very bad of the police—'

'The cops never got called,' said Eric, clearly glad of the chance to steer the conversation onto more normal lines. 'When Martin saw Miz Cage grabbed in Mealey he thought it was just a sort of…pro-fessional disagreement. You know?'

'What?' Holly gaped at him.

'Like, you'd double-crossed your co-lleagues, or something?' said Eric, slouching to the door with the dustpan, brush and noxious bag held well out in front of him. 'We both saw the four-wheel drive tailing you yesterday. Martin saw it come with you into Mealey Marshes. I saw it following us here. Never occurred to us you didn't know. It was pretty obvious.'

'I just thought there were a lot of black four-wheel drives around.' Holly shook her head. It would have been laughable if it hadn't been so deeply embarrassing.

'Yeah, well, our mistake,' said Eric, leading the way into the entrance hall. 'But the way we saw it, cops would've just complicated things, so we thought we'd handle it ourselves. We didn't know about the guns then, o' course. Or Miz Purse. Or the psycho-path.'

'I see,' Holly said weakly. 'Well…thanks for the thought.'

She heard the sound of the Mazda starting up. Martin had wasted no time in getting the Purses on their way. But as Eric had said, the Purses were really the least of her worries.

Eric glanced around and lowered his voice. 'Miz M still thinks the cops are going to turn up, but she'll twig sooner or later and put in a call. And Allnut will be here soon. Just slip out and get down to the lay-by. I'll cover for you.'

'Well, Eric, at least that establishes where *your* loyalties lie,' a voice rasped from the other side of the hall.

Una Maggott appeared in the doorway of her room. Her eyes were blazing. Andrew's mobile phone and the box of teaspoons rested on her knees. Behind her, the python slid behind glass.

Eric swore under his breath. At the same moment, Sheena emerged from the back of the house, carrying a tea tray. Seeing the confrontation, she halted, her eyes wary. Outside, a car horn tooted and there was the screech of tires on bitumen, but no one looked around.

'You can get out, Eric,' Una said coldly. 'Now. And you can take your snake and the hearse with you!'

'But I've got nowhere to keep them!' Eric protested, looking panic-stricken. 'You know I haven't!'

'You should have thought of that before you decided to transfer your loyalties to Ms. Cage, or whatever her name is,' Una spat, wheeling herself further into the hall. 'I want you out, and I'm not bound to give house room to your property.'

Eric was white to the lips. 'You can't do this,' he said. 'Not with no warning. Cleopatra and the hearse were Mr. M's most—'

'Prized possessions,' sneered Una Maggott. 'Yes. So the will said. That's why he left them to you, isn't it?'

She looked at the smirking portrait on the wall and her face darkened. 'Just as he left every stick of furniture, every pot and pan, every portable object in *my* house, to *Sheena*.'

'It was all he *could* leave me, Una!' Sheena exclaimed, her knuckles whitening on the handles of the tray. 'By the end it was all he had, except for the pension!'

'Keep out of this!' Una said, without looking around. 'This has nothing to do with you. You got what you could out of me, then stayed on while it suited you, and gave notice when it suited you. And now Eric is leaving too. Well, good riddance! Good riddance to both of you!'

She faced Eric with her chin jutting out, her lips set. She was icy. Hateful. Or so Holly would have thought if she hadn't glimpsed, beneath that bitter mask, the face of the girl in the old snapshot—the girl who had grown up to lose her mother, her father and her home in a single year, and decided that trust led only to pain. The girl who had eventually transformed herself into La Dragonne, and ended up old, crippled and alone.

'Ms. Maggott, Eric knows I didn't mean you any harm,' Holly said. 'That's the only reason he—'

'Don't speak to me, girl!' Una rasped. 'Save your lies for the police.' She glanced through the open front door. 'Ah, there you are, Allnut!' she called. 'Just in time, for a change.'

Cliff Allnut, red and startled-looking but impeccable in his natty golfing gear, was hurrying over the churned-up gravel. Dulcie, Sebastian and Lily, having finally decided it was safe to emerge from hiding, were trailing after him, all looking as if they had been rolling in a compost heap.

The gang's all here, Holly thought, and felt a bubble of laughter rise from her chest to her throat where it stuck and burned.

'What's been happening here?' Allnut panted, nimbly skirting the abandoned green van and jogging up the steps to the verandah. 'A madman in a white car just nearly ran me down! What's this about *gangsters*? Dulcie says the Cage woman—'

'I finally got the house searched, Allnut!' Una crowed. 'We found the spoons! And Andrew's bag! We also found out that it was the boy who stole Dulcie's money. Put that in your pipe and smoke it!'

Allnut stopped dead. His mouth fell open. Behind him, Dulcie made an incomprehensible gobbling sound.

'*Now* try telling the police I should be locked up!' Una shouted, picking up the blue box and shaking it at him. '*Now* try telling them I'm senile, Allnut! I've got my proof. There'll be sniffer dogs here before you know it.'

Well, it was now or never. Holly took a small step forward, pulling Abigail with her.

'You don't need to wait for a sniffer dog, Una,' she said. 'If Andrew's body is here, Abigail can find it.'

Una's lip curled. 'Oh, yes,' she jeered. 'Eric told me you shared your office with a mind-reader. He thought it would put me off you, no doubt, but I was desperate enough to think it didn't matter. So this is her, is it? And you're offering her services?

In return for not prosecuting you for swindling me out of my money, I suppose.'

'What?' Allnut suddenly looked alert and ten times more intelligent, as if the word 'money' had activated a light switch in his brain. He strode into the hall.

'This is absurd!' cried Dulcie, dodging and weaving to get a clear view around him. 'Una, you can't possibly—'

'Keep quiet!' Una snapped. 'Well, Ms. Love?'

A satisfyingly sharp, pious retort along the lines of: *No strings, Ms. Maggott—I only want to find out the truth* flashed across Holly's mind, but she dismissed it. No point in cutting off your nose to spite your face, as her mother always said. Still, her spirit revolted against the idea of using Abigail as a bargaining chip. She thought of a dignified compromise and seized on it.

'I'm not asking for any promises,' she said, lifting her chin. 'I'm just asking you to keep an open mind for now. About me—and about Eric as well. That's all.'

'How generous!' Una was still sneering.

Holly heard Eric suppress a sigh. She glanced at Abigail and her heart quailed. Abigail was looking far from impressive. Her emerald green dress and purple scarf looked garish and tawdry in these surroundings. She still had leaves in her plainly dyed hair. Her eyes no longer looked dramatically haunted, but rather vacant and confused. She was, in fact, the very picture of a middle-aged charlatan who had floundered way out of her depth.

Beside her, Mrs. Moss teetered on her high heels, looking rather wistfully toward the front door. Holly looked, too, and saw Martin leaning against the doorjamb, exactly as he had done the day before when he came to report on the fenceline. Meeting her eyes, he shrugged slightly: *Well, I offered. Too late now.*

'So what does your tame mind-reader have to tell us from beyond, Ms. Love?' Una enquired nastily. 'Can she speak for herself? So far she's done nothing but stare into space. Is that part of the act? If so—'

'The chandelier fell,' Abigail suddenly declared in a hollow voice. 'It was huge. Glittering. It fell—here, where I'm standing now.' She shivered all over.

'Oh, spare us,' Sheena muttered.

Lily laughed derisively.

But Una had sat up, her face as shocked as if she'd just been slapped.

'Don't be taken in, Una,' Cliff Allnut said with contempt. 'This is how these people work. Any fool can see there was a chandelier here once. The chains are still hanging from the ceiling!'

Holly saw Mrs. Moss give him a surprised, appraising look. Yes, she thought. Allnut shouldn't be underestimated. He was a solicitor, after all.

'Those chains could have been for any sort of light fitting,' she said. 'It didn't have to be a chandelier.' This argument sounded feeble, even to her. She wished heartily that Abigail had experienced a more convincing vision at this moment. No doubt a psychic couldn't pick and choose, but a pool of blood, for example, or a sinister locked chest, would have made more of an impression.

'It was a chandelier,' Allnut insisted, suddenly reverting to stupidity. 'It fell years ago, in my father's time. He told me.'

'Oh, she must have seen the old pictures in the kitchen!' Dulcie shrieked. 'Una, there are *pictures* in the *kitchen* showing that chandelier hanging at the foot of the stairs!'

'Shut up, Mum,' Sebastian muttered, staring at Abigail in fascination.

'She hasn't been in the kitchen,' Una said.

'That one probably has,' Lily put in, looking down her nose at Holly.

Holly took an angry breath to deny it, but before she could burst into speech, Una held up her hand.

'That's enough,' she said. 'I think...I'd like to try this.' She looked straight at Abigail. 'Will you do it?'

Abigail nodded slowly. 'There is an unquiet soul in this house,' she said. 'We have to set it free.'

'Oh, Lord,' Holly heard Sheena groan. At the front door, Martin slightly adjusted his position and stared down at his boots. Holly felt herself blushing, wished fervently that Abigail could do her stuff without resorting to melodrama, then was appalled at her own disloyalty.

'Do you need something of Andrew's to help you look, Abigail?' she whispered. 'Like with Lancelot?'

'Who's Lancelot?' Sebastian asked eagerly.

Abigail shook her head. 'The call is very clear,' she said, and looked up the stairs.

'I knew it!' hissed Una Maggott, clenching her fists. 'Go up, then! Go and look! Go!'

Chapter Twenty-four

Holly had expected the search for Andrew McNish to be similar to the hunt for Lancelot the cat, but it wasn't. This time there was no indecision at all. Abigail's face grew more and more sombre as she climbed the squeaking stairs with Holly and Mrs. Moss close behind her. At the top, where doors hung open exposing ransacked rooms, and the faint, sweet smell of death drifted in the air, she paused only to catch her breath before turning to the right.

Swiftly she led the way past Sheena's room, and the room with the leaky roof. Toward Andrew's room? Toward the room where Rollo Maggott had kept watch on his gates? Toward the bathroom doorway, where a black leather bag lay gaping on its side like a disembowelled corpse, its contents spilling raggedly onto the chipped mosaic tiles?

It was when Holly saw that bag, recognised it as Andrew's, recognised the red T-shirt on top of the pile—never one of Andrew's favourites, but the very one he had been wearing in the photograph she had given to O'Brien—that everything suddenly threatened to become real, and her heart began to fail her. She found she was panting. The odour of death was making her head swim. The corridor seemed thick with it. She wanted to call to Abigail to wait, to slow down, but the swirling dust motes, gleaming in the light from the bathroom window, seemed to have caught in her throat.

Abigail stopped abruptly. 'Here,' she said.

She was pointing at the half-open door of the linen storeroom from which Sheena had danced backwards only the day before, and in which Sebastian had tried to hide his stash.

Andrew can't be in there, Holly thought, and was disconcerted to feel a wave of relief so powerful that it almost overwhelmed her disappointment. This wouldn't do. Gingerly she swung the storeroom door wide, releasing a powerful smell of mothballs.

The little room was in chaos. Skinner, Fen and Bernie had left no pillowcase unturned in their fruitless search for the money they could not believe was gone. The cream-painted shelves that lined the walls had been stripped bare. Bed linen, blankets, quilts, towels, embroidered tray cloths, rust-spotted tablecloths and napkins, a multitude of doilies and a few unsavoury-looking spare pillows encased in brittle, yellowed plastic, lay tangled and trampled on the floor.

'Are you sure, Abby?' Mrs. Moss asked anxiously.

Abigail nodded, but a little furrow had appeared between her eyebrows. She turned to Holly in mute appeal.

Holly stared into the uncompromisingly corpse-free space and gnawed at her lip.

What now, O'Brien?

And an answer came to her, wafting through her mind like a soft, chill breath. But it wasn't the ghost of O'Brien who whispered to her. It was the remembered voice of Una Maggott—mad Una Maggott: *He'll be under the floorboards, or walled in by now. They're not silly.*

Holly bent and gathered up an armful of blankets. Mothballs rained from the scratchy pink folds, making her sneeze. 'Let's get this stuff out,' she said.

With the three of them working together, it took only a minute to transfer the chaos from storeroom to corridor. When they had finished, they were walled in by a small mountain range of cloth, and a bleak, empty space yawned before them, somehow looking more menacing than it had before.

Holly crept in, fruitlessly scanning the floor for signs of recent cuts or nailing, shuffling her feet to feel for loosened boards, kicking mothballs out of her way. She looked up at the ceiling, which was cobwebby and mottled with age but otherwise unmarked. She peered at the strips of wall visible between the empty shelves and saw no sign of disturbance.

Acutely aware that Abigail and Mrs. Moss were watching her, she felt the need to do something more positive. She reached between shelves to knock on the nearest wall, the one to her left, felt a raised pattern beneath the skin of cream paint, and realised what it meant. The storeroom walls were covered with the same embossed wallpaper that darkened the corridor, but the paper had been painted over. To make the little room lighter and cleaner-looking, perhaps? It seemed an odd expenditure of effort in a house that had otherwise been so neglected. But what other reason could there be?

She thought of one, and her stomach gave a little lurch. What if the wallpaper had been painted to conceal the fact that a section of it had been *damaged*? Had vanished, in fact, when a body-sized cavity was hollowed out of the wall?

Holly realised almost instantly that this theory was deeply flawed. The Maggott house was old, and no doubt sturdily built, but surely even a double brick wall, however lavishly plastered, would not be thick enough to absorb a fully grown man without showing a very obvious bulge?

Once the idea of a wall burial had taken root in her mind, however, it proved impossible to dislodge. She had, after all, found it hard to believe that the cat Lancelot could fit under the divan bed. Yet he had done it.

She had to check, if only because she couldn't think of anything else to do. Deciding that if the excavation had been done at all, it would have been done as close to the floor as possible, she crouched, reached under the lowest shelf and edged crabwise along the wall, trailing her fingertips over the paint, feeling for a place where the texture of the wallpaper stopped and the smoothness of new plaster or board began. By the time she reached the corner her thighs and calves were in agony, she had repeatedly bumped her head against the second-lowest shelf, and she had discovered no break in the wallpaper whatsoever.

Well, of course, she told herself bitterly. The image of Sheena, Lily, Dulcie or Eric huddled in the linen room, chipping away at plaster and brick while the body of Andrew McNish lay cooling in a corner, was ludicrous. It was tempting to give up and admit defeat. But with a kind of masochistic stubbornness, as if completing the search was a moral obligation, a kind of penance for stupidity, she ignored the protests from her thighs and waddled herself into a turn. Stretching forward again, she began on the back wall.

And felt her fingers glide over glacial smoothness.

It was like being struck by lightning. It gave her such a shock that she yelled, rocked on her heels, and fell backwards. Mrs. Moss and Abigail darted forward with little cries of alarm. It was impossible for them to crowd around her in the confined space, but they tried.

'Was it a spider, dear?' asked Mrs. Moss, as Holly clambered to her feet.

Holly shook her head. 'This wall,' she managed to say. 'It's different—at the bottom—or maybe...' She ran her hands experimentally over the space between the second and third shelves, the third and the fourth. No wallpaper. Thick cream paint, but definitely no wallpaper.

'Abigail! Can I borrow your scarf?'

Mrs. Moss raised her eyebrows, but Abigail pulled off the long strip of purple silk and handed it over without a word. They both retreated into the corridor as Holly used the scarf to measure the length of the storeroom from front to back. Then they followed her as she ran into Rollo Maggott's room. She could see at once that she was right. The storeroom wall on this side looked longer. She measured, just to be sure, and found that the difference was a little over half the length of the scarf. About a metre. More than enough.

'There's a cavity at the back of the storeroom,' she said, putting into words what by now they all knew.

'You *are* clever, dear,' said Mrs. Moss.

Abigail shivered.

Holly felt as if a million butterflies were trapped in her stomach and trying to get out. 'I should have checked this room yesterday,' she said, to stop herself from thinking.

Was it only yesterday? It seemed incredible. She made herself look at the grotesque carved bed that hulked beside the window, in the niche created by the storeroom. She found it repellent. She wondered how Cliff Allnut could have agreed to spend the night in it, however drunk he was. She would have taken the sofa downstairs any day. She would rather have slept on the floor.

Mrs. Moss shook her head. 'No one who wasn't actually looking for a difference in the walls would have noticed. The shelves in the storeroom confuse the eye.'

Abigail moved restlessly. 'Someone with a very strange mind spent time in this room,' she said, wrinkling her nose. 'Someone mad, I think.'

That seemed as good a cue as any to retire to the corridor and move back to the space encircled by the linen store contents.

'So, what now?' Mrs. Moss asked eagerly.

The fact was, Holly felt reluctant to do anything at all. For two pins she would have lain down among the sheets and towels, pulled something over her head and gone to sleep. But she knew she couldn't do that. She couldn't escape. And neither could she breathe a word of the craven fear that, despite everything, they were about to make perfect fools of themselves. She couldn't express the doubts that still niggled deep in her mind.

Could mothballs and lavender air-freshener really mask the smell of fresh paint? Could it really be that no one in the house had noticed that the linen cupboard had lost a metre in length, however tightly packed the shelves were? Could an amateur, however determined, really remove shelves and reposition them on a false wall in a single night without disturbing a soul? So when she replied to Mrs. Moss, she restricted herself to outlining her most obvious dilemma—one that she knew would be understood and appreciated.

'The minute we tell Una about this she'll freak out,' she said. 'Una will want action. She won't want to wait for the police. But she should. There might be trouble otherwise.'

'Interfering with a crime scene.' Mrs. Moss nodded knowledgeably.

'But the police won't believe it *is* a crime scene unless they actually see the body,' Abigail protested.

The body.

This is Andrew we're talking about, Holly told herself. *Andrew!* The man I was going to marry. In what now seemed another life.

She swallowed. 'Actually, I was thinking about another sort of trouble. If Andrew is behind that false wall, it means that one of those people downstairs killed him. Who knows what the killer might do if we go rushing down there and announce…?'

She watched the faces before her become extremely thoughtful.

'Too bad,' said Abigail, after a moment. 'I think we should take the bull by the horns.'

'Softly softly catchee monkey,' Mrs. Moss demurred obscurely.

Holly stood irresolute. Monkey or bull, she found herself pondering. Monkey, bull or chicken?

Raised voices floated up from the entrance hall: Una's rasp, Dulcie's high twitter, Allnut's rumble. The stairs squeaked.

Sebastian Maggott appeared on the landing. He peered down the corridor at them, at the contents of the linen store heaped on the floor.

'Auntie Una says have you found anything yet?' he called self-consciously.

Holly felt the spirit of O'Brien poke her left shoulderblade. She made her decision. Bugger the monkeys. And the chickens. It was red rag time.

'Tell her yes, we think so,' she called back. 'If Martin's still there, could you ask him to come up? And bring some tools? We have to demolish a wall.'

◇◇◇

And so it was that ten minutes later, Martin was ripping into the back wall of the linen room with the aid of a sledgehammer and a crowbar. Una, her wheelchair forming the apex of a ragged triangle of onlookers that included everyone in the house, watched avidly from the corridor, the giant black torch in her lap.

Holly, Abigail and Mrs. Moss stood a little apart from the others, or rather, the others stood a little apart from them. It was as if the three had been instinctively quarantined, as if an invisible barrier had been set up between the hunters and the hunted, the accusers and the accused.

Mrs. Moss and Abigail, rigid with tension, had their eyes fixed on Martin. Holly, the spirit of O'Brien still hovering at her back, was covertly surveying the cast of suspects, searching in vain for signs of obvious guilt.

No one had tried to make a getaway. No one was acting out of character. Sheena and Dulcie had protested vigorously about the proposed destruction but, having quickly realised they were powerless to prevent it, now stood silently, wincing at each blow of the hammer, each shelf prised from its moorings, each sound of cracking plasterboard and splintering wood.

Lily was slightly smiling but watching attentively, as if she were memorising every detail of the lunacy in order to be able to recount it later to an interested audience. Cliff Allnut had restricted himself to pursing his lips and glaring huffily at Holly, as if warning her of retribution to come. Sebastian had passionately resisted his mother's attempts to make him stay downstairs, but having got his way had remembered his chosen persona and now skulked at the edge of the group, occasionally kicking at the piles of sheets and towels in a bored sort of way that deceived no one.

Eric stood expressionless behind Una's wheelchair. He had lugged the chair upstairs, but Martin had carried Una. Una had insisted on that. It could have been because she was genuinely afraid that Eric would drop her accidentally on purpose, as she loudly claimed, or simply because she quite liked the idea of Martin's strong arms around her. Holly suspected the latter.

'There's something in here, all right,' Martin called over his shoulder.

Everyone leaned forward. Someone drew a shuddering breath, but Holly did not see who it was. The moment Martin spoke she had looked toward the sound of his voice. She felt breathless, and there was a tightness in her chest as if her heart were being squeezed.

The plasterboard, boldly striped with the pitted white bars that showed where the shelves had been torn away, was now partially broken on the right-hand side. Martin was peering through the gap into darkness.

'Can I have the torch?' he called, turning a little and stretching out his hand.

Holly waited for Eric to move, but Eric remained motionless. Una was panting, her face no longer avid but taut with strain. Her hands gripped the arms of her wheelchair, the knuckles white, the veins standing out knotted and blue.

Holly stepped forward and took the torch from Una's lap. She had the strangest feeling that she was standing back and watching herself as she went into the ravaged storeroom, slapping the torch into Martin's waiting hand like a nurse passing an instrument to a surgeon at the climax of a delicate operation.

Martin bent to the hole in the plasterboard, turned the torch on and shone the powerful white beam through the gap, directing it down.

'What...?' Una's voice was strangled, almost unrecognisable.

Martin's head and hand, and the stem of the torch, were blocking the hole. Holly couldn't see what he was looking at. But she could hear him swearing under his breath. When he straightened and turned his face had blanched under the tan, and his eyes had darkened to indigo. He thrust the torch at Holly.

'Wait and give me a hand, will you?' he muttered. 'Just stand back a bit.'

He waited while Holly stowed the torch on the shelf at her elbow and retreated a little. Then he picked up the hammer, hooked the claw end into the gap in the plasterboard, and began breaking the board up, cracking it then snapping broken sections free. He worked rapidly downwards, passing each ragged, powdery piece of waste to Holly for her to put aside. It took only a minute or two before the whole lower part of the wall was gone.

And then Martin swung the torch around on its shelf and switched it on, so that its cruel white beam shone directly into the cavity.

The picture was to stay with Holly, vivid in every detail, for the rest of her life. It was as if, like the flash of a camera, the shock had imprinted the image on her brain. Against a background of shredded black satin draperies, through which glimpses of embossed wallpaper could be seen, a statue of a jackal-headed god brooded over a white coffin with a glass lid and tarnished brass handles. Several small, blackened caskets, a flat box tied with ragged ribbon, a flute glass and a bottle of French champagne had been arranged at the statue's feet.

'It's a coffin,' Holly heard Cliff Allnut say from the corridor. 'Why would they put him in a coffin?' He sounded primly accusing, as if somehow the discovery was a ploy designed to deceive him.

Holly took a step forward, then another. She looked down at the coffin, through the film that frosted the inside of the glass lid. And then she felt Martin's hand on her arm and she turned away and let him lead her out of the storeroom to where Una sat waiting in her chair, her face immobile as a carved mask.

'It's not Andrew, Una,' Holly heard herself say.

Martin murmured something about calling the police, and left her. Mrs. Moss and Abigail were hovering beside her, but she couldn't find the words to speak to them. Without surprise she noticed Lily melting away, no doubt bent on making herself scarce now that a police visit was inevitable and questions about the source of Sebastian's stash might be asked. She barely noticed Dulcie and Sheena pushing past her into the storeroom.

'W—what do you mean it isn't him?' Eric stammered, looking dumbfounded. 'Who is it then?'

The image of what she had seen through the coffin lid rose before Holly's eyes. Again she saw that wizened brown face lightly dusted with mould, the brittle cloud of white-blonde hair, the small, clawed hands, no more than fragile bones gloved in leathery skin, raised slightly from the sunken breast where gold, diamonds and rubies glinted, horribly undimmed, amid the remains of a red evening gown edged with nylon tulle.

'Lois!' screamed Dulcie from the storeroom. 'Oh, my God! It's *Lois!*'

She blundered out into the corridor, threw herself into her son's unwilling arms and burst into hysterical sobs.

And as Sheena stumbled out after her, with her hand pressed to her mouth, as Cliff Allnut stood rooted to the spot, his lips stretched into a comical O, Eric moved from behind the wheel-chair and went to stare in his turn at Rollo Maggott's second wife, so lovingly and so intensely embalmed that she was still recognisable after thirty-five years.

But Una Maggott continued to sit immobile, her face almost as rigid as the face in the coffin, except that the corner of her mouth was twitching uncontrollably, and tears were slowly rolling down her cheeks.

Holly bent over her, put a tentative hand on her shoulder. 'I'm sorry,' she said, and meant it with all her heart.

Una made no response. Was she thinking about her father, romancing on his deathbed about his lost love, embroidering fantastically on the lie he had probably come to believe as his mind decayed? Or was she thinking about Andrew McNish, the charming, cunning stranger with the boyish smile who had not been her half-brother, never *could* have been her half-brother, because Lois Maggott had not run away, pregnant or otherwise, but had died in this house long ago?

Holly didn't ask. What did it matter anyway? All Una's extraordinary energy, her fervent belief, her refusal to give in, had led only to the dead end of betrayal. Yet another betrayal. The long, sad, story of her life.

'He left champagne for her.'

Holly looked up. Eric was beside her. His face was inexpressibly sad.

'Ol' Maggott,' Eric said. 'He left Lois all the things she liked. Champagne and jewellery and chocolates and money and stuff. For the afterlife. Like they used to do for the pharaohs. And he put the god of the underworld to watch over her. An-ubis. You know?'

There was a paralysed silence.

'Are you saying you *knew*—?' Dulcie began.

Eric shook his head. 'He never told me. Never said a word. All those years...' He sighed, shrugged. 'Still, maybe by the time I started working for him he'd forgot she was there. He was pretty far gone.'

'It's criminal!' puffed Allnut. 'Rollo Maggott lied to my father! He lied to the police! Keeping a dead body in the house...'

'He must have killed her,' said Sebastian with relish.

Dulcie wailed.

'No,' said Eric soberly. 'He was a nutter, but he wouldn't have killed anyone. Lois must've just—died. Heart attack, or accident, or—'

'But he hid the body!' Sebastian persisted. 'Why would he hide the body unless—?'

'He wanted to keep her,' said Eric. 'See where he put her? Right next to his bed, so he could sleep beside her, with just a wall between them.'

'The old devil!' Sheena muttered. 'The crazy old devil! And to think I—' She gagged, pressed her hand to her mouth again and bolted for the bathroom.

Holly felt Una's shoulder move. She looked down and was astonished to see that the rigid face had cracked into a grim smile.

'It seems that even Sheena draws the line at sex in the graveyard,' Una said.

Dulcie gave a little scream of horror. Her son sniggered.

'Una, *really!*' Allnut protested.

'You slept in that bed yourself, the other night, Allnut,' Una reminded him. 'Makes you think, doesn't it?'

Allnut goggled at her, went several shades paler, and turned, shuddering, away.

This time Una actually laughed. 'Take me downstairs, would you, Eric?' she said. 'I could do with a brandy.'

Chapter Twenty-five

'Imagine that being old Rollo Maggott's house!' said Mrs. Moss the following morning as she, Holly and Abigail sat drinking coffee and eating Danish pastries at one of the rickety tables outside the Mealey Marshes cake shop. 'I had no idea till Trevor Purse told me—he'd been there before, to exterminate rats. I'd heard the garden was full of pyramids and statues and so on, but it wasn't.'

'Una had them all pulled down,' said Holly. 'It was the first thing she did.'

'You'd think she'd have dealt with the rats first.' Mrs. Moss wrinkled her nose. 'Trevor said the place was crawling with them. He found that very absorbing, of course—he seems to like a challenge—but I don't think he enjoyed working for Miss Maggott very much. She was on his back all the time, apparently, pestering him for progress reports and so on. It upset him. He's not accustomed to being supervised by clients, he says.'

'Una's like that,' Holly murmured. 'She gets crazes on things and goes over the top.' She chewed pastry mechanically, registering that it melted in her mouth but taking no joy in it.

She knew she should be grateful just to be alive. She also knew that it was natural for someone who had been kidnapped and menaced with a knife and who had, moreover, discovered two dead bodies in two days, to feel a little emotionally drained. But she felt more than emotionally drained. She felt tense, unsatisfied and baffled.

The parrot had glared at her balefully when she'd come home the night before. It hadn't said a word as she filled up its seed and water containers and covered its cage with O'Brien's blue shirt. She had probably just been extremely overtired, but she hadn't been able to shake off the feeling that it was sulking not because she was late, but because she had let it down.

All night, it seemed, she had dreamed of shrivelled mummy faces, snakes, jackal-headed gods, emerald rings, silver teaspoons, knives and falling chandeliers. She had woken feeling unrested and jittery, with the weak impulse to pull her quilt over her head and stay where she was.

The lure of coffee, the oppression of the jungle mural and the knowledge that Abigail and Mrs. Moss would certainly come to get her if she didn't show her face at the time appointed the night before, had eventually prised her from the bed. Now she was telling herself she might have done better to stay there. The coffee was wonderful, the pastries were good, and Mealey Marshes looked quaint and bright in the crisp autumn morning, but none of these things had improved her mood.

'Well, the poor woman isn't normal, is she?' Mrs. Moss said comfortably, putting down her cup. 'Still, she must have been very embarrassed last night. Imagine finding the wrong body after all the fuss she'd made about her brother being murdered and so on.'

'Andrew never was her brother,' said Holly.

'He's not dead, either,' said Abigail, pressing her finger to the last flakes of pastry on her plate and putting them into her mouth. 'Not in that house, anyway. There was only one unquiet spirit there, and we found her.'

'I keep thinking about O'Brien,' Holly blurted out, and blinked defiantly as her companions both stared at her in some alarm.

'I don't see why Mr. O'Brien would be an unquiet spirit, Holly,' Abigail said gently. 'His body wasn't hidden.'

'Far from it,' said Mrs. Moss. 'You aren't saying you think the quack was wrong and Mr. O'Brien was chilled off after all, are you, dear?'

'No!' Holly muttered, already regretting her outburst but feeling she had no alternative but to explain herself. 'Nothing like that. It's just...there are too many unanswered questions. Too many loose ends. Andrew's mobile. The missing tea mug. Una's lost rings. Una's fall. The hidden teaspoons. The bag of clothes. The dead rat. The warning note...'

And where is Andrew? she thought, but didn't say.

'O'Brien wouldn't have liked the loose ends,' she said instead. 'He would have *done* something about them. I can't stop thinking about it.'

'I think you have post-traumatic stress syndrome,' said Mrs. Moss, with the assurance of the late-night TV viewer.

'We probably all do,' said Abigail. 'That's why it was a good idea to have cakes this morning. In fact, I think we should all have another one. We need to raise our sugar levels.'

'We always have pastries on Sundays, Abby,' said Mrs. Moss, getting to her feet. 'And we always end up having two. My turn.'

She gave Holly a little pat on the shoulder and disappeared through the screen door, which rattled and banged behind her.

They operate like a tag team, Holly thought with dreary amusement. She's giving Abigail a chance to talk some sense into me. Holly didn't resent it. On the contrary, she was warmed by their concern, though she doubted Abigail could say anything that would help. She drank the last of her coffee and waited.

'Holly, I do understand how you feel,' Abigail began. 'It's terribly frustrating not to get to the bottom of things, or find out how stories end. It happens to me all the time when clients don't come back. But it can't be helped. As far as Una Maggott is concerned, the investigation is over, isn't it? Once she found out that Andrew couldn't have been her brother, she lost interest in him and everything to do with him. That was obvious last night.'

'Yes.' Holly looked down at the brown froth remaining in her coffee cup, tilting the cup from side to side to make the froth slide back and forth. 'It's like Eric said—she gets obsessed, then loses interest and just goes on to the next thing. Mrs. Moss said she must be embarrassed by what happened last night, but I honestly don't think she's capable of embarrassment. Yesterday morning she was accusing everyone in the house of trying to kill her. By last night she'd forgotten all about that and was quite happy to be left alone with Eric, Dulcie and Sheena—oh, and Sebastian, of course. It was as if none of the stuff that had happened before mattered.'

'Well, let's face it, she's…unusual,' Abigail said, with professional tact. 'Her father was the same way, I gather. According to Enid, he was quite notorious.'

'He'll be even more notorious now.' Holly looked up, saw Abigail watching her, and smiled.

'It's okay, Abigail. I know there's nothing I can do. It's just frustrating, that's all. I'll get over it.'

'Of course you will. You just need to keep busy. Find a new focus.'

A white ute with a brown dog in the back swung past the war memorial and did a U-turn, pulling up outside the cake shop. Martin jumped out and strode toward the shop door.

Holly's heart gave a nervous little flutter. She told herself it was the coffee.

'Oh, hello, Martin!' called Abigail. 'I was just thinking about you.'

Holly gave her a sharp look and she smiled blandly.

'Hi,' Martin said, stopping by their table. 'Recovered from yesterday?'

He spoke as if they had been doing a spot of bushwalking instead of being terrorised by a gang of toughs and discovering an embalmed corpse in a cupboard.

'Up to a point,' Holly said. 'Now I'm just waiting for the police to turn up and charge me with false pretences or something.'

Martin laughed. 'Don't hold your breath. They've got plenty to do with a dead body to play with and four bad guys to nail. Anyhow, Una's not going to make a complaint. She's moved on.'

'What's the new big thing?'

'Would you believe eBay? After last night's entertainment, she's decided she can't rest until she's cleared the house of everything that wasn't in it when her grandparents were alive, and she thinks eBay might be the best way to go. According to Eric, she and the kid stayed up most of the night talking about it.'

'Right.' Holly shook her head. Una really was incredible.

'Neck okay?' Martin asked.

'Oh, yes,' Holly said, her fingers flying instinctively to the sticking plaster on her throat. 'It was just a nick. It's fine.'

She swallowed, quelling an inward shudder at the thought of Bernie's knife, and saw Martin's eyes darken.

Mrs. Moss pushed her way through the screen door bearing a tray onto which three more Danish pastries and three more coffees had been squeezed.

'You do all right for yourselves, you Mealey people,' said Martin, instantly back in casual mode.

'Hello, Martin,' Mrs. Moss said absently, as she began transferring the fresh goodies to the table and stacking the used cups and plates onto the tray. 'You know, I was thinking while I was waiting in there, it was really very lucky that Rollo Maggott left that poem in his wife's coffin.'

'It was an awful poem,' Holly couldn't help saying. 'Conceited and self-justifying and...and talking about Lois as if she'd only existed for his benefit. *And* it didn't scan.' She caught herself thinking that Martin would probably regard this as a very callous remark, and told herself he'd have to like it or lump it. She'd given up pretending to be something she wasn't.

'It wasn't exactly Shakespeare,' Martin agreed mildly. 'But at least it explained how she died. If it hadn't been there the police might have suspected murder, and that would have complicated things.'

'It certainly wouldn't have been very nice for the family,' Mrs. Moss said primly.

Martin grinned. 'Dulcie didn't seem to think it was particularly nice that the lady was flattened when the chandelier she was swinging on fell on her. Una wasn't impressed either. But it's a lot better than murder. In fact, I can think of worse ways to go. I'd rather die laughing any day.'

'Me, too,' said Holly.

He smiled at her as comfortably as if they had known each other for years. 'So it's not all bad. And think of all that Maggott jewellery and cash finding its way back into the Maggott coffers! Not to mention a tasteful statue of Anubis and a bottle of French champagne.'

'Would thirty-five-year-old champagne be drinkable?'

'Depends how desperate you are, I guess.'

He wandered off into the cake shop after that, taking the tray of used cups with him, leaving Abigail and Mrs. Moss to exchange knowing, indulgent glances and Holly to take a self-conscious sip of coffee and think how very compelling blue eyes were when they were warm, instead of like two chips of ice.

'I wonder if the Purses have made it up this morning,' she remarked eventually, in the hope of breaking up her companions' wordless communication about her putative love life.

'Oh, they probably made it up last night,' said Abigail. 'They're obviously a very devoted couple. And the minute Leanne told Trevor she was pregnant he'd have been—'

Holly choked on her coffee.

'—putty in her hands,' Abigail finished serenely. 'When we were tied to that post together she told me that's why she'd been working—to make a bit of extra money for the baby. She's opened a special purpose bank account and everything. She was waiting until she had a good amount in there before she told Trevor, because he'd been very insistent that they had to wait for a baby until they felt absolutely secure financially, but—'

'He'll be over the moon!' Holly laughed.

Abigail nodded. 'That's what I told her. So we found out the ending to that story, at least, Holly. And, oh, that reminds me! There's another one. It was on my answering machine last night. Poor April—you know, my client whose partner moved another woman into the house? Well, she's finally walked out on him.'

'So she came to her senses at last!' said Mrs. Moss, clapping her hands. 'I don't believe it! Or did Saul move *another* girl in? Trying for a foursome? I wouldn't put it past him.'

Abigail shook her head. 'April raided his computer while he was out. She found out he'd been quietly transferring their money and shares into his own name. It had been going on for years. He'd even bought himself a holiday house on the South Coast.'

'The swine!' gasped Mrs. Moss.

'It was lucky you told April to check the finances, Abigail,' Holly said grimly.

'Yes,' Abigail agreed. 'That was thanks to you. If I hadn't spoken to you first, I'd never have thought of it. April has had a lot of Pentacles in her cards ever since she started coming to me, but she always said that money didn't mean anything to her, and all she wanted was love, spiritual connection with nature, and the simple life.'

She frowned and thoughtfully licked a line of cappuccino froth from her top lip.

'You know, April's the gentlest person, but she was just about incoherent with rage on the phone,' she said. 'It's strange, isn't it? She wouldn't leave Saul when she knew perfectly well that he'd robbed her of security, and trust, and peace of mind, and privacy in her own home, and quite a lot of hair. But when she found out he'd robbed her of a few dollars, that was it!'

'Well, people can be very peculiar, Abby,' soothed Mrs. Moss. 'No one knows that better than we do.'

'All that talk about love,' sighed Abigail. 'Love, love, love! But all the time it was the money that counted.'

It always comes down to money in the end, Love.

O'Brien was right all along, Holly thought soberly. In the end, Andrew's and my wonderful, romantic affair came down to his stealing my money, and my trying to get it back. O'Brien himself wasn't ever really on my side—he only promised to help me because there was money in it for him. Skinner and his thugs were willing to kidnap two people and raid the Maggott house because of money. Leanne Purse deceived Trevor because he worried so much about money. And money had been at the root of all Una's problems. *Bloodsuckers...*

Eric's low, contemptuous voice seemed to echo in Holly's ears: *It wouldn't matter if she didn't have so much bloody money. If she was like her old man and didn't have a bean Dulcie and co wouldn't give a stuff about what she did...*

Andrew, Dulcie, Lily, Allnut—they had all battened onto Una because she was rich. And no doubt Sebastian, Una's guide in her latest craze, was out for all he could get.

Eric probably didn't class himself or Sheena in the bloodsucker category, but the fact was, protective of Una as he claimed to be, Eric only went on working for her because he didn't have enough money to house his snake and his hearse elsewhere. Sheena had gladly sold her entire inheritance from fond, foolish old Rollo Maggott to his daughter in return for a 'little nest egg'...

And suddenly, Holly's stomach dropped as if she were in a plane that had hit an air pocket. The world seemed to be spinning around her—not slowly like a merry-go-round this time, but as fast as a ride she had once been sick on at Luna Park. She gripped the table with her free hand for balance, carefully put down her coffee cup and stood up.

'Good heavens, Holly, what is it?' cried Mrs. Moss in alarm. 'You look awful! Do you feel faint, dear? Have you got a pain?'

But Holly was looking at Abigail. 'You told me the night before last. When you read the cards. You said you saw secrets and lies around me. Secrets, lies, shadows...and a snake. You told me to trust my instincts.'

Her mouth full of sweet almond pastry, her eyes wide, Abigail nodded dumbly.

'There was a man upside-down, too,' Holly said. She began groping in her shoulder bag.

'This is our treat, dear,' said Mrs. Moss nervously. 'Abby, I really think we should get Holly back—'

Holly's fingers closed on her car keys. She pulled them out. 'I'm all right,' she said, backing away from the table. 'Really. It's

only—everything's just made sense. A weird kind of sense, but…
sense. I have to go. Sorry. Thanks for the coffee.'

'But where are you going?' cried Mrs. Moss, scrambling to
her feet.

'Back to Horsetrough Lane, I think,' Holly heard Abigail
answer for her placidly. 'Following her instincts. Do you want
to go halves on her Danish, Enid?'

◇◇◇

The old house looked deserted. The front gates gaped wide.
Trevor Purse's van had gone from the churned gravel apron.
Presumably it had already been towed away.

Holly knocked at the front door. When, after a few minutes,
no one came, she retreated to the gravel and trudged around to
the back, skirting the left-hand light post that still bore ragged
pieces of duct tape.

Behind a humdrum clutter of clothesline, garbage bins and
garage, new lawn ran primly to the black railing fence. Beyond
the fence the ground fell away, and bush-clad hills, one folding in on the other, stretched into the far distance to meet the
perfect blue sky.

Not far from the corner of the house, a rectangular grid of bars
set into in a metal frame was propped beside a naked window.
Holly stepped up to the window and looked in. She saw a large,
old-fashioned kitchen, with table, chairs, a dresser and a black
fuel stove as well as a gas stove that probably also qualified as
antique. The only concessions to modernity appeared to be a
refrigerator, a microwave oven, a toaster and an electric jug.

A figure in jeans and T-shirt was cooking something in the
microwave. Holly tapped on the windowpane. The figure turned
and she saw it was Eric, almost unrecognisable in mufti. He waved
and pointed to his right. Holly continued along the house until
she came to the back door, which opened just as she reached it.

'Didn't expect you back,' said Eric, standing aside to let her
into the kitchen and closing the door behind her. 'Thought
you'd have had enough of this place. Everyone else has. They've
all gone. The place is like a tomb.'

'I hardly knew you without your Elvis gear,' Holly said.

'Yeah, well, it's Sunday, isn't it?'

The microwave beeped to indicate it had finished its task. Words began running along its display panel. ENJOY YOUR MEAL...ENJOY YOUR MEAL...ENJOY YOUR...

Eric slouched to the microwave and opened it. When he turned around again he was holding a limp rat by the tail.

Holly felt a wave of dizziness.

'I was just defrosting this,' Eric said. 'Cleo's due for a feed. Do you want to watch?'

'Not really, thanks.'

It would be hard to think of anything Holly would like less.

Eric swung the rat between his fingers. 'Ol' Maggott used to give her live rats, but I persuaded him to stop.'

'That's good.'

'Yeah. Live feed can do snakes a lot of damage. Clawing and biting. You know.'

'Right.'

Holly was feeling unreal again. She tore her eyes away from the rat and looked instead around the kitchen, noting the framed photographs that covered the walls. Most of the oldest were dim and foxed, but she could still make out the people in their old-fashioned clothes posed in various places around the house. Sitting at dinner in what was now the library. Promenading arm in arm on the front verandah. Standing at the bottom of the grand staircase, beneath a huge crystal chandelier.

'There were others,' said Eric, pointing at a few rectangular patches on the greasy cream paint. 'They were of the outside. Una took them to show Martin what the yard looked like in the old days.'

Holly nodded. She knew she should get on with it—could almost feel the spirit of O'Brien nudging her in the ribs—but found she was strangely unwilling to take the next step. Her eyes fell on the fuel stove. One of the little black doors was slightly open, displaying a mound of white ash. Through the gap, against the white background, Holly saw a tiny gleam of red.

She moved to the stove, crouched and pulled the small door wide. She felt no excitement. She knew what she would find.

'That old thing hasn't been used for years,' said Eric.

Holly reached into the space beyond the little door. Ash fell in a soft shower onto her knees as she crooked her forefinger around the handle of the red mug and pulled it free.

She stood, holding up her find for Eric to see, shaking ash from the red glaze to reveal the word 'Andrew' marked out in white.

'Lordy!' whispered Eric, abruptly back in Elvis mode. He attempted to cross himself, forgetting about the rat in his hand.

'Well, that puts the lid on it,' Holly said, dusting off her jeans. 'So, Eric, where's Una?'

Chapter Twenty-six

Una Maggott was sitting at her desk in front of her computer when Holly came into the room. She looked up, her lips faintly smiling, her small eyes cold. Holly felt that atavistic repulsion, that instinctive distrust, that she had felt the very first time she saw this woman and had suppressed so many times since.

'So you came back,' Una said. 'I thought you might.'

'I found the *Andrew* mug,' said Holly, lifting her hand to display the mug.

'So I see. A bit late, though, don't you think?'

'A bit late, yes. If I'd found it before I'd have smelled a rat much sooner. The fuel stove was a ridiculously obvious hiding place. Anyone searching the kitchen would have found it. And it's inconceivable that a woman like you, however besotted, would buy a clumsy, kitschy thing like this as a gift unless there was a very good reason for it. As you told Cliff Allnut, Una, when you lie it's a mistake to over-elaborate.'

Una's eyes strayed back to her computer screen. 'It's a shame Dulcie insisted on taking that boy away,' she murmured. 'He's a sharp one. A real Maggott. I could have used him.'

'Like you use everyone,' Holly said. 'Like you used Andrew McNish. And me!'

Una shrugged. 'McNish was in a hole and I offered him a way out of it. He knew exactly what he was doing.'

'But I didn't,' said Holly.

'Yes, well…' Una's lip curled.

Holly felt her face grow hot, and fought down her anger. 'You even used yourself, Una, when it suited you,' she said. 'You told me a very personal story about seeing your father for the last time. You did it to play on my feelings. You're good at seeing people's weaknesses—or what you think of as weaknesses. You wanted to make me feel sorry for you, to make sure I'd keep my promise to search the house, so I'd find the things you and Andrew had planted between you to make the police believe your crazy story he'd been murdered!'

Una turned to look at her. 'You seem to have it all worked out, Ms. Cage—oh, I'm sorry, it's Ms. Love, actually, isn't it? I still haven't got round to talking to the police about that.'

Holly refused to be diverted by the implied threat. Una wasn't going to go to the police.

'I believed you completely when you told me about arguing with your dying father. You were so upset—so obviously upset. But that was because what you told me was the truth.'

'Indeed it was.'

'Except for one thing. The secret your father told you on his deathbed wasn't that Lois had had a child. It was that Lois hadn't run away thirty-five years ago, but had been killed when the chandelier fell. And that he'd embalmed her body and hidden it in this house!'

Una's mouth twitched.

'Just thinking about it made you angry all over again,' Holly went on. 'That's why you were so convincing. As if it wasn't bad enough that your stepmother's body was hidden somewhere in the house you were about to take possession of at last, that dying old man told you he'd disposed of Lois as if she were an Egyptian queen, with all the treasure he thought she deserved. All the jewellery he'd heaped on her while she was alive. All the cash he'd been able to scrape together, converted to gold sovereigns. The Anubis statue, which I'll bet is the genuine article—'

'You surprise me, Ms. Love,' Una Maggott sneered. 'To be able to tell a real antiquity from a cheap copy! You appear to have hidden depths.'

And the supercilious contempt in the woman's voice was enough to make Holly throw away all thought of sparing her anything.

'But the thing that really got under your skin, Una, was that you knew that by that time Rollo Maggott was so far gone that he thought he was talking to Sheena—Sheena who he loved, and wanted to provide for, and to whom he'd left *the entire contents* of this house! And you were angry, so angry, because he was rambling and confused and wouldn't get to the point about where Lois' body actually was, no matter how you raged at him, no matter what you did…'

'Are you trying to blackmail me, Ms. Love?' Una asked curtly. 'Because if you are, I can assure you—'

Holly felt her hands curling into fists. Deliberately she relaxed them.

'You can't think of anything but money, can you?' she said. 'You can't think of a single reason why anyone would do anything, except for money.'

'Then why are you here?'

'Because I wanted to face you with it. I wanted you to know you didn't get away with it. I wanted you to know I *know*.'

It sounded feeble, when she put it into words. And suddenly all the things she'd been planning to say seemed pointless. *You had to be so patient, at first. Knowing Cliff Allnut, the bequest to Sheena would have been watertight. You had to persuade Sheena to sign over her inheritance to you. And only after that was done, done by Allnut again, in exactly the same punctilious, watertight way, could you begin searching for Lois' body and the goodies buried with it. You had the garden dug up first, and when Martin didn't strike gold, you started clearing out the attic, the storerooms, everywhere a body could possibly be hidden. And when still nothing was found, you hired a pest exterminator to poke into all the secret holes and corners in the house.*

Una was sneering at her again. 'And what *do* you know, Ms. Love?'

'For one thing, I know you can't be nearly as rich as people here think you are,' said Holly, stung into speech. 'If you have money to burn, why would you bother hiring a small-time detective you thought you could get cheap, then work so hard to keep her? Why are your clothes expensive, but slightly out of date? Why would you live with these—' she gestured at the stalking gods on the walls '—when you obviously loathe them, and a decent paint job would cover them up?'

Una abruptly turned her chair around and wheeled herself to the window. The back of her neck was rigid. Holly felt a little rush of triumph. She knew she was right.

'Your money was supposed to have come from shares in that company you ran with Alexis Delafont. But maybe that company wasn't as solvent as people thought. Maybe you and Alexis took one too many risks, went a bit too close to the edge. And when he was killed it all fell in a heap.'

There was silence in the room. The Egyptian figures stalked toward the bay window. The snake's forked tongue flickered in and out, tasting the air.

At last, Una stirred.

'The French taxation people were vicious,' she said, staring through the limp lace curtain, the smudgy glass, the black iron bars. 'They took everything. I lost my Paris apartment. My shares were worthless.'

'Then Cliff Allnut rang and told you your father was dying.'

'Yes. The old *cochon* was finally on his last legs. I thanked *le bon dieu*, sold the last of my jewellery and came home.' Una laughed bitterly. '*Home!* A draughty ruin in the middle of nowhere. But worth a bit of money, at least, I thought. Enough to give me a roof over my head, and some sort of income. And then, when I got here—'

'You found out there was buried treasure in the house too.'

'Yes!' The voice was like a sigh. 'The fortune everyone thought had been stolen by that little whore Lois. It was here, buried

with her! All I had to do was find it. As soon as Sheena's claim
had been sorted out, I started looking.'

'And you never told anyone what you were really doing,'
Holly said, shaking her head. 'I suppose even you didn't have
the stomach to admit you'd tricked Sheena out of what your
father meant her to have.'

'Not till I'd secured it, anyway,' Una said coolly. 'Sheena was
useful to me. So was Eric. And they were cheap. I wanted to hold
on to them for as long as I could. I was starting to run out of
money. Then I saw a television program about sniffer dogs and
realised that was the answer. If I could get some trained corpse
dogs into this house, they'd find the woman's tomb for me. And
it would cost me nothing.'

She swung her chair around. Holly saw that she was grinning,
and felt cold fingers run down her spine.

'They all thought I was mad, like my father,' Una said. 'I let
them think it. What did I care, as long as I got what I wanted?
Now I can sell this house and get away from here. When I'm
back to somewhere civilised, I can buy as much help as I need.'

'You *are* mad, Una,' said Holly evenly. 'Or what I call mad.
No sane person would have staged a charade like you did with
Andrew McNish. No sane person would invite guests into her
house specifically to accuse them of murder! You even kept Lily
on when you obviously despised her, to give yourself another
potential suspect. And I suppose you drugged Cliff Allnut, to
make sure he stayed overnight.'

'It was just a couple of my sleeping pills. They didn't do him
any harm.'

Holly shook her head. 'No one with any sense of reality at all
would think a plan like that would work. I'm sure Andrew didn't.
He just went along with you for what he could get out of it.'

'I don't doubt it,' said Una, her face darkening. 'What a
twister that man was! He cheated me, as well as lying about his
contacts. He didn't sprinkle blood on the bedclothes as he was
supposed to do before he came down to dinner—too squeam-
ish, I suppose, to cut himself. And he left his phone in a stupid

place, where it could be brushed back by the opening door. He could have ruined everything. He nearly did!'

She leaned back in her chair, perfectly relaxed now. 'But in the end the plan *did* work, Ms. Love, thanks to you. I must admit it wouldn't have occurred to me to use a psychic to locate the tomb. I'd assumed all psychics were frauds.'

'*You're* the fraud, Una!' Holly spat, finally losing control of her temper. 'You're the fraud, and the user, and the snake! You accused *six* people of murder—including Eric, who really cares about you. You even staged a little accident to yourself to convince me there was a killer in the house. And planted a dead rat and a warning note for me, because you knew I'd react just the way I did to being threatened. How could you do it? If Andrew *had* left blood on the bedclothes, Eric and all the others might have been living under a shadow for the rest of their lives!'

Una snorted. 'Now you're lurching into melodrama, Ms. Love. Andrew McNish is certain to surface sometime. He's too cocky to do otherwise. Eric and the rest of them would have been exonerated eventually.'

'It might have taken *years*—'

'Oh, stop whining!' Una snapped, wheeling herself back to her desk. 'Sentiment has no place in matters of business. Now, will you please leave? I'm expecting a visitor. And you have nothing to complain of. You were paid for your services—that two hundred and fifty I gave you was the last ready cash I had.'

She turned back to the computer screen, but Holly stood her ground.

'And what did you pay Andrew for his...services?'

'It's none of your business, but I'll tell you if that will get rid of you. He got what he asked for—money, in the form of my mother's rings, a new phone, and a car he'd taken a liking to, full of petrol and parked in the lay-by, ready to go.'

Her lip curled. 'A secondhand gold Mercedes is not the vehicle *I* would have chosen if I wanted to disappear, but McNish is far from prudent. It's in very good condition, apparently, according to the mechanic in Springwood who checked it over. He's a surly type, but seems to know what he's about. So McNish told me, anyway.'

Holly considered the irony of her own sighting of what was almost certainly Andrew's getaway car at the Springwood service centre, and decided it was not worth mentioning.

'So you just let Andrew out of the gates on Tuesday night, after all the others had gone to bed, and off he went,' she said instead. 'Where is he now?'

Una shrugged. 'I have absolutely no idea. As far as he can get from our thuggish friends of yesterday, I suppose.' She smiled thinly. 'Not perhaps, as far as he'd like,' she added. 'The best of the stones in my mother's rings were replaced with imitations long before I left France.'

'Maybe you and Andrew *are* related after all,' Holly said, and left her.

◇◇◇

Returning to Stillwaters Road, Holly found Mrs. Moss and Abigail waiting for her in Mrs. Moss' blue and beige living room. Rufus the cat sat on guard by the security screen, gazing across the stairwell, his amber eyes fixed on the red heart door behind which the parrot was singing variations of 'My Bonny Lies Over the Ocean.'

'Well, I've never heard of anything so devious!' said Mrs. Moss, when Holly had finished telling her story. 'More tea, dear?'

'The woman's a snake,' Holly agreed, accepting her refilled cup with a smile of thanks.

'I suppose she was desperate,' said Abigail. 'And reading about Andrew McNish at the critical time—'

'Actually, I think Lily was her first candidate as a potential murderee,' said Holly. 'Una would have sized Lily up as someone who had her eye on the main chance, and Lily had told her she had no ties. She got Lily installed in the house, established herself as Lily's doting patron, and was probably just getting ready to put the idea of playing the disappearing protégée to her when Allnut ferreted out the information that Lily in fact had plenty of ties in the area—a mother and aunties, not to mention a coven! Una would have realised then that whatever else Lily might do for money, she wasn't going to disappear. So she was back to square one.'

'Bummer,' said Mrs. Moss, pouring more tea for herself.

'Yes,' Holly agreed. 'Her money was running out. She didn't have time to develop another believeable protégée. *Then* she read about Andrew, and got the idea of pretending she believed he was her half-brother. That would make a very quick decision to write a will in his favour seem quite natural. Well, natural for Una, anyway.'

The mobile phone rang in the kitchen. Mrs. Moss didn't move.

'I must have forgotten to turn it off,' Mrs. Moss said, noticing Holly's enquiring look. 'All the excitement. But I never work on Sundays. I don't feel it's appropriate. Going back to what we were saying before, I just hate to think of that woman getting away with what she did.'

'She won't get away with it forever, Enid,' said Abigail serenely. 'There is such a thing as karma.'

'Possibly,' said Mrs. Moss, looking unconvinced.

'It might be working already,' Holly told her. 'It turned out Eric was eavesdropping. He heard everything she said. He's furious, and he's leaving. Today. He and Cleopatra are going to move into his old dad's garage till he's fixed something else up, and he'll buy a tarpaulin for the hearse. Una won't find life so pleasant all alone in that house, with no one to run her messages for her.'

'She'll have her money to comfort her,' snapped Mrs. Moss.

'Not for quite a while. The police will probably hold on to the things that were buried with Lois for ages. And the house will take a long time to sell, according to Len Land. He's the real estate agent Una's using. I met him on the way out.'

She smiled involuntarily, thinking of Len Land's startled look of recognition, of his hand reaching into the breast pocket of his sagging suit jacket, and the rather worn-looking, yellow-stickered envelope he handed over.

'This was in the letterbox at Clover Road when I called in there yesterday, Miss Love,' Land said. 'Redirected mail for you. I thought I'd have to return it to sender, but here you are! What a coincidence, eh?'

'It's a small world,' Holly had agreed faintly, tearing the envelope open and finding inside, to her great surprise, a note from her cousin Liz.

> *...snail mail because your phone seems to be off, and emails keep bouncing. What do you think about Lloyd and Angie getting engaged? I was so surprised. Hope you're not upset. Also, I don't know if you're still seeing Andrew McNish, but if you are, could you possibly remind him that he owes Leah forty dollars for that sponsorship thing? I know it's a lot, but he did promise and Leah's already written to him twice...*

Forty dollars...

'Well, it's nice to see you smiling, anyway, dear,' said Mrs. Moss.

'It's good to get the loose ends tidied up,' said Holly. 'Most of them, anyway.'

'And you will stay, Holly, won't you?' asked Abigail. 'Till old Droopy Drawers comes for the rent at the end of the month, anyway? Someone's got to look after the parrot, after all. I feel you two have formed a genuine bond.'

'I'd love to stay,' Holly said sincerely. 'But I really think I'd better go. Una won't report me to the police, and Dulcie's taken Sebastian back to Queensland, but Cliff Allnut isn't going to let it drop.'

'Oh, I think he will,' said Mrs. Moss complacently. 'I had a little word with him. I told him that there's nothing illegal about using a pseudonym for professional reasons, as long as you diligently perform the service you advertise, and pay your taxes.'

Holly smiled at her. 'That's really kind of you, Mrs. Moss, but I don't think...'

'It's not as if Cliff and I are strangers,' said Mrs. Moss. 'We're quite old friends, in a way. I knew it the very first time I heard his voice—probably because he was saying something about chains at the time.'

'Oh, Enid!' cried Abigail, clasping her hands. 'You don't mean...'

'Certainly,' said Mrs. Moss, beaming. 'Cliff—every Tuesday night, around ten-thirty, almost without fail. Mind you, I mightn't be hearing from him again. I think he was quite surprised to find out how old I was. I thought he was going to faint when he heard my voice, the naughty boy. And when I told him my second name was Natasha, after my mother's sister, he—'

'Enid, you blackmailed him!' Abigail shrieked joyfully, and from behind the red-heart door the parrot screeched a maniacal reply, in a sort of Indian love call across the stairwell.

'Abby, *really!*' said Mrs. Moss with dignity. 'I would *never* put the black on a client. I simply told poor Cliff that Holly was a good friend of mine, and reminded him that we all have our little weaknesses, which it was just as well to keep private, between friends. Especially when we are solicitors, and respectable members of the golf club, with reputations to keep.'

Holly stared at her, open-mouthed.

'So you can stay, Holly!' said Abigail.

'And you mustn't worry about money,' Mrs. Moss chimed in. 'On the way back from breakfast we ran into that lovely girl Dimity—who looks so much *better* now she's got two eyebrows, by the way, doesn't she, Abby?'

Abigail nodded. 'And Dimity told us that her grandmother thinks someone is embezzling the church funds, and she wants to hire me to find out who it is. So of course I told her that wasn't a job for me. It was a job for a private detective, and it just so happened that I knew the perfect—'

'Abigail, I'm not a detective,' Holly protested, laughing.

'Well, you do a very good imitation of one,' said Mrs. Moss. 'And you get results. That's all that counts. After all, I'm not a dominatrix or a busty blonde with a warm, caring nature, but I get by.'

Holly slumped back in her chair. She felt dizzy again.

'Give us a biscuit!' the parrot shrieked across the stairwell.

'O'Brien senses you're staying,' said Abigail. 'He's overjoyed.'

'Bless him,' said Mrs. Moss fondly. 'More tea, anyone?'

Author's Note

Writing about your home territory, the Blue Mountains in my case, is vastly satisfying and enjoyable, but fraught with danger. We are a relatively small community. For those who don't read or don't believe the routine disclaimers on publishers' imprint pages, may I state here, unequivocally, that no investigator, financial advisor, mechanic, taxi driver, bank teller, clairvoyant, mural painter, police officer, doctor, solicitor, butcher, Elvis impersonator, funeral director, landscaper, pest exterminator, receptionist, bookseller, sex worker, or any other character in this book is anything like anyone I know. While major town names are real, specific locations like streets, shops, pubs and motels are not. May I also say that the village of Mealey Marshes does not exist in the real world, though it would be nice if it did.

To receive a free catalog of Poisoned Pen Press titles, please contact us in one of the following ways:

Phone: 1-800-421-3976
Facsimile: 1-480-949-1707
Email: info@poisonedpenpress.com
Website: www.poisonedpenpress.com

Poisoned Pen Press
6962 E. First Ave. Ste 103
Scottsdale, AZ 85251